THE HUGO WINNERS

THE HUGO WINNERS

EDITED BY

Isaac Asimov

LONDON : DENNIS DOBSON

THE DARFSTELLER by Walter M. Miller, Jr. Copyright © 1955 by Street & Smith Publications, Inc. Reprinted by courtesy of the author. Appeared originally in *Astounding Science Fiction*, January 1955. ALLAMAGOOSA by Eric Frank Russell. Copyright © 1955 by Street & Smith Publications, Inc. Reprinted by courtesy of Scott Meredith and the author. Appeared originally in *Astounding Science Fiction*, May 1955 and in FAR STARS, Dobson, 1961. EXPLORATION TEAM by Murray Leinster. Copyright © 1956 by Street & Smith Publications, Inc. Reprinted by courtesy of the author. Appeared originally in *Astounding Science Fiction*, March 1956. Included in COLONIAL SURVEY by Murray Leinster, Gnome Press 1957. THE STAR by Arthur C. Clarke. Copyright 1955 by Royal Publications, Inc. Reprinted by courtesy of Scott Meredith and the author. Appeared originally in *Infinity Science Fiction*, November 1955. Included in THE OTHER SIDE OF THE SKY by Arthur C. Clarke, Harcourt, Brace, 1957, Gollancz, 1961 and A CENTURY OF SCIENCE FICTION edited by Damon Knight, Simon & Schuster, 1962, Gollancz, 1963. OR ALL THE SEAS WITH OYSTERS by Avram Davidson. Copyright © 1958 by Galaxy Publishing Corp. Reprinted by courtesy of Robert P. Mills and the author. Appeared originally in *Galaxy Science Fiction*, May 1958. Included in THE FOURTH GALAXY READER edited by H. L. Gold, Doubleday, 1959, and in SCIENCE FICTION-59 edited by Judith Merril, Gnome Press, 1959. THE BIG FRONT YARD by Clifford D. Simak. Copyright © 1958 by Street & Smith Publications, Inc. Reprinted by courtesy of Robert P. Mills and the author. Appeared originally in *Astounding Science Fiction*, October 1958. Included in THE WORLDS OF CLIFFORD SIMAK by Clifford D. Simak, Simon & Schuster, 1960. THE HELL-BOUND TRAIN by Robert Bloch. Copyright © 1958 by Mercury Press, Inc. Reprinted by courtesy of Harry Altshuler and the author. Appeared originally in *The Magazine of Fantasy and Science Fiction*, September 1958. Included in PLEASANT DREAMS by Robert Bloch, Arkham House, 1960. FLOWERS FOR ALGERNON by Daniel Keyes. Copyright © 1959 by Daniel Keyes. Reprinted by courtesy of Robert P. Mills and the author. Appeared originally in *The Magazine of Fantasy and Science Fiction*, April 1959. Included in THE BEST FROM FANTASY AND SCIENCE FICTION – Ninth Series edited by Robert P. Mills, Doubleday, 1960. 5TH ANNUAL OF THE YEAR'S BEST SCIENCE FICTION edited by Judith Merril, Simon & Schuster, 1960; *Best Articles and Stories*, February 1961, *Literary Cavalcade*, November 1961 and in BEST S.F. 4 edited by Edmund Crispin, Faber, 1961. THE LONGEST VOYAGE by Poul Anderson. Copyright © 1960 by Street & Smith Publications, Inc. Reprinted by courtesy of Scott Meredith and the author. Appeared originally in *Analog Science Fact and Fiction*, December 1960.

Second Impression 1963

Third Impression 1964

Fourth Impression 1971

SBN 234 777354

Copyright © 1962 by Isaac Asimov

First published in Great Britain in 1963 by Dennis Dobson
80 Kensington Church Street
London, W.8

Printed in Great Britain by A. Wheaton & Co. Ltd., Exeter

To all the True Conventioneers,
and, particularly,
to Pittsburgh

ACKNOWLEDGMENTS

For help in the preparation of this book, the kindly services of Robert P. Mills and Sam Moskowitz are most gratefully acknowledged.

CONTENTS

Let me introduce this book my own way, please; by which I mean I will begin by introducing myself.

I am Isaac Asimov and I am an old-timer.

Not, you understand, that I am (ha, ha) really old. Quite the contrary. I am rather young actually, being only mumblety-mumble years old and looking even younger!

I call myself an old-timer only because I started reading science fiction in 1929. Now this was only three years after Hugo Gernsback had inaugurated what is known to all True Believers as the Age of Science Fiction.

Gernsback was a Luxemburger who arrived in the United States in 1904. Fascinated by the new field of electronics, he ventured into publishing and put out a magazine devoted to the new science. Unable to keep himself down to the petty pace of actual events, he tried his hand at writing science fiction in order that he might forecast future developments in electronics and in science generally.

His own output, however, was insufficient for himself and, in 1926, he began publication of a magazine called *Amazing Stories*, the first periodical in the world to be devoted, exclusively, to tales of science fiction.

In the next few years a group of notable youngsters gathered about the magazine, and about a few more like it (*Wonder*

Stories, Astounding Stories) that arose in *Amazing*'s wake. That group made up the first science fiction fans.

The typical science fiction fan was an early teen-ager or even a pre-teener who worshipped science the way almost all his peers worshipped baseball. He dreamed of rocketships and new electronic marvels as others dreamed of homeruns and double-plays. And where his comrades shot cattle-rustlers with vigor, he himself blasted down the treacherous, be-tentacled monsters of Ganymede.

In short, among others, he was I!

At the start, we (myself and the others) had very little company in our specialized reveries. You can imagine the laughter to which we were subjected when sensible, hard-headed, practical, every-day people discovered we were reading crazy stories about atomic bombs, television, guided missiles, and rockets to the moon. All this was obvious crackpotism that could never come to pass, you see.

So we kept quiet about our lunacy and lived each month for those days when a new issue of one of our magazines was scheduled to reach the newsstands. We haunted the stands patiently on those days, and when the garish cover of the new issue finally came into sight, suffusing all the air about it with an electric glow, we passed over our quarter and reached out in trembling delight. (It is easy to duplicate the sensation in full adulthood. Everyone who has had a rich uncle die and leave him a million dollars after taxes knows exactly what the sensation is.)

Happiness reached a peak even more excessive when the astonishing discovery was made (as it eventually always was) that somewhere there existed another person who was interested in science fiction. Mind you, one always knew that somewhere, *in other cities*, they existed. After all, fans wrote endlessly to the various magazines, reporting on stories, criticizing the science content, demanding weekly publication, sneering at each other's views—and the magazine printed all the letters in microscopic print, with jovial asides from the editor.

But to find a fellow-fan in your own city, even in your own neighborhood!

It was a love affair on the spot. It was the tight union of a common interest unshared by the Philistines. The next step was a determined search for still other brethren, and the founding of a club. At weekly gatherings, the momentous issues of the day (Would *Astounding* adopt smooth edges? Was E. E. Smith's latest serial the equal of his immortal "Skylark of Space"?) were thrashed out.

The clubs grew larger and more active. Inter-city leagues of clubs were founded. Then, in 1939, the inevitable climax was reached. It was decided to hold a World Science Fiction Convention.

It was held in New York. Two hundred eager teen-agers attended, some coming from as far away as California. Editors attended and were astonished at the ardor and enthusiasm. The Guest of Honor was Frank R. Paul, the illustrator who had turned Gernsback's science fiction magazine covers into glowing dreams of fanciful machinery and horrid extra-terrestrial monsters.

I was there, too, already an "old-time fan" and now a writer, with three published stories to my credit. It made me a celebrity and I loved it. I signed autographs with a lofty dignity that was softened at the corners by just a touch of kindly condescension.

The success of that great gathering was enormous. We watched the old German science fiction movie, *Metropolis.* Fans shook hands with various editors and writers who, to their amazement, were not ten feet tall—but only seven or eight. We listened to talks on science fiction and, in fact, we could and did speak about science fiction and nothing but science fiction to anyone we met. For one short, golden day, we inhabited a tiny world in which science fiction was the exclusive interest.

I imagine Heaven must be a feeble imitation of that day.

There was nothing to do but repeat. In 1940, the 2nd Convention was held in Chicago; in 1941, the 3rd Convention was held in Denver.

Then came a pause called World War II. The lonely teen-agers of the '30s who had at last found each other, were now mostly in the Army, and those few who, for one reason or another, remained at home, initiated drives to send them science fiction magazines. (Pinup girls and letters from home are all very well in their way, but *our* boys in the foxholes needed those magazines to keep up their morale.)

In 1946, with peace restored and the atom bomb shedding a

horrid glare of rationality over our crackpotism, the conventions were resumed and not a year has been missed since.

The 4th Convention was held at Los Angeles, and others have ranged as far north as Toronto (the 6th, in 1948), as far west as Seattle (the 19th, in 1961) and as far south as New Orleans (the 9th, in 1951). The 15th Convention crossed the ocean and was held in London. In 1952, no less than a thousand fans and professionals attended the 10th Convention held, like the 2nd, in Chicago.

Every Convention is notable and lovable, but the 1955 Convention is particularly memorable for two reasons.

It was held in Cleveland and it was the THIRTEENTH Convention. The organizing fans of the Cleveland area were therefore faced with the task of selecting a guest of honor who would not object to the evil connotations of the number, 13.

Someone was needed who was particularly sane and rational; some gentleman known to be fearless and intrepid. Naturally, he had also to be a witty and forceful speaker and, above all, he had to be devilishly handsome.

All this narrowed the field of possibilities in drastic fashion. In fact, only one candidate met all the requirements, and I accepted with my usual grace and charm.

With myself as Guest of Honor, the 13th Convention was obviously slated for immortality, but the organizing fans did not rest upon their laurels.

Until the 13th Convention, fans had occasionally voted on favorite novels, novelettes, short stories, artists, fan magazines, and so on. The results would be announced amid great jubilation. At the 11th Convention (Philadelphia, 1953) little space-ship models were handed out to winners. This, however, was a one-shot. At the 12th Convention (San Francisco, 1954) no awards of this type were made.

Well, then, the 13th Convention decided to make the spaceship award permanent. Mr. Ben Jason of Cleveland designed a new statuette, classic in its smooth simplicity, which at once— unofficially—was dubbed the Hugo after the immortal Gernsback. By 1958, the name was official.

Let the Philistines have their Oscars and their Emmys. *We* have the Hugos.

Hugos have been handed out at every convention since that epoch-making 13th. They have been reverently handed out on seven rafter-ringing occasions.

I watched the Hugos given out at the 13th Convention, smiling blandly from my post in the center of the head table. The next year, at the 14th Convention (New York, 1956), I watched more given out, again from a seat at the head table, a place that was mine by virtue of the fact that I was one of the featured speakers.

At both the 17th Convention (Detroit, 1959) and the 18th Convention (Pittsburgh, 1960) I was toastmaster and I handed out the Hugos with my very own hands.

But by the time the 19th Convention (Seattle, 1961) was over, a certain gnawing suspicion had found its way into the regions of my heart. I thought deeply and checked statistics and slowly the conviction grew and strengthened that a peculiar and unnatural situation prevailed in the science fiction world.

What it was, I can state simply. Although Hugos had been given out by car lots to all sorts of relatively insignificant personages, none—not one—had ever been awarded to *me*.

For months now I have brooded over the possibilities of revenge; as any red-blooded American boy would. I have discarded complicated schemes that involved poison-pen letters, mysterious and untraceable South American toxins, plastic bomb booby traps, and was almost at my wits' end, when the perfect opportunity presented itself.

The suggestion was made that someone collect the Hugo winners among the novelettes and short stories and place all of them within the pages of a single book. At least one story, sometimes two, had been given an award in this category on every occasion when Hugos were handed out except for the 11th Convention (Philadelphia, 1953) and the 15th Convention (London, 1957). Nine different stories were involved, winners at six different conventions. Thus the readers would find themselves with a lavish treat of the best-by-vote: over 100,000 words of superior fiction.

The person qualifying as editor for such an anthology would naturally have to be someone who had not himself received a Hugo, so that he could approach the job with the proper detachment. At the same time, he would have to be a person of note, sane and rational, fearless and intrepid, witty and forceful, and, above all, devilishly handsome.

All this was pointed out to Mr. Timothy Seldes at Doubleday and Company, and that fine gentleman agreed in every particular. Once again, the stringent requirements for the post seemed to cut down the possibilities to a single individual and I accepted with that lovable modesty that suits me so well.

And so here I have my revenge. If those wise guys, herein included among the authors, had not been so eager to grab at the Hugos, but had modestly held back the way I did, *they* might have edited this anthology.

I hope they have learned their lesson.

Anyway, here I am, and here are the Hugo winners.

Isaac Asimov
West Newton, Massachusetts

1955
13th Convention
Cleveland

Walter M. Miller, Jr.

I ought to have met Walter Miller at the 13th Convention (Cleveland, 1955) when his novelette "The Darfsteller" won its author a Hugo, but I didn't. When his name was called out by Anthony Boucher, (the toastmaster upon that occasion) a proxy came up to accept it. My disappointment was soothed a bit by the fact that the proxy was the charming Judith Merril, one of science fiction's best anthologists.

Things were different at the 14th Convention (New York, 1956). Walt wasn't taking a Hugo that time but he was there and he and I and Robert P. Mills had lunch together. Mills was editor of a new magazine *Venture Science Fiction* (an excellent venture indeed, which should have made out better than it did) and Walt and I were trying to write stories for it, so there was a great deal to discuss.

For this purpose, Mills took us both to a beautiful French restaurant for he spared no expense on such occasions, since he never picked up a check. I was at my most charming, witty, genial and learned, and interrupted my discourse only long enough to order the meal, which, naturally, I did in a French of the most elegant Parisian variety. This, after all, is only to be expected of one who, like myself, speaks, in ordinary life, that delightful patois that can only be described as High Brooklyn.

Now imagine that five years have passed, five years during which Walt and I have not met again. It is now time to write to Walt for permission to use "The Darfsteller." In doing so, I delicately recalled myself to him. Of course, I felt sure he could not have forgotten me. My only uncertainty was which of my many mind-stimulating comments he would lovingly cite as evidence that lunch with me was an occasion he would cherish in his memory forever.

In answering (and giving permission), he said, "Of course, I remember you. You ordered chitlin's in French."

But then, what can you expect of a Hugo-winner? Just to show you the greediness of this variety of writer, Walt did it again at the 19th Convention (Seattle, 1961) only worse. He carried off the biggest prize of all and won a Hugo for his novel, *A Canticle for Leibowitz.*

Fortunately, we can't include novels in this anthology. I wouldn't want to encourage Walt in this callous business of monopolizing Hugos

1

THE DARFSTELLER

"Judas, Judas" was playing at the Universal on Fifth Street, and the cast was entirely human. Ryan Thornier had been saving up for it for several weeks, and now he could afford the price of a matinée ticket. It had been a race for time between his piggy bank and the wallets of several "public-spirited" angels who kept the show alive, and the piggy bank had won. He could see the show before the wallets went flat and the show folded, as any such show was bound to do after a few limping weeks. A glow of anticipation suffused him. After watching the wretched mockery of dramaturgical art every day at the New Empire Theater where he worked as janitor, the chance to see real theater again would be like a breath of clean air.

He came to work an hour early on Wednesday morning and sped through his usual chores on overdrive. He finished his work before one o'clock, had a shower backstage, changed to street clothes, and went nervously upstairs to ask Imperio D'Uccia for the rest of the day off.

D'Uccia sat enthroned at a rickety desk before a wall plastered with photographs of lightly clad female stars of the old days. He heard the janitor's petition with a faint, almost oriental smile of apparent sympathy, then drew himself up to his full height of sixty-five inches, leaned on the desk with chubby hands to study Thornier with beady eyes.

"Off? So you wanna da day off? Mmmph—" He shook his head as if mystified by such an incomprehensible request.

The gangling janitor shifted his feet uneasily. "Yes, sir. I've fin-

ished up, and Jigger'll come over to stand by in case you need
anything special." He paused. D'Uccia was studying his nails,
frowning gravely. "I haven't asked for a day off in two years, Mr.
D'Uccia," he added, "and I was sure you wouldn't mind after all
the overtime I've—"

"Jigger," D'Uccia grunted. "Whoosa t'is Jigger?"

"Works at the Paramount. It's closed for repairs, and he doesn't
mind—"

The theater manager grunted abruptly and waved his hands.
"I don' pay no Jigger, I pay you. Whassa this all about? You swip
the floor, you putsa things away, you all finish now, ah? You
wanna day off. Thatsa whass wrong with the world, too mucha
time loaf. Letsa machines work. More time to mek trouble." The
theater manager came out from behind his desk and waddled to
the door. He thrust his fat neck outside and looked up and down
the corridor, then waddled back to confront Thornier with a short
fat finger aimed at the employee's long and majestic nose.

"Whensa lass time you waxa the upstairs floor, hah?"

Thornier's jaw sagged forlornly. "Why, I—"

"Don'ta tell me no lie. Looka that hall. Sheeza feelth. *Look!* I
want you to look." He caught Thornier's arm, tugged him to
the doorway, pointed excitedly at the worn and ancient oak flooring. "Sheeza feelth ground in! See? When you wax, hah?"

A great shudder seemed to pass through the thin elderly man.
He sighed resignedly and turned to look down at D'Uccia with
weary gray eyes.

"Do I get the afternoon off, or don't I?" he asked hopelessly,
knowing the answer in advance.

But D'Uccia was not content with a mere refusal. He began to
pace. He was obviously deeply moved. He defended the system
of free enterprise and the cherished traditions of the theater. He
spoke eloquently of the golden virtues of industriousness and
dedication to duty. He bounced about like a furious Pekingese
yapping happily at a scarecrow. Thornier's neck reddened, his
mouth went tight.

"Can I go now?"

"When you waxa da floor? Palisha da seats, fixa da lights?
When you clean op the dressing room, hah?" He stared up at
Thornier for a moment, then turned on his heel and charged to

the window. He thrust his thumb into the black dirt of the window box, where several prize lilies were already beginning to bloom. "*Ha!*" he snorted. "Dry, like I thought! You think the bulbs a don't need a drink, hah?"

"But I watered them this morning. The sun—"

"Hah! You letsa little *fiori* wilt an die, hah? And you wanna the day off?"

It was hopeless. When D'Uccia drew his defensive mantle of calculated deafness or stupidity about himself, he became impenetrable to any request or honest explanation. Thornier sucked in a slow breath between his teeth, stared angrily at his employer for a moment, and seemed briefly ready to unleash an angry blast. Thinking better of it, he bit his lip, turned, and stalked wordlessly out of the office. D'Uccia followed him triumphantly to the door.

"Don' you go sneak off, now!" he called ominously, and stood smiling down the corridor until the janitor vanished at the head of the stairs. Then he sighed and went back to get his hat and coat. He was just preparing to leave when Thornier came back upstairs with a load of buckets, mops, and swabs.

The janitor stopped when he noticed the hat and coat, and his seamed face went curiously blank. "Going home, Mr. D'Uccia?" he asked icily.

"Yeh! I'ma worka too hard, the doctor say. I'ma need the sunshine. More frash air. I'ma go relax on the beach a while."

Thornier leaned on the mop handle and smiled nastily. "Sure," he said. "Letsa machines do da work."

The comment was lost on D'Uccia. He waved airily, strode off toward the stairway, and called an airy "*A rivederci!*" over his shoulder.

"*A rivederci, padrone,*" Thornier muttered softly, his pale eyes glittering from their crow's-feet wrappings. For a moment his face seemed to change—and once again he was Chaubrec's Adolfo, at the exit of the Commandant, Act II, scene *iv*, from "A Canticle for the Marsman."

Somewhere downstairs, a door slammed behind D'Uccia.

"Into death!" hissed Adolfo-Thornier, throwing back his head to laugh Adolfo's laugh. It rattled the walls. When its reverberations had died away, he felt a little better. He picked up his buckets and brooms and walked on down the corridor to the door of D'Uccia's office.

Unless "Judas, Judas" hung on through the week end, he wouldn't get to see it, since he could not afford a ticket to the evening performance, and there was no use asking D'Uccia for favors. While he waxed the hall, he burned. He waxed as far as D'Uccia's doorway, then stood staring into the office for several vacant minutes.

"I'm fed up," he said at last.

The office remained silent. The window-box lilies bowed to the breeze.

"You little creep!" he growled. "I'm through!"

The office was speechless. Thornier straightened and tapped his chest.

"I, Ryan Thornier, am walking out, you hear? The show is finished!"

When the office failed to respond, he turned on his heel and stalked downstairs. Minutes later, he came back with a small can of gold paint and a pair of artists' brushes from the storeroom. Again he paused in the doorway.

"Anything else I can do, Mr. D'Uccia?" he purred.

Traffic murmured in the street; the breeze rustled the lilies; the building creaked.

"Oh? You want me to wax in the wall-cracks, too? How could I have forgotten!"

He clucked his tongue and went over to the window. Such lovely lilies. He opened the paint can, set it on the window ledge, and then very carefully he gilded each of the prize lilies, petals, leaves, and stalks, until the flowers glistened like the work of Midas' hands in the sunlight. When he finished, he stepped back to smile at them in admiration for a moment, then went to finish waxing the hall.

He waxed it with particular care in front of D'Uccia's office. He waxed under the throw rug that covered the worn spot on the floor where D'Uccia had made a sharp left turn into his sanctum every morning for fifteen years, and then he turned the rug over and dusted dry wax powder into the pile. He replaced it carefully and pushed at it a few times with his foot to make cer-

tain the lubrication was adequate. The rug slid about as if it rode
on a bed of bird-shot.

Thornier smiled and went downstairs. The world was suddenly
different somehow. Even the air smelled different. He paused
on the landing to glance at himself in the decorative mirror.

Ah! the old trouper again. No more of the stooped and haggard
menial. None of the wistfulness and weariness of self-perpetuated
slavery. Even with the gray at the temples and the lines in the
face, here was something of the old Thornier—or one of the *many*
old Thorniers of earlier days. Which one? Which one'll it be?
Adolfo? Or Hamlet? Justin, or J. J. Jones, from "The Electrocu-
tioner"? Any of them, all of them; for he was Ryan Thornier, star,
in the old days.

"Where've you been, baby?" he asked his image with a tight
smile of approval, winked, and went on home for the evening.
Tomorrow, he promised himself, a new life would begin.

"But you've been making that promise for years, Thorny," said
the man in the control booth, his voice edged with impatience.
"What do you mean, 'you quit?' Did you tell D'Uccia you quit?"

Thornier smiled loftily while he dabbed with his broom at a
bit of dust in the corner. "Not exactly, Richard," he said. "But the
padrone will find it out soon enough."

The technician grunted disgust. "I don't understand you,
Thorny. Sure, if you *really* quit, that's swell—if you don't just
turn around and get another job like this one."

"Never!" the old actor proclaimed resonantly, and glanced up
at the clock. Five till ten. Nearly time for D'Uccia to arrive for
work. He smiled to himself.

"If you really quit, what are you doing here today?" Rick
Thomas demanded, glancing up briefly from the Maestro. His
arms were thrust deep into the electronic entrails of the machine, and he wore a pencil-sized screwdriver tucked behind one
ear. "Why don't you go home, if you quit?"

"Oh, don't worry, Richard. This time it's for real."

"Pssss!" An amused hiss from the technician. "Yeah, it was for
real when you quit at the Bijou, too. Only then a week later you
come to work here. So what now, Mercutio?"

"To the casting office, old friend. A bit part somewhere, per-

haps." Thornier smiled on him benignly. "Don't concern yourself
about me."

"Thorny, can't you get it through your head that theater's
dead? There isn't any theater! No movies, no television either—
except for dead men and the Maestro here." He slapped the
metal housing of the machine.

"I *meant*," Thorny explained patiently, "'employment office,'
and 'small job,' you . . . you machineage flintsmith. Figures of
speech, solely."

"Yah."

"I thought you *wanted* me to resign my position, Richard."

"Yes! If you'll do something worthwhile with yourself. Ryan
Thornier, star of 'Walkaway,' playing martyr with a scrub-bucket!
Aaaak! You give me the gripes. And you'll do it again. You can't
stay away from the stage, even if all you can do about it is mop
up the oil drippings."

"You couldn't possibly understand," Thornier said stiffly.

Rick straightened to look at him, took his arms out of the
Maestro and leaned on top of the cabinet. "I dunno, Thorny,"
he said in a softer voice. "Maybe I do. You're an actor, and you're
always playing roles. Living them, even. You can't help it, I
guess. But you *could* do a saner job of picking the parts you're
going to play."

"The world has cast me in the role I play," Thornier announced
with a funereal face.

Rick Thomas clapped a hand over his forehead and drew it
slowly down across his face in exasperation. "I give up!" he
groaned. "Look at you! Matinée idol, pushing a broom. Eight
years ago, it made sense—*your* kind of sense, anyhow. Dramatic
gesture. Leading actor defies autodrama offer, takes janitor's job.
Loyal to tradition, and the guild—and all that. It made small
headlines, maybe even helped the legit stage limp along a little
longer. But the audiences stopped bleeding for you after a while,
and then it stopped making even *your* kind of sense!"

Thornier stood wheezing slightly and glaring at him. "What
would *you* do," he hissed, "if they started making a little black
box that could be attached to the wall up there"—he waved to a
bare spot above the Maestro's bulky housing—"that could repair,
maintain, operate, and adjust—do all the things you do to that

. . . that contraption. Suppose nobody needed electronicians any more."

Rick Thomas thought about it a few moments, then grinned. "Well, I guess I'd get a job making the little black boxes, then."

"You're not funny, Richard!"

"I didn't intend to be."

"You're . . . you're not an artist." Flushed with fury, Thornier swept viciously at the floor of the booth.

A door slammed somewhere downstairs, far below the above-stage booth. Thorny set his broom aside and moved to the window to watch. The *clop, clop, clop* of bustling footsteps came up the central aisle.

"Hizzoner, da Imperio," muttered the technician, glancing up at the clock. "Either that clock's two minutes fast, or else this was his morning to take a bath."

Thornier smiled sourly toward the main aisle, his eyes traveling after the waddling figure of the theater manager. When D'Uccia disappeared beneath the rear balcony, he resumed his sweeping.

"I don't see why you don't get a sales job, Thorny," Rick ventured, returning to his work. "A good salesman is just an actor, minus the temperament. There's *lots* of demand for good actors, come to think of it. Politicians, top executives, even generals—some of them seem to make out on *nothing but* dramatic talent. History affirms it."

"Bah! I'm no schauspieler." He paused to watch Rick adjusting the Maestro, and slowly shook his head. "Ease your conscience, Richard," he said finally.

Startled, the technician dropped his screwdriver, looked up quizzically. "*My* conscience? What the devil is uneasy about *my* conscience?"

"Oh, don't pretend. That's why you're always so concerned about me. I know *you* can't help it that your . . . your trade has perverted a great art."

Rick gaped at him in disbelief for a moment. "*You* think *I*—" He choked. He colored angrily. He stared at the old ham and began to curse softly under his breath.

Thornier suddenly lifted a finger to his mouth and went *shhhhh!* His eyes roamed toward the back of the theater.

"That was only D'Uccia on the stairs," Rick began. "What—?"

"*Shhhh!*"

They listened. The janitor wore a rancid smile. Seconds later it came—first a faint yelp, then—

Bbbrroom*mmpb!*

It rattled the booth windows. Rick started up frowning.

"What the—?"

"*Shhhh!*"

The jolting jar was followed by a faint mutter of profanity. "That's D'Uccia. What happened?"

The faint mutter suddenly became a roaring stream of curses from somewhere behind the balconies.

"Hey!" said Rick. "He must have hurt himself."

"Naah. He just found my resignation, that's all. See? I told you I'd quit."

The profane bellowing grew louder to the accompaniment of an elephantine thumping on carpeted stairs.

"He's not *that* sorry to see you go," Rick grunted, looking baffled.

D'Uccia burst into view at the head of the aisle. He stopped with his feet spread wide, clutching at the base of his spine with one hand and waving a golden lily aloft in the other.

"Lily gilder!" he screamed. "Pansy painter! You fancy-pantsy bom! Come out, you fonny fonny boy!"

Thornier thrust his head calmly through the control-booth window, stared at the furious manager with arched brows. "You calling me, Mr. D'Uccia?"

D'Uccia sucked in two or three gasping breaths before he found his bellow again.

"*Thornya!*"

"Yes, sir?"

"Itsa finish, you hear?"

"What's finished, boss?"

"Itsa finish. I'ma go see the servo man. I'ma go get me· a swip-op machine. You gotta two wiks notice."

"Tell him you don't want any notice," Rick grunted softly from nearby. "Walk out on him."

"All right, Mr. D'Uccia," Thornier called evenly.

D'Uccia stood there sputtering, threatening to charge, waving the lily helplessly. Finally he threw it down in the aisle with a curse and whirled to limp painfully out.

"*Whew!*" Rick breathed. "What did you do?"

Thornier told him sourly. The technician shook his head.

"He won't fire you. He'll change his mind. It's too hard to hire anybody to do dirty-work these days."

"You heard him. He can buy an autojan installation. 'Swip-op' machine."

"Baloney! Dooch is too stingy to put out that much dough. Besides, he can't get the satisfaction of screaming at a machine."

Thornier glanced up wryly. "Why *can't* he?"

"Well—" Rick paused. "Ulp! . . . You're right. He can. He came up here and bawled out the Maestro once. Kicked it, yelled at it, shook it—like a guy trying to get his quarter back out of a telephone. Went away looking pleased with himself, too."

"Why not?" Thorny muttered gloomily. "People are machines to D'Uccia. And he's *fair* about it. He's willing to treat them all alike."

"But you're not going to stick around two weeks, are you?"

"Why not? It'll give me time to put out some feelers for a job."

Rick grunted doubtfully and turned his attention back to the machine. He removed the upper front panel and set it aside. He opened a metal canister on the floor and lifted out a foot-wide foot-thick roll of plastic tape. He mounted it on a spindle inside the Maestro, and began feeding the end of the tape through several sets of rollers and guides. The tape appeared worm-eaten —covered with thousands of tiny punch-marks and wavy grooves. The janitor paused to watch the process with cold hostility.

"Is that the script-tape for the 'Anarch'?" he asked stiffly.

The technician nodded. "Brand new tape, too. Got to be careful how I feed her in. It's still got fuzz on it from the recording cuts." He stopped the feed mechanism briefly, plucked at a punch-mark with his awl, blew on it, then started the feed motor again.

"What happens if the tape gets nicked or scratched?" Thorny grunted curiously. "Actor collapse on stage?"

Rick shook his head. "Naa, it happens all the time. A scratch

or a nick'll make a player muff a line or maybe stumble, then the
Maestro catches the goof, and compensates. Maestro gets feed-
back from the stage, continuously directs the show. It can do a
lot of compensating, too."

"I thought the whole show came from the tape."

The technician smiled. "It does, in a way. But it's more than
a recorded mechanical puppet show, Thorny. The Maestro
watches the stage . . . no, more than that . . . the Maestro *is*
the stage, an electronic analogue of it." He patted the metal housing. "All the actors' personality patterns are packed in here. It's
more than a remote controller, the way most people think of it.
It's a creative directing machine. It's even got pickups out in the
audience to gauge reactions to—"

He stopped suddenly, staring at the old actor's face. He swallowed nervously. "Thorny *don't* look that way. I'm sorry. Here,
have a cigarette."

Thorny accepted it with trembling fingers. He stared down
into the gleaming maze of circuitry with narrowed eyes, watched
the script-belt climb slowly over the rollers and down into the
bowels of the Maestro.

"Art!" he hissed. "Theater! What'd they give you your degree
in, Richard? Dramaturgical engineering?"

He shuddered and stalked out of the booth. Rick listened to
the angry rattle of his heels on the iron stairs that led down to
stage level. He shook his head sadly, shrugged, went back
to inspecting the tape for rough cuts.

Thorny came back after a few minutes with a bucket and a
mop. He looked reluctantly repentant. "Sorry, lad," he grunted.
"I know you're just trying to make a living, and—"

"Skip it," Rick grunted curtly.

"It's just . . . well . . . this particular show. It gets me."

"This—? 'The Anarch,' you mean? What about it, Thorny? You
play in it once?"

"Uh-uh. It hasn't been on the stage since the Nineties, except
—well, it was almost revived ten years ago. We rehearsed for
weeks. Show folded before opening night. No dough."

"You had a good part in it?"

"I was to play Andreyev," Thornier told him with a faint smile.
Rick whistled between his teeth. "The lead. That's too bad."

He hoisted his feet to let Thorny mop under them. "Big disappointment, I guess."

"It's not that. It's just . . . well . . . 'The Anarch' rehearsals were the last time Mela and I were on stage together. That's all."

"Mela?" The technician paused, frowning. "Mela *Stone?*"

Thornier nodded.

Rick snatched up a copy of the uncoded script, waved it at him. "But she's in *this* version, Thorny! Know that! She's playing Marka."

Thornier's laugh was brief and brittle.

Rick reddened slightly. "Well, I mean her mannequin's playing it."

Thorny eyed the Maestro distastefully. "Your mechanical Svengali's playing its airfoam zombies in *all* roles, you mean."

"Oh, cut it out, Thorny. Be sore at the world if you want to, but don't blame me for what audiences want. And I didn't invent autodrama anyhow."

"I don't blame anybody. I merely detest that . . . that—" He punched at the base of the Maestro with his wet mop.

"You and D'Uccia," Rick grunted disgustedly. "Except—D'Uccia loves it when it's working O.K. It's just a machine, Thorny. Why hate it?"

"Don't need a reason to hate it," he said, snarly-petulant. "I hate air-cabs, too. It's a matter of taste, that's all."

"All right, but the public likes autodrama—whether it's by TV, stereo, or on stage. And they get what they want."

"*Why?*"

Rick snickered. "Well, it's their dough. Autodrama's portable, predictable, duplicatable. And flexible. You can run 'Macbeth' tonight, the 'Anarch' tomorrow night, and 'King of the Moon' the next night—in the same house. No actor-temperament problems. No union problems. Rent the packaged props, dolls, and tapes from Smithfield. Packaged theater. Systematized, mass-produced. In Coon Creek, Georgia, yet."

"Bah!"

Rick finished feeding in the script tape, closed the panel, and opened an adjacent one. He ripped the lid from a cardboard carton and dumped a heap of smaller tape-spools on the table.

"Are *those* the souls they sold to Smithfield?" Thornier asked, smiling at them rather weirdly.

The technician's stool scraped back and he exploded: "You know what they are!"

Thornier nodded, leaned closer to stare at them as if fascinated. He plucked one of them out of the pile, sighed down at it.

"If you say 'Alas, poor Yorick,' I'll heave you out of here!" Rick grated.

Thornier put it back with a sigh and wiped his hand on his coveralls. Packaged personalities. Actor's egos, analogized on tape. Real actors, once, whose dolls were now cast in the roles. The tapes contained complex psychophysiological data derived from months of psychic and somatic testing, after the original actors had signed their Smithfield contracts. Data for the Maestro's personality matrices. Abstractions from the human psyche, incarnate in glass, copper, chromium. The souls they rented to Smithfield on a royalty basis, along with their flesh and blood likenesses in the dolls.

Rick loaded a casting spool onto its spindle, started it feeding through the pickups.

"What happens if you leave out a vital ingredient? Such as Mela Stone's tape, for instance," Thornier wanted to know.

"The doll'd run through its lines like a zombie, that's all," Rick explained. "No zip. No interpretation. Flat, deadpan, like a robot."

"They are robots."

"Not exactly. Remote marionettes for the Maestro, but interpreted. We did a run-through on 'Hamlet' once, without any actor tapes. Everybody talked in flat monotones, no expressions. It was a scream."

"Ha, ha," Thornier said grimly.

Rick slipped another tape on the spindle, clicked a dial to a new setting, started the feed again. "This one's Andreyev, Thornier—played by Peltier." He cursed suddenly, stopped the feed, inspected the tape anxiously, flipped open the pickup mechanism, and inspected it with a magnifier.

"What's wrong?" asked the janitor.

"Take-off's about worn out. Hard to keep its spacing right. I'm nervous about it getting hung up and chewing up the tape."

"No duplicate tapes?"

"Yeah. One set of extras. But the show opens tonight." He cast another suspicious look at the pickup glideway, then closed it and switched the feed again. He was replacing the panel when the feed mechanism stalled. A ripping sound came from inside. He muttered fluent profanity, shut off the drive, jerked away the panel. He held up a shredded ribbon of tape for Thorny to see, then flung it angrily across the booth. "Get out of here! You're a jinx!"

"Not till I finish mopping."

"Thorny, get D'Uccia for me, will you? We'll have to get a new pickup flown in from Smithfield before this afternoon. This is a helluva mess."

"Why not hire a human stand-in?" he asked nastily, then added: "Forgive me. That would be a perversion of your art, wouldn't it? Shall I get D'Uccia?"

Rick threw the Peltier spool at him. He ducked out with a chuckle and went to find the theater manager. Halfway down the iron stairs, he paused to look at the wide stage that spread away just beyond the folded curtains. The footlights were burning, and the gray-green floor looked clean and shimmering, with its checkerboard pattern of imbedded copper strips. The strips were electrified during the performance, and they fed the mannequins' energy-storage packs. The dolls had metallic disks in their soles, and rectifiers in their insteps. When batteries drained low, the Maestro moved the actor's foot an inch or so to contact the floor electrodes for periodic recharging during the play, since a doll would grow wobbly and its voice indistinct after a dozen minutes on internal power alone.

Thorny stared at the broad expanse of stage where no humans walked on performance night. D'Uccia's Siamese tomcat sat licking itself in the center of the stage. It glanced up at him haughtily, seemed to sniff, began licking itself again. He watched it for a moment, then called back upstairs to Rick.

"Energize the floor a minute, will you, Rick?"

"Huh? Why?"—a busy grunt.

"Want to check something."

"O.K., but then fetch D'Uccia."

He heard the technician snap a switch. The cat's calm hauteur exploded. The cat screamed, scrambled, barrel-rolled, amid a faint sputter of sparks. The cat did an Immelmann turn over the footlights, landed in the pit with a clawing crash, then scampered up the aisle with fur erect toward its haven beneath Imperio's desk.

"Whatthehell?" Rick growled, and thrust his head out of the booth.

"Shut it off now," said the janitor. "D'Uccia'll be here in a minute."

"With fangs showing!"

Thornier went to finish his routine clean-up. Gloom had begun to gather about him. He was leaving—leaving even this last humble role in connection with the stage. A fleeting realization of his own impotence came to him. Helpless. Helpless enough to seek petty revenges like vandalizing D'Uccia's window box and tormenting D'Uccia's cat, because there was not any real enemy at which he could strike out.

He put the realization down firmly, and stamped on it. *He* was Ryan Thornier, and never helpless, unless he willed it so. I'll make them know who I am just *once,* he thought, before I go. I'll make them remember, and they won't ever forget.

But that line of thought about playing one last great role, one last masterful interpretation, he knew was no good. "Thorny, if you ever played a one-last-great," Rick had said to him once, "there wouldn't be a thing left to live for, would there?" Rick had said it cynically, but it was true anyhow. And the pleasant fantasy was somehow alarming as well as pleasant.

The chic little woman in the white-plumed hat was explaining things carefully—with round vowels and precise enunciation—to the Playwright of the Moment, up-and-coming, with awed worshipfulness in his gaze as he listened to the pert little producer. "Stark realism, you see, is the milieu of autodrama," she said. "Always remember, Bernie, that consideration for the actors is a thing of the past. Study the drama of Rome—ancient Rome. If a play had a crucifixion scene, they got a slave for the part and crucified him. On stage, but *really!*"

The Playwright of the Moment laughed dutifully around his

long cigarette holder. "So that's where they got the line: 'It's superb, but it's hell on the actors.' I must rewrite the murder scene in my 'George's Wake.' Do it with a hatchet, this time."

"Oh, now, *Bernie!* Mannequins don't bleed."

They both laughed heartily. "And they *are* expensive. Not hell on the actors, but hell on the budget."

"The Romans probably had the same problem. I'll bear it in mind."

Thornier saw them—the producer and the Playwright of the Moment—standing there in the orchestra when he came from backstage and across toward the center aisle. They lounged on the arms of their seats, and a crowd of production personnel and technicians milled about them. The time for the first run-through was approaching.

The small woman waved demurely to Thorny when she saw him making his way slowly through the throng, then turned to the playwright again. "Bernie, be a lamb and get me a drink, will you? I've got a butterfly."

"Surely. Hard, or soft?"

"Oh, hard. Scotch mist in a paper cup, please. There's a bar next door."

The playwright nodded a nod that was nearly a bow and shuffled away up the aisle. The woman caught at the janitor's sleeve as he passed.

"Going to snub me, Thorny?"

"Oh, hello, Miss Ferne," he said politely.

She leaned close and muttered: "Call me 'Miss Ferne' again and I'll claw you." The round vowels had vanished.

"O.K., Jade, but—" He glanced around nervously. Technicians milled about them. Ian Feria, the producer, watched them curiously from the wings.

"What's been doing with you, Thorny? Why haven't I seen you," she complained.

He gestured with the broom handle, shrugged. Jade Ferne studied his face a moment and frowned. "Why the agonized look, Thorny? Mad at me?"

He shook his head. "This play, Jade—'The Anarch,' well—" He glanced miserably toward the stage.

Memory struck her suddenly. She breathed a compassionate

ummm. "The attempted revival, ten years ago—you were to be Andreyev. Oh, Thorny, I'd forgotten."

"It's all right." He wore a carefully tailored martyr's smile.

She gave his arm a quick pat. "I'll see you after the run-through, Thorny. We'll have a drink and talk old times."

He glanced around again and shook his head. "You've got new friends now, Jade. They wouldn't like it."

"The crew? Nonsense! They're not snobs."

"No, but they want your attention. Feria's trying to catch your eye right now. No use making them sore."

"All right, but after the run-through I'll see you in the mannequin room. I'll just slip away."

"If you want to."

"I do, Thorny. It's been so long."

The playwright returned with her Scotch mist and gave Thornier a hostilely curious glance.

"Bless your heart, Bernie," she said, the round vowels returning, then to Thornier: "Thorny, would you do me a favor? I've been trying to corner D'Uccia, but he's tied up with a servo salesman somewhere. Somebody's got to run and pick up a mannequin from the depot. The shipment was delivered, but the trucker missed a doll crate. We'll need it for the run-through. Could you—"

"Sure, Miss Ferne. Do I need a requisition order?"

"No, just sign the delivery ticket. And Thorny, see if the new part for the Maestro's been flown in yet. Oh, and one other thing—the Maestro chewed up the Peltier tape. We've got a duplicate, but we should have two, just to be safe."

"I'll see if they have one in stock," he murmured, and turned to go.

D'Uccia stood in the lobby with the salesman when he passed through. The theater manager saw him and smirked happily.

". . . Certain special features, of course," the salesman was saying. "It's an old building, and it wasn't designed with autojanitor systems in mind, like buildings are now. But we'll tailor the installation to fit your place, Mr. D'Uccia. We want to do the job *right*, and a packaged unit wouldn't do it."

"Yah, you gimme da price, hah?"

"We'll have an estimate for you by tomorrow. I'll have an engineer over this afternoon to make the survey, and he'll work up a layout tonight."

"Whatsa 'bout the demonstration, uh? Whatsa 'bout you show how da swip-op machine go?"

The salesman hesitated, eying the janitor who waited nearby. "Well, the floor-cleaning robot is only a small part of the complete service, but . . . I tell you what I'll do. I'll bring a packaged char-all over this afternoon, and let you have a look at it."

"Fine. Datsa fine. You bring her, den we see."

They shook hands. Thornier stood with his arms folded, haughtily inspecting a bug that crawled across the frond of a potted palm, and waiting for a chance to ask D'Uccia for the keys to the truck. He felt the theater manager's triumphant gaze, but gave no indication that he heard.

"We can do the job for you all right, Mr. D'Uccia. Cut your worries in half. And that'll cut your doctor bills in half, too, like you say. Yes, sir! A man in your position gets ground down with just plain human inefficiency—other people's inefficiency. You'll never have to worry about that, once you get the building auto-janitored, no sir!"

"T'ank you kindly."

"Thank *you*, Mr. D'Uccia, and I'll see you later this afternoon." The salesman left.

"Well, bom?" D'Uccia grunted to the janitor.

"The keys to the truck. Miss Ferne wants a pickup from the depot."

D'Uccia tossed them to him. "You hear what the man say? Letsa machines do alla work, hah? Always you wantsa day off. O.K., you takka da day off, ever'day pretty soon. Nice for you, hah, ragazzo?"

Thornier turned away quickly to avoid displaying the surge of unwanted anger. "Be back in an hour," he grunted, and hurried away on his errand, his jaw working in sullen resentment. Why wait around for two humiliating weeks? Why not just walk out? Let D'Uccia do his own chores until the autojan was installed. He'd never be able to get another job around the theater anyhow, so D'Uccia's reaction wouldn't matter.

I'll walk out now, he thought—and immediately knew that he wouldn't. It was hard to explain to himself, but—when he thought of the final moment when he would be free to look for a decent job and a comfortable living—he felt a twinge of fear that was hard to understand.

The janitor's job had paid him only enough to keep him alive in a fourth floor room where he cooked his own meager meals and wrote memoirs of the old days, but it had kept him close to the lingering remnants of something he loved.

"Theater," they called it. Not *the* theater—as it was to the scalper's victim, the matinée housewife, or the awestruck hick—but just "theater." It wasn't a place, wasn't a business, wasn't the name of an art. "Theater" was a condition of the human heart and soul. Jade Ferne was theater. So was Ian Feria. So was Mela, poor kid, before her deal with Smithfield. Some had it, others didn't. In the old days, the ones that didn't have it soon got out. But the ones that had it, still had it, ever after *the* theater was gobbled up by technological change. And they hung around. Some of them, like Jade and Ian and Mela, adapted to the change, profited by the prostitution of the stage, and developed ulcers and a guilty conscience. Still, they were theater, and because they were, he, Thornier, hung around, too, scrubbing the floors they walked on, and feeling somehow that he was still in theater. Now he was leaving. And now he felt the old bitterness boiling up inside again. The bitterness had been chronic and passive, and now it threatened to become active and acute.

If I could only give them one last performance! he thought. One last great role—

But *that* thought led to the fantasy-plan for revenge, the plan that came to him often as he wandered about the empty theater. Revenge was no good. And the plan was only a daydream. And yet—he wasn't going to get another chance.

He set his jaw grimly and drove on to the Smithfield depot.

The depot clerk had hauled the crated mannequin to the fore, and it was waiting for Thornier when he entered the stock room. He rolled it out from the wall on a dolly, and the janitor helped him wrestle the coffin-sized packing case onto the counter.

"Don't take it to the truck yet," the clerk grunted around the fat stub of a cigar. "It ain't a new doll, and you gotta sign a release."

"What kind of a release?"

"Liability for malfunction. If the doll breaks down during the show, you can't sue Smithfield. It's standard prack for used-doll rentals."

"Why didn't they send a new one, then?"

"Discontinued production on this model. You want it, you take a used one, and sign the release."

"Suppose I don't sign?"

"No siggy, no dolly."

"Oh." He thought for a moment. Obviously, the clerk had mistaken him for production personnel. His signature wouldn't mean anything—but it was getting late, and Jade was rushed. Since the release wouldn't be valid anyhow he reached for the form.

"Wait," said the clerk. "You better look at what you're signing for." He reached for a wrecking claw and slipped it under a metal binding strap. The strap broke with a screechy snap. "It's been overhauled," the clerk continued. "New solenoid fluid injected, new cosmetic job. Nothing really wrong. A few fatigue spots in the padding, and one toe missing. But you oughta have a look, anyhow."

He finished breaking the lid-fastenings loose and turned to a wall-control board. "We don't have a complete Maestro here," he said as he closed a knife switch, "but we got the control transmitters, and some taped sequences. It's enough to pre-flight a doll."

Equipment hummed to life somewhere behind the panel. The clerk adjusted several dials while Thornier waited impatiently.

"Let's see—" muttered the clerk. "Guess we'll start off with the Frankenstein sequence." He flipped a switch.

A purring sound came faintly from within the coffinlike box. Thornier watched nervously. The lid stirred, began to rise. A woman's hands came into view, pushing the lid up from within. The purring increased. The lid clattered aside to hang by the metal straps.

The woman sat up and smiled at the janitor.

Thornier went white. "Mela!" he hissed.

"Ain't that a chiller?" chuckled the clerk. "Now for the hoochy-coochy sequence—"

"No—"

The clerk flipped another switch. The doll stood up slowly, chastely nude as a window-dummy. Still smiling at Thorny, the doll did a bump and a grind.

"Stop it!" he yelled hoarsely.

"Whassa matter, buddy?"

Thorny heard another switch snap. The doll stretched gracefully and yawned. It stretched out in its packing case again, closed its eyes and folded its hands over its bosom. The purring stopped.

"What's eating you?" the clerk grumbled, slapping the lid back over the case again. "You sick or something?"

"I . . . I knew her," Ryan Thornier wheezed. "I used to work—" He shook himself angrily and seized the crate.

"Wait, I'll give you a hand."

Fury awakened new muscles. He hauled the crate out on the loading dock without assistance and dumped in it the back of the truck, then came back to slash his name across the release forms.

"You sure get sore easy," the clerk mumbled. "You better take it easy. You sure better take it easy."

Thorny was cursing softly as he nosed the truck out into the river of traffic. Maybe Jade thought it was funny, sending him after Mela's doll. Jade remembered how it had been between them—if she bothered to think about it. Thornier and Stone—a team that had gotten constant attention from the gossip columnists in the old days. Rumors of engagement, rumors of secret marriage, rumors squabbles and reunions, break-ups and patch-ups, and some of the rumors were almost true. Maybe Jade thought it was a howl, sending him to fetch the mannequin.

But no—his anger faded as he drove along the boulevard—she hadn't thought about it. Probably she tried hard not to think of old times any more.

Gloom settled over him again, replacing rage. Still it haunted him—the horrified shock of seeing her sit up like an awakened corpse to smile at him. *Mela . . . Mela—*

They'd had it good together and bad together. Bit parts and beans in a cold-water flat. Starring roles and steaks at Sardi's. And

—love? Was that what it was? He thought of it uneasily. Hypnotic absorption in each other, perhaps, and in the mutual intoxication of their success—but it wasn't necessarily love. Love was calm and even and lasting, and you paid for it with a dedicated lifetime, and Mela wouldn't pay. She'd walked out on them. She'd walked to Smithfield and bought security with sacrifice of principle. There'd been a name for what she'd done. "Scab," they used to say.

He shook himself. It was no good, thinking about those times. Times died with each passing minute. Now they paid $8.80 to watch Mela's figurine move in her stead, wearing Mela's face, moving with Mela's gestures, walking with the same lilting walk. And the doll was still young, while Mela had aged ten years, years of collecting quarterly royalties from her dolls and living comfortably.

Great Actors Immortalized—that was one of Smithfield's little slogans. But they had discontinued production on Mela Stone, the depot clerk had said. Overstocked.

The promise of relative immortality had been quite a bait. Actors unions had resisted autodrama, for obviously the bit players and the lesser-knowns would not be in demand. By making dozens—even hundreds—of copies of the same leading star, top talent could be had for every role, and the same actor-mannequin could be playing simultaneously in dozens of shows all over the country. The unions had resisted—but only a few were wanted by Smithfield anyhow, and the lure was great. The promise of fantastic royalties was enticing enough, but in addition—immortality for the actor, through duplication of mannequins. Authors, artists, playwrights had always been able to outlive the centuries, but actors were remembered only by professionals, and their names briefly recorded in the annals of the stage. Shakespeare would live another thousand years, but who remembered Dick Burbage who trouped in the day of the bard's premiers? Flesh and bone, heart and brain, these were the trouper's media, and his art could not outlive them.

Thorny knew the yearnings after lastingness, and he could no longer hate the ones who had gone over. As for himself, the autodrama industry had made him a tentative offer, and he had resisted—partly because he was reasonably certain that the offer would have been withdrawn during testing procedures. Some actors were not "cybergenic"—could not be adequately sculptured into electronic-robotic analogues. These were the portrayers, whose art was inward, whose roles had to be lived rather than played. No polygraphic analogue could duplicate their talents, and Thornier knew he was one of them. It had been easy for him to resist.

At the corner of Eighth Street, he remembered the spare tape and the replacement pickup for the Maestro. But if he turned back now, he'd hold up the run-through, and Jade would be furious. Mentally he kicked himself, and drove on to the delivery entrance of the theater. There he left the crated mannequin with the stage crew, and headed back for the depot without seeing the producer.

"Hey, bud," said the clerk, "your boss was on the phone. Sounded pretty unhappy."

"Who . . . D'Uccia?"

"No . . . well, yeah, D'Uccia, too. He wasn't unhappy, just having fits. I meant Miss Ferne."

"Oh . . . where's your phone?"

"Over there. The lady was near hysterical."

Thorny swallowed hard and headed for the booth. Jade Ferne was a good friend, and if his absent-mindedness had goofed up her production—

"I've got the pickup and the tape ready to go," the clerk called after him. "She told me about it on the phone. Boy, you're sure on the ball today, ain't ya—the greasy eight ball."

Thorny reddened and dialed nervously.

"Thank God!" she groaned. "Thorny, we did the run-through with Andreyev a walking zombie. The Maestro chewed up our duplicate Peltier tape, and we're running without an actor-analogue in the starring role. Baby, I could murder you!"

"Sorry, Jade. I slipped a cog, I guess."

"Never mind! Just get the new pickup mechanism over here for Thomas. And the Peltier tape. And don't have a wreck. It's two o'clock, and tonight's opening, and we're still short our leading man. And there's no time to get anything else flown in from Smithfield."

"In some ways, nothing's changed, has it, Jade?" he grunted, thinking of the eternal backstage hysteria that lasted until the lights went low and beauty and calm order somehow emerged miraculously out of the prevailing chaos.

"Don't philosophize, just *get* here!" she snapped, and hung up.

The clerk had the cartons ready for him as he emerged. "Look, chum, better take care of that Peltier tape," the clerk advised. "It's the last one in the place. I've got more on order, but they won't be here for a couple of days."

Thornier stared at the smaller package thoughtfully. The last Peltier?

The plan, he remembered the plan. *This* would make it easy. Of course, the plan was only a fantasy, a vengeful dream. He couldn't go through with it. To wreck the show would be a stab at Jade—

He heard his own voice like a stranger's, saying: "Miss Ferne also asked me to pick up a Wilson Granger tape, and a couple of three-inch splices."

The clerk looked surprised. "Granger? He's not in the 'Anarch,' is he?"

Thornier shook his head. "No—guess she wants it for a trial casting. Next show, maybe."

The clerk shrugged and went to get the tape and the splices. Thornier stood clenching and unclenching his fists. He wasn't going to go through with it, of course. Only a silly fantasy.

"I'll have to make a separate ticket on these," said the clerk, returning.

He signed the delivery slips in a daze, then headed for the truck. He drove three blocks from the depot, then parked in a loading zone. He opened the tape cartons carefully with his pen-knife, peeling back the glued flaps so that they could be sealed again. He removed the two rolls of pattern perforated tape from their small metal canisters, carefully plucked off the masking-tape seals and stuck them temporarily to the dashboard. He unrolled the first half-yard of the Peltier tape; it was unperforated, and printed with identifying codes and manufacturer's data. Fortunately, it was not a brand-new tape; it had been used before, and he could see the wear-marks. A splice would not arouse suspicion.

He cut off the identifying tongue with his knife, laid it aside. Then he did the same to the Granger tape.

Granger was fat, jovial, fiftyish. His mannequin played comic supporting roles.

Peltier was young, gaunt, gloomy—the intellectual villain, the dedicated fanatic. A fair choice for the part of Andreyev.

Thornier's hands seemed to move of their own volition, playing reflexively in long-rehearsed roles. He cut the tapes. He took out one of the hot-splice packs and jerked the tab that started the chemical action. He clocked off fifteen seconds by his watch, then opened the pack and fitted into it the cut ends of the Granger tape and the Peltier identifying tongue, butted them carefully end to end, and closed the pack. When it stopped smoking, he opened it to inspect the splice. A neat patch, scarcely visible on the slick plastic tape. Granger's analogue, labeled as Peltier's. And the body of the mannequin was Peltier's. He resealed it in its canister.

He wadded the Peltier tape and the Granger label and the extra delivery receipt copy into the other box. Then he pulled the truck out of the loading zone and drove through the heavy traffic like a racing jockey, trusting the anti-crash radar to see him safely through. As he crossed the bridge, he threw the Peltier tape out the window into the river. And then there was no retreat from what he had done.

Jade and Feria sat in the orchestra, watching the final act of the run-through with a dud Andreyev. When Thorny slipped in beside them, Jade wiped mock sweat from her brow.

"Thank God you're back!" she whispered as he displayed the delayed packages. "Sneak backstage and run them up to Rick in the booth, will you? Thorny, I'm out of my mind!"

"Sorry, Miss Ferne." Fearing that his guilty nervousness hung about him like a ragged cloak, he slipped quickly backstage and delivered the cartons to Thomas in the booth. The technician hovered over the Maestro as the play went on, and he gave Thornier only a quick nod and a wave.

Thorny retreated into misty old corridors and unused dressing rooms, now heaped with junk and remnants of other days. He had to get a grip on himself, had to quit quaking inside. He

wandered alone in the deserted sections of the building, opening
old doors to peer into dark cubicles where great stars had preened
in other days, other nights. Now full of trunks and cracked mir-
rors and tarpaulins and junked mannequins. Faint odors lingered
—nervous smells—perspiration, make-up, dim perfume that pervaded the walls. Mildew and dust—the aroma of time. His footsteps sounded hollowly through the unpeopled rooms, while
muffled sounds from the play came faintly through the walls—
the hysterical pleading of Marka, the harsh laughter of Piotr, the
marching boots of the revolutionist guards, a burst of music toward the end of the scene.

He turned abruptly and started back toward the stage. It was
no good, hiding away like this. He must behave normally, must
do what he usually did. The falsified Peltier tape would not
wreak its havoc until after the first run-through, when Thomas
fed it into the Maestro, reset the machine, and prepared to start
the second trial run. Until then, he must remain casually himself,
and afterwards—?

Afterwards, things would have to go as he had planned. Afterwards, Jade would have to come to him, as he believed she
would. If she didn't, then he had bungled, he had clumsily
wrecked, and to no avail.

He slipped through the power-room where converters hummed
softly, supplying power to the stage. He stood close to the entrance, watching the beginnings of scene *iii*, of the third act.
Andreyev—the Peltier doll—was on alone, pacing grimly in his
apartment while the low grumble of a street mob and the distant
rattle of machine-gun fire issued from the Maestro-managed
sound effect system. After a moment's watching, he saw that
Andreyev's movements were not "grim" but merely methodical
and lifeless. The tapeless mannequin, going through the required
motions, robotlike, without interpretation of meaning. He heard a
brief burst of laughter from someone in the production row, and
after watching the zombielike rendering of Andreyev in a sus-
penseful scene, he, too, found himself grinning faintly.

The pacing mannequin looked toward him suddenly with a
dead-pan face. It raised both fists toward its face.

"Help," it said in a conversational monotone. "Ivan, where are
you? Where? Surely they've come; they must come." It spoke

quietly, without inflection. It ground its fists casually against its temples, paced mechanically again.

A few feet away, two mannequins that had been standing frozen in the off-stage lineup, clicked suddenly to life. As ghostly calm as display window dummies, they galvanized suddenly at a signal pulse command from the Maestro. Muscles—plastic sacs filled with oil-suspended magnetic powder and wrapped with elastic coils of wire, like flexible solenoids—tightened and strained beneath the airfoam flesh, working spasmodically to the pulsing rhythms of the polychromatic u.h.f. commands of the Maestro. Expressions of fear and urgency leaped to their faces. They crouched, tensed, looked around, then burst on stage, panting wildly.

"Comrade, she's come, she's come!" one of them screamed. "She's come with *him*, with Boris!"

"What? She has him prisoner?" came the casual reply.

"No, no, comrade. We've been betrayed. She's with him. She's a traitor, she's sold out to them."

There was no feeling in the uninterpreted Andreyev's responses, even when he shot the bearer of bad tidings through the heart.

Thornier grew fascinated with watching as the scene progressed. The mannequins moved gracefully, their movements sinuous and more evenly flowing then human, they seemed boneless. The ratio of mass-to-muscle power of their members was carefully chosen to yield the flow of a dance with their every movement. Not clanking mechanical robots, not stumbling puppets, the dolls sustained patterns of movement and expression that would have quickly brought fatigue to a human actor, and the Maestro coördinated the events on stage in a way that would be impossible to a group of humans, each an individual and thinking independently.

It was as always. First, he looked with a shudder at the Machine moving in the stead of flesh and blood, at Mechanism sitting in the seat of artistry. But gradually his chill melted away, and the play caught him, and the actors were no longer machines. He lived in the role of Andreyev, and breathed the lines off stage, and he knew the rest of them: Mela and Peltier, Sam Dion and

Peter Repplewaite. He tensed with them, gritted his teeth in anticipation of difficult lines, cursed softly at the dud Andreyev, and forgot to listen for the faint crackle of sparks as the mannequins' feet stepped across the copper-studded floor, drinking energy in random bites to keep their storage packs near full charge.

Thus entranced, he scarcely noticed the purring and brushing and swishing sounds that came from behind him, and grew louder. He heard a quiet mutter of voices nearby, but only frowned at the distraction, kept his attention rooted to the stage.

Then a thin spray of water tickled his ankles. Something soggy and spongelike slapped against his foot. He whirled.

A gleaming metal spider, three feet high came at him slowly on six legs, with two grasping claws extended. It clicked its way toward him across the floor, throwing out a thin spray of liquid which it promptly sucked up with the spongelike proboscis. With one grasping claw, it lifted a ten-gallon can near his leg, sprayed under it, swabbed, and set the can down again.

Thornier came unfrozen with a howl, leaped over the thing, hit the wet-soapy deck off balance. He skidded and sprawled. The spider scrubbed at the floor toward the edge of the stage, then reversed directions and came back toward him.

Groaning, he pulled himself together, on hands and knees. D'Uccia's cackling laughter spilled over him. He glanced up. The chubby manager and the servo salesman stood over him, the salesman grinning, D'Uccia chortling.

"Datsa ma boy, datsa ma boy! Always, he watcha the show, then he don't swip-op around, then he wantsa day off. Thatsa ma boy, for sure." D'Uccia reached down to pat the metal spider's chassis. "Hey, *ragazzo*," he said again to Thornier, "want you should meet my new *boy* here. This one, he don't watcha the show like you."

He got to his feet, ghost-white and muttering. D'Uccia took closer note of his face, and his grin went sick. He inched back a step. Thornier glared at him briefly, then whirled to stalk away. He whirled into near collision with the Mela Stone mannequin, recovered, and started to pass in back of it.

Then he froze.

The Mela Stone mannequin was on stage, in the final scene.

And this one looked older, and a little haggard. It wore an expression of shocked surprise as it looked him up and down. One hand darted to its mouth.

"Thorny—!" A frightened whisper.

"*Mela!*" Despite the play, he shouted it, opening his arms to her. "Mela, how *wonderful!*"

And then, he noticed she winced away from his sodden coveralls. And she wasn't glad to see him at all.

"Thorny, how nice," she managed to murmur, extending her hand gingerly. The hand flashed with jewelry.

He took it for an empty second, stared at her, then walked hurriedly away, knots twisting up inside him. Now he could play it through. Now he could go on with it, and even enjoy executing his plan against all of them.

Mela had come to watch opening night for her doll in "The Anarch," as if its performance were her own. *I'll arrange,* he thought, *for it not to be a dull show.*

"No, no, *nooo!*" came the monotone protest of the dud Andreyev, in the next-to-the-last scene. The bark of Marka's gun, and the Peltier mannequin crumpled to the stage; and except for a brief triumphant denouement, the play was over.

At the sound of the gunshot, Thornier paused to smile tightly over his shoulder, eyes burning from his hawklike face. Then he vanished into the wings.

She got away from them as soon as she could, and she wandered around backstage until she found him in the storage room of the costuming section. Alone, he was sorting through the contents of an old locker and muttering nostalgically to himself. She smiled and closed the door with a thud. Startled, he dropped an old collapsible top-hat and a box of blank cartridges back into the trunk. His hand dived into his pocket as he straightened.

"Jade! I didn't expect—"

"Me to come?" She flopped on a dusty old chaise longue with a weary sigh and fanned herself with a program, closing her eyes. She kicked off her shoes and muttered: "Infuriating bunch. I hate 'em!"—made a retching face, and relaxed into little-girlhood. A little girl who had trouped with Thornier and the rest of them —the *actress* Jade Ferne, who had begged for bit parts and haunted the agencies and won the roles through endless rehearsals and shuddered with fright before opening curtain like the rest of them. Now she was a pert little woman with shrewd eyes, streaks of gray at the temples, and hard lines around her mouth. As she let the executive cloak slip away, the shrewdness and the hard lines melted into weariness.

"Fifteen minutes to get my sanity back, Thorny," she muttered, glancing at her watch as if to time it.

He sat on the trunk and tried to relax. She hadn't seemed to notice his uneasiness, or else she was just too tired to attach any significance to it. If she found him out, she'd have him flayed and pitched out of the building on his ear, and maybe call the police. She came in a small package, but so did an incendiary grenade. *It won't hurt you, Jade, what I'm doing*, he told himself. *It'll cause a big splash, and you won't like it, but it won't hurt you, nor even wreck the show.*

He was doing it for show business, the old kind, the kind they'd both known and loved. And in that sense, he told himself further, he was doing it as much for her as he was for himself.

"How was the run-through, Jade?" he asked casually. "Except for Andreyev, I mean."

"Superb, simply superb," she said mechanically.

"I mean *really*."

She opened her eyes, made a sick mouth. "Like always, Thorny, like always. Nauseating, overplayed, perfectly directed for a gum-chewing bag-rattling crowd. A crowd that wants it overplayed so that it won't have to think about what's going on. A crowd that doesn't want to reach *out* for a feeling or a meaning. It wants to be clubbed in the head with the meaning, so it doesn't have to reach. I'm sick of it."

He looked briefly surprised. "That figures," he grunted wryly.

She hooked her bare heels on the edge of the longue, hugged her shins, rested her chin on her knees, and blinked at him. "Hate me for producing the stuff, Thorny?"

He thought about it for a moment, shook his head. "I get sore at the set-up sometimes, but I don't blame you for it."

"That's good. Sometimes I'd trade places with you. Sometimes I'd rather be a charwoman and scrub D'Uccia's floors instead."

"Not a chance," he said sourly. "The Maestro's relatives are taking *that* over, too."

"I know. I heard. You're out of a job, thank God. Now you can get somewhere."

He shook his head. "I don't know where. I can't do anything but act."

"Nonsense. I can get you a job tomorrow."

"Where?"

"With Smithfield. Sales promotion. They're hiring a number of old actors in the department."

"No." He said it flat and cold.

"Not so fast. This is something new. The company's expanding."

"Ha."

"Autodrama for the home. A four-foot stage in every living room. Miniature mannequins, six inches high. Centralized Maestro service. Great plays piped to your home by concentric cable. Just dial Smithfield, make your request. Sound good?"

He stared at her icily. "Greatest thing in show business since Sarah Bernhardt," he offered tonelessly.

"Thorny! Don't get nasty with me!"

"Sorry. But what's so new about having it in the home? Autodrama took over TV years ago."

"I know, but this is different. Real miniature theater. Kids go wild for it. But it'll take good promotion to make it catch on."

"Sorry, but you know me better than that."

She shrugged, sighed wearily, closed her eyes again. "Yes, I do. You've got portrayer's integrity. You're a darfsteller. A director's ulcer. You can't play a role without living it, and you won't live it unless you believe it. So go ahead and starve." She spoke crossly, but he knew there was grudging admiration behind it.

"I'll be O.K.," he grunted, adding to himself: *after tonight's performance.*

"Nothing I can do for you?"

"Sure. Cast me. I'll stand in for dud mannequins."

She gave him a sharp glance, hesitated. "You know, I believe you *would!*"

He shrugged. "Why not?"

She stared thoughtfully at a row of packing cases, waggled her dark head. "Hmmp! What a spectacle that'd be—a human actor, incognito, playing in an autodrama."

"It's been done—in the sticks."

"Yes, but the audience knew it was being done, and that always spoils the show. It creates contrasts that don't exist or wouldn't be noticed otherwise. Makes the dolls seem snaky, birdlike, too rubbery quick. With no humans on stage for contrast, the dolls just seem wistfully graceful, ethereal."

"But if the audience didn't know—"

Jade was smiling faintly. "I wonder," she mused. "I wonder if they'd guess. They'd notice a difference, of course—in one mannequin."

"But they'd think it was just the Maestro's interpretation of the part."

"Maybe—if the human actor were careful."

He chuckled sourly. "If it fooled the critics—"

"Some ass would call it 'an abysmally unrealistic interpretation' or 'too obviously mechanical.'" She glanced at her watch, shook herself, stretched wearily, and slipped into her shoes again. "Anyway," she added, "there's no reason to do it, since the Maestro's *really* capable of rendering a better-than-human performance anyhow."

The statement brought an agonized gasp from the janitor. She looked at him and giggled. "Don't be shocked, Thorny. I said '*capable* of'—not 'in the habit of.' Autodrama entertains audiences on the level they *want* to be entertained on."

"But—"

"*Just*," she added firmly, "as show business has always done."

"But—"

"Oh, retract your eyeballs, Thorny. I didn't mean to blaspheme." She preened, began slipping back into her producer's mold as she prepared to return to her crowd. "The only thing wrong with autodrama is that it's scaled down to the moron-level —but show business always has been, and probably should be. Even if it gives us kids a pain." She smiled and patted his cheek. "Sorry I shocked you. Au 'voir, Thorny. And luck."

When she was gone, he sat fingering the cartridges in his pocket and staring at nothing. Didn't any of them have any sensibilities? Jade too, a seller of principle. And he had always thought of her as having merely compromised with necessity, against her real wishes. The idea that she could really believe autodrama capable of rendering a better-than-human performance—

But she didn't. Of course she needed to rationalize, to excuse what she was doing—

He sighed and went to lock the door, then to recover the old "Anarch" script from the trunk. His hands were trembling slightly. Had he planted enough of an idea in Jade's mind; would she remember it later? Or perhaps remember it too clearly, and suspect it?

He shook himself sternly. No apprehensions allowed. When Rick rang the bell for the second run-through, it would be his entrance-cue, and he must be in-character by then. Too bad he was no schauspieler, too bad he couldn't switch himself on-and-off the way Jade could do, but the necessity for much inward preparation was the burden of the darfsteller. He could not change into a role without first changing himself, and letting the revision seep surfaceward as it might, reflecting the inner state of the man.

Strains of "Moussorgsky" pervaded the walls. He closed his eyes to listen and feel. Music for empire. Music at once brutal and majestic. It was the time of upheaval, of vengeance, of overthrow. Two times, superimposed. It was the time of opening night, with Ryan Thornier—ten years ago—cast in the starring role.

He fell into a kind of trance as he listened and clocked the pulse of his psyche and remembered. He scarcely noticed when the music stopped, and the first few lines of the play came through the walls.

"Cut! Cut!" A worried shout. Feria's.

It had begun.

Thornier took a deep breath and seemed to come awake. When he opened his eyes and stood up, the janitor was gone. The janitor had been a nightmare role, nothing more.

And Ryan Thornier, star of "Walkaway," favored of the critics, confident of a bright future, walked out of the storage room with a strange lightness in his step. He carried a broom, he still wore the dirty coveralls, but now as if to a masquerade.

The Peltier mannequin lay sprawled on the stage in a grotesque heap. Ryan Thornier stared at it calmly from behind the set and listened intently to the babble of stage hands and technicians that milled about him:

"Don't know. Can't tell yet. It came out staggering and gibbering—like it was drunk. It reached for a table, then it fell on its face—"

"Acted like the trouble might be a mismatched tape, but Rick rechecked it. Really Peltier's tape—"

"Can't figure it out. Miss Ferne's having kittens."

Thornier paused to size up his audience. Jade, Ian, and their staff milled about in the orchestra section. The stage was empty, except for the sprawled mannequin. Too much frantic conversation, all around. His entrance would go unnoticed. He walked slowly on-stage and stood over the fallen doll with his hands in his pockets and his face pulled down in a somber expression. After a moment, he nudged the doll with his toe, paused, nudged it again. A faint giggle came from the orchestra. The corner of his eye caught Jade's quick glance toward the stage. She paused in the middle of a sentence.

Assured that she watched, he played to an imaginary audience-friend standing just off stage. He glanced toward the friend, lifted his brows questioningly. The friend apparently gave him the nod. He looked around warily, then knelt over the fallen doll. He took its pulse, nodded eagerly to the off-stage friend. Another giggle came from orchestra. He lifted the doll's head, sniffed its breath, made a face. Then, gingerly, he rolled it.

He reached deep into the mannequin's pocket, having palmed his own pocket watch beforehand. His hand paused there, and he smiled to his off-stage accomplice and nodded eagerly. He withdrew the watch and held it up by its chain for his accomplice's approval.

A light burst of laughter came from the production personnel. The laughter frightened the thief. He shot an apprehensive glance around the stage, hastily returned the watch to the fallen dummy, felt its pulse again. He traded a swift glance with his confederate, whispered "Aha!" and smiled mysteriously. Then he helped the doll to its feet and staggered away with it—a friend leading a drunk home to its family. In the doorway, he paused to frame his exit with a wary backward glance that said he was taking it to a dark alley where he could rob it in safety.

Jade was gaping at him.

Three technicians had been watching from just off the set, and they laughed heartily and clapped his shoulder as he passed, providing the off-stage audience to which he had seemed to be playing.

Good-natured applause came from Jade's people out front, and as Thorny carried the doll away to storage, he was humming softly to himself.

At five minutes till six, Rick Thomas and a man from the Smithfield depot climbed down out of the booth, and Jade pressed forward through the crowd to question him with her eyes.

"The tape," he said. "Defective."

"But it's too late to get another!" she squawked.

"Well, it's the tape, anyway."

"How do you *know?*"

"Well—trouble's bound to be in one of three places. The doll, the tape, or the analogue tank where the tape-data gets stored. We cleared the tank and tried it with another actor. Worked O.K. And the doll works O.K. on an uninterpreted run. So, by elimination, the tape."

She groaned and slumped into a seat, covering her face with her hands.

"No way at *all* to locate another tape?" Rick asked.

"We called every depot within five hundred miles. They'd have to cut one from a master. Take too long."

"So we call off the show!" Ian Feria called out resignedly, throwing up his hands in disgust. "Refund on tickets, open tomorrow."

"Wait!" snapped the producer, looking up suddenly. "Dooch—the house is sold out, isn't it?"

"Yah." D'Uccia grunted irritably. "She'sa filled op. Wassa matter with you pipple, you don' getsa Maestro fix? Wassa matter? We lose the money, hah?"

"Oh, shut up. Change curtain time to nine, offer refunds if they won't wait. Ian, keep at it. Get things set up for tonight." She spoke with weary determination, glancing around at them. "There

may be a slim chance. Keep at it. I'm going to try something."
She turned and started away.

"Hey!" Feria called.

"Explain later," she muttered over her shoulder.

She found Thornier replacing burned-out bulbs in the wall fixtures. He smiled down at her while he reset the clamps of an amber glass panel. "Need me for something, Miss Ferne?" he called pleasantly from the stepladder.

"I might," she said tersely. "Did you mean that offer about standing in for dud mannequins?"

A bulb exploded at her feet after it slipped from his hand. He came down slowly, gaping at her.

"You're not serious!"

"Think you could try a run-through as Andreyev?"

He shot a quick glance toward the stage, wet his lips, stared at her dumbly.

"Well—*can* you?"

"It's been ten years, Jade . . . I—"

"You can read over the script, and you can wear an earplug radio—so Rick can prompt you from the booth."

She made the offer crisply and matter-of-factly, and it made Thorny smile inwardly. It was theater—calmly asking the outrageously impossible, gambling on it, and getting it.

"The customers—they're expecting Peltier."

"Right now I'm only asking you to try a run-through, Thorny. After that, we'll see. But remember it's our only chance of going on tonight."

"Andreyev," he breathed. "The lead."

"Please, Thorny, will you try?"

He looked around the theater, nodded slowly. "I'll go study my lines," he said quietly, inclining his head with what he hoped was just the proper expression of humble bravery.

I've got to make it good, I've got to make it great. The last chance, the last great role—

Glaring footlights, a faint whisper in his ear, and the cold panic of the first entrance. It came and passed quickly. Then the stage was a closed room, and the audience—of technicians and production personnel—was only the fourth wall, somewhere beyond the lights. He was Andreyev, commissioner of police, party whip, loyal servant of the regime, now tottering in the revolutionary storm of the Eighties. The last Bolshevik, no longer a rebel, no longer a radical, but now the loyalist, the conservatist, the defender of the status quo, champion of the Marxist ruling classes. No longer conscious of a self apart from that of the role, he lived the role. And the others, the people he lived it with, the people whose feet crackled faintly as they stepped across the floor, he acted and reacted with them and against them as if they, too, shared life, and while the play progressed he forgot their lifelessness for a little time.

Caught up by the magic, enfolded in scheme of the inevitable, borne along by the tide of the drama, he felt once again the sense of belonging as a part in a whole, a known and predictable whole that moved as surely from scene *i* to the final curtain as man from womb to tomb, and there were no lost years, no lapse or sense of defeated purpose between the rehearsals of those many years ago and this the fulfillment of opening night. Only when at last he muffed a line, and Rick's correction whispered in his ear did the spell that was gathered about him briefly break —and he found himself unaccountably frightened, frightened by the sudden return of realization that all about him was Machine, and frightened, too, that he had forgotten. He had been conforming to the flighty mechanical grace of the others, reflexively imitating the characteristic lightness of the mannequins' movements, the dancelike qualities of their playing. To know suddenly, having forgotten it, that the mouth he had just kissed was not a woman's, but the rubber mouth of a doll, and that dancing patterns of high frequency waves from the Maestro had controlled the solenoid currents that turned her face lovingly up toward his, had lifted the cold soft hands to touch his face. The faint rubbery smell-taste hung about his mouth.

When his first exit came, he went off trembling. He saw Jade coming toward him, and for an instant, he felt a horrifying certainty that she would say, "Thorny, you were almost as good as a mannequin!" Instead, she said nothing, but only held out her hand to him.

"Was it too bad, Jade?"

"Thorny, you're in! Keep it up, and you might have more than a one-night stand. Even Ian's convinced. He squealed at the idea, but now he's sold."

"No kicks? How about the lines with Piotr?"

"Wonderful. Keep it up. Darling, you were marvelous."

"It's settled, then?"

"Darling, it's *never* settled until the curtain comes up. You know that." She giggled. "We had one *kick* all right—or maybe I shouldn't tell you."

He stiffened slightly. "Oh? Who from?"

"Mela Stone. She saw you come on, turned white as a sheet, and walked out. I can't imagine!"

He sank slowly on a haggard looking couch and stared at her. "The hell you can't," he grated softly.

"She's here on a personal appearance contract, you know. To give an opening and an intermission commentary on the author and the play." Jade smirked at him gleefully. "Five minutes ago she called back, tried to cancel her appearance. Of course, she can't pull a stunt like that. Not while Smithfield owns her."

Jade winked, patted his arm, tossed an uncoded copy of the script at him, then headed back toward the orchestra. Briefly he wondered what Jade had against Mela. Nothing serious, probably. Both had been actresses. Mela got a Smithfield contract; Jade didn't get one. It was enough.

By the time he had reread the scene to follow, his second cue was approaching, and he moved back toward the stage.

Things went smoothly. Only three times during the first act did he stumble over lines he had not rehearsed in ten years. Rick's prompting was in his ear, and the Maestro could compensate to some extent for his minor deviations from the script. This time he avoided losing himself so completely in the play; and this time the weird realization that he had become one with the machine-set pattern did not disturb him. This time he remembered, but when the first break came—

"Not quite so good, Thorny," Ian Feria called. "Whatever you were doing in the first scene, do it again. That was a little wooden. Go through that last bit again, and play it down. Andreyev's no mad bear from the Urals. It's Marka's moment, anyhow. Hold in."

He nodded slowly and looked around at the frozen dolls. He

had to forget the machinery. He had to lose himself in it and live it, even if it meant being a replacement link in the mechanism. It disturbed him somehow, even though he was accustomed to subordinating himself to the total gestalt of the scene as in other days. For no apparent reason, he found himself listening for laughter from the production people, but none came.

"All right," Feria called. "Bring 'em alive again."

He went on with it, but the uneasy feeling nagged at him. There was self-mockery in it, and the expectation of ridicule from those who watched. He could not understand why, and yet—

There was an ancient movie—one of the classics—in which a man named Chaplin had been strapped into a seat on a production line where he performed a perfectly mechanical task in a perfectly mechanical fashion, a task that could obviously have been done by a few cams and a linkage or two, and it was one of the funniest comedies of all times—yet tragic. A task that made him a part in an overall machine.

He sweated through the second and third acts in a state of compromise with himself—overplaying it for purposes of self-preparation, yet trying to convince Feria and Jade that he could handle it and handle it well. Overacting was necessary in spots, as a learning technique. Deliberately ham up the rehearsal to impress lines on memory, then underplay it for the real performance—it was an old trick of troupers who had to do a new show each night and had only a few hours in which to rehearse and learn lines. But would they know why he was doing it?

When it was finished, there was no time for another runthrough, and scarcely time for a nap and a bite to eat before dressing for the show.

"It was terrible, Jade," he groaned. "I muffed it. I know I did."

"Nonsense. You'll be in tune tonight, Thorny. I knew what you were doing, and I can see past it."

"Thanks. I'll try to pull in."

"About the final scene, the shooting—"

He shot her a wary glance. "What about it?"

"The gun'll be loaded tonight, blanks, of course. And this time you'll have to fall."

"So?"

"So be careful where you fall. Don't go down on the copper bus-lugs. A hundred and twenty volts mightn't kill you, but we don't want a dying Andreyev bouncing up and spitting blue sparks. The stagehands'll chalk out a safe section for you. And one other thing—"

"Yes?"

"Marka fires from close range. Don't get burned."

"I'll watch it."

She started away, then paused to frown back at him steadily for several seconds. "Thorny, I've got a queer feeling about you. I can't place it exactly."

He stared at her evenly, waiting.

"Thorny, are you going to wreck the show?"

His face showed nothing, but something twisted inside him. She looked beseeching, trusting, but worried. She was counting on him, placing faith in him—

"Why should I botch up the performance, Jade? Why should I do a thing like that?"

"I'm asking you."

"O.K. I promise you—you'll get the best Andreyev I can give you."

She nodded slowly. "I believe you. I didn't doubt *that*, exactly."

"Then what worries you?"

"I don't know. I know how you feel about autodrama. I just got a shuddery feeling that you had something up your sleeve. That's all. I'm sorry. I know you've got too much integrity to wreck your own performance, but—" She stopped and shook her head, her dark eyes searching him. She was still worried.

"Oh, all right. I was going to stop the show in the third act. I was going to show them my appendectomy scar, do a couple of card tricks, and announce that I was on strike. I was going to walk out." He clucked his tongue at her, looked hurt.

She flushed slightly, and laughed. "Oh, I know you wouldn't pull anything shabby. Not that you wouldn't do anything you *could* to take a swat at autodrama generally, but . . . there's nothing you could do tonight that would accomplish anything. Except sending the customers home mad. That doesn't fit you, and I'm sorry I thought of it."

"Thanks. Stop worrying. If you lose dough, it won't be my fault."

"I believe you, but—"

"But what?"

She leaned close to him. "But you look too triumphant, that's what!" she hissed, then patted his cheek.

"Well, it's my last role. I—"

But she had already started away, leaving him with his sandwich and a chance for a nap.

Sleep would not come. He lay fingering the .32 caliber cartridges in his pocket and thinking about the impact of his final exit upon the conscience of the theater. The thoughts were pleasant.

It struck him suddenly as he lay drowsing that they would call it suicide. How silly. Think of the jolting effect, the dramatic punch, the audience reaction. Mannequins don't bleed. And later, the headlines: Robot Player Kills Old Trouper, Victim of Mechanized Stage. Still, they'd call it suicide. How silly.

But maybe that's what the paranoid on the twentieth story window ledge thought about, too—the audience reaction. Wasn't every self-inflicted wound really aimed at the conscience of the world?

It worried him some, but—

"*Fifteen minutes until curtain,*" the sound system was croaking. "*Fifteen minutes—*"

"Hey, Thorny!" Feria called irritably. "Get back to the costuming room. They've been looking for you."

He got up wearily, glanced around at the backstage bustle, then shuffled away toward the make-up department. One thing was certain: he had to go on.

The house was less than packed. A third of the customers had taken refunds rather than wait for the postponed curtain and a substitute Andreyev, a substitute unknown or ill-remembered at best, with no Smithy index rating beside his name in lights. Nevertheless, the bulk of the audience had planned their evenings and stayed to claim their seats with only suppressed bad humor about the delay. Scalpers' customers who had overpaid and who could not reclaim more than half the bootleg price from the box-office were forced to accept the show or lose money and get nothing. They came, and shifted restlessly, and glanced at their watches while an m.c.'s voice made apologies and introduced orchestral numbers, mostly from the Russian composers. Then, finally—

"Ladies and gentlemen, tonight we have with us one of the best loved actresses of stage, screen, and autodrama, co-star of our play tonight, as young and lovely as she was when first immortalized by Smithfield—Mela *Stone!*"

Thornier watched tight-lipped from shadows as she stepped gracefully into the glare of the footlights. She seemed abnormally pale, but make-up artistry had done a good job; she looked only slightly older than her doll, still lovely, though less arrogantly beautiful. Her flashing jewelry was gone, and she wore a simple dark gown with a deep-slit neck, and her tawny hair was wrapped high in a turbanlike coiffure that left bare a graceful neck.

"Ten years ago," she began quietly, "I rehearsed for a production of 'The Anarch' which never appeared, rehearsed it with a man named Ryan Thornier in the starring role, the actor who fills that role tonight. I remember with a special sort of glow the times—"

She faltered, and went on lamely. Thorny winced. Obviously the speech had been written by Jade Ferne and evidently the words were like bits of poisoned apples in Mela's mouth. She gave the impression that she was speaking them only because it wasn't polite to retch them. Mela was being punished for her attempt to back out, and Jade had forced her to appear only by threatening to fit out the Stone mannequin with a gray wig and have the doll read her curtain speeches. The small producer had a vicious streak, and she exercised it when crossed.

Mela's introductory lines were written to convince the audience that it was indeed lucky to have Thornier instead of Peltier, but there was nothing to intimate his flesh-and-blood status. She did not use the words "doll" or "mannequin," but allowed the audience to keep its preconceptions without confirming them. It was short. After a few anecdotes about the show's first presentation more than a generation ago, she was done.

"And with no further delay, my friends, I give you—Pruchev's 'The Anarch.'"

She bowed away and danced behind the curtains and came off crying. A majestic burst of music heralded the opening scene. She saw Thornier and stopped, not yet off stage. The curtain started up. She darted toward him, hesitated, stopped to stare up at him apprehensively. Her eyes were brimming, and she was biting her lip.

On stage, a telephone jangled on the desk of Commissioner Andreyev. His cue was still three minutes away. A lieutenant came on to answer the phone.

"Nicely done, Mela," he whispered, smiling sourly.

She didn't hear him. Her eyes drifted down to his costume— very like the uniform he'd worn for a dress rehearsal ten years ago. Her hand went to her throat. She wanted to run from him, but after a moment she got control of herself. She looked at her own mannequin waiting in the line-up, then at Thornier.

"Aren't you going to say something appropriate?" she hissed.

"I—" His icy smile faded slowly. The first small triumph—triumph over Mela, a sick and hag-ridden Mela who had bought security at the expense of integrity and was still paying for it in small installments like this, Mela whom he once had loved. The first small "triumph" coiled into a sick knot in his throat.

She started away, but he caught her arm.

"I'm sorry, Mela," he muttered hoarsely. "I'm really sorry."

"It's not your fault."

But it was. She didn't know what he'd done, of course; didn't know he'd switched the tapes and steered his own selection as a replacement for the Peltier doll, so that she'd have to watch him playing opposite the doll-image of a Mela who had ceased to exist ten years ago, watch him relive a mockery of something.

"I'm sorry," he whispered again.

She shook her head, pulled her arm free, hurried away. He watched her go and went sick inside. Their frigid meeting earlier in the day had been the decisive moment, when in a surge of bitterness he'd determined to go through with it and even excuse himself for doing it. Maybe bitterness had fogged his eyesight, he thought. Her reaction to bumping into him that way hadn't been snobbery; it had been horror. An old ghost in dirty coveralls and motley, whose face she'd probably fought to forget, had sprung up to confront her in a place that was too full of memories anyhow. No wonder she seemed cold. Probably he symbolized some of her own self-accusations, for he knew he had affected others that way. The successful ones, the ones who had profited by autodrama—they often saw him with mop and bucket, and if they remembered Ryan Thornier, turned quickly away. And at each turning away, he had felt a small glow of satisfaction as he imagined them thinking: *Thornier wouldn't compromise*—and hating him, because they had compromised and lost something thereby. But being hated by Mela—was different somehow. He didn't want it.

Someone nudged his ribs. "Your cue, Thorny!" hissed a tense voice. "You're *on!*"

He came awake with a grunt. Feria was shoving him frantically toward his entrance. He made a quick grab for his presence of mind, straightened into character, and strode on.

He muffed the scene badly. He knew that he muffed it even before he made his exit and saw their faces. He had missed two cues and needed prompting several times from Rick in the booth. His acting was wooden—he felt it.

"You're doing fine, Thorny, just fine!" Jade told him, because there was nothing else she *dared* tell him during a performance. Shock an actor's ego during rehearsal, and he had time to recover; shock it during a performance, and he might go sour for the night. He knew, though, without being told, the worry that seethed behind her mechanical little smile. "But just calm down a little, eh?" she advised. "It's going fine."

She left him to seethe in solitude. He leaned against the wall and glowered at his feet and flagellated himself. *You failure, you miserable crumb, you janitor-at-heart, you stage-struck charwoman—*

He had to straighten out. If he ruined this one, there'd never be another chance. But he kept thinking of Mela, and how he had wanted to hurt her, and how now that she was being hurt he wanted to stop.

"Your cue, Thorny—wake up!"

And he was on again, stumbling over lines, being terrified of the sea of dim faces where a fourth wall should be.

She was waiting for him after his second exit. He came off pale and shaking, perspiration soaking his collar. He leaned back and lit a cigarette and looked at her bleakly. She couldn't talk. She took his arm in both hands and kneaded it while she rested her forehead against his shoulder. He gazed down at her in dismay. She'd stopped feeling hurt; she couldn't feel hurt when she watched him make a fool of himself out there. She might have been vengefully delighted by it, and he almost wished that she were. Instead, she was pitying him. He was numb, sick to the core. He couldn't go on with it.

"Mela, I'd better tell *you;* I can't tell Jade what I—"

"Don't talk, Thorny. Just do your best." She peered up at him. "Please do your best?"

It startled him. Why should she feel that way?

"Wouldn't you really rather see me flop?" he asked.

She shook her head quickly, then paused and nodded it. "Part of me would, Thorny. A vengeful part. I've got to believe in the automatic stage. I . . . I do believe in it. But I don't want you to flop, not really." She put her hands over her eyes briefly. "You don't know what it's like seeing you out there . . . in the middle of all that . . . that—" She shook herself slightly. "It's a mockery, Thorny, you don't belong out there, but—as long as you're there, don't muff it. Do your best?"

"Yeah, sure."

"It's a precarious thing. The effect, I mean. If the audience starts realizing you're not a doll—" She shook her head slowly.

"What if they do?"

"They'll laugh. They'll laugh you right off the stage."

He was prepared for anything but that. It confirmed the nagging hunch he'd had during the run-through.

"Thorny, that's all I'm really concerned about. I don't care whether you play it well or play it lousy, as long as they don't find out what you are. I don't want them to laugh at you; you've been hurt enough."

"They wouldn't laugh if I gave a good performance."

"But they *would!* Not in the same way, but they would. Don't you see?"

His mouth fell open. He shook his head. It wasn't true. "Human actors have done it before," he protested. "In the sticks, on small stages with undersized Maestros."

"Have you ever seen such a play?"

He shook his head.

"I have. The audience knows about the human part of the cast in advance. So it doesn't strike them as funny. There's no jolt of discovering an incongruity. Listen to me Thorny—do your best, but you don't dare make it *better* than a doll could do."

Bitterness came back in a flood. Was this what he had hoped for? To give as machinelike a performance as possible, to do as good a job as the Maestro, but no better, and above all, *no different?* So that they wouldn't find out?

She saw his distressed expression and felt for his hand. "Thorny, don't hate me for telling you. I want you to bring it off O.K., and I thought you ought to realize. I think I know what's been wrong. You're afraid—down deep—that they *won't* recognize you for who you are, and that makes your performance un-doll-like. You better start being afraid they will recognize you, Thorny."

As he stared at her, it began to penetrate that she was still capable of being the woman he'd once known and loved. Worse, she wanted to save him from being laughed at. Why? If she felt motherly, she might conceivably want to shield him against wrath, criticism, or rotten tomatoes, but not against loss-of-dignity. Motherliness thrived on the demise of male dignity, for it sharpened the image of the child in the man.

"Mela—?"

"Yes, Thorny."

"I guess I never quite got over you."

She shook her head quickly, almost angrily.

"Darling, you're living ten years ago. I'm not, and I won't. Maybe I don't like the present very well, but I'm in it, and I can only change it in little ways. I can't make it the past again, and I won't try." She paused a moment, searching his face. "Ten years ago, we weren't living in the present either. We were living in a mythical, magic, wonderful future. Great talent, just starting to bloom. We were living in dream-plans in those days. The future we lived in never happened, and you can't go back and make it

C

happen. And when a dream-plan stops being possible, it turns into a pipe dream. I won't live in a pipe dream. I want to stay sane, even if it hurts."

"Too bad you had to come tonight," he said stiffly.

She wilted. "Oh, Thorny, I didn't mean that the way it sounded. And I wouldn't say it that strongly unless"—she glanced through the soundproof glass toward the stage where her mannequin was on in the scene with Piotr—"unless I had trouble too, with too much wishing."

"I wish you were with me out there," he said softly. "With no dolls and no Maestro. I know how it'd be then."

"Don't! Please, Thorny, don't."

"Mela, I loved you—"

"No!" She got up quickly. "I . . . I want to see you after the show. Meet me. But don't talk that way. Especially not here and not now."

"I can't help it."

"Please! Good-by for now, Thorny, and—do your best."

My best to be a mechanism, he thought bitterly as he watched her go.

He turned to watch the play. Something was wrong out there on the stage. Badly wrong. The Maestro's interpretation of the scene made it seem unfamiliar somehow. He frowned. Rick had spoken of the Maestro's ability to compensate, to shift interpretations, to redirect. Was that what was happening? The Maestro compensating—for *his* performance?

His cue was approaching. He moved closer to the stage.

Act I had been a flop. Feria, Ferne, and Thomas conferred in an air of tension and a haze of cigarette smoke. He heard heated muttering, but could not distinguish words. Jade called a stagehand, spoke to him briefly, and sent him away. The stagehand wandered through the group until he found Mela Stone, spoke to her quickly and pointed. Thorny watched her go to join the production group, then turned away. He slipped out of their line-of-sight and stood behind some folded backdrops, waiting for the end of a brief intermission and trying not to think.

"Great act, Thorny," a costumer said mechanically, and clapped his shoulder in passing.

He suppressed an impulse to kick the costumer. He got out a copy of the script and pretended to read his lines. A hand tugged at his sleeve.

"Jade!" He looked at her bleakly, started to apologize.

"Don't," she said. "We've talked it over. Rick, you tell him."

Rick Thomas who stood beside her grinned ruefully and waggled his head. "It's not altogether your fault, Thorny. Or haven't you noticed?"

"What do you mean?" he asked suspiciously.

"Take scene five, for example," Jade put in. "Suppose the cast had been entirely human. How would you feel about what happened?"

He closed his eyes for a moment and relived it. "I'd probably be sore," he said slowly. "I'd probably accuse Kovrin of jamming my lines and Aksinya of killing my exit—as an excuse," he added with a lame grin. "But I can't accuse the dolls. They can't steal."

"As a matter of fact, old man, they *can*," said the technician. "And your excuse is exactly right."

"Whh—what?"

"Sure. You *did* muff the first scene or two. The audience reacted to it. And the Maestro reacts to audience-reaction—by compensating through shifts in interpretation. It sees the stage as a whole, you included. As far as the Maestro's concerned, you're an untaped dud—like the Peltier doll we used in the first runthrough. It sends you only the script-tape signals, uninterpreted. Because it's got no analogue tape on you. Now without an audience, that'd be O.K. But with an audience reaction to go by, it starts compensating, and since it can't compensate through *you*, it works on the others."

"I don't understand."

"Bluntly, Thorny, the first scene or two stunk. The audience didn't like you. The Maestro started compensating by emphasizing other roles—and recharacterizing *you*, through the others."

"Recharacterize? How can it do that?"

"Easily, darling," Jade told him. "When Marka says 'I hate him; he's a beast'—for example—she can say it like it's true, or she can say it like she's just temporarily furious with Andreyev. And it affects the light in which the audience see you. Other actors affect *your* role. You know that's true of the old stage. Well, it's true of autodrama, too."

He stared at them in amazement. "Can't you stop it? Readjust the Maestro, I mean?"

"Not without clearing the whole thing out of the machine and starting over. The effect is cumulative. The more it compensates, the tougher it gets for you. The tougher it gets for you, the worse you look to the crowd. And the worse you look to the crowd, the more it tries to compensate."

He stared wildly at the clock. Less than a minute until the first scene of Act II. "What'll I do?"

"Stick it," said Jade. "We've been on the phone to Smithfield. There's a programming engineer in town, and he's on his way over in a heliocab. Then we'll see."

"We may be able to nurse it back in tune," Rick added, "a little at a time—by feeding in a fake set of audience-restlessness factors, and cutting out its feeler circuits out in the crowd. We'll try, that's all."

The light flashed for the beginning of the act.

"Good luck, Thorny."

"I guess I'll need it." Grimly he started toward his entrance.

The thing in the booth was watching him. It watched and measured and judged and found wanting. *Maybe,* he thought wildly, *it even hated him.* It watched, it planned, it regulated, and it was wrecking him.

The faces of the dolls, the hands, the voices—belonged to *it.* The wizard circuitry in the booth rallied them against him. It saw him, undoubtedly, as one of them, but not answering to its pulsing commands. It saw him, perhaps, as a malfunctioning doll, and it tried to correct the effects of his misbehavior. He thought of the old conflict between director and darfsteller, the self-directed actor—and it was the same conflict, aggravated by an electronic director's inability to understand that such things could be. The darfsteller, the undirectable portrayer whose acting welled from unconscious sources with no external strings—directors were inclined to hate them, even when the portrayal was superb. A mannequin, however, was the perfect schauspieler, the actor that a director could play like an instrument.

It would have been easier for him now had he been a schau-spieler, for perhaps he could adapt. But he was Andreyev, *his* Andreyev, as he had prepared himself for the role. Andreyev was incarnate as an *alter anima* within him. He had never "played" a role. He had always become the role. And now he could adapt to the needs of the moment on stage only as Andreyev, in and through his identity with Andreyev, and without changing the feel of his portrayal. To attempt it, to try to fall into conformity with what the Maestro was doing, would mean utter confusion. Yet, the machine was forcing him—through the others.

He stood stonily behind his desk, listening coldly to the denials of the prisoner—a revolutionary, an arsonist associated with Piotr's guerrilla band.

"I tell you, Comrade, I had nothing to do with it!" the prisoner shouted. "*Nothing!*"

"Haven't you questioned him thoroughly?" Andreyev growled at the lieutenant who guarded the man. "Hasn't he signed a confession?"

"There was no need, Comrade. His accomplice confessed," protested the lieutenant.

Only it wasn't supposed to be a protest. The lieutenant made it sound like a monstrous thing to do—to wring another confession, by torture perhaps, from the prisoner, when there was already sufficient evidence to convict. The words were right, but their meaning was wrenched. It should have been a crisp statement of fact: No need, Comrade; his accomplice confessed.

Thorny paused, reddening angrily. His next line was, "See that this one confesses, too." But he wasn't going to speak it. It would augment the effect of the lieutenant's tone of shocked protest. He thought rapidly. The lieutenant was a bit-player, and didn't come back on until the third act. It wouldn't hurt to jam him.

He glowered at the doll, demanded icily: "And what have you done with the accomplice?"

The Maestro could not invent lines, nor comprehend an ad lib. The Maestro could only interpret a deviation as a malfunction, and try to compensate. The Maestro backed up a line, had the lieutenant repeat his cue.

"I told you—he *confessed.*"

"*So!*" roared Andreyev. "You killed him, eh? Couldn't survive the questioning, eh? And you killed him."

Thorny, what are you doing? came Rick's frantic whisper in his earplug.

"He confessed," repeated the lieutenant.

"You're under arrest, Nichol!" Thorny barked. "Report to Major Malin for discipline. Return the prisoner to his cell." He paused. The Maestro couldn't go on until he cued it, but now there was no harm in speaking the line. "Now—see that this one confesses, too."

"Yes, sir," the lieutenant replied stonily, and started off-stage with the prisoner.

Thorny took glee in killing his exit by calling after him: "And see that he lives through it!"

The Maestro marched them out without looking back, and Thorny was briefly pleased with himself. He caught a glimpse of Jade with her hands clasped over her head, giving him a "the-winnah" signal from concealment. But he couldn't keep ad libbing his way out of it every time.

Most of all, he dreaded the entrance of Marka, Mela's doll. The Maestro was playing her up, ennobling her, subtly justifying her treachery, at the expense of Andreyev's character. He didn't want to fight back. Marka's role was too important for tampering, and besides, it would be like slapping at Mela to confuse the performance of her doll.

The curtain dipped. The furniture revolved. The stage became a living room. And the curtain rose again.

He barked: "No more arrests; after curfew, shoot on sight!" at the telephone, and hung up.

When he turned, she stood in the doorway, listening. She shrugged and entered with a casual walk while he watched her in suspicious silence. It was the consummation of her treachery. She had come back to him, but as a spy for Piotr. He suspected her only of infidelity and not of treason. It was a crucial scene, and the Maestro could play her either as a treacherous wench, or a reluctant traitor with Andreyev seeming a brute. He watched her warily.

"Well—hello," she said petulantly, after walking around the room.

He grunted coldly. She stayed flippant and aloof. So far, it was as it should be. But the vicious argument was yet to come.

She went to a mirror and began straightening her windblown hair. She spoke nervously, compulsively, rattling about trivia, concealing her anxiety in his presence after her betrayal. She looked furtive, haggard, somehow more like the real Mela of today; the Maestro's control of expression was masterful.

"What are you doing here?" he exploded suddenly, interrupting her disjointed spiel.

"I still live here, don't I?"

"You got out."

"Only because you ordered me out."

"You made it clear you wanted to leave."

"Liar!"

"Cheat!"

It went on that way for a while; then he began dumping the contents of several drawers into a suitcase.

"I live here, and I'm staying," she raged.

"Suit yourself, Comrade."

"What're you doing?"

"Moving out, of course."

The battle continued. Still there was no attempt by the Maestro to revise the scene. Had the trouble been corrected? Had his exchange with the lieutenant somehow affected the machine? Something was different. It was becoming a good scene, his best so far.

She was still raving at him when he started for the door. She stopped in mid-sentence, breathless—then shrieked his name and flung herself down on the sofa, sobbing violently. He stopped. He turned and stood with his fists on his hips staring at her. Gradually, he melted. He put the suitcase down and walked back to stand over her, still gruff and glowering.

Her sobbing subsided. She peered up at him, saw his inability to escape, began to smile. She came up slowly, arms sliding around his neck.

"Sasha . . . oh, my Sasha—"

The arms were warm, the lips moist, the woman alive in his

embrace. For a moment he doubted his senses. She giggled at him and whispered, "You'll break a rib."

"Mela—"

"Let go, you fool—the scene!" Then, aloud: "Can I stay, darling?"

"Always," he said hoarsely.

"And you won't be jealous again?"

"Never."

"Or question me everytime I'm gone an hour or two?"

"Or sixteen. It *was* sixteen hours."

"I'm sorry." She kissed him. The music rose. The scene ended.

"How did you swing it?" he whispered in the clinch. "And why?"

"They asked me to. Because of the Maestro." She giggled. "You looked devastated. Hey, you can let go now. The curtain's down."

The mobile furniture had begun to rearrange itself. They scurried off-stage, side-stepping a couch as it rolled past. Jade was waiting for them.

"Great!" she whispered, taking their hands. "That was just great."

"Thanks . . . thanks for sliding me in," Mela answered.

"Take it from here out, Mela—the scenes with Thorny, at least."

"I don't know," she muttered. "It's been so long. Anybody could have ad libbed through that fight scene."

"You can do it. Rick'll keep you cued and prompted. The engineer's here, and they're fussing around with the Maestro. But it'll straighten *itself* out, if you give it a couple more scenes like that to watch."

The second act had been rescued. The supporting cast was still a hazard, and the Maestro still tried to compensate according to audience reaction during Act I, but with a human Marka, the compensatory attempts had less effect, and the interpretive distortions seemed to diminish slightly. The Maestro was piling up new data as the play continued, and reinterpreting.

"It wasn't great," he sighed as they stretched out to relax between acts. "But it was passable."

"Act Three'll be better, Thorny," Mela promised. "We'll rescue it yet. It's just too bad about the first act."

"I wanted it to be tops," he breathed. "I wanted to give them something to think about, something to remember. But now we're fighting to rescue it from being a total flop."

"Wasn't it always like that? You get steamed up to make history, but then you wind up working like crazy just to keep it passable."

"Or to keep from ducking flying groceries sometimes."

She giggled. "Jiggie used to say, 'I went on like the main dish and came off like the toss salad.'" She paused, then added moodily: "The *tough* part of it is—you've *got* to aim high just to hit anywhere at all. It can get to be heartbreaking, too—trying for the sublime every time, and just escaping the ridiculous, or the mediocre."

"No matter how high you aim, you can't hit escape velocity. Ambition is a trajectory with its impact point in oblivion, no matter how high the throw."

"Sounds like a quote."

"It is. From the Satyricon of an ex-Janitor."

"Thorny—?"

"What?"

"I'm going to be sorry tomorrow—but I *am* enjoying it tonight —going through it all again I mean. Living it like a pipe dream. It's no good though. It's opium."

He stared at her for a moment in surprise, said nothing. Maybe it was opium for Mela, but she hadn't started out with a crazy hope that tonight would be the climax and the high-point of a lifetime on the stage. She was filling in to save the show, and it meant nothing to her in terms of a career she had deliberately abandoned. He, however, had hoped for a great portrayal. It *wasn't* great, though. If he worked hard at Act III, it might—as a whole—stand up to his performances of the past. Unless—

"Think anybody in the audience has guessed yet? About us, I mean?"

She shook her head. "Haven't seen any signs of it," she murmured drowsily. "People see what they expect to see. But it'll leak out tomorrow."

"Why?"

"Your scene with the lieutenant. When you ad libbed out of a jam. There's bound to be a drama critic or maybe a professor out there who read the play ahead of time, and started frowning when you pulled that off. He'll go home and look up his copy of the script just to make sure, and then the cat's out."

"It won't matter by then."

"No."

She wanted a nap or a drowse, and he fell silent. As he watched her relax, some of his bitter disappointment slipped away. It was good just to be acting again, even for one opiate evening. And maybe it was best that he wasn't getting what he wanted. He was even ready to admit to a certain insanity in setting out on such a course.

Perfection and immolation. Now that the perfection wasn't possible, the whole scheme looked like a sick fanatic's nightmare, and he was ashamed. Why had he done it—given in to what had always been only a petulant fantasy, a childish dream? The wish, plus the opportunity, plus the impulse, in a framework of bitterness and in a time of personal transition—it had been enough to bring the crazy yearning out of its cortical wrinkle and start him acting on a dream. A child's dream.

And then the momentum had carried him along. The juggled tapes, the loaded gun, the dirty trick on Jade—and now fighting to keep the show from dying. He had gone down to the river and climbed up on the bridge rail and looked down at the black and swirling tide—and finally climbed down again because the wind would spoil his swan dive.

He shivered. It scared him a little, to know he could lose himself so easily. What had the years done to him, or what had he done to himself?

He had kept his integrity maybe, but what good was integrity in a vacuum? He had the soul of an actor, and he'd hung onto it when the others were selling theirs, but the years had wiped out the market and he was stuck with it. He had stood firm on principle, and the years had melted the cold glacier of reality from under the principle; still, he stood on it, while the reality ran on down to the sea. He had dedicated himself to the living stage, and carefully tended its grave, awaiting the resurrection.

Old ham, he thought, you've been flickering into mad warps and staggering into dimensions of infrasanity. You took unreality

by the hand and led her gallantly through peril and confusion
and finally married her before you noticed that she was dead.
Now the only decent thing to do was bury her, but her inter-
ment would do nothing to get him back through the peril and
confusion and on the road again. He'd have to hike. Maybe it was
too late to do anything with the rest of a lifetime. But there was
only one way to find out. And the first step was to put some
mileage between himself and the stage.

If a little black box took over my job, Rick had said, I'd go to
work making little black boxes.

Thorny realized with a slight start that the technician had
meant it. Mela had done it, in a sense. So had Jade. Especially
Jade. But that wasn't the answer for him, not now. He'd hung
around too long mourning the dead, and he needed a clean, sharp
break. Tomorrow he'd fade out of sight, move away, pretend he
was twenty-one again, and start groping for something to do with
a lifetime. How to keep eating until he found it—that would be
the pressing problem. Unskilled laborers were hard to find these
days, but so were unskilled jobs. Selling his acting talent for commercial purposes would work only if he could find a commercial
purpose he could believe in and live for, since his talent was not
the surface talent of a schauspieler. It would be a grueling search,
for he had never bothered to believe in anything but theater.

Mela stirred suddenly. "Did I hear somebody call me?" she
muttered. "This racket—!" She sat up to look around.

He grunted doubtfully. "How long till curtain?" he asked.

She arose suddenly and said, "Jade's waving me over. See you
in the act, Thorny."

He watched Mela hurry away, he glanced across the floor at
Jade who waited for her in the midst of a small conference, he
felt a guilty twinge. He'd cost them money, trouble, and nervous
sweat, and maybe the performance endangered the run of the
show. It was a rotten thing to do, and he was sorry, but it couldn't
be undone, and the only possible compensation was to deliver a
best-possible Act III and then get out. Fast. Before Jade found
him out and organized a lynch mob.

After staring absently at the small conference for a few moments, he closed his eyes and drowsed again.

Suddenly he opened them. Something about the conference group—something peculiar. He sat up and frowned at them again. Jade, Mela, Rick, and Feria, and three strangers. Nothing peculiar about that. Except . . . let's see . . . the thin one with the scholarly look—that would be the programming engineer, probably. The beefy, healthy fellow with the dark business suit and the wandering glance—Thorny couldn't place him—he looked out of place backstage. The third one seemed familiar somehow, but he, too, looked out of place—a chubby little man with no necktie and a fat cigar, he seemed more interested in the backstage rush than in the proceedings of the group. The beefy gent kept asking him questions, and he muttered brief answers around his cigar while watching the stagehands' parade.

Once when answering he took his cigar out of his mouth and glanced quickly across the floor in Thorny's direction. Thorny stiffened, felt bristles rise along his spine. The chubby little gent was—

—The depot clerk!

Who had issued him the extra tape and the splices. Who could put the finger on the trouble right away, and was undoubtedly doing it.

Got to get out. Got to get out fast. The beefy fellow was either a cop or a private investigator, one of several hired by Smithfield. Got to run, got to hide, got to— Lynch mob.

"Not through that door, buddy, *that's* the stage; what're you— Oh, Thorny! It's not time to go on."

"Sorry," he grunted at the prop man and turned away.

The light flashed, the buzzer sounded faintly.

"*Now* it's time," the prop man called after him.

Where was he going? And what good would it do?

"Hey, Thorny! The buzzer. Come back. It's line-up. You're on when the curtain lifts . . . *hey!*"

He paused, then turned around and went back. He went onstage and took his place. She was already there, staring at him strangely as he approached.

"You didn't do it, did you, Thorny?" she whispered.

He gazed at her in tight-lipped silence, then nodded.

She looked puzzled. She looked at him as if he were no longer a person, but a peculiar object to be studied. Not scornful, nor angry, nor righteous—just puzzled.

"Guess I was nuts," he said lamely.

"Guess you were."

"Not too much harm done, though," he said hopefully.

"The wrong people saw the second act, Thorny. They walked out."

"Wrong people?"

"Two backers and a critic."

"Oh?"

He stood stunned. She stopped looking at him then and just stood waiting for the curtain to rise, her face showing nothing but a puzzled sadness. It wasn't her show, and she had nothing in it but a doll that would bring a royalty check or two, and now herself as a temporary substitute for the doll. The sadness was for him. Contempt he could have understood.

The curtain lifted. A sea of dim faces beyond the footlights. And he was Andreyev, chief of a Soviet police garrison, loyalist servant of a dying cause. It was easy to stay in the role this time, to embed his ego firmly in the person of the Russian cop and live a little of the last century. For the ego was more comfortable there than in the skin of Ryan Thornier—a skin that might soon be sent to the tannery, judging the furtive glances that were coming from backstage. It might even be comfortable to remain Andreyev after the performance, but that was a sure way to get Napoleon Bonaparte for a roommate.

There was no change of setting between scenes *i* and *ii*, but only a dip of the curtain to indicate a time-lapse and permit a change of cast. He stayed on stage, and it gave him a moment to think. The thoughts weren't pleasant.

Backers had walked out. Tomorrow the show would close unless the morning teleprint of the *Times* carried a rave review. Which seemed wildly improbable. Critics were jaded. Jaded tastes were apt to be impatient. They would not be eager to forgive the first act. He had wrecked it, and he couldn't rescue it.

Revenge wasn't sweet. It tasted like rot and a sour stomach.

Give them a good third act. There's nothing more you can do. But even that wouldn't take away the rotten taste.

Why did you do it, Thorny? Rick's voice, whispering from the booth and in his earplug prompter.

He glanced up and saw the technician watching him from the small window of the booth. He spread his hands in a wide shrugging gesture, as if to ask: How can I tell you, what can I do?

Go on with it, what else? Rick whispered, and withdrew from the window.

The incident seemed to confirm that Jade intended for him to finish it, anyhow. She could scarcely intend otherwise. She was in it with him, in a sense. If the audience found out the play had a human stand-in, and if the critics didn't like the show, they might pounce on the producer who "perpetrated such an impossible substitution"—even harder than they'd pounce on him. She had gambled on him, and in spite of his plot to force her into such a gamble, it was her show, and her responsibility, and she'd catch the brunt of it. Critics, owners, backers, and public—they didn't care about "blame," didn't care about excuses or reasons. They cared about the finished product, and if they didn't like it, the responsibility for it was clear.

As for himself? A cop waiting backstage. Why? He hadn't studied the criminal code, but he couldn't think of any neat little felonious label that could be pinned on what he'd done. Fraud? Not without an exchange of money or property, he thought. He'd been after intangibles, and the law was an earthy thing; it became confused when motives carried men beyond assaults on property or person, into assaults on ideas or principles. Then it passed the buck to psychiatry.

Maybe the beefy gent wasn't a cop at all. Maybe he was a collector of maniacs.

Thorny didn't much care. The dream had tumbled down, and he'd just have to let the debris keep falling about him until he got a chance to start climbing out of the wreckage. It was the end of something that should have ended years ago, and he couldn't get out until it finished collapsing.

The curtain lifted. Scene *ii* was good. Not brilliant, but good enough to make them stop snapping their gum and hold them locked in their seats, absorbed in their identity with Andreyev. Scene *iii* was his Gethsemane—when the mob besieged the

public offices while he waited for word of Marka and an answer
to his offer of a truce with the guerrilla forces. The answer came
in one word.

"*Nyet.*"

His death sentence. The word that bound him over to the jack-
als in the streets, the word that cast him to the ravening mob.
The mob had a way: the mob was collecting officials and mount-
ing them. He could see their collection from the window, looking
across the square, and he discussed it with an aide. Nine men
impaled on the steel spikes of the heavy grillwork fence in front
of the Regional Soviet offices. The mob seized another specimen
with its thousand hands and mounted it carefully. It lifted the
specimen into a sitting position over a two-foot spike, then
dropped him on it. Two specimens still squirmed.

He'd cheat the mob, of course. There were the barricades in
the building below, and there would be plenty of time to meet
death privately and chastely before the mob tore its way inside.
But he delayed. He waited for word from Marka.

Word came. Two guards burst in.

"She's here, Comrade, she's come!"

Come with the enemy, they said. Come betraying him, betraying the state. *Impossible!* But the guard insisted.

Berserk fury, and refusal to believe. With a low snarl, he drew
the automatic, shot the bearer of bad tidings through the heart.

With the crash of the gunshot, the mannequin crumpled. The
explosion startled a sudden memory out of hiding, and he remembered: the second cartridge in the clip—*not a blank!* He had forgotten to unload the deadly round.

For an instant he debated firing it into the fallen mannequin
as a way to get rid of it, then dismissed the notion and obeyed
the script. He stared at his victim and wilted, letting the gun slip
from his fingers and fall to the floor. He staggered to the window
to stare out across the square. He covered his face with his hands,
awaited the transition curtain.

The curtain came. He whirled and started for the gun.

No, Thorny, no! came Rick's frantic whisper from the booth.
To the ikon . . . the ikon!

He stopped in mid-stage. No time to retrieve the gun and unload. The curtain had only dipped and was starting up again. Let

Mela get rid of the round, he thought. He crossed to the shrine, tearing open his collar, rumpling his hair. He fell to his knees before the ancient ikon, in dereliction before the God of an older Russia, a Russia that survived as firmly in fierce negation as it had survived in fierce affirmation. The cultural soul was a living thing, and it survived as well in downfall as in victory; it could never be excised, but only eaten away or slowly transmuted by time and gentle pressures of rain wearing the rock.

There was a bust of Lenin beneath the ikon. And there was a bust of Harvey Smithfield beneath the Greek players' masks on the wall of D'Uccia's office. The signs of the times, and the signs of the timeless, and the cultural heartbeat pulsed to the rhythm of centuries. He had resisted the times as they took a sharp turn in direction, but no man could swim long against the tide as it plodded its zigzag course into timelessness. And the sharp deflections in the course were deceptive—for all of them really wound their way downstream. No man ever added his bit to the flow by spending all his effort to resist the current. The tide would tire him and take him into oblivion while the world flowed on.

Marka, Boris, Piotr had entered, and he had turned to stare at them without understanding. The mockery followed, and the harsh laughter, as they pushed the once haughty but now broken chieftain about the stage like a dazed animal unable to respond. He rebounded from one to another of them, as they prodded him to dispel the trancelike daze.

"Finish your prayer, Comrade," said Mela, picking up the gun he'd dropped.

As he staggered close to Mela, he found his chance, and whispered quickly: "The gun, Mela—eject the first cartridge. Eject it, quickly."

He was certain she heard him, although she showed no reaction—unless the slight flicker of her eyes had been a quick glance at the gun. Had she understood? A moment later, another chance to whisper.

"The next bullet's real. Work the slide. Eject it."

He stumbled as Piotr pushed him, fell against a heavy couch, slid down, and stared at them. Piotr went to open the window and shout an offer to the mob below. A bull-roar arose from the herd outside. They hauled him to the window as a triumphal display.

"See, Comrade?" growled the guerrilla. "Your faithful congregation awaits you."

Marka closed the windows. "I can't stand that sight!" she cried.

"Take him to his people," the leader ordered.

"No—" Marka brought up the gun, shook her head fiercely. "I won't let you do that. Not to the mob."

Piotr growled a curse. "They'll have him anyway. They'll be coming up here to search."

Thorny stared at the actress with a puzzled frown. Still she hadn't ejected the cartridge. And the moment was approaching —a quick bullet to keep him from the mob, a bit of hot mercy flung hastily to him by the woman who had enthralled him and used him and betrayed him.

She turned toward him with the gun, and he began to back away.

"All right, Piotr—if they'll get him anyway—"

She moved a few steps toward him as he backed to a corner. *The live round, Mela, eject it!*

Then her foot brushed a copper bus-lug, and he saw the faint little jet of sparks. Eyes of glass, flesh of airfoam plastic, nerves of twitching electron streams.

Mela was gone. This was her doll. Maybe the real Mela couldn't stomach it after she'd found what he'd done, or maybe Jade had called her off after the first scene of the third act. A plastic hand held the gun, and a tiny flexible solenoid awaited the pulse that would tighten the finger on the trigger. Terror lanced through him.

Cue, Thorny, *cue!* whispered his earplug.

The doll had to wait for his protest before it could fire. It had to be cued. His eyes danced about the stage, looking for a way out. Only an instant to decide.

He could walk over and take the gun out of the doll's hand without giving it a cue—betraying himself to the audience and wrecking the final moment of the show.

He could run for it, cue her, and hope she missed, falling after the shot. But he'd fall on the lugs that way, and come up shrieking.

For God's sake, Thorny! Rick was howling. *The cue, the cue!*

He stared at the gun and swayed slightly from side to side. The gun swayed with him—slightly out of phase. A second's delay, no more—

"Please, Marka—" he called, swaying faster.

The finger tensed on the trigger. The gun moved in a search pattern, as he shifted to and fro. It was risky. It had to be precisely timed. It was like dancing with a cobra. He wanted to flee.

You faked the tape, you botched the show, you came out second best to a system you hated, he reminded himself. *And you even loaded the gun. Now if you can't risk it—*

He gritted his teeth, kept up the irregular weaving motion, then—

"Please, Marka . . . no, no, *nooo!*"

A spiked fist hit him somewhere around the belt, spun him around, and dropped him. The sharp cough of the gun was only a part of the blow. Then he was lying crumpled on his side in the chalked safety area, bleeding and cursing softly. The scene continued. He started to cry out, but checked the shout in his throat. Through a haze, he watched the others move on toward the finale, saw the dim sea of faces beyond the lights. Bullet punched through his side somewhere.

Got to stop squirming. Can't have a dead Andreyev floundering about like a speared fish on the stage. Wait a minute—just another minute—hang on.

But he couldn't. He clutched at his side and felt for the wound. Hard to feel through all the stickiness. He wanted to tear his clothes free to get at it and stop the bleeding, but that was no good either. They'd accept a mannequin fumbling slightly in a death agony, but the blood wouldn't go over so well. Mannequins didn't bleed. Didn't they see it anyway? They had to see it. Clever gimmick, they'd think. Tube of red ink, maybe. Realism is the milieu of—

He twisted his hand in his belt, drew it up strangle-tight around his waist. The pain got worse for a moment, but it seemed to slow the flow of blood. He hung onto it, gritting his teeth, waiting.

He knew about where it hit him, but it was harder to tell

where it had come out. And what it had taken with it on the way. Thank God for the bleeding. Maybe he wasn't doing much of it inside.

He tried to focus on the rest of the stage. Music was rising somewhere. Had they all walked off and left him? But no—there was Piotr, through the haze. Piotr approached his chair of office —heavy, ornate, antique. Once it had belonged to a noble of the czar. Piotr, perfectly cold young machine, in his triumph—inspecting the chair.

A low shriek came from backstage somewhere. Mela. Couldn't she keep her mouth shut for half a minute? Probably spotted the blood. Maybe the music drowned the squeal.

Piotr mounted the single step and turned. He sat down gingerly in the chair of empire, testing it, and smiling victory. He seemed to find the chair comfortable.

"I must keep this, Marka," he said.

Thorny wheezed a low curse at him. He'd keep it all right, until the times went around another twist in the long old river. And welcome to it—judging by the thundering applause.

And the curtain fell slowly to cover the window of the stage.

Feet trouped past him, and he croaked "Help!" a couple of times, but the feet kept going. The mannequins, marching off to their packing cases.

He got to his feet alone, and went black. But when the blackness dissolved, he was still standing there, so he staggered toward the exit. They were rushing toward him—Mela and Rick and a couple of the crew. Hands grabbed for him, but he fought them off.

"I'll walk by myself now!" he growled.

But the hands took him anyway. He saw Jade and the beefy gent, tried to lurch toward them and explain everything, but she went even whiter and backed away. *I must look a bloody mess,* he thought.

"I was trying to duck. I didn't want to—"

"Save your breath," Rick told him. "I saw you. Just hang on."

They got him onto a doll packing case, and he heard somebody yelling for a doctor from the departing audience, and then a lot of hands started scraping at his side and tugging at him.

"Mela—"

"Right here, Thorny. I'm here."

And after a while she was still there, but sunlight was spilling across the bed, and he smelled faint hospital odors. He blinked at her for several seconds before he found a voice.

"The show?" he croaked.

"They panned it," she said softly.

He closed his eyes again and groaned.

"But it'll make dough."

He blinked at her and gaped.

"Publicity. Terrific. Shall I read you the reviews?"

He nodded, and she reached for the papers. All about the madman who bled all over the stage. He stopped her halfway through the first article. It was enough. The audience had begun to catch on toward the last lines of the play, and the paging of a surgeon had confirmed the suspicion.

"You missed the bedlam backstage," she told him. "It was quite a mess."

"But the show won't close?"

"How can it? With all the morbidity for pulling power. If it closes, it'll be with the Peltier performance to blame."

"And Jade—?"

"Sore. Plenty sore. Can you blame her?"

He shook his head. "I didn't want to hurt anybody. I'm sorry."

She watched him in silence for a moment, then: "You can't flounder around like you've been doing, Thorny, without somebody getting hurt, without somebody hating your guts, getting trampled on. You just can't."

It was true. When you hung onto a piece of the past, and just hung onto it quietly, you only hurt yourself. But when you started trying to bludgeon a place for it in the present, you began knocking over the bystanders.

"Theater's dead, Thorny. Can't you believe that now?"

He thought about it a little, and shook his head. It wasn't dead. Only the form was changed, and maybe not permanently at that. He'd thought of it first last night, before the ikon. There were things of the times, and a few things that were timeless. The times came as a result of a particular human culture. The timeless came as a result of any human culture at all. And Cultural Man was a showman. He created display windows of culture for an audience of men, and paraded his aspirations and ideals and purposes thereon, and the displays were necessary to the continuity of the culture, to the purposeful orientation of the species.

Beyond one such window, he erected an altar, and placed a priest before it to chant a liturgical description of the heart-reasoning of his times. And beyond another window, he built a stage and set his talking dolls upon it to live a dramaturgical sequence of wishes and woes of his times.

True, the priests would change, the liturgy would change, and the dolls, the dramas, the displays—but the windows would never —no never—be closed as long as Man outlived his members, for only through such windows could transient men see themselves against the background of a broader sweep, see man encompassed by Man. A perspective not possible without the windows.

Dramaturgy. Old as civilized Man. Outlasting forms and techniques and applications. Outlasting even current popular worship of the Great God Mechanism, who was temporarily enshrined while still being popularly misunderstood. Like the Great God Commerce of an earlier century, and the God Agriculture before him.

Suddenly he laughed aloud. "If they used human actors today, it would be a pretty moldy display. Not even *true,* considering the times."

By the time another figure lounged in his doorway, he had begun to feel rather expansive and heroic about it all. When a small cough caused him to glance up, he stared for a moment, grinned broadly, then called: "Ho, Richard! Come in. Here . . . sit down. Help me decide on a career, eh? Heh heh—" He waved the classified section and chuckled. "What kind of little black boxes can an old ham—"

He paused. Rick's expression was chilly, and he made no move to enter. After a moment he said: "I guess there'll always be a sucker to rerun this particular relay race."

"Race?" Thorny gathered a slow frown.

"Yeah. Last century, it was between a Chinese abacus operator and an IBM machine. They really had a race, you know."

"Now see here—"

"And the century before that, it was between a long-hand secretary and a typewriting machine."

"If you came here to—"

"And before that, the hand-weavers against the automatic looms."

"Nice to have seen you, Richard. On your way out, would you ask the nurse to—"

"Break up the looms, smash the machines, picket the offices with typewriters, keep adding machines out of China! So then what? Try to be a better tool than a tool?"

Thorny rolled his head aside and glowered at the wall. "All right. I was wrong. What do you want to do? Gloat? Moralize?"

"No. I'm just curious. It keeps happening—a specialist trying to compete with a high-level specialist's tools. Why?"

"*Higher* level?" Thorny sat up with a snarl, groaned, caught at his side and sank back again, panting.

"Easy, old man," Rick said quietly. "Sorry. Higher organizational-level, I meant. Why do you keep on doing it?"

Thorny lay silent for a few moments, then: "Status jealousy. Even hawks try to drive other hawks out of their hunting grounds. Fight off competition."

"But you're no hawk. And a machine isn't competition."

"Cut it out, Rick. What did you come here for?"

Rick glanced at the toe of his shoe, snickered faintly, and came on into the room. "Thought you might need some help finding a job," he said. "When I looked in the door and saw you lying there looking like somebody's King Arthur, I got sore again." He sat restlessly on the edge of a chair and watched the old man with mingled sadness, irritation, and affection.

"You'd help me . . . find a job?"

"Maybe. A job, not a permanent niche."

"It's too late to find a permanent niche."

"It was too late when you were born, old man! There isn't any such thing—hasn't been, for the last century. Whatever you specialize in, another specialty will either gobble you up, or find a way to replace you. If you get what looks like a secure niche, somebody'll come along and wall you up in it and write your epitaph on it. And the more specialized a society gets, the more dangerous it is for the pure specialist. You think an electronic engineer is any safer than an actor? Or a ditch-digger?"

"I don't know. It's not fair. A man's career—"

"You've always got one specialty that's safe."

"What's that?"

"The specialty of creating new specialties. Continuously. Your own."

"But that's—" He started to protest, to say that such a concept belonged to the highly trained few, to the technical elite of the era, and that it wasn't specialization, but generalization. But why to the few? The specialty of creating new specialties—

"But that's—"

"More or less a definition of Man, isn't it?" Rick finished for him. "Now about the job—"

"Yes, about the job—"

So maybe you don't start from the bottom after all, he decided. You start considerably above the lemur, the chimpanzee, the orangutan, the Maestro—if you ever start at all.

Eric Frank Russell

I met Eric Frank Russell only once but that was under the most impressive possible circumstances. It was in 1939 at a meeting of a fan club in Queens. I had sold a couple of small stories and Russell, on the other hand, had just had published a novel called *Sinister Barriers* which was remarkable on two counts. In the first place, it was a tale that was immediately recognized as a classic. In the second, it appeared in the first issue of a new magazine called *Unknown*, the like of which had never been seen before and will never be seen again. It featured fantasy fiction, but adult and sensible and clever and literate fantasy.

Alas, *Unknown* did not survive World War II and the paper shortages it inflicted on publishers. And if anything can intensify the agony of this catastrophe, it is the thought that its downfall carried with it a story of mine, sold but not published, and now forever lost to humanity.

But Russell survived, I am glad to say, and continued to write amazingly well.

I am trying now to re-create in my mind the picture of the man as I saw him in 1939—he, the revered author of *Sinister Barriers*, I the novice. I think I can rely on my near-photographic memory for the purpose. (I call it "near-photographic" because I can only remember things that happen to be lying around near photographs.)

Let's see, as I recall, he is six-feet seven-inches tall (when he is sitting down, that is) with a long and majestic English face. Then, too, I distinctly remember, there was a small flashing golden aura about his head, the occasional play of hissing lightning flashes when he moved it suddenly, and the distant rumble of thunder when he spoke.

Sinister Barriers would have won a Hugo, hands down, had

such baubles been awarded back in 1939. But Russell knew perfectly well how to bide his time (the dog) and on the very first occasion that Hugos *were* awarded—at the 13th Convention (Cleveland, 1955) he walked off with one for his short story, "Allamagoosa."

2

ALLAMAGOOSA

It was a long time since the *Bustler* had been so silent. She lay in the Sirian spaceport, her tubes cold, her shell particle-scarred, her air that of a long-distance runner exhausted at the end of a marathon. There was good reason for this: she had returned from a lengthy trip by no means devoid of troubles.

Now, in port, well-deserved rest had been gained if only temporarily. Peace, sweet peace. No more bothers, no more crises, no more major upsets, no more dire predicaments such as crop up in free flight at least twice a day. Just peace.

Hah!

Captain McNaught reposed in his cabin, feet up on desk, and enjoyed the relaxation to the utmost. The engines were dead, their hellish pounding absent for the first time in months. Out there in the big city four hundred of his crew were making whoopee under a brilliant sun. This evening, when First Officer Gregory returned to take charge, he was going to go into the fragrant twilight and make the rounds of neon-lit civilization.

That was the beauty of making landfall at long last. Men could give way to themselves, blow off surplus steam, each according to his fashion. No duties, no worries, no dangers, no responsibilities in spaceport. A haven of safety and comfort for tired rovers.

Again, hah!

Burman, the chief radio officer, entered the cabin. He was one of the half-dozen remaining on duty and bore the expression of a man who can think of twenty better things to do.

"Relayed signal just come in, sir." Handing the paper across he waited for the other to look at it and perhaps dictate a reply.

Taking the sheet, McNaught removed the feet from his desk, sat erect and read the message aloud.

Terran Headquarters to Bustler. *Remain Siriport pending further orders. Rear Admiral Vane W. Cassidy due there seventeenth. Feldman. Navy Op. Command, Sirisec.*

He looked up, all happiness gone from his leathery features, and groaned.

"Something wrong?" asked Burman, vaguely alarmed.

McNaught pointed at three thin books on his desk. "The middle one. Page twenty."

Leafing through it, Burman found an item that said: *Vane W. Cassidy, R-Ad. Head Inspector Ships and Stores.*

Burman swallowed hard. "Does that mean—?"

"Yes, it does," said McNaught without pleasure. "Back to training-college and all its rigmarole. Paint and soap, spit and polish." He put on an officious expression, adopted a voice to match it. "Captain, you have only seven ninety-nine emergency rations. Your allocation is eight hundred. Nothing in your log-book accounts for the missing one. Where is it? What happened to it? How is it that one of the men's kit lacks an officially issued pair of suspenders? Did you report his loss?"

"Why does he pick on us?" asked Burman, appalled. "He's never chivvied us before."

"That's why," informed McNaught, scowling at the wall. "It's our turn to be stretched across the barrel." His gaze found the calendar. "We have three days—and we'll need 'em! Tell Second Officer Pike to come here at once."

Burman departed gloomily. In short time Pike entered. His face reaffirmed the old adage that bad news travels fast.

"Make out an indent," ordered McNaught, "for one hundred gallons of plastic paint, Navy-gray, approved quality. Make out another for thirty gallons of interior white enamel. Take them to spaceport stores right away. Tell them to deliver by six this evening along with our correct issue of brushes and sprayers. Grab up any cleaning material that's going for free."

"The men won't like this," remarked Pike, feebly.

"They're going to love it," McNaught asserted. "A bright and shiny ship, all spic and span, is good for morale. It says so in that book. Get moving and put those indents in. When you come back, find the stores and equipment sheets and bring them here. We've got to check stocks before Cassidy arrives. Once he's here we'll have no chance to make up shortages or smuggle out any extra items we happened to find in our hands."

"Very well, sir." Pike went out wearing the same expression as Burman's.

Lying back in his chair McNaught muttered to himself. There was a feeling in his bones that something was sure to cause a last-minute ruckus. A shortage of any item would be serious enough unless covered by a previous report. A surplus would be bad, very bad. The former implied carelessness or misfortune. The latter suggested barefaced theft of government property in circumstances condoned by the commander.

For instance, there was that recent case of Williams of the heavy cruiser *Swift*. He'd heard of it over the spacevine when out around Bootes. Williams had been found in unwitting command of eleven reels of electric-fence wire when his official issue was ten. It had taken a court-martial to decide that the extra reel—which had formidable barter-value on a certain planet—had not been stolen from space-stores, or, in sailor jargon, "teleportated aboard." But Williams had been reprimanded. And that did not help promotion.

He was still rumbling discontentedly when Pike returned bearing a folder of foolscap sheets.

"Going to start right away, sir?"

"We'll have to." He heaved himself erect, mentally bidded good-by to time off and a taste of the bright lights. "It'll take long enough to work right through from bow to tail. I'll leave the men's kit inspection to the last."

Marching out of the cabin, he set forth toward the bow, Pike following with broody reluctance.

As they passed the open main lock Peaslake observed them, bounded eagerly up the gangway and joined behind. A pukka member of the crew, he was a large dog whose ancestors had been more enthusiastic than selective. He wore with pride a big collar inscribed: *Peaslake—Property of S. S. Bustler*. His chief duties, ably performed, were to keep alien rodents off the ship and, on rare occasions, smell out dangers not visible to human eyes.

The three paraded forward, McNaught and Pike in the manner of men grimly sacrificing pleasure for the sake of duty, Peaslake with the panting willingness of one ready for any new game no matter what.

Reaching the bow-cabin, McNaught dumped himself in the pilot's seat, took the folder from the other. "You know this stuff better than me—the chart room is where I shine. So I'll read them out while you look them over." He opened the folder, started on the first page. "K1. Beam compass, type D, one of."

"Check," said Pike.

"K2. Distance and direction indicator, electronic, type JJ, one of."

"Check."

"K3. Port and starboard gravitic meters, Casini models, one pair."

"Check."

Peaslake planted his head in McNaught's lap, blinked soulfully and whined. He was beginning to get the others' viewpoint. This tedious itemizing and checking was a hell of a game. McNaught consolingly lowered a hand and played with Peaslake's ears while he ploughed his way down the list.

"K187. Foam rubber cushions, pilot and co-pilot, one pair."

"Check."

By the time First Officer Gregory appeared they had reached the tiny intercom cubby and poked around it in semidarkness. Peaslake had long departed in disgust.

"M24. Spare minispeakers, three inch, type T2, one set of six."

"Check."

Looking in, Gregory popped his eyes and said, "What's going on?"

"Major inspection due soon." McNaught glanced at his watch. "Go see if stores has delivered a load and if not why not. Then you'd better give me a hand and let Pike take a few hours off."

"Does this mean land-leave is canceled?"

"You bet it does—until after Hizonner has been and gone." He glanced at Pike. "When you get into the city search around and send back any of the crew you can find. No arguments or excuses. Also no alibis and/or delays. It's an order."

Pike registered unhappiness. Gregory glowered at him, went away, came back and said, "Stores will have the stuff here in twenty minutes' time." With bad grace he watched Pike depart.

"M47. Intercom cable, woven-wire protected, three drums."

"Check," said Gregory, mentally kicking himself for returning at the wrong time.

The task continued until late in the evening, was resumed early next morning. By that time three-quarters of the men were hard at work inside and outside the vessel, doing their jobs as though sentenced to them for crimes contemplated but not yet committed.

Moving around the ship's corridors and catwalks had to be done crab-fashion, with a nervous sidewise edging. Once again it was being demonstrated that the Terran life form suffers from ye fear of wette paynt. The first smearer would have ten years willed off his unfortunate life.

It was in these conditions, in midafternoon of the second day, that McNaught's bones proved their feelings had been prophetic. He recited the ninth page while Jean Blanchard confirmed the presence and actual existence of all items enumerated. Two-thirds of the way down they hit the rocks, metaphorically speaking, and commenced to sink fast.

McNaught said boredly, "V1097. Drinking bowl, enamel, one of."

"Is zis," said Blanchard, tapping it.

"V1098. Offog, one."

"*Quoi?*" asked Blanchard, staring.

"V1098. Offog, one," repeated McNaught. "Well, why are you looking thunderstruck? This is the ship's galley. You're the head cook. You know what's supposed to be in the galley, don't you? Where's this offog?"

"Never hear of heem," stated Blanchard, flatly.

"You must have. It's on this equipment-sheet in plain, clear type. Offog, one, it says. It was here when we were fitted-out four years ago. We checked it ourselves and signed for it."

"I signed for nossings called offog," Blanchard denied. "In the cuisine zere is no such sing."

"Look!" McNaught scowled and showed him the sheet.

Blanchard looked and sniffed disdainfully. "I have here zee electronic oven, one of. I have jacketed boilers, graduated capacities, one set. I have bain marie pans, seex of. But no offog. Never heard of heem. I do not know of heem." He spread his hands and shrugged. "No offog."

"There's got to be," McNaught insisted. "What's more, when Cassidy arrives there'll be hell to pay if there isn't."

"You find heem," Blanchard suggested.

"You got a certificate from the International Hotels School of Cookery. You got a certificate from the Cordon Bleu College of Cuisine. You got a certificate with three credits from the Space-Navy Feeding Center," McNaught pointed out. "All that—and you don't know what an offog is."

"*Nom d'un chien!*" ejaculated Blanchard, waving his arms around. "I tell you ten t'ousand time zere is no offog. Zere never was an offog. Escoffier heemself could not find zee offog of vich zere is none. Am I a magician perhaps?"

"It's part of the culinary equipment," McNaught maintained. "It must be because it's on page nine. And page nine means its proper home is in the galley, care of the head cook."

"Like hail it does," Blanchard retorted. He pointed at a metal box on the wall. "Intercom booster. Is zat mine?"

McNaught thought it over, conceded, "No, it's Burman's. His stuff rambles all over the ship."

"Zen ask heem for zis bloody offog," said Blanchard, triumphantly.

"I will. If it's not yours it must be his. Let's finish this checking first. If I'm not systematic and thorough Cassidy will jerk off my insignia." His eyes sought the list. "V1099. Inscribed collar, leather, brass studded, dog, for the use of. No need to look for that. I saw it myself five minutes ago." He ticked the item, continued, "V1100. Sleeping basket, woven reed, one of."

"Is zis," said Blanchard, kicking it into a corner.

"V1101. Cushion, foam rubber, to fit sleeping basket, one of."

"Half of," Blanchard contradicted. "In four years he has chewed away other half."

"Maybe Cassidy will let us indent for a new one. It doesn't matter. We're O. K. so long as we can produce the half we've got." McNaught stood up, closed the folder. "That's the lot for here. I'll go see Burman about this missing item."

The inventory party moved on.

Burman switched off a UHF receiver, removed his earplugs and raised a questioning eyebrow.

"In the galley we're short an offog," explained McNaught. "Where is it?"

"Why ask me? The galley is Blanchard's bailiwick."

"Not entirely. A lot of your cables run through it. You've two terminal boxes in there, also an automatic switch and an intercom booster. Where's the offog?"

"Never heard of it," said Burman, baffled.

McNaught shouted, "Don't tell me that! I'm already fed up hearing Blanchard saying it. Four years back we had an offog. It says so here. This is our copy of what we checked and signed for. It says we signed for an offog. Therefore we must have one. It's got to be found before Cassidy gets here."

"Sorry, sir," sympathized Burman. "I can't help you."

"You can think again," advised McNaught. "Up in the bow there's a direction and distance indicator. What do *you* call it?"

"A didin," said Burman, mystified.

"And," McNaught went on, pointing at the pulse transmitter, "what do you call *that?*"

"The opper-popper."

"Baby names, see? Didin and opper-popper. Now rack your brains and remember what you called an offog four years ago."

"Nothing," asserted Burman, "has ever been called an offog to my knowledge."

"Then," demanded McNaught, "why did we sign for one?"

"I didn't sign for anything. You did all the signing."

"While you and others did the checking. Four years ago, presumably in the galley, I said, 'Offog, one,' and either you or Blanchard pointed to it and said, 'Check.' I took somebody's word for it. I have to take other specialists' words for it. I am an expert navigator, familiar with all the latest navigational gadgets but not

D

with other stuff. So I'm compelled to rely on people who know what an offog is—or ought to."

Burman had a bright thought. "All kinds of oddments were dumped in the main lock, the corridors and the galley when we were fitted-out. We had to sort through a deal of stuff and stash it where it properly belonged, remember? This offog-thing might be any place today. It isn't necessarily my responsibility or Blanchard's."

"I'll see what the other officers say," agreed McNaught, conceding the point. "Gregory, Worth, Sanderson or one of the others may be coddling the item. Wherever it is, it's got to be found. Or accounted for in full if it's been expended."

He went out. Burman pulled a face, inserted his earplugs, resumed fiddling with his apparatus. An hour later McNaught came back wearing a scowl.

"Positively," he announced with ire, "there is no such thing on the ship. Nobody knows of it. Nobody can so much as guess at it."

"Cross it off and report it lost," Burman suggested.

"What, when we're hard aground? You know as well as I do that loss and damage must be signaled at time of occurrence. If I tell Cassidy the offog went west in space, he'll want to know when, where, how and why it wasn't signaled. There'll be a real ruckus if the contraption happens to be valued at half a million credits. I can't dismiss it with an airy wave of the hand."

"What's the answer then?" inquired Burman, innocently ambling straight into the trap.

"There's one and only one," McNaught announced. "*You* will manufacture an offog."

"Who? Me?" said Burman, twitching his scalp.

"You and no other. I'm fairly sure the thing is your pigeon, anyway."

"Why?"

"Because it's typical of the baby names used for your kind of stuff. I'll bet a month's pay that an offog is some sort of scientific allamagoosa. Something to do with fog, perhaps. Maybe a blind-approach gadget."

"The blind-approach transceiver is called 'the fumbly,'" Burman informed.

"There you are!" said McNaught as if that clinched it. "So you will make an offog. It will be completed by six tomorrow evening and ready for my inspection then. It had better be convincing, in fact pleasing. In fact its function will be convincing."

Burman stood up, let his hands dangle, and said in hoarse tones, "How can I make an offog when I don't even know what it is?"

"Neither does Cassidy know," McNaught pointed out, leering at him. "He's more of a quantity surveyor than anything else. As such he counts things, looks at things, certifies that they exist, accepts advice on whether they are functionally satisfactory or worn out. All we need do is concoct an imposing allamagoosa and tell him it's the offog."

"Holy Moses!" said Burman, fervently.

"Let us not rely on the dubious assistance of Biblical characters," McNaught reproved. "Let us use the brains that God has given us. Get a grip on your soldering-iron and make a topnotch offog by six tomorrow evening. That's an order!"

He departed, satisfied with this solution. Behind him, Burman gloomed at the wall and licked his lips once, twice.

Rear Admiral Vane W. Cassidy arrived right on time. He was a short, paunchy character with a florid complexion and eyes like those of a long-dead fish. His gait was an important strut.

"Ah, captain, I trust that you have everything shipshape."

"Everything usually is," assured McNaught, glibly. "I see to that." He spoke with conviction.

"Good!" approved Cassidy. "I like a commander who takes his responsibilities seriously. Much as I regret saying so, there are a few who do not." He marched through the main lock, his cod-eyes taking note of the fresh white enamel. "Where do you prefer to start, bow or tail?"

"My equipment-sheets run from bow backward. We may as well deal with them the way they're set."

"Very well." He trotted officiously toward the nose, paused on the way to pat Peaslake and examine his collar. "Well cared-for, I see. Has the animal proved useful?"

"He saved five lives on Mardia by barking a warning."

"The details have been entered in your log, I suppose?"

"Yes, sir. The log is in the chart room awaiting your inspection."

"We'll get to it in due time." Reaching the bow-cabin, Cassidy took a seat, accepted the folder from McNaught, started off at businesslike pace. "K1. Beam compass, type D, one of."

"This is it, sir," said McNaught, showing him.

"Still working properly?"

"Yes, sir."

They carried on, reached the intercom-cubby, the computer room, a succession of other places back to the galley. Here, Blanchard posed in freshly laundered white clothes and eyed the newcomer warily.

"V147. Electronic oven, one of."

"Is zis," said Blanchard, pointing with disdain.

"Satisfactory?" inquired Cassidy, giving him the fishy-eye.

"Not beeg enough," declared Blanchard. He encompassed the entire galley with an expressive gesture. "Nossings beeg enough. Place too small. Eversings too small. I am chef de cuisine an' she is a cuisine like an attic."

"This is a warship, not a luxury liner," Cassidy snapped. He frowned at the equipment-sheet. "V148. Timing device, electronic oven, attachment thereto, one of."

"Is zis," spat Blanchard, ready to sling it through the nearest port if Cassidy would first donate the two pins.

Working his way down the sheet, Cassidy got nearer and nearer while nervous tension built up. Then he reached the critical point and said, "V1098. Offog, one."

"*Morbleu!*" said Blanchard, shooting sparks from his eyes, "I have say before an' I say again, zere never was—"

"The offog is in the radio room, sir," McNaught chipped in hurriedly.

"Indeed?" Cassidy took another look at the sheet. "Then why is it recorded along with galley equipment?"

"It was placed in the galley at time of fitting-out, sir. It's one of those portable instruments left to us to fix up where most suitable."

"Hm-m-m! Then it should have been transferred to the radio room list. Why didn't you transfer it?"

"I thought it better to wait for your authority to do so, sir."

The fish-eyes registered gratification. "Yes, that is quite proper

of you, captain. I will transfer it now." He crossed the item from
sheet nine, initialed it, entered it on sheet sixteen, initialed that.
"V1099. Inscribed collar, leather . . . oh, yes, I've seen that. The
dog was wearing it."

He ticked it. An hour later he strutted into the radio room.
Burman stood up, squared his shoulders but could not keep his
feet or hands from fidgeting. His eyes protruded slightly and
kept straying toward McNaught in silent appeal. He was like a
man wearing a porcupine in his britches.

"V1098. Offog, one," said Cassidy in his usual tone of brooking
no nonsense.

Moving with the jerkiness of a slightly uncoördinated robot,
Burman pawed a small box fronted with dials, switches and
colored lights. It looked like a radio ham's idea of a fruit machine.
He knocked down a couple of switches. The lights came on,
played around in intriguing combinations.

"This is it, sir," he informed with difficulty.

"Ah!" Cassidy left his chair and moved across for a closer look.
"I don't recall having seen this item before. But there are so many
different models of the same things. Is it still operating effi-
ciently?"

"Yes, sir."

"It's one of the most useful things in the ship," contributed Mc-
Naught, for good measure.

"What does it *do?*" inquired Cassidy, inviting Burman to cast a
pearl of wisdom before him.

Burman paled.

Hastily, McNaught said, "A full explanation would be rather
involved and technical but, to put it as simply as possible, it en-
ables us to strike a balance between opposing gravitational fields.
Variations in lights indicate the extent and degree of unbalance
at any given time."

"It's a clever idea," added Burman, made suddenly reckless
by this news, "based upon Finagle's Constant."

"I see," said Cassidy, not seeing at all. He resumed his seat,
ticked the offog and carried on. "Z44. Switchboard, automatic,
forty-line intercom, one of."

"Here it is, sir."

Cassidy glanced at it, returned his gaze to the sheet. The others used his momentary distraction to mop perspiration from their foreheads.

Victory had been gained.

All was well.

For the third time, hah!

Rear Admiral Vane W. Cassidy departed pleased and complimentary. Within one hour the crew bolted to town. McNaught took turns with Gregory at enjoying the gay lights. For the next five days all was peace and pleasure.

On the sixth day Burman brought in a signal, dumped it upon McNaught's desk and waited for the reaction. He had an air of gratification, the pleasure of one whose virtue is about to be rewarded.

Terran Headquarters to Bustler. *Return here immediately for overhaul and refitting. Improved power plant to be installed. Feldman. Navy Op. Command. Sirisec.*

"Back to Terra," commented McNaught, happily. "And an overhaul will mean at least one month's leave." He eyed Burman. "Tell all officers on duty to go to town at once and order the crew aboard. The men will come running when they know why."

"Yes, sir," said Burman, grinning.

Everyone was still grinning two weeks later when the Siriport had receded far behind and Sol had grown to a vague speck in the sparkling mist of the bow starfield. Eleven weeks still to go, but it was worth it. Back to Terra. Hurrah!

In the captain's cabin the grins abruptly vanished one evening when Burman suddenly developed the willies. He marched in, chewed his bottom lip while waiting for McNaught to finish writing in the log.

Finally, McNaught pushed the book away, glanced up, frowned. "What's the matter with you? Got a bellyache or something?"

"No, sir. I've been thinking."

"Does it hurt that much?"

"I've been thinking," persisted Burman in funereal tones. "We're going back for overhaul. You know what that means?

We'll walk off the ship and a horde of experts will walk onto it."
He stared tragically at the other. "Experts, I said."

"Naturally they'll be experts," McNaught agreed. "Equipment
cannot be tested and brought up to scratch by a bunch of dopes."

"It will require more than a mere expert to bring the offog up
to scratch," Burman pointed out. "It'll need a genius."

McNaught rocked back, swapped expressions like changing
masks. "Jumping Judas! I'd forgotten all about that thing. When
we get to Terra we won't blind *those* boys with science."

"No, sir, we won't," endorsed Burman. He did not add "any
more" but his face shouted aloud, "You got me into this. You get
me out of it." He waited a time while McNaught did some intense thinking, then prompted, "What do you suggest, sir?"

Slowly the satisfied smile returned to McNaught's features as
he answered, "Break up the contraption and feed it into the disin-
tegrator."

"That doesn't solve the problem," said Burman. "We'll still be
short an offog."

"No we won't. Because I'm going to signal its loss owing to the
hazards of space-service." He closed one eye in an emphatic wink.
"We're in free flight right now." He reached for a message-pad
and scribbled on it while Burman stood by vastly relieved.

*Bustler to Terran Headquarters. Item V1098, Offog one, came
apart under gravitational stress while passing through twin-sun
field Hector Major-Minor. Material used as fuel. McNaught, Commander. Bustler.*

Burman took it to the radio room and beamed it Earthward.
All was peace and progress for another two days. The next time
he went to the captain's cabin he went running and worried.

"General call, sir," he announced breathlessly and thrust the
message into the other's hands.

*Terran Headquarters for relay all sectors. Urgent and Impor-
tant. All ships grounded forthwith. Vessels in flight under official
orders will make for nearest spaceport pending further instructions. Welling. Alarm and Rescue Command. Terra.*

"Something's gone bust," commented McNaught, undisturbed.
He traipsed to the chart room, Burman following. Consulting the

charts, he dialed the intercom phone, got Pike in the bow and ordered, "There's a panic. All ships grounded. We've got to make for Zaxtedport, about three days' run away. Change course at once. Starboard seventeen degrees, declination ten." Then he cut off, griped, "Bang goes that sweet month on Terra. I never did like Zaxted, either. It stinks. The crew will feel murderous about this and I don't blame them."

"What d'you think has happened, sir?" asked Burman. He looked both uneasy and annoyed.

"Heaven alone knows. The last general call was seven years ago when the *Starider* exploded halfway along the Mars run. They grounded every ship in existence while they investigated the cause." He rubbed his chin, pondered, went on, "And the call before that one was when the entire crew of the *Blowgun* went nuts. Whatever it is this time, you can bet it's serious."

"It wouldn't be the start of a space war?"

"Against whom?" McNaught made a gesture of contempt. "Nobody has the ships with which to oppose us. No, it's something technical. We'll learn of it eventually. They'll tell us before we reach Zaxted or soon afterward."

They did tell him. Within six hours. Burman rushed in with face full of horror.

"What's eating you now?" demanded McNaught, staring at him.

"The offog," stuttered Burman. He made motions as though brushing off invisible spiders.

"What of it?"

"It's a typographical error. In your copy it should read off. dog."

The commander stared owlishly.

"Off. dog?" echoed McNaught, making it sound like foul language.

"See for yourself." Dumping the signal on the desk, Burman bolted out, left the door swinging. McNaught scowled after him, picked up the message.

Terran Headquarters to Bustler. *Your report V1098, ship's official dog Peaslake. Detail fully circumstances and manner in which animal came apart under gravitational stress. Cross-examine crew and signal all coincidental symptoms experienced* by them. *Urgent and Important. Welling. Alarm and Rescue Command. Terra.*

In the privacy of his cabin McNaught commenced to eat his nails. Every now and again he went a little cross-eyed as he examined them for nearness to the flesh.

1956
14th Convention
New York

Murray Leinster

Murray Leinster is the acknowledged dean of science fiction. He is a *real* old-timer. I look up to him with the respect and reverence due one of such ancient and patriarchal grandeur. After all, in the 1930s, when all the world was green and new, Murray Leinster wrote some of the stories that set my young and eager heart to pounding wildly. Little did I imagine then that the day would come I would meet, and even touch, so god-like a man.

I must admit, though, that it is deucedly irritating to be part of a field with so uncharacteristic a dean, however god-like.

After all, you know what a dean is *supposed* to be like. He should be a benign greybeard who makes an impressive appearance and who knows how to smile benevolently at awed looks and humble greetings. Above all, he does not sully the sanctity of his position by competing with younger men.

Certainly, Leinster should be just such a dean. He had a story, "The Runaway Skyscraper," in the June 1926 issue of *Amazing Stories*, which was only the third issue of the oldest science fiction magazine. Surely he should be entitled to take his ease now.

Isn't it hard then, that Leinster, quick and spry as any young squirt, has continued to write copiously to this very day, and manages to do it so well that at the 14th Convention (New York, 1956) he carried off a Hugo for "Exploration Team."

I pointed out the inappropriateness of his behavior, and, more in sorrow than in anger, explained that as dean he had his dignity to think of. I urged him to return the Hugo and offered to keep it for him.

It pains me to report that he merely laughed at this and skipped gaily off, holding his Hugo so that anyone might see it— completely lost to shame.

3

EXPLORATION TEAM

I

The nearer moon went by overhead. It was jagged and irregular in shape, and was probably a captured asteroid. Huyghens had seen it often enough, so he did not go out of his quarters to watch it hurtle across the sky with seemingly the speed of an atmosphere-flier, occulting the stars as it went. Instead, he sweated over paper work, which should have been odd because he was technically a felon and all his labors on Loren Two felonious. It was odd, too, for a man to do paper work in a room with steel shutters and a huge bald eagle—untethered—dozing on a three-inch perch set in the wall. But paper work was not Huyghens' real task. His only assistant had tangled with a nightwalker and the furtive Kodius Company ships had taken him away to where Kodius Company ships came from. Huyghens had to do two men's work in loneliness. To his knowledge, he was the only man in this solar system.

Below him, there were snufflings. Sitka Pete got up heavily and padded to his water pan. He lapped the refrigerated water and sneezed violently. Sourdough Charley waked and complained in a rumbling growl. There were divers other rumblings and mutterings below. Huyghens called reassuringly, "Easy there!" and went on with his work. He finished a climate report, and fed figures to a computer, and while it hummed over them he entered the inventory totals in the station log, showing what supplies remained. Then he began to write up the log proper.

"Sitka Pete," he wrote, "*has apparently solved the problem of killing individual sphexes. He has learned that it doesn't do to hug them and that his claws can't penetrate their hide—not the top hide, anyhow. Today Semper notified us that a pack of sphexes had found the scent-trail to the station. Sitka hid downwind until they arrived. Then he charged from the rear and brought his paws together on both sides of a sphex's head in a terrific pair of slaps. It must have been like two twelve-inch shells arriving from opposite directions at the same time. It must have scrambled the sphex's brains as if they were eggs. It dropped dead. He killed two more with such mighty pairs of wallops. Sourdough Charley watched, grunting, and when the sphexes turned on Sitka, he charged in his turn. I, of course, couldn't shoot too close to him, so he might have fared badly but that Faro Nell came pouring out of the bear quarters to help. The diversion enabled Sitka Pete to resume the use of his new technic, towering on his hind legs and swinging his paws in the new and grisly fashion. The fight ended promptly. Semper flew and screamed above the scrap, but as usual did not join in. Note: Nugget, the cub, tried to mix in but his mother cuffed him out of the way. Sourdough and Sitka ignored him as usual. Kodius Champion's genes are sound!*"

The noises of the night went on outside. There were notes like organ tones—song lizards. There were the tittering giggling cries of night-walkers—not to be tittered back at. There were sounds like tack hammers, and doors closing, and from every direction came noises like hiccups in various keys. These were made by the improbable small creatures which on Loren Two took the place of insects.

Huyghens wrote out:

"*Sitka seemed ruffled when the fight was over. He painstakingly used his trick on every dead or wounded sphex, except those he'd killed with it, lifting up their heads for his pile-driver-like blows from two directions at once, as if to show Sourdough how it was done. There was much grunting as they hauled the carcasses to the incinerator. It almost seemed—*"

The arrival bell clanged, and Huyghens jerked up his head to stare at it. Semper, the eagle, opened icy eyes. He blinked.

Noises. There was a long, deep, contented snore from below. Something shrieked, out in the jungle. Hiccups. Clatterings, and organ notes—

The bell clanged again. It was a notice that a ship aloft somewhere had picked up the beacon beam—which only Kodius Company ships should know about—and was communicating for a landing. But there shouldn't be any ships in this solar system just now! This was the only habitable planet of the sun, and it had been officially declared uninhabitable by reason of inimical animal life. Which meant sphexes. Therefore no colony was permitted, and the Kodius Company broke the law. And there were few graver crimes than unauthorized occupation of a new planet.

The bell clanged a third time. Huyghens swore. His hand went out to cut off the beacon—but that would be useless. Radar would have fixed it and tied it in with physical features like the nearby sea and the Sere Plateau. The ship could find the place, anyhow, and descend by daylight.

"The devil!" said Huyghens. But he waited yet again for the bell to ring. A Kodius Company ship would double-ring to reassure him. But there shouldn't be a Kodius Company ship for months.

The bell clanged singly. The space phone dial flickered and a voice came out of it, tinny from stratospheric distortion:

"*Calling ground! Calling ground! Crete Line ship* Odysseus *calling ground on Loren Two. Landing one passenger by boat. Put on your field lights.*"

Huyghens' mouth dropped open. A Kodius Company ship would be welcome. A Colonial Survey ship would be extremely unwelcome, because it would destroy the colony and Sitka and Sourdough and Faro Nell and Nugget—and Semper—and carry Huyghens off to be tried for unauthorized colonization and all that it implied.

But a commercial ship, landing one passenger by boat— There was simply no circumstances under which that would happen. Not to an unknown, illegal colony. Not to a furtive station!

Huyghens flicked on the landing-field lights. He saw the glare in the field outside. Then he stood up and prepared to take the measures required by discovery. He packed the paper work he'd been doing into the disposal safe. He gathered up all personal documents and tossed them in. Every record, every bit of evidence that the Kodius Company maintained this station went into the safe. He slammed the door. He touched his finger to the disposal button, which would destroy the contents and melt down even the ashes past their possible use for evidence in court.

Then he hesitated. If it were a Survey ship, the button had to be pressed and he must resign himself to a long term in prison. But a Crete Line ship—if the space phone told the truth—was not threatening. It was simply unbelievable.

He shook his head. He got into travel garb and armed himself. He went down into the bear quarters, turning on lights as he went. There were startled snufflings and Sitka Pete reared himself very absurdly to a sitting position to blink at him. Sourdough Charley lay on his back with his legs in the air. He'd found it cooler, sleeping that way. He rolled over with a thump. He made snorting sounds which somehow sounded cordial. Faro Nell padded to the door of her separate apartment—assigned her so that Nugget would not be underfoot to irritate the big males.

Huyghens, as the human population of Loren Two, faced the work force, fighting force, and—with Nugget—four-fifths of the terrestrial nonhuman population of the planet. They were mutated Kodiak bears, descendants of the Kodius Champion for whom the Kodius Company was named. Sitka Pete was a good twenty-two hundred pounds of lumbering, intelligent carnivore. Sourdough Charley would weigh within a hundred pounds of that figure. Faro Nell was eighteen hundred pounds of female charm—and ferocity. Then Nugget poked his muzzle around his mother's furry rump to see what was toward, and he was six hundred pounds of ursine infancy. The animals looked at Huyghens expectantly. If he'd had Semper riding on his shoulder, they'd have known what was expected of them.

"Let's go," said Huyghens. "It's dark outside, but somebody's coming. And it may be bad!"

He unfastened the outer door of the bear quarters. Sitka Pete went charging clumsily through it. A forthright charge was the best way to develop any situation—if one was an oversized male Kodiak bear. Sourdough went lumbering after him. There was nothing hostile immediately outside. Sitka stood up on his hind legs—he reared up a solid twelve feet—and sniffed the air. Sour-dough methodically lumbered to one side and then the other, sniffing in his turn. Nell came out, nine-tenths of a ton of dainti-ness, and rumbled admonitorily at Nugget, who trailed her closely. Huyghens stood in the doorway, his night-sighted gun ready. He felt uncomfortable at sending the bears ahead into a Loren Two jungle at night. But they were qualified to scent danger, and he was not.

The illumination of the jungle in a wide path toward the land-ing field made for weirdness in the look of things. There were arching giant ferns and columnar trees which grew above them, and the extraordinary lanceolate underbrush of the jungle. The flood lamps, set level with the ground, lighted everything from below. The foliage, then, was brightly lit against the black night-sky—brightly lit enough to dim-out the stars. There were astonish-ing contrasts of light and shadow everywhere.

"On ahead!" commanded Huyghens, waving. "Hup!"

He swung the bear-quarters door shut. He moved toward the landing field through the lane of lighted forest. The two giant male Kodiaks lumbered ahead. Sitka Pete dropped to all fours and prowled. Sourdough Charley followed closely, swinging from side to side. Huyghens came alertly behind the two of them, and Faro Nell brought up the rear with Nugget following her closely.

It was an excellent military formation for progress through dan-gerous jungle. Sourdough and Sitka were advance-guard and point, respectively, while Faro Nell guarded the rear. With Nug-get to look after, she was especially alert against attack from behind. Huyghens was, of course, the striking force. His gun fired explosive bullets which would discourage even sphexes, and his night-sight—a cone of light which went on when he took up the trigger-slack—told exactly where they would strike. It was not a sportsmanlike weapon, but the creatures of Loren Two were not sportsmanlike antagonists. The night-walkers, for example— But night-walkers feared light. They attacked only in a species of hysteria if it were too bright.

Huyghens moved toward the glare at the landing field. His mental state was savage. The Kodius Company station on Loren Two was completely illegal. It happened to be necessary, from one point of view, but it was still illegal. The tinny voice on the space phone was not convincing, in ignoring that illegality. But if a ship landed, Huyghens could get back to the station before men could follow, and he'd have the disposal safe turned on in time to protect those who'd sent him here.

But he heard the faraway and high harsh roar of a landing-boat rocket—not a ship's bellowing tubes—as he made his way through the unreal-seeming brush. The roar grew louder as he pushed on, the three big Kodiaks padding here and there, sniffing thoughtfully, making a perfect defensive-offensive formation for the particular conditions of this planet.

He reached the edge of the landing field, and it was blindingly bright, with the customary divergent beams slanting skyward so a ship could check its instrument landing by sight. Landing fields like this had been standard, once upon a time. Nowadays all developed planets had landing grids—monstrous structures which drew upon ionospheres for power and lifted and drew down star ships with remarkable gentleness and unlimited force. This sort of landing field would be found where a survey-team was at work, or where some strictly temporary investigation of ecology or bacteriology was under way, or where a newly authorized colony had not yet been able to build its landing grid. Of course it was un-thinkable that anybody would attempt a settlement in defiance of the law!

Already, as Huyghens reached the edge of the scorched open space, the night-creatures had rushed to the light like moths on Earth. The air was misty with crazily gyrating, tiny flying things. They were innumerable and of every possible form and size, from the white midges of the night and multi-winged flying worms to those revoltingly naked-looking larger creatures which might have passed for plucked flying monkeys if they had not been carnivorous and worse. The flying things soared and whirred and danced and spun insanely in the glare. They made peculiarly plaintive humming noises. They almost formed a lamp-lit ceiling over the cleared space. They did hide the stars. Staring upward, Huyghens could just barely make out the blue-white flame of the space-boat's rocket through the fog of wings and bodies.

The rocket-flame grew steadily in size. Once, apparently, it tilted to adjust the boat's descending course. It went back to normal. A speck of incandescence at first, it grew until it was like a great star, and then a more-than-brilliant moon, and then it was a pitiless glaring eye. Huyghens averted his gaze from it. Sitka Pete sat lumpily—more than a ton of him—and blinked wisely at the dark jungle away from the light. Sourdough ignored the deepening, increasing rocket roar. He sniffed the air delicately. Faro Nell held Nugget firmly under one huge paw and licked his head as if tidying him up to be seen by company. Nugget wriggled.

The roar became that of ten thousand thunders. A warm breeze below outward from the landing-field. The rocket boat hurled downward, and its flame touched the mist of flying things, and they shriveled and burned and were hot. Then there were churning clouds of dust everywhere, and the center of the field blazed terribly—and something slid down a shaft of fire, and squeezed it flat, and sat on it—and the flame went out. The rocket boat sat there, resting on its tail fins, pointing toward the stars from which it came.

There was a terrible silence after the tumult. Then, very faintly, the noises of the night came again. There were sounds like those of organ pipes, and very faint and apologetic noises like hiccups. All these sounds increased, and suddenly Huyghens could hear quite normally. Then a side-port opened with a quaint sort of clattering, and something unfolded from where it had been inset into the hull of the space boat, and there was a metal passageway across the flame-heated space on which the boat stood.

A man came out of the port. He reached back in and shook hands very formally. He climbed down the ladder rungs to the walkway. He marched above the steaming baked area, carrying a craveling bag. He reached the end of the walk and stepped gingerly to the ground. He moved hastily to the edge of the clearing. He waved to the space boat. There were ports. Perhaps someone returned the gesture. The walkway folded briskly back up to the hull and vanished in it. A flame exploded into being under the tail fins. There were fresh clouds of monstrous, choking dust and a brightness like that of a sun. There was noise past the possibility of endurance. Then the light rose swiftly through the dust cloud, and sprang higher and climbed more swiftly still. When Huyghens' ears again permitted him to hear anything, there was only a diminishing mutter in the heavens and a small bright speck of light ascending to the sky and swinging eastward as it rose to intercept the ship which had let it descend.

The night noises of the jungle went on. Life on Loren Two did not need to heed the doings of men. But there was a spot of incandescence in the day-bright clearing, and a short, brisk man looked puzzledly about him with a traveling bag in his hand.

Huyghens advanced toward him as the incandescence dimmed. Sourdough and Sitka preceded him. Faro Nell trailed faithfully, keeping a maternal eye on her offspring. The man in the clearing stared at the parade they made. It would be upsetting, even after preparation, to land at night on a strange planet, and to have the ship's boat and all links with the rest of the cosmos depart, and then to find one's self approached—it might seem stalked—by two colossal male Kodiak bears, with a third bear and a cub behind them. A single human figure in such company might seem irrelevant.

The new arrival gazed blankly. He moved, startled. Then Huyghens called:

"Hello, there! Don't worry about the bears! They're friends!"

Sitka reached the newcomer. He went warily downwind from him and sniffed. The smell was satisfactory. Man-smell. Sitka sat down with the solid impact of more than a ton of bear-meat landing on packed dirt. He regarded the man amiably. Sourdough said *"Whoosh!"* and went on to sample the air beyond the clearing. Huyghens approached. The newcomer wore the uniform of the Colonial Survey. That was bad. It bore the insignia of a senior officer. Worse.

"Hah!" said the just-landed man. "Where are the robots? What in all the nineteen hells are these creatures? Why did you shift your station? I'm Roane, here to make a progress report on your colony."

Huyghens said:

"What colony?"

"Loren Two Robot Installation—" Then Roane said indignantly, "Don't tell me that that idiot skipper dropped me at the wrong place! This is Loren Two, isn't it? And this is the landing field.

But where are your robots? You should have the beginning of a grid up! What the devil's happened here and what are these beasts?"

Huyghens grimaced.

"This," he said politely, "is an illegal, unlicensed settlement. I'm a criminal. These beasts are my confederates. If you don't want to associate with criminals you needn't, of course, but I doubt if you'll live till morning unless you accept my hospitality while I think over what to do about your landing. In reason, I ought to shoot you."

Faro Nell came to a halt behind Huyghens, which was her proper post in all out-door movement. Nugget, however, saw a new human. Nugget was a cub, and, therefore, friendly. He ambled forward ingratiatingly. He was four feet high at the shoulders, on all fours. He wriggled bashfully as he approached Roane. He sneezed, because he was embarrassed.

His mother overtook him swiftly and cuffed him to one side. He wailed. The wail of a six-hundred-pound Kodiak bear-cub is a remarkable sound. Roane gave ground a pace.

"I think," he said carefully, "that we'd better talk things over. But if this is an illegal colony, of course you're under arrest and anything you say will be used against you."

Huyghens grimaced again.

"Right," he said. "But now if you'll walk close to me, we'll head back to the station. I'd have Sourdough carry your bag—he likes to carry things—but he may need his teeth. We've half a mile to travel." He turned to the animals. "Let's go!" he said commandingly. "Back to the station! Hup!"

Grunting, Sitka Pete arose and took up his duties as advanced point of a combat team. Sourdough trailed, swinging widely to one side and another. Huyghens and Roane moved together. Faro Nell and Nugget brought up the rear. Which, of course, was the only relatively safe way for anybody to travel on Loren Two, in the jungle, a good half mile from one's fortresslike residence.

But there was only one incident on the way back. It was a night-walker, made hysterical by the lane of light. It poured through the underbrush, uttering cries like maniacal laughter. Sourdough brought it down, a good ten yards from Huyghens.

When it was all over, Nugget bristled up to the dead creature, uttering cub-growls. He feigned to attack it.

His mother whacked him soundly.

II

There were comfortable, settling-down noises below. The bears grunted and rumbled, but ultimately were still. The glare from the landing field was gone. The lighted lane through the jungle was dark again. Huyghens ushered the man from the space boat up into his living quarters. There was a rustling stir, and Semper took his head from under his wing. He stared coldly at the two humans. He spread monstrous, seven-foot wings and fluttered them. He opened his beak and closed it with a snap.

"That's Semper," said Huyghens. "Semper Tyrannis. He's the rest of the terrestrial population here. Not being a fly-by-night sort of creature, he didn't come out to welcome you."

Roane blinked at the huge bird, perched on a three-inch-thick perch set in the wall.

"An eagle?" he demanded. "Kodiak bears—mutated ones you say, but still bears—and now an eagle? You've a very nice fighting unit in the bears."

"They're pack animals, too," said Huyghens. "They can carry some hundreds of pounds without losing too much combat efficiency. And there's no problem of supply. They live off the jungle. Not sphexes, though. Nothing will eat a sphex, even if it can kill one."

He brought out glasses and a bottle. He indicated a chair. Roane put down his traveling bag. He took a glass.

"I'm curious," he observed. "Why Semper Tyrannis? I can understand Sitka Pete and Sourdough Charley as names. The home of their ancestors makes them fitting. But why Semper?"

"He was bred for hawking," said Huyghens. "You sic a dog on something. You sic Semper Tyrannis. He's too big to ride on a hawking glove, so the shoulders of my coats are padded to let him ride there. He's a flying scout. I've trained him to notify us of sphexes, and in flight he carries a tiny television camera. He's useful, but he hasn't the brains of the bears."

Roane sat down and sipped at his glass.

"Interesting . . . very interesting! But this is an illegal settlement. I'm a Colonial Survey officer. My job is reporting on progress according to plan, but nevertheless I have to arrest you. Didn't you say something about shooting me?"

Huyghens said doggedly:

"I'm trying to think of a way out. Add up all the penalties for illegal colonization and I'd be in a very bad fix if you got away and reported this set-up. Shooting you would be logical."

"I see that," said Roane reasonably. "But since the point has come up—I have a blaster trained on you from my pocket."

Huyghens shrugged.

"It's rather likely that my human confederates will be back here before your friends. You'd be in a very tight fix if my friends came back and found you more or less sitting on my corpse."

Roane nodded.

"That's true, too. Also it's probable that your fellow terrestrials wouldn't co-operate with me as they have with you. You seem to have the whip hand, even with my blaster trained on you. On the other hand, you could have killed me quite easily after the boat left, when I'd first landed. I'd have been quite unsuspicious. So you may not really intend to murder me."

Huyghens shrugged again.

"So," said Roane, "since the secret of getting along with people is that of postponing quarrels—suppose we postpone the question of who kills whom? Frankly, I'm going to send you to prison if I can. Unlawful colonization is very bad business. But I suppose you feel that you have to do something permanent about me. In your place I probably should, too. Shall we declare a truce?"

Huyghens indicated indifference. Roane said vexedly:

"Then I do! I have to! So—"

He pulled his hand out of his pocket and put a pocket blaster on the table. He leaned back, defiantly.

"Keep it," said Huyghens. "Loren Two isn't a place where you live long unarmed." He turned to a cupboard. "Hungry?"

"I could eat," admitted Roane.

Huyghens pulled out two mealpacks from the cupboard and inserted them in the readier below. He set out plates.

"Now—what happened to the official, licensed, authorized

colony here?" asked Roane briskly. "License issued eighteen
months ago. There was a landing of colonists with a drone fleet of
equipment and supplies. There've been four ship-contacts since.
There should be several thousand robots being industrious under
adequate human supervision. There should be a hundred-mile-
square clearing, planted with food plants for later human arrivals.
There should be a landing grid at least half-finished. Obviously
there should be a space beacon to guide ships to a landing. There
isn't. There's no clearing visible from space. That Crete Line ship
has been in orbit for three days, trying to find a place to drop me.
Her skipper was fuming. Your beacon is the only one on the
planet, and we found it by accident. What happened?"

Huyghens served the food. He said dryly:

"There could be a hundred colonies on this planet without any
one knowing of any other. I can only guess about your robots,
but I suspect they ran into sphexes."

Roane paused, with his fork in his hand.

"I read up on this planet, since I was to report on its colony. A
sphex is part of the inimical animal life here. Cold-blooded bel-
ligerent carnivore, not a lizard but a genus all its own. Hunts in
packs. Seven to eight hundred pounds, when adult. Lethally
dangerous and simply too numerous to fight. They're why no
license was ever granted to human colonists. Only robots could
work here, because they're machines. What animal attacks machines?"

Huyghens said:

"What machine attacks animals? The sphexes wouldn't bother
robots, of course, but would robots bother the sphexes?"

Roane chewed and swallowed.

"Hold it! I'll agree that you can't make a hunting-robot. A machine can discriminate, but it can't decide. That's why there's no
danger of a robot revolt. They can't decide to do something for
which they have no instructions. But this colony was planned
with full knowledge of what robots can and can't do. As ground
was cleared, it was enclosed in an electric fence which no sphex
could touch without frying."

Huyghens thoughtfully cut his food. After a moment:

"The landing was in the wintertime," he observed. "It must
have been, because the colony survived a while. And at a guess,

the last ship-landing was before thaw. The years are eighteen months long here, you know."

Roane admitted:

"It was in winter that the landing was made. And the last ship-landing was before spring. The idea was to get mines in operation for material, and to have ground cleared and enclosed in sphex-proof fence before the sphexes came back from the tropics. They winter there, I understand."

"Did you ever see a sphex?" Huyghens asked. Then added, "No, of course not. But if you took a spitting cobra and crossed it with a wildcat, painted it tan-and-blue and then gave it hydrophobia and homicidal mania at once—why you might have one sphex. But not the race of sphexes. They can climb trees, by the way. A fence wouldn't stop them."

"An electrified fence," said Roane. "Nothing could climb that!"

"No one animal," Huyghens told him. "But sphexes are a race. The smell of one dead sphex brings others running with blood in their eyes. Leave a dead sphex alone for six hours and you've got them around by the dozen. Two days and there are hundreds. Longer, and you've got thousands of them! They gather to caterwaul over their dead pal and hunt for whoever or whatever killed him."

He returned to his meal. A moment later he said:

"No need to wonder what happened to your colony. During the winter the robots burned out a clearing and put up an electrified fence according to the book. Come spring, the sphexes came back. They're curious, among their other madnesses. A sphex would try to climb the fence just to see what was behind it. He'd be electrocuted. His carcass would bring others, raging because a sphex was dead. Some of them would try to climb the fence—and die. And their corpses would bring others. Presently the fence would break down from the bodies hanging on it, or a bridge of dead beasts' carcasses would be built across it—and from as far downwind as the scent carried there'd be loping, raging, scent-crazed sphexes racing to the spot. They'd pour into the clearing through or over the fence, squalling and screeching for something to kill. I think they'd find it."

Roane ceased to eat. He looked sick.

"There were . . . pictures of sphexes in the data I read. I suppose that would account for . . . everything."

He tried to lift his fork. He put it down again.

"I can't eat," he said abruptly.

Huyghens made no comment. He finished his own meal, scowling. He rose and put the plates into the top of the cleaner. There was a whirring. He took them out of the bottom and put them away.

"Let me see those reports, eh?" he asked dourly. "I'd like to see what sort of a set-up they had—those robots."

Roane hesitated and then opened his traveling bag. There was a microviewer and reels of films. One entire reel was labeled "Specifications for Construction, Colonial Survey," which would contain detailed plans and all requirements of material and workmanship for everything from desks, office, administrative personnel, for use of, to landing grids, heavy-gravity planets, lift-capacity one hundred thousand Earth-tons. But Huyghens found another. He inserted it and spun the control swiftly here and there, pausing only briefly at index frames until he came to the section he wanted. He began to study the information with growing impatience.

"Robots, robots, robots!" he snapped. "Why don't they leave them where they belong—in cities to do the dirty work, and on airless planets where nothing unexpected ever happens! Robots don't belong in new colonies! Your colonists depended on them for defense! Dammit, let a man work with robots long enough and he thinks all nature is as limited as they are! This is a plan to set up a controlled environment! On Loren Two! Controlled environment—" He swore, luridly. "Complacent, idiotic, deskbound half-wits!"

"Robots are all right," said Roane. "We couldn't run civilization without them."

"But you can't tame a wilderness with 'em!" snapped Huyghens. "You had a dozen men landed, with fifty assembled robots to start with. There were parts for fifteen hundred more—and I'll bet anything I've got that the ship-contacts landed more still."

"They did," admitted Roane.

"I despise 'em," growled Huyghens. "I feel about 'em the way the old Greeks and Romans felt about slaves. They're for menial work—the sort of work a man will perform for himself, but that he won't do for another man for pay. Degrading work!"

"Quite aristocratic!" said Roane with a touch of irony. "I take it that robots clean out the bear quarters downstairs."

"No!" snapped Huyghens. "I do! They're my friends! They fight for me! They can't understand the necessity and no robot would do the job right!"

He growled, again. The noises of the night went on outside. Organ tones and hiccupings and the sound of tack hammers and slamming doors. Somewhere there was a singularly exact replica of the discordant squeaking of a rusty pump.

"I'm looking," said Huyghens at the micro-viewer, "for the record of their mining operations. An open-pit operation wouldn't mean a thing. But if they had driven a tunnel, and somebody was there supervising the robots when the colony was wiped out, there's an off-chance he survived a while."

Roane regarded him with suddenly intent eyes.

"And—"

"Dammit," snapped Huyghens, "if so I'll go see! He'd . . . they'd have no chance at all, otherwise. Not that the chance is good in any case!"

Roane raised his eyebrows.

"I'm a Colonial Survey officer," he said. "I've told you I'll send you to prison if I can. You've risked the lives of millions of people, maintaining non-quarantined communication with an unlicensed planet. If you did rescue somebody from the ruins of the robot colony, does it occur to you that they'd be witnesses to your unauthorized presence here?"

Huyghens spun the viewer again. He stopped. He switched back and forth and found what he wanted. He muttered in satisfaction: "They did run a tunnel!" Aloud he said, "I'll worry about witnesses when I have to."

He pushed aside another cupboard door. Inside it were the odds and ends a man makes use of to repair the things about his house that he never notices until they go wrong. There was an assortment of wires, transistors, bolts, and similar stray items that a man living alone will need. When to his knowledge he's the only inhabitant of a solar system, he especially needs such things.

"What now?" asked Roane mildly.

"I'm going to try to find out if there's anybody left alive over there. I'd have checked before if I'd known the colony existed. I can't prove they're all dead, but I may prove that somebody's still alive. It's barely two weeks' journey away from here! Odd that two colonies picked spots so near!"

He absorbedly picked over the oddments he'd selected. Roane said vexedly:

"Confound it! How can you check whether somebody's alive some hundreds of miles away—when you didn't know he existed half an hour ago?"

Huyghens threw a switch and took down a wall panel, exposing electronic apparatus and circuits behind. He busied himself with it.

"Ever think about hunting for a castaway?" he asked over his shoulder. "There's a planet with some tens of millions of square miles on it. You know there's a ship down. You've no idea where. You assume the survivors have power—no civilized man will be without power very long, so long as he can smelt metals!—but making a space beacon calls for high-precision measurements and workmanship. It's not to be improvised. So what will your ship-wrecked civilized man do, to guide a rescue ship to the one or two square miles he occupies among some tens of millions on the planet?"

Roane fretted visibly.

"What?"

"He's had to go primitive, to begin with," Roane explained. "He cooks his meat over a fire, and so on. He has to make a strictly primitive signal. It's all he can do without gauges and micrometers and very special tools. But he can fill all the planet's atmosphere with a signal that searchers for him can't miss. You see?"

Roane thought irritably. He shook his head.

"He'll make," said Huyghens, "a spark transmitter. He'll fix its output at the shortest frequency he can contrive—it'll be somewhere in the five-to-fifty-meter wave-band, but it will tune very broad—and it will be a plainly human signal. He'll start it broadcasting. Some of those frequencies will go all around the planet under the ionosphere. Any ship that comes in under the radio roof will pick up his signal, get a fix on it, move and get another fix, and then go straight to where the castaway is waiting placidly in a hand-braided hammock, sipping whatever sort of drink he's improvised out of the local vegetation."

Roane said grudgingly:

"Now that you mention it, of course—"

"My space phone picks up microwaves," said Huyghens, "I'm shifting a few elements to make it listen for longer stuff. It won't be efficient, but it will pick up a distress signal if one's in the air. I don't expect it, though."

He worked. Roane sat still a long time, watching him. Down below, a rhythmic sort of sound arose. It was Sourdough Charley, snoring. He lay on his back with his legs in the air. He'd discovered that he slept cooler that way. Sitka Pete grunted in his sleep. He was dreaming. In the general room of the station Semper, the eagle, blinked his eyes rapidly and then tucked his head under a gigantic wing and went to sleep. The noises of the Loren Two jungle came through the steel-shuttered windows. The nearer moon—which had passed overhead not long before the ringing of the arrival bell—again came soaring over the eastern horizon. It sped across the sky at the apparent speed of an atmosphere-flier. Overhead, it could be seen to be a jagged irregular mass of rock or metal, plunging blindly about the great planet forever.

Inside the station, Roane said angrily:

"See here, Huyghens! You've reason to kill me. Apparently you don't intend to. You've excellent reason to leave that robot colony strictly alone. But you're preparing to help, if there's anybody alive to need it. And yet you're a criminal—and I mean a criminal! There've been some ghastly bacteria exported from planets like Loren Two! There've been plenty of lives lost in consequence, and you're risking more! Why do you do it? Why do you do something that could produce monstrous results to other beings?"

Huyghens grunted.

"You're only assuming there are no sanitary and quarantine precautions taken in my communications. As a matter of fact, there are. They're taken, all right! As for the rest, you wouldn't understand."

"I don't understand," snapped Roane, "but that's no proof I can't! Why are you a criminal?"

Huyghens painstakingly used a screwdriver inside the wall panel. He delicately lifted out a small electronic assembly. He carefully began to fit in a spaghettied new assembly with larger units.

"I'm cutting my amplification here to hell-and-gone," he observed, "but I think it'll do. I'm doing what I'm doing," he added calmly, "I'm being a criminal because it seems to me befitting what I think I am. Everybody acts according to his own real notion of himself. You're a conscientious citizen, and a loyal official, and a well-adjusted personality. You consider yourself an intelligent rational animal. But you don't act that way! You're reminding me of my need to shoot you or something similar, which a merely rational animal would try to make me forget. You happen, Roane, to be a man. So am I. But I'm aware of it. Therefore, I deliberately do things a merely rational animal wouldn't, because they're my notion of what a man who's more than a rational animal should do."

He very carefully tightened one small screw after another. Roane said annoyedly:

"Oh. Religion."

"Self-respect," corrected Huyghens. "I don't like robots. They're too much like rational animals. A robot will do whatever it can that its supervisor requires it to do. A merely rational animal will do whatever it can that circumstances require it to do. I wouldn't like a robot unless it had some idea of what was befitting it and would spit in my eye if I tried to make it do something else. The bears downstairs, now— They're no robots! They are loyal and honorable beasts, but they'd turn and tear me to bits if I tried to make them do something against their nature. Faro Nell would fight me and all creation together, if I tried to harm Nugget. It would be unintelligent and unreasonable and irrational. She'd lose out and get killed. But I like her that way! And I'll fight you and all creation when you make me try to do something against my nature. I'll be stupid and unreasonable and irrational about it." Then he grinned over his shoulder. "So will you. Only you don't realize it."

He turned back to his task. After a moment he fitted a manual-control knob over a shaft in his haywire assembly.

"What did somebody try to make you do?" asked Roane shrewdly. "What was demanded of you that turned you into a criminal? What are you in revolt against?"

Huyghens threw a switch. He began to turn the knob which controlled the knob of his makeshift-modified receiver.

"Why," he said amusedly, "when I was young the people around me tried to make me into a conscientious citizen and a loyal employee and a well-adjusted personality. They tried to make me into a highly intelligent rational animal and nothing more. The difference between us, Roane, is that I found it out. Naturally, I rev—"

He stopped short. Faint, crackling, crisp frying sounds came from the speaker of the space phone now modified to receive what once were called short waves.

Huyghens listened. He cocked his head intently. He turned the knob very, very slowly. Then Roane made an arrested gesture, to call attention to something in the sibilant sound. Huyghens nodded. He turned the knob again, with infinitesimal increments.

Out of the background noise came a patterned mutter. As Huyghens shifted the tuning, it grew louder. It reached a volume where it was unmistakable. It was a sequence of sounds like discordant buzzing. There were three half-second buzzings with half-second pauses between. A two-second pause. Three full-second buzzings with half-second pauses between. Another two-second pause and three half-second buzzings, again. Then silence for five seconds. Then the pattern repeated.

"The devil!" said Huyghens. "That's a human signal! Mechanically made, too! In fact, it used to be a standard distress-call. It was termed an S O S, though I've no idea what that meant. Anyhow, somebody must have read old-fashioned novels, some time, to know about it. And so someone is still alive over at your licensed, but now smashed-up, robot colony. And they're asking for help. I'd say they're likely to need it."

He looked at Roane.

"The intelligent thing to do is sit back and wait for a ship—either of my friends or yours. A ship can help survivors or castaways much better than we can. A ship can even find them more easily. But maybe time is important to the poor devils! So I'm going to take the bears and see if I can reach them. You can wait here, if you like. What say? Travel on Loren Two isn't a picnic! I'll be fighting nearly every foot of the way. There's plenty of 'inimical animal life' here!"

Roane snapped angrily:

"Don't be a fool! Of course I'm coming! What do you take me for? And two of us should have four times the chance of one!"

Huyghens grinned.

"Not quite. You forget Sitka Pete and Sourdough Charley and Faro Nell. There'll be five of us if you come, instead of four. And, of course, Nugget has to come—and he'll be no help—but Semper may make up for him. You won't quadruple our chances, Roane, but I'll be glad to have you if you want to be stupid and unreasonable and not at all rational—and come along."

III

There was a jagged spur of stone looming precipitously over a river-valley. A thousand feet below, a broad stream ran westward to the sea. Twenty miles to the east, a wall of mountains rose sheer against the sky. Its peaks seemed to blend to a remarkable evenness of height. There was rolling, tumbled ground between for as far as the eye could see.

A speck in the sky came swiftly downward. Great pinions spread, and flapped, and icy eyes surveyed the rocky space. With more great flappings, Semper the eagle came to ground. He folded his huge wings and turned his head jerkily, his eyes unblinking. A tiny harness held a miniature camera against his chest. He strutted over the bare stone to the highest point. He stood there, a lonely and arrogant figure in the vastness.

There came crashings and rustlings, and then snuffling sounds. Sitka Pete came lumbering out into the clear space. He wore a harness too, and a pack. The harness was complex, because it had not only to hold a pack in normal travel, but, when he stood on his hind legs, it must not hamper the use of his forepaws in combat.

He went cagily all over the open area. He peered over the edge of the spur's farthest tip. He prowled to the other side and looked down. He scouted carefully. Once he moved close to Semper and the eagle opened his great curved beak and uttered an indignant noise. Sitka paid no attention.

He relaxed, satisfied. He sat down untidily, his hind legs sprawling. He wore an air approaching benevolence as he surveyed the landscape about and below him.

More snufflings and crashings. Sourdough Charley came into view with Huyghens and Roane behind him. Sourdough carried a pack, too. Then there was a squealing and Nugget scurried up from the rear, impelled by a whack from his mother. Faro Nell appeared, with the carcass of a staglike animal lashed to her harness.

"I picked this place from a space photo," said Huyghens, "to make a directional fix from. I'll get set up."

He swung his pack from his shoulders to the ground. He extracted an obviously self-constructed device which he set on the ground. It had a whip aerial, which he extended. Then he plugged in a considerable length of flexible wire and unfolded a tiny, improvised directional aerial with an even tinier booster at its base. Roane slipped his pack from his shoulders and watched. Huyghens slipped headphones over his ears. He looked up and said sharply:

"Watch the bears, Roane. The wind's blowing up the way we came. Anything that trails us—sphexes, for example—will send its scent on before. The bears will tell us."

He busied himself with the instruments he'd brought. He heard the hissing, frying, background noise which could be anything at all except a human signal. He reached out and swung the small aerial around. Rasping, buzzing tones came in, faintly and then loudly. This receiver, though, had been made for this particular wave band. It was much more efficient than the modified space phone had been. It picked up three short buzzes, three long ones, and three short ones again. Three dots, three dashes, and three dots. Over and over again. S O S. S O S. S O S.

Huyghens took a reading and moved the directional aerial a

carefully measured distance. He took another reading. He shifted
it yet again and again, carefully marking and measuring each
spot and taking notes of the instrument readings. When he finished, he had checked the direction of the signal not only by
loudness but by phase—he had as accurate a fix as could possibly
be had with portable apparatus.

Sourdough growled softly. Sitka Pete whiffed the air and arose
from his sitting position. Faro Nell whacked Nugget, sending him
whimpering to the farthest corner of the flea place. She stood
bristling, facing down-hill the way they'd come.

"Damn!" said Huyghens.

He got up and waved his arm at Semper, who had turned his
head at the stirrings. Semper squawked in a most un-eaglelike
fashion and dived off the spur and was immediately fighting the
down-draught beyond it. As Huyghens reached his weapon, the
eagle came back overhead. He went magnificently past, a hundred feet high, careening and flapping in the tricky currents. He
screamed, abruptly, and circled and screamed again. Huyghens
swung a tiny vision plate from its strap to where he could look
into it. He saw, of course, what the little camera on Semper's
chest could see—reeling, swaying terrain as Semper saw it,
though without his breadth of field. There were moving objects
to be seen through the shifting trees. Their coloring was unmistakable.

"Sphexes," said Huyghens dourly. "Eight of them. Don't look
for them to follow our track, Roane. They run parallel to a trail
on either side. That way they attack in breadth and all at once
when they catch up. And listen! The bears can handle anything
they tangle with! It's our job to pick off the loose ones! And aim
for the body! The bullets explode."

He threw off the safety of his weapon. Faro Nell, uttering thunderous growls, went padding to a place between Sitka Pete and
Sourdough. Sitka glanced at her and made a whuffing noise, as if
derisive of her blood-curdling sounds. Sourdough grunted in a
somehow solid fashion. He and Sitka moved farther away from
Nell to either side. They would cover a wider front.

There was no other sign of life than the shrillings of the incredibly tiny creatures which on this planet were birds, and Faro

Nell's deep-bass, raging growls, and then the click of Roane's safety going off as he got ready to use the weapon Huyghens had given him.

Semper screamed again, flapping low above the treetops, following parti-colored, monstrous shapes beneath.

Eight blue-and-tan fiends came racing out of the underbrush. They had spiny fringes, and horns, and glaring eyes, and they looked as if they had come straight out of hell. On the instant of their appearance they leaped, emitting squalling, spitting squeals that were like the cries of fighting tomcats ten thousand times magnified. Huyghens' rifle cracked, and its sound was wiped out in the louder detonation of its bullet in sphexian flesh. A tan-and-blue monster tumbled over, shrieking. Faro Nell charged, the very impersonation of white-hot fury. Roane fired, and his bullet exploded against a tree. Sitka Pete brought his massive forepaws in a clapping, monstrous ear-boxing motion. A sphex died.

Then Roane fired again. Sourdough Charley whuffed. He fell forward upon a spitting bi-colored fiend, rolled him over, and raked with his hind claws. The belly-hide of the sphex was tenderer than the rest. The creature rolled away, snapping at its own wounds. Another sphex found itself shaken loose from the tumult about Sitka Pete. It whirled to leap on him from behind—and Huyghens fired very coldly—and two plunged upon Faro Nell and Roane blasted one and Faro Nell disposed of the other in truly awesome fury. Then Sitka Pete heaved himself erect—seeming to drip sphexes—and Sourdough waddled over and pulled one off and killed it and went back for another. And both rifles cracked together and there was suddenly nothing left to fight.

The bears prowled from one to another of the corpses. Sitka Pete rumbled and lifted up a limp head. Crash! Then another. He went over the lot, whether or not they showed signs of life. When he had finished, they were wholly still.

Semper came flapping down out of the sky. He had screamed and fluttered overhead as the fight went on. Now he landed with a rush. Huyghens went soothingly from one bear to another, calming them with his voice. It took longest to calm Faro Nell, licking Nugget with impassioned solicitude and growling horribly as she licked.

"Come along, now," said Huyghens, when Sitka showed signs of intending to sit down again. "Heave these carcasses over a cliff. Come along! Sitka! Sourdough! Hup!"

He guided them as the two big males somewhat fastidiously lifted up the nightmarish creatures they and the guns together had killed, and carried them to the edge of the spur of stone. They let the dead beasts go bouncing and sliding down into the valley.

"That," said Huyghens, "is so their little pals will gather round them and caterwaul their woe where there's no trail of ours to give them ideas. If we'd been near a river, I'd have dumped them in to float down-river and gather mourners wherever they stranded. Around the station I incinerate them. If I had to leave them, I'd make tracks away. About fifty miles upwind would be a good idea."

He opened the pack Sourdough carried and extracted giant sized swabs and some gallons of antiseptic. He tended the three Kodiaks in turn, swabbing not only the cuts and scratches they'd received, but deeply soaking their fur where there could be suspicion of spilled sphex blood.

"This antiseptic deodorizes, too," he told Roane. "Or we'd be trailed by any sphex who passed to leeward of us. When we start off, I'll swab the bears' paws for the same reason."

Roane was very quiet. He'd missed his first shot with a bullet-firing weapon—a beam hasn't the stopping-power of an explosive bullet—but he'd seemed to grow savagely angry with himself. The last few seconds of the fight, he'd fired very deliberately and every bullet hit. Now he said bitterly:

"If you're instructing me so I can carry on should you be killed, I doubt that it's worth while!"

Huyghens felt in his pack and unfolded the enlargements he'd made of the space photos of this part of the planet. He carefully oriented the map with distant landmarks. He drew a painstakingly accurate line across the photo.

"The S O S signal comes from somewhere close to the robot colony," he reported. "I think a little to the south of it. Probably from a mine they'd opened up, on the far side—of course—of the Sere Plateau. See how I've marked this map? Two fixes, one from the station and one from here. I came away off-course to get a fix here so we'd have two position-lines to the transmitter. The signal could have come from the other side of the planet. But it doesn't."

"The odds would be astronomical against other castaways," protested Roane.

"No-o-o-o," said Huyghens. "Ships have been coming here. To the robot-colony. One could have crashed. And I have friends, too."

He repacked his apparatus and gestured to the bears. He led them beyond the scene of combat and very carefully swabbed off their paws, so they could not possibly leave a trail of sphex-blood scent behind them. He waved Semper, the eagle, aloft.

"Let's go," he told the Kodiaks. "Yonder! Hup!"

The party headed downhill and into the jungle again. Now it was Sourdough's turn to take the lead, and Sitka Pete prowled more widely behind him. Faro Nell trailed the men, with Nugget. She kept an extremely sharp eye upon the cub. He was a baby, still. He only weighed six hundred pounds. And of course she watched against danger from the rear.

Overhead, Semper fluttered and flew in giant circles and spirals, never going very far away. Huyghens referred constantly to the screen which showed what the air-borne camera saw. The image tilted and circled and banked and swayed. It was by no means the best air-reconnaissance that could be imagined. But it was the best that would work. Presently Huyghens said:

"We swing to the right, here. The going's bad straight ahead, and it looks like a pack of sphexes has killed and is feeding."

Roane was upset. He was dissatisfied with himself. So he said:

"It's against reason for carnivores to be as thick as you say! There has to be a certain amount of other animal life for every meat-eating beast! Too many of them would eat all the game and starve!"

"They're gone all winter," explained Huyghens, "which around here isn't as severe as you might think. And a good many animals seem to breed just after the sphexes go south. Also, the sphexes aren't around all the warm weather. There's a sort of peak, and then for a matter of weeks you won't see a one of them, and suddenly the jungle swarms with them again. Then, presently, they head south. Apparently they're migratory in some fashion, but nobody knows." He said dryly: "There haven't been many naturalists around on this planet. The animal life is inimical."

Roane fretted. He was a senior officer in the Colonial Survey, and he was accustomed to arrival at a partly or completely-finished colonial set-up, and to pass upon the completion or non-completion of the planned installation as designed. Now he was in an intolerably hostile environment, depending upon an illegal colonist for his life, engaged upon a demoralizingly indefinite enterprise—because the mechanical spark-signal could be working long after its constructors were dead—and his ideas about a number of matters were shaken. He was alive, for example, because of three giant Kodiak bears and a bald eagle. He and Huyghens could have been surrounded by ten thousand robots, and they'd have been killed. Sphexes and robots would have ignored each other, and sphexes would have made straight for the men, who'd have had less than four seconds in which to discover for themselves that they were attacked, prepare to defend themselves, and kill eight sphexes.

Roane's convictions as a civilized man were shaken. Robots were marvelous contrivances for doing the expected: accomplishing the planned; coping with the predicted. But they also had defects. Robots could only follow instructions—if this thing happens, do this, if that thing happens do that. But before something else, neither this or that, robots were helpless. So a robot civilization worked only in an environment where nothing unanticipated ever turned up, and human supervisors never demanded anything unexpected. Roane was appalled. He'd never encountered the truly unpredictable before in all his life and career.

He found Nugget, the cub, ambling uneasily in his wake. The cub flattened his ears miserably when Roane glanced at him. It occurred to the man that Nugget was receiving a lot of disciplinary thumpings from Faro Nell. He was knocked about physically, pretty much as Roane was being knocked about psychologically. His lack of information and unfitness for independent survival in this environment was beng hammered into him.

"Hi, Nugget," said Roane ruefully. "I feel just about the way you do!"

Nugget brighted visibly. He frisked. He tended to gambol. He looked very hopefully up into Roane's face—and he stood four feet high at the shoulder and would overtop Roane if he stood erect.

Roane reached out and patted Nugget's head. It was the first time in all his life that he'd ever petted an animal.

He heard a snuffling sound behind him. Skin crawled at the back of his neck. He whirled.

Faro Nell regarded him—eighteen hundred pounds of she-bear only ten feet away and looking into his eyes. For one panicky instant Roane went cold all over. Then he realized that Faro Nell's eyes were not burning. She was not snarling. She did not emit those blood-curdling sounds which the bare prospect of danger to Nugget had produced up on the rocky spur. She looked at him blandly. In fact, after a moment she swung off on some independent investigation of a matter that had aroused her curiosity.

The traveling party went on, Nugget frisking beside Roane and tending to bump into him out of pure cub-clumsiness. Now and again he looked adoringly at Roane, in the instant and overwhelming affection of the very young.

Roane trudged on. Presently he glanced behind again. Faro Nell was now ranging more widely. She was well satisfied to have Nugget in the immediate care of a man. From time to time he got on her nerves.

A little while later, Roane called ahead.

"Huyghens! Look here! I've been appointed nursemaid to Nugget!"

Huyghens looked back.

"Oh, slap him a few times and he'll go back to his mother."

"The devil I will!" said Roane querulously. "I like it!"

The traveling party went on.

When night fell, they camped. There could be no fire, of course, because all the minute night-things about would come eagerly to dance in the glow. But there could not be darkness, equally, because night-walkers hunted in the dark. So Huyghens set out the barrier lamps which made a wall of twilight about their halting place, and the staglike creature Faro Nell had carried became their evening meal. Then they slept—at least the

men did—and the bears dozed and snorted and waked and dozed
again. But Semper sat immobile with his head under his wing on
a tree limb. And presently there was a glorious cool hush and
all the world glowed in morning light diffused through the jungle
by a newly risen sun. And they arose, and traveled again.

This day they stopped stock-still for two hours while sphexes
puzzled over the trail the bears had left. Huyghens discoursed
calmly on the need for an anti-scent, to be used on the boots of
men and the paws of bears, which would make the following of
their trails unpopular with sphexes. And Roane seized upon the
idea and absorbedly suggested that a sphex-repellent odor might
be worked out, which would make a human revolting to a sphex.
If that were done—why—humans could go freely about un-
molested.

"Like stink-bugs," sad Huyghens, sardonically. "A very intelligent idea! Very rational! You can feel proud!"

And suddenly Roane, very obscurely, was not proud of the idea
at all.

They camped again. On the third night they were at the base
of that remarkable formation, the Sere Plateau, which from a distance looked like a mountain-range but was actually a desert
tableland. And it was not reasonable for a desert to be raised
high, while lowlands had rain, but on the fourth morning they
found out why. They saw, far, far away, a truly monstrous moun-
tain-mass at the end of the long-way expanse of the plateau. It
was like the prow of a ship. It lay, so Huyghens observed, directly
in line with the prevailing winds, and divided them as a ship's
prow divides the waters. The moisture-bearing air-currents
flowed beside the plateau, not over it, and its interior was pure
sere desert in the unscreened sunshine of high altitudes.

It took them a full day to get halfway up the slope. And here,
twice as they climbed, Semper flew screaming over aggregations
of sphexes to one side of them or the other. These were much
larger groups than Huyghens had ever seen before—fifty to a
hundred monstrosities together, where a dozen was a large
hunting-pack elsewhere. He looked in the screen which showed
him what Semper saw, four to five miles away. The sphexes

padded uphill toward the Sere Plateau in a long line. Fifty—sixty —seventy tan-and-azure beasts out of hell.

"I'd hate to have that bunch jump us," he said candidly to Roane. "I don't think we'd stand a chance."

"Here's where a robot tank would be useful," Roane observed.

"Anything armored," conceded Huyghens. "One man in an armored station like mine would be safe. But if he killed a sphex he'd be besieged. He'd have to stay holed up, breathing the smell of dead sphex, until the odor had gone away. And he mustn't kill any others or he'd be besieged until winter came."

Roane did not suggest the advantages of robots in other directions. At that moment, for example, they were working their way up a slope which averaged fifty degrees. The bears climbed without effort despite their burdens. For the men it was infinite toil. Semper, the eagle, manifested impatience with bears and men alike, who crawled so slowly up an incline over which he soared.

He went ahead up the mountainside and teetered in the air-currents at the plateau's edge. Huyghens looked in the vision-plate by which he reported.

"How the devil," panted Roane—they had stopped for a breather, and the bears waited patiently for them—"do you train bears like these? I can understand Semper."

"I don't train them," said Huyghens, staring into the plate. "They're mutations. In heredity the sex-linkage of physical characteristics is standard stuff. But there's been some sound work done on the gene-linkage of psychological factors. There was need, on my home planet, for an animal who could fight like a fiend, live off the land, carry a pack and get along with men at least as well as dogs do. In the old days they'd have tried to breed the desired physical properties into an animal who already had the personality they wanted. Something like a giant dog, say. But back home they went at it the other way about. They picked the wanted physical characteristics and bred for the personality —the psychology. The job got done over a century ago—a Kodiak bear named Kodius Champion was the first real success. He had everything that was wanted. These bears are his descendants."

"They look normal," commented Roane.

"They are!" said Huyghens warmly. "Just as normal as an honest dog! They're not trained, like Semper. They train themselves!"

He looked back into the plate in his hands, which showed the ground five and six and seven thousand feet higher. "Semper, now, is a trained bird without too much brains. He's educated—a glorified hawk. But the bears want to get along with men. They're emotionally dependent on us! Like dogs. Semper's a servant, but they're companions and friends. He's trained, but they're loyal. He's conditioned. They love us. He'd abandon me if he ever realized he could—he thinks he can only eat what men feed him. But the bears wouldn't want to. They like us. I admit that I like them. Maybe because they like me."

Roane said deliberately:

"Aren't you a trifle loose-tongued, Huyghens? I'm a Colonial Survey officer. I have to arrest you sooner or later. You've told me something that will locate and convict the people who set you up here. It shouldn't be hard to find where bears were bred for psychological mutations, and where a bear named Kodius Champion left descendants! I can find out where you came from now, Huyghens!"

Huyghens looked up from the plate with its tiny swaying television image, relayed from where Semper floated impatiently in mid-air.

"No harm done," he said amiably. "I'm a criminal there, too. It's officially on record that I kidnaped these bears and escaped with them. Which, on my home planet, is about as heinous a crime as a man can commit. It's worse than horse-theft back on Earth in the old days. The kin and cousins of my bears are highly thought of. I'm quite a criminal, back home."

Roane stared.

"Did you steal them?" he demanded.

"Confidentially," said Huyghens, "no. But prove it!" Then he said: "Take a look in this plate. See what Semper can see up at the plateau's edge."

Roane squinted aloft, where the eagle flew in great sweeps and dashes. Somehow, by the experience of the past few days, Roane knew that Semper was screaming fiercely as he flew. He made a dart toward the plateau's border.

Roane looked at the transmitted picture. It was only four inches by six, but it was perfectly without grain and in accurate color. It moved and turned as the camera-bearing eagle swooped and circled. For an instant the screen showed the steeply sloping mountainside, and off at one edge the party of men and bears could be seen as dots. Then it swept away and showed the top of the plateau.

There were sphexes. A pack of two hundred trotted toward the desert interior. They moved at leisure, in the open. The viewing camera reeled, and there were more. As Roane watched and as the bird flew higher, he could see still other sphexes moving up over the edge of the plateau from a small erosion-defile here and another one there. The Sere Plateau was alive with the hellish creatures. It was inconceivable that there should be game enough for them to live on. They were visible as herds of cattle would be visible on grazing planets.

It was simply impossible.

"Migrating," observed Huyghens. "I said they did. They're headed somewhere. Do you know, I doubt that it would be healthy for us to try to cross the plateau through such a swarm of sphexes?"

Roane swore, in abrupt change of mood.

"But the signal's still coming through! Somebody's alive over at the robot colony! Must we wait till the migration's over?"

"We don't know," Huyghens pointed out, "that they'll stay alive. They may need help badly. We have to get to them. But at the same time—"

He glanced at Sourdough Charley and Sitka Pete, clinging patiently to the mountainside while the men rested and talked. Sitka had managed to find a place to sit down, though one massive paw anchored him in his place.

Huyghens waved his arm, pointing in a new direction.

"Let's go!" he called briskly. "Let's go! Yonder! Hup!"

IV

They followed the slopes of the Sere Plateau, neither ascending to its level top—where sphexes congregated—nor descending into the foothills where sphexes assembled. They moved along hillsides and mountain-flanks which sloped anywhere from thirty to sixty degrees, and they did not cover much distance. They practically forgot what it was to walk on level ground. Semper, the eagle, hovered overhead during the daytime, not far away. He descended at nightfall for his food from the pack of one of the bears.

"The bears aren't doing too well for food," said Huyghens dryly. "A ton of bear needs a lot to eat. But they're loyal to us. Semper hasn't any loyalty. He's too stupid. But he's been conditioned to think that he can only eat what men feed him. The bears know better, but they stick to us regardless. I rather like these bears."

It was the most self-evident of understatements. This was at an encampment on the top of a massive boulder which projected from a mountainous stony wall. This was six days from the start of their journey. There was barely room on the boulder for all the party. And Faro Nell fussily insisted that Nugget should be in the safest part, which meant near the mountain-flank. She would have crowded the men outward, but Nugget whimpered for Roane. Wherefore, when Roane moved to comfort him, Faro Nell contentedly drew back and snorted at Sitka and Sourdough and they made room for her near the edge.

It was a hungry camp. They had come upon tiny rills upon occasion, flowing down the mountain side. Here the bears had drunk deeply and the men had filled canteens. But this was the third night, and there had been no game at all. Huyghens made no move to bring out food for Roane or himself. Roane made no comment. He was beginning to participate in the relationship between bears and men, which was not the slavery of the bears but something more. It was two-way. He felt it.

"It would seem," he said fretfully, "that since the sphexes don't seem to hunt on their way uphill, that there should be some game. They ignore everything as they file uphill."

This was true enough. The normal fighting formation of sphexes was line abreast, which automatically surrounded anything which offered to flee and outflanked anything which offered fight. But here they ascended the mountain in long lines, one after the other, following apparently long-established trails. The wind blew along the slopes and carried scent only sidewise. But the sphexes were not diverted from their chosen paths. The long processions of hideous blue-and-tawny creatures—it was hard to think of them as natural beasts, male and female and laying eggs like reptiles on other planets—simply climbed.

"There've been other thousands of beasts before them," said Huyghens. "They must have been crowding this way for days or even weeks. We've seen tens of thousands in Semper's camera. They must be uncountable, altogether. The first-comers ate all the game there was, and the last-comers have something else on whatever they use for minds."

Roane protested: "But so many carnivores in one place is impossible! I know they are here, but they can't be!"

"They're cold-blooded," Huyghens pointed out. "They don't burn food to sustain body-temperature. After all, lots of creatures go for long periods without eating. Even bears hibernate. But this isn't hibernation—or estivation, either."

He was setting up the radiation-wave receiver in the darkness. There was no point in attempting a fix here. The transmitter was on the other side of the Sere Plateau, which inexplicably swarmed with the most ferocious and deadly of all the creatures of Loren Two. The men and bears would commit suicide by crossing here.

But Huyghens turned on the receiver. There came the whispering, scratchy sound of background-noise. Then the signal. Three dots, three dashes, three dots. Three dots, three dashes, three dots. It went on and on and on. Huyghens turned it off. Roane said:

"Shouldn't we have answered that signal before we left the station? To encourage them?"

"I doubt they have a receiver," said Huyghens. "They won't expect an answer for months, anyhow. They'd hardly listen all the time, and if they're living in a mine-tunnel and trying to sneak out for food to stretch their supplies—why, they'll be too busy to try to make complicated recorders or relays."

Roane was silent for a moment or two.

"We've got to get food for the bears," he said presently. "Nugget's weaned, and he's hungry."

"We will," Huyghens promised. "I may be wrong, but it seems to me that the number of sphexes climbing the mountain is less than yesterday and the day before. We may have just about crossed the path of their migration. They're thinning out. When we're past their trail, we'll have to look out for night-walkers and the like again. But I think they wiped out all animal life on their migration-route."

He was not quite right. He was waked in darkness by the sound of slappings and the grunting of bears. Feather-light puffs of breeze beat upon his face. He struck his belt-lamp sharply and the world was hidden by a whitish film which snatched itself away. Something flapped. Then he saw the stars and the emptiness on the edge of which they camped. Then big white things flapped toward him.

Sitka Pete whuffed mightily and swatted. Faro Nell grunted and swung. She caught something in her claws. She crunched. The light went off as Huyghens realized. Then he said:

"Don't shoot, Roane!" He listened, and heard the sounds of feeding in the dark. It ended. "Watch this!" said Huyghens.

The belt-light came on again. Something strangely-shaped and pallid like human skin reeled and flapped crazily toward him. Something else. Four. Five—ten—twenty—more . . .

A huge hairy paw reached up into the light-beam and snatched a flying thing out of it. Another great paw. Huyghens shifted the light and the three great Kodiaks were on their hind legs, swatting at creatures which flittered insanely, unable to resist the fascination of the glaring lamp. Because of their wild gyrations it was impossible to see them in detail, but they were those unpleasant night-creatures which looked like plucked flying monkeys but were actually something quite different.

The bears did not snarl or snap. They swatted, with a remarkable air of businesslike competence and purpose. Small mounds of broken things built up about their feet.

Suddenly there were no more. Huyghens snapped off the light. The bears crunched and fed busily in the darkness.

"Those things are carnivores *and* blood-suckers, Roane," said Huyghens calmly. "They drain their victims of blood like vampire bats—they've some trick of not waking them—and when they're dead the whole tribe eats. But bears have thick furs, and they wake when they're touched. And they're omnivorous—they'll eat anything but sphexes, and like it. You might say that those night-creatures came to lunch. But they stayed. They are it—for the bears, who are living off the country as usual."

Roane uttered a sudden exclamation. He made a tiny light, and blood flowed down his hand. Huyghens passed over his pocket kit of antiseptic and bandages. Roane stanched the bleeding and bound up his hand. Then he realized that Nugget chewed on something. When he turned the light, Nugget swallowed convulsively. It appeared that he had caught and devoured the creature which had drawn blood from Roane. But Roane had lost none to speak of, at that.

In the morning they started along the sloping scarp of the plateau once more. During the morning, Roane said painfully:

"Robots wouldn't have handled those vampire-things, Huyghens."

"Oh, they could be built to watch for them," said Huyghens, tolerantly. "But you'd have to swat for yourself. I prefer the bears."

He led the way on. Here their jungle-formation could not apply. On a steep slope the bears ambled comfortably, the tough pads of their feet holding fast on the slanting rock, but the men struggled painfully. Twice Huyghens halted to examine the ground about the mountains' bases through binoculars. He looked encouraged as they went on. The monstrous peak which was like the bow of a ship at the end of the Sere Plateau was visibly nearer. Toward midday, indeed, it looked high above the horizon, no more than fifteen miles away. And at midday Huyghens called a final halt.

"No more congregations of sphexes down below," he said cheerfully, "and we haven't seen a climbing line of them in miles." The crossing of a sphex-trail meant simply waiting until one party had passed, and then crossing before another came in view. "I've a hunch we've crossed their migration-route. Let's see what Semper tells us!"

He waved the eagle aloft. And Semper, like all creatures other than men, normally functioned only for the satisfaction of his appetite, and then tended to loaf or sleep. He had ridden the last few miles perched on Sitka Pete's pack. Now he soared upward and Huyghens watched in the small vision-plate.

Semper went soaring—and the image on the plate swayed and

turned and turned—and in minutes was above the plateau's edge. And here there was some vegetation and the ground rolled somewhat, and there were even patches of brush. But as Semper towered higher still, the inner desert appeared. But nearby it was clear of beasts. Only once, when the eagle banked sharply and the camera looked along the long dimension of the plateau, did Huyghens see any sign of the blue-and-tan beasts. There he saw what looked like masses amounting to herds. But, of course, carnivores do not gather in herds.

"We go straight up," said Huyghens in satisfaction. "We cross the plateau here—and we can edge downwind a bit, even. I think we'll find something interesting on our way to your robot colony."

He waved to the bears to go ahead uphill.

They reached the top hours later—barely before sunset. And they saw game. Not much, but game at the grassy, brushy border of the desert. Huyghens brought down a shaggy ruminant which surely would not live on a desert. When night fell there was an abrupt chill in the air. It was much colder than night-temperatures on the slopes. The air was thin. Roane thought confusedly and presently guessed at the cause. In the lee of the prow-mountain the air was calm. There were no clouds. The ground radiated its heat to empty space. It could be bitterly cold in the nighttime, here.

"And hot by day," Huyghens agreed when he mentioned it. "The sunshine's terrifically hot where the air is thin, but on most mountains there's wind. By day, here, the ground will tend to heat up like the surface of a planet without atmosphere. It may be a hundred and forty or fifty degrees on the sand at midday. But it should be cold at night."

It was. Before midnight Huyghens built a fire. There could be no danger of night-walkers where the temperature dropped to freezing.

In the morning the men were stiff with cold, but the bears snorted and moved about briskly. They seemed to revel in the morning chill. Sitka and Sourdough Charley, in fact, became festive and engaged in a mock fight, whacking each other with blows that were only feigned, but would have crushed in the skull of any man. Nugget sneezed with excitement as he watched them. Faro Nell regarded them with female disapproval.

They went on. Semper seemed sluggish. After a single brief flight he descended and rode on Sitka's pack, as on the previous day. He perched there, surveying the landscape as it changed from semi-arid to pure desert in their progress. His air was arrogant. But he would not fly. Soaring birds do not like to fly when there are no winds to make currents of which to take advantage. On the way, Huyghens painstakingly pointed out to Roane exactly where they were on the enlarged photograph taken from space, and the exact spot from which the distress-signal seemed to come.

"You're doing it in case something happens to you," said Roane. "I admit it's sense, but—what could I do to help those survivors even if I got to them, without you?"

"What you've learned about sphexes would help," said Huyghens. "The bears would help. And we left a note back at my station. Whoever grounds at the landing field back there—and the beacon's working again—will find instructions to come to the place we're trying to reach."

Roane plodded alongside him. The narrow non-desert border of the Sere Plateau was behind them, now. They marched across powdery desert sand.

"See here," said Roane, "I want to know something! You tell me you're listed as a bear-thief on your home planet. You tell me it's a lie—to protect your friends from prosecution by the Colonial Survey. You're on your own, risking your life every minute of every day. You took a risk in not shooting me. Now you're risking more in going to help men who'd have to be witnesses that you were a criminal. What are you doing it for?"

Huyghens grinned.

"Because I don't like robots. I don't like the fact that they're subduing men—making men subordinate to them."

"Go on," insisted Roane. "I don't see why disliking robots should make you a criminal. Nor men subordinating themselves to robots, either!"

"But they are," said Huyghens mildly. "I'm a crank, of course. But—I live like a man on this planet. I go where I please and do what I please. My helpers, the bears, are my friends. If the robot colony had been a success, would the humans in it have lived like men? Hardly! They'd have to live the way the robots let them! They'd have to stay inside a fence the robots built. They'd have to eat foods that robots could raise, and no others. Why—a man couldn't move his bed near a window, because if he did the house-tending robots couldn't work! Robots would serve them— the way the robots determined—but all they'd get out of it would be jobs servicing the robots!"

Roane shook his head.

"As long as men want robot service, they have to take the service that robots can give. If you don't want those services—"

"I want to decide what I want," said Huyghens, again mildly, "instead of being limited to choose among what I'm offered. On my home planet we halfway tamed it with dogs and guns. Then we developed the bears, and we finished the job with them. Now there's population-pressure and the room for bears and dogs—and men—is dwindling. More and more people are being deprived of the power of decision, and being allowed only the power of choice among the things robots allow. The more we depend on robots, the more limited those choices become. We don't want our children to limit themselves to wanting what robots can provide! We don't want them shriveling to where they abandon everything robots can't give—or won't! We want them to be men —and women. Not damned automatons who live *by* pushing robot-controls so they can live *to* push robot-controls. If that's not subordination to robots—"

"It's an emotional argument," protested Roane. "Not everybody feels that way."

"But I feel that way," said Huyghens. "And so do a lot of others. This is a big galaxy and it's apt to contain some surprises. The one sure thing about a robot and a man who depends on them is that they can't handle the unexpected. There's going to come a time when we need men who can. So on my home planet, some of us asked for Loren Two, to colonize. It was refused—too dangerous. But men can colonize anywhere if they're men. So I came here to study the planet. Especially the sphexes. Eventually, we expected to ask for a license again, with proof that we could handle even those beasts. I'm already doing it in a mild way. But the Survey licensed a robot colony—and where is it?"

Roane made a sour face.

"You picked the wrong way to ~~go about it, Huyghens. It was~~ illegal. It is. It was the pioneer spirit, which is admirable enough, but wrongly directed. After all, it was pioneers who left Earth for the stars. But—"

Sourdough raised up on his hind legs and sniffed the air. Huyghens swung his rifle around to be handy. Roane slipped off the safety-catch of his own. Nothing happened.

"In a way," said Roane vexedly, "you're talking about liberty and freedom, which most people think is politics. You say it can be more. In principle, I'll concede it. But the way you put it, it sounds like a freak religion."

"It's self-respect," corrected Huyghens.

"You may be—"

Faro Nell growled. She bumped Nugget with her nose, to drive him closer to Roane. She snorted at him. She trotted swiftly to where Sitka and Sourdough faced toward the broader, sphex-filled expanse of the Sere Plateau. She took up her position between them.

Huyghens gazed sharply beyond them and then all about.

"This could be bad!" he said softly. "But luckily there's no wind. Here's a sort of hill. Come along, Roane!"

He ran ahead, Roane following and Nugget plumping heavily with him. They reached the raised place—actually a mere hillock no more than five or six feet above the surrounding sand, with a distorted cactuslike growth protruding from the ground. Huyghens stared again. He used his binoculars.

"One sphex," he said curtly. "Just one! And it's out of all reason for a sphex to be alone! But it's not rational for them to gather in hundreds of thousands, either!" He wetted his finger and held it up. "No wind at all."

He used the binoculars again.

"It doesn't know we're here," he added. "It's moving away. Not another one in sight—" He hesitated, biting his lips. "Look here, Roane! I'd like to kill that one lone sphex and find out something. There's a fifty per cent chance I could find out something really important. But—I might have to run. If I'm right—" Then he said grimly, "It'll have to be done quickly. I'm going to ride Faro Nell

—for speed. I doubt Sitka or Sourdough would stay behind. But Nugget can't run fast enough. Will you stay here with him?"

Roane drew in his breath. Then he said calmly:

"You know what you're doing. Of course."

"Keep your eyes open. If you see anything, even at a distance, shoot and we'll be back—fast! Don't wait until something's close enough to hit. Shoot the instant you see anything—if you do!"

Roane nodded. He found it peculiarly difficult to speak again. Huyghens went over to the embattled bears. He climbed up on Faro Nell's back, holding fast by her shaggy fur.

"Let's go!" he snapped. "That way! Hup!"

The three Kodiaks plunged away at a dead run, Huyghens lurching and swaying on Faro Nell's back. The sudden rush dislodged Semper from his perch. He flapped wildly and got aloft. Then he followed effortfully, flying low.

It happened very quickly. A Kodiak bear can travel as fast as a race horse on occasion. These three plunged arrow-straight for a spot perhaps half a mile distant, where a blue-and-tawny shape whirled to face them. There was the crash of Huyghens' weapon from where he rode on Faro Nell's back—the explosion of the weapon and the bullet was one sound. The somehow unnatural spiky monster leaped and died.

Huyghens jumped down from Faro Nell. He became feverishly busy at something on the ground—where the parti-colored sphex had fallen. Semper banked and whirled and came down to the ground. He watched, with his head on one side.

Roane stared, from a distance. Huyghens was doing something to the dead sphex. The two male bears prowled about. Faro Nell regarded Huyghens with intense curiosity. Back at the hillock, Nugget whimpered a little. Roane patted him roughly. Nugget whimpered more loudly. In the distance, Huyghens straightened up and took three steps toward Faro Nell. He mounted. Sitka turned his head back toward Roane. He seemed to see or sniff something dubious. He reared upward. He made a noise, apparently, because Sourdough ambled to his side. The two great beasts began to trot back. Semper flapped wildly and—lacking wind—lurched crazily in the air. He landed on Huyghens' shoulder and his talons clung there.

Then Nugget howled hysterically and tried to swarm up Roane, as a cub tries to swarm up the nearest tree in time of danger. Roane collapsed, and the cub upon him—and there was a flash of stinking scaly hide, while the air was filled with the snarling, spitting squeals of a sphex in full leap. The beast had overjumped, aiming at Roane and the cub while both were upright and arriving when they had fallen. It went tumbling.

Roane heard nothing but the fiendish squalling, but in the distance Sitka and Sourdough were coming at rocketship speed. Faro Nell let out a roar and fairly split the air. And then there was a furry cub streaking toward her, bawling, while Roane rolled to his feet and snatched up his gun. He raged through pure instinct. The sphex crouched to pursue the cub and Roane swung his weapon as a club. He was literally too close to shoot—and perhaps the sphex had only seen the fleeing bear-cub. But he swung furiously.

And the sphex whirled. Roane was toppled from his feet. An eight-hundred-pound monstrosity straight out of hell—half wildcat and half spitting cobra with hydrophobia and homicidal mania added—such a monstrosity is not to be withstood when in whirling its body strikes one in the chest.

That was when Sitka arrived, bellowing. He stood on his hind legs, emitting roars like thunder, challenging the sphex to battle. He waddled forward. Huyghens arrived, but he could not shoot with Roane in the sphere of an explosive bullet's destructiveness. Faro Nell raged and snarled, torn between the urge to be sure that Nugget was unharmed, and the frenzied fury of a mother whose offspring has been endangered.

Mounted on Faro Nell, with Semper clinging idiotically to his shoulder, Huyghens watched helplessly as the sphex spat and squalled at Sitka, having only to reach out one claw to let out Roane's life.

v

They got away from there, though Sitka seemed to want to lift the limp carcass of his victim in his teeth and dash it repeatedly to the ground. He seemed doubly raging because a man—with whom all Kodius Champion's descendants had an emotional relationship—had been mishandled. But Roane was not grievously hurt. He bounced and swore as the bears raced for the horizon. Huyghens had flung him up on Sourdough's pack and snapped for him to hold on. He bumped and chattered furiously:

"Dammit, Huyghens! This isn't right! Sitka got some deep scratches! That horror's claws may be poisonous!"

But Huyghens snapped, "Hup! Hup!" to the bears, and they continued their race against time. They went on for a good two miles, when Nugget wailed despairingly of his exhaustion and Faro Nell halted firmly to nuzzle him.

"This may be good enough," said Huyghens. "Considering that there's no wind and the big mass of beasts is down the plateau and there were only those two around here. Maybe they're too busy to hold a wake, even! Anyhow—"

He slid to the ground and extracted the antiseptic and swabs.

"Sitka first," snapped Roane. "I'm all right!"

Huyghens swabbed the big bear's wounds. They were trivial, because Sitka Pete was an experienced sphex-fighter. Then Roane grudgingly let the curiously-smelling stuff—it reeked of ozone—be applied to the slashes on his chest. He held his breath as it stung. Then he said dourly:

"It was my fault, Huyghens. I watched you instead of the landscape. I couldn't imagine what you were doing."

"I was doing a quick dissection," Huyghens told him. "By luck, that first sphex was a female, as I hoped. And she was just about to lay her eggs. Ugh! And now I know why the sphexes migrate, and where, and how it is that they don't need game up here."

He slapped a quick bandage on Roane. He led the way eastward, still putting distance between the dead sphexes and his party. It was a crisp walk, only, but Semper flapped indignantly overhead, angry that he was not permitted to ride again.

"I'd dissected them before," said Huyghens. "Not enough's been known about them. Some things needed to be found out if men were ever to be able to live here."

"With bears?" asked Roane ironically.

"Oh, yes," said Huyghens. "But the point is that sphexes come to the desert here to breed—to mate and lay their eggs for the sun to hatch. It's a particular place. Seals return to a special place to mate—and the males at least don't eat for weeks on end.

Salmon return to their native streams to spawn. They don't eat, and they die afterward. And eels—I'm using Earth examples, Roane—travel some thousands of miles to the Sargasso to mate and die. Unfortunately, sphexes don't appear to die, but it's clear that they have an ancestral breeding place and that they come here to the Sere Plateau to deposit their eggs!"

Roane plodded onward. He was angry: angry with himself because he hadn't taken elementary precautions; because he'd felt too safe, as a man in a robot-served civilization forms the habit of doing; because he hadn't used his brain when Nugget whimpered, in even a bear-cub's awareness that danger was near.

"And now," Huyghens added, "I need some equipment that the robot colony had. With it, I think we can make a start toward making this a planet that men can live like men on!"

Roane blinked.

"What's that?"

"Equipment," said Huyghens impatiently. "It'll be at the robot colony. Robots were useless because they wouldn't pay attention to sphexes. They'd still be. But take out the robot controls and the machines will do! They shouldn't be ruined by a few months' exposure to weather!"

Roane marched on and on. Presently he said:

"I never thought you'd want anything that came from that colony, Huyghens!"

"Why not?" demanded Huyghens impatiently. "When men make machines do what they want, that's all right. Even robots—when they're where they belong. But men will have to handle flame-casters in the job I want them for. There have to be some, because there was a hundred-mile clearing to be burned off. And Earth-sterilizers—intended to kill the seeds of any plants that robots couldn't handle. We'll come back up here, Roane, and at the least we'll destroy the spawn of these infernal beasts! If we can't do more than that—just doing that every year will wipe out the race in time. There are probably other hordes than this, with other breeding places. But we'll find them, too. We'll make this planet into a place where men from my world can come—and still be men!"

Roane said sardonically:

"It was sphexes that beat the robots. Are you sure you aren't planning to make this world safe for robots?"

Huyghens laughed shortly.

"You've only seen one night-walker," he said. "And how about those things on the mountain-slope—which would have drained you of blood and then feasted? Would you care to wander about this planet with only a robot bodyguard, Roane? Hardly! Men can't live on this planet with only robots to help them—and stop them from being fully men! You'll see!"

They found the colony after only ten days more of travel and after many sphexes and more than a few staglike creatures and shaggy ruminants had fallen to their weapons and the bears. But first they found the survivors of the colony.

There were three of them, hard-bitten and bearded and deeply embittered. When the electrified fence went down, two of them were away at a mine-tunnel, installing a new control-panel for the robots who worked in it. The third was in charge of the mining operation. They were alarmed by the stopping of communication with the colony and went back in a tank-truck to find out what had happened, and only the fact that they were unarmed saved them. They found sphexes prowling and caterwauling about the fallen colony, in numbers they still did not wholly believe. And the sphexes smelled men inside the armored vehicle, but couldn't break in. In turn, the men couldn't kill them, or they'd have been trailed to the mine and besieged there for as long as they could kill an occasional monster.

The survivors stopped all mining—of course—and tried to use remote-controlled robots for revenge and to get supplies for them. Their mining-robots were not designed for either task. And they had no weapons. They improvised miniature throwers of burning rocket-fuel, and they sent occasional prowling sphexes away screaming with scorched hides. But this was useful only because it did not kill the beasts. And it cost fuel. In the end they barricaded themselves and used the fuel only to keep a spark-signal going against the day when another ship came to seek the colony. They stayed in the mine as in a prison, on short rations, waiting without real hope. For diversion they could only contemplate the mining-robots they could not spare fuel to run and which could not do anything but mine.

When Huyghens and Roane reached them, they wept. They hated robots and all things robotic only a little less than they hated sphexes. But Huyghens explained, and armed them with weapons from the packs of the bears, and they marched to the dead colony with the male Kodiaks as point and advance-guard, and with Faro Nell bringing up the rear. They killed sixteen sphexes on the way. In the now overgrown clearing there were four more. In the shelters of the colony they found only foulness and the fragments of what had been men. But there was some food—not much, because the sphexes clawed at anything that smelled of men, and had ruined the plastic packets of radiation-sterilized food. But there were some supplies in metal containers which were not destroyed.

And there was fuel, which men could dispense when they got to the control-panels of the equipment. There were robots everywhere, bright and shining and ready for operation, but immobile, with plants growing up around and over them.

They ignored those robots. But lustfully they fueled tracked flame-casters—adapting them to human rather than robot operation—and the giant soil-sterilizer which had been built to destroy vegetation that robots could not be made to weed out or cultivate. And they headed back for the Sere Plateau, burning-eyed and filled with hate.

But Nugget became a badly spoiled bear-cub, because the freed men approved passionately of anything that would even grow up to kill sphexes. They petted him to excess, when they camped.

And they reached the plateau by a sphex-trail to the top. And Semper scouted for sphexes, and the giant Kodiaks disturbed them and the sphexes came squalling and spitting to destroy them—and while Roane and Huyghens fired steadily, the great machines swept up with their special weapons. The Earth-sterilizer, it was found, was deadly against animal life as well as seeds, when its diathermic beam was raised and aimed. But it had to be handled by a man. No robot could decide just when it was to be used, and against what target.

Presently the bears were not needed, because the scorched

corpses of sphexes drew live ones from all parts of the plateau even in the absence of noticeable breezes. The official business of the sphexes was presumably finished, but they came to cater-waul and seek vengeance—which they did not find. Presently the survivors of the robot colony drove machines—as men needed to do, here—in great circles around the hugest heap of slaughtered fiends, destroying new arrivals as they came. It was such a killing as men had never before made on any planet, but there would not be many left of the sphex-horde which had bred in this par-ticular patch of desert. There might be other hordes elsewhere, and other breeding places, but the normal territory of this mass of monsters would see few of them this year.

Or next year, either. Because the soil-sterilizer would go over the dug-up sand where the sphex-spawn lay hidden for the sun to hatch. And the sun would never hatch them.

But Huyghens and Roane, by that time, were camped on the edge of the plateau with the Kodiaks. They were technically up-wind from the scene of slaughter—and somehow it seemed more befitting for the men of the robot colony to conduct it. After all, it was those men whose companions had been killed.

There came an evening when Huyghens amiably cuffed Nug-get away from where he sniffed too urgently at a stag-steak cooking on the campfire. Nugget ambled dolefully behind the protecting form of Roane and sniveled.

"Huyghens," said Roane painfully, "we've got to come to a set-tlement of our affairs. I'm a Colonial Survey officer. You're an illegal colonist. It's my duty to arrest you."

Huyghens regarded him with interest.

"Will you offer me lenience if I tell on my confederates," he ask mildly, "or may I plead that I can't be forced to testify against myself?"

Roane said vexedly:

"It's irritating! I've been an honest man all my life, but—I don't believe in robots as I did, except in their place. And their place isn't here. Not as the robot colony was planned, anyhow. The sphexes are nearly wiped out, but they won't be extinct and robots can't handle them. Bears and men will have to live here or—the people who do will have to spend their lives behind sphex-proof fences, accepting only what robots can give them. And there's much too much on this planet for people to miss it! To live in a robot-managed controlled environment on a planet like Loren Two wouldn't . . . it wouldn't be self-respecting!"

"You wouldn't be getting religious, would you?" asked Huyghens dryly. "That was your term for self-respect before."

Semper, the eagle, squawked indignantly as Sitka Pete almost stepped on him, approaching the fire. Sitka Pete sniffed, and Huyghens spoke to him sharply, and he sat down with a thump. He remained sitting in an untidy lump, looking at the steak and drooling.

"You don't let me finish!" protested Roane querulously. "I'm a Colonial Survey officer, and it's my job to pass on the work that's done on a planet before any but the first-landed colonists may come there to live. And of course to see that specifications are followed. Now—the robot colony I was sent to survey was practically destroyed. As designed, it wouldn't work. It couldn't survive."

Huyghens grunted. Night was falling. He turned the meat over the fire.

"Now, in emergencies," said Roane carefully, "colonists have the right to call on any passing ship for aid. Naturally! So— I've always been an honest man before, Huyghens—my report will be that the colony as designed was impractical, and that it was overwhelmed and destroyed except for three survivors who holed up and signaled for help. They did, you know!"

"Go on," grunted Huyghens.

"So," said Roane querulously, "it just happened—just happened, mind you—that a ship with you and Sitka and Sourdough and Faro Nell on board—and Nugget and Semper, too, of course—picked up the distress-call. So you landed to help the colonists. And you did. That's the story. Therefore it isn't illegal for you to be here. It was only illegal for you to be here when you were needed. But we'll pretend you weren't."

Huyghens glanced over his shoulder in the deepening night. He said calmly:

"I wouldn't believe that if I told it myself. Do you think the Survey will?"

"They're not fools," said Roane tartly. "Of course they won't!

But when my report says that because of this unlikely series of events it is practical to colonize the planet, whereas before it wasn't—and when my report proves that a robot colony alone is stark nonsense, but that with bears and men from your world added, so many thousand colonists can be received per year— And when that much is true, anyhow—"

Huyghens seemed to shake a little as a dark silhouette against the flames. A little way off, Sourdough sniffed the air hopefully. With a bright light like the fire, presently naked-looking flying things might appear to be slapped down out of the air. They were succulent—to a bear.

"My reports carry weight," insisted Roane. "The deal will be offered, anyhow! The robot colony organizers will have to agree or they'll have to fold up. It's true! And your people can hold them up for nearly what terms they choose."

Huyghens' shaking became understandable. It was laughter.

"You're a lousy liar, Roane," he said, chuckling. "Isn't it unintelligent and unreasonable and irrational to throw away a lifetime of honesty just to get me out of a jam? You're not acting like a rational animal, Roane. But I thought you wouldn't, when it came to the point."

Roane squirmed.

"That's the only solution I can think of. But it'll work."

"I accept it," said Huyghens, grinning. "With thanks. If only because it means another few generations of men living like men on a planet that is going to take a lot of taming. And—if you want to know—because it keeps Sourdough and Sitka and Nell and Nugget from being killed because I brought them here illegally."

Something pressed hard against Roane. Nugget, the cub, pushed urgently against him in his desire to get closer to the fragrantly cooking meat. He edged forward. Roane toppled from where he squatted on the ground. He sprawled. Nugget sniffed luxuriously.

"Slap him," said Huyghens. "He'll move back."

"I won't!" said Roane indignantly from where he lay. "I won't do it! He's my friend!"

Arthur C. Clarke

If Arthur C. Clarke had more hair and were considerably more handsome, he could easily be mistaken for me.

He is just about my age and has been writing just about as long. He has written science fiction novels and has published collections of his science fiction short stories, as I have. He has been professionally trained in science as I have (he in astronomy, I in chemistry) and has published books on "straight science" as I have.

On top of that, where I was Guest of Honor at the 13th Convention (Cleveland, 1955), he was Guest of Honor at the 14th Convention (New York, 1956). It was at the 14th Convention that I grew to know Arthur well and learned to love him, for, indeed, he is a lovable fellow and a witty conversationalist.

From one standpoint, however, he leaves much to be desired as a friend. Ordinarily, I am in an impregnable position when it comes to conserving my tender ego. When I find myself in the company of someone whose fiction I suspect to be more successful than mine, I cleverly change the subject to non-fiction. When it is non-fiction at which I am about to take a back seat, I discourse learnedly on fiction.

Only with Arthur are both approaches rudely blocked. His science fiction, alas, is among the most imaginative and carefully thought out you can find anywhere; while his non-fiction is both authoritative, clear, and written with fascinating skill. Worst of all, I cannot even fall back on the last resort of sheer quantity, since Arthur is almost as prolific in both fact and fiction as I am.

The final straw was the fact that Arthur did with ease and aplomb what I could not. At the Convention at which *he* was the Guest of Honor, he rose from his seat to accept a Hugo for his short story "The Star," and so excellent a story was it and so well-deserved was the award, that I found my traitorous hands applauding with wild joy.

Nevertheless, I must admit that some mornings, as I comb my luxuriant shock of brown, wavy hair, I find myself rather pleased that Arthur is a bit on the bald side. Serves him right, say I.

4

THE STAR

It is three thousand light-years to the Vatican. Once I believed that space could have no power over Faith. Just as I believed that the heavens declared the glory of God's handiwork. Now I have seen that handiwork, and my faith is sorely troubled.

I stare at the crucifix that hangs on the cabin wall above the Mark VI computer, and for the first time in my life I wonder if it is no more than an empty symbol.

I have told no one yet, but the truth cannot be concealed. The data are there for anyone to read, recorded on the countless miles of magnetic tape and the thousands of photographs we are carrying back to Earth. Other scientists can interpret them as easily as I can—more easily, in all probability. I am not one who would condone that tampering with the Truth which often gave my Order a bad name in the olden days.

The crew is already sufficiently depressed, I wonder how they will take this ultimate irony. Few of them have any religious faith, yet they will not relish using this final weapon in their campaign against me—that private, good-natured but fundamentally serious war which lasted all the way from Earth. It amused them to have a Jesuit as chief astrophysicist: Dr. Chandler, for instance, could never get over it (why are medical men such notorious atheists?). Sometimes he would meet me on the observation deck, where the lights are always low so that the stars shine with undiminished glory. He would come up to me in the gloom and stand staring out of the great oval port, while the heavens

crawled slowly round us as the ship turned end over end with
the residual spin we had never bothered to correct.

"Well, Father," he would say at last. "It goes on forever and
forever, and perhaps *Something* made it. But how you can believe that Something has a special interest in us and our miserable little world—that just beats me." Then the argument would
start, while the stars and nebulae would swing around us in silent,
endless arcs beyond the flawlessly clear plastic of the observation
port.

It was, I think, the apparent incongruity of my position which
. . . yes, *amused* . . . the crew. In vain I would point to my
three papers in the *Astrophysical Journal,* my five in the *Monthly
Notices of the Royal Astronomical Society.* I would remind them
that our Order has long been famous for its scientific works. We
may be few now, but ever since the eighteenth century we have
made contributions to astronomy and geophysics out of all pro-
portions to our numbers.

Will my report on the Phoenix Nebula end our thousand years
of history? It will end, I fear, much more than that.

I do not know who gave the Nebula its name, which seems to
me a very bad one. If it contains a prophecy, it is one which
cannot be verified for several thousand million years. Even the
word nebula is misleading: this is a far smaller object than those
stupendous clouds of mist—the stuff of unborn stars—which are
scattered throughout the length of the Milky Way. On the cosmic
scale, indeed, the Phoenix Nebula is a tiny thing—a tenuous shell
of gas surrounding a single star.

Or what is left of a star . . .

The Rubens engraving of Loyola seems to mock me as it hangs
there above the spectrophotometer tracings. What would *you,*
Father, have made of this knowledge that has come into my keeping, so far from the little world that was all the universe you
knew? Would your faith have risen to the challenge, as mine has
failed to do?

You gaze into the distance, Father, but I have traveled a distance beyond any that you could have imagined when you
founded our Order a thousand years ago. No other survey ship
has been so far from Earth: we are at the very frontiers of the

explored universe. We set out to reach the Phoenix Nebula, we succeeded, and we are homeward bound with our burden of knowledge. I wish I could lift that burden from my shoulders, but I call to you in vain across the centuries and the light-years that lie between us.

On the book you are holding the words are plain to read. AD MAIOREM DEI GLORIAM the message runs, but it is a message I can no longer believe. Would you still believe it, if you could see what we have found?

We knew, of course, what the Phoenix Nebula was. Every year, in *our* galaxy alone, more than a hundred stars explode, blazing for a few hours or days with thousands of times their normal brilliance before they sink back into death and obscurity. Such are the ordinary novae—the commonplace disasters of the universe. I have recorded the spectrograms and light-curves of dozens, since I started working at the lunar observatory.

But three or four times in every thousand years occurs something beside which even a nova pales into total insignificance.

When a star becomes a *supernova*, it may for a little while outshine all the massed suns of the galaxy. The Chinese astronomers watched this happen in 1054 A.D., not knowing what it was they saw. Five centuries later, in 1572, a supernova blazed in Cassiopeia so brilliantly that it was visible in the daylight sky. There have been three more in the thousand years that have passed since then.

Our mission was to visit the remnants of such a catastrophe, to reconstruct the events that led up to it, and, if possible, to learn its cause. We came slowly in through the concentric shells of gas that had been blasted out six thousand years before, yet were expanding still. They were immensely hot, radiating still with a fierce violet light, but far too tenuous to do us any damage. When the star had exploded, its outer layers had been driven upwards with such speed that they had escaped completely from its gravitational field. Now they formed a hollow shell large enough to engulf a thousand solar systems, and at its center burned the tiny, fantastic object which the star had now become—a white dwarf, smaller than the Earth yet weighing a million times as much.

The glowing gas shells were all around us, banishing the normal night of interstellar space. We were flying into the center of a cosmic bomb that had detonated millennia ago and whose incandescent fragments were still hurtling apart. The immense scale of the explosion, and the fact that the debris already covered a volume of space many billions of miles across, robbed the scene of any visible movement. It would take decades before the unaided eye could detect any motion in these tortured wisps and eddies of gas, yet the sense of turbulent expansion was overwhelming.

We had checked our primary drive hours before, and were drifting slowly towards the fierce little star ahead. Once it had been a sun like our own, but it had squandered in a few hours the energy that should have kept it shining for a million years. Now it was a shrunken miser, hoarding its resources as if trying to make amends for its prodigal youth.

No one seriously expected to find planets. If there had been any before the explosion, they would have been boiled into puffs of vapor, and their substance lost in the greater wreckage of the star itself. But we made the automatic search, as always when approaching an unknown sun, and presently we found a single small world circling the star at an immense distance, It must have been the Pluto of this vanished solar system, orbiting on the frontiers of the night. Too far from the central sun ever to have known life, its remoteness had saved it from the fate of all its lost companions.

The passing fires had seared its rocks and burnt away the mantle of frozen gas that must have covered it in the days before the disaster. We landed, and we found the Vault.

Its builders had made sure that we should. The monolithic marker that stood above the entrance was now a fused stump, but even the first long-range photographs told us that here was the work of intelligence. A little later we detected the continent-wide pattern of radioactivity that had been buried in the rock. Even if the pylon above the Vault had been destroyed, this would have remained, an immovable and all but eternal beacon calling to the stars. Our ship fell towards this gigantic bull's-eye like an arrow into its target.

The pylon must have been a mile high when it was built, but now it looked like a candle that had melted down into a puddle of wax. It took us a week to drill through the fused rock, since we did not have the proper tools for a task like this. We were astronomers, not archaeologists, but we could improvise. Our original program was forgotten: this lonely monument, reared at such labor at the greatest possible distance from the doomed sun, could have only one meaning. A civilization which knew it was about to die had made its last bid for immortality.

It will take us generations to examine all the treasures that were placed in the Vault. *They* had plenty of time to prepare, for their sun must have given its first warnings many years before the final detonation. Everything that they wished to preserve, all the fruits of their genius, they brought here to this distant world in the days before the end, hoping that some other race would find them and that they would not be utterly forgotten.

If only they had had a little more time! They could travel freely enough between the planets of their own sun, but they had not yet learned to cross the interstellar gulfs, and the nearest solar system was a hundred light-years away.

Even if they had not been so disturbingly human as their sculpture shows, we could not have helped admiring them and grieving for their fate. They left thousands of visual records and the machines for projecting them, together with elaborate pictorial instructions from which it will not be difficult to learn their written language. We have examined many of these records, and brought to life for the first time in six thousand years the warmth and beauty of a civilization which in many ways must have been superior to our own. Perhaps they only showed us the best, and one can hardly blame them. But their worlds were very lovely, and their cities were built with a grace that matches anything of ours. We have watched them at work and play, and listened to their musical speech sounding across the centuries. One scene is still before my eyes—a group of children on a beach of strange blue sand, playing in the waves as children play on Earth.

And sinking into the sea, still warm and friendly and life-giving, is the sun that will soon turn traitor and obliterate all this innocent happiness.

Perhaps if we had not been so far from home and so vulnerable to loneliness, we should not have been so deeply moved. Many of us had seen the ruins of ancient civilizations on other worlds, but they had never affected us so profoundly.

This tragedy was unique. It was one thing for a race to fail and die, as nations and cultures have done on Earth. But to be destroyed so completely in the full flower of its achievement, leaving no survivors—how could that be reconciled with the mercy of God?

My colleagues have asked me that, and I have given what answers I can. Perhaps you could have done better, Father Loyola, but I have found nothing in the *Exercitia Spiritualia* that helps me here. They were not an evil people: I do not know what gods they worshipped, if indeed they worshipped any. But I have looked back at them across the centuries, and have watched while the loveliness they used their last strength to preserve was brought forth again into the light of their shrunken sun.

I know the answers that my colleagues will give when they get back to Earth. They will say that the universe has no purpose and no plan, that since a hundred suns explode every year in our galaxy, at this very moment some race is dying in the depths of space. Whether that race has done good or evil during its lifetime will make no difference in the end: there is no divine justice, *for there is no God.*

Yet, of course, what we have seen proves nothing of the sort. Anyone who argues thus is being swayed by emotion, not logic. God has no need to justify His actions to man. He who built the universe can destroy it when He chooses. It is arrogance—it is perilously near blasphemy—for us to say what He may or may not do.

This I could have accepted, hard though it is to look upon whole worlds and peoples thrown into the furnace. But there comes a point when even the deepest faith must falter, and now, as I look at my calculations, I know I have reached that point at last.

We could not tell, before we reached the nebula, how long ago the explosion took place. Now, from the astronomical evidence and the record in the rocks of that one surviving planet, I have been able to date it very exactly. I know in what year the light of this colossal conflagration reached Earth. I know how brilliantly the supernova whose corpse now dwindles behind our speeding ship once shone in terrestrial skies. I know how it must have blazed low in the East before sunrise, like a beacon in that Oriental dawn.

There can be no reasonable doubt: the ancient mystery is solved at last. Yet—O God, there were so many stars you *could* have used.

What was the need to give these people to the fire, that the symbol of their passing might shine above Bethlehem?

1958
16th Convention
Los Angeles

Avram Davidson

Avram Davidson won his way into my heart with a short story in *The Magazine of Fantasy and Science Fiction* in which a character refers to *me*.

It was with no little dismay then, that I met the gentleman himself at the 17th Convention (Detroit, 1959) for it was then I found out exactly what it was that had gained entrance to my heart. It explained the tickling sensation in my chest and the periodic sieges of heartburn that had been overcoming me; for be it known, oh, gentle readers, that Avram is mostly Beard.

Now there are beards and beards. There are prissy Vandykes that bespeak the scholarly man of culture; there are the little token bits of hair that spell beatnik; there are the oddly shaped beavers that mark the Civil War general.

Here, however, we have a full black beard, rippling its mighty length down Avram's majestically rotund figure. Avram need wear no tie, collar nor shirt stud. In fact, Avram need wear no belt buckle. It is only necessary for a man with a red lantern to precede Avram wherever he goes, lest the sight of the Beard coming upon people unexpectedly produce fainting spells and, in crowds, destructive panic.

But the Beard has its uses. Avram is a dangerous man in any battle of wits, and a sharp retort delivered in his deceptively sweet voice could wreak real damage, were it not softened and gentled by passage through the numerous filter-like crannies and byways of the Beard. His deftest repartee is in that way turned into mellifluously caressing remarks that make him beloved by all.

Furthermore, at those times when he chooses to knot his Beard around his waist and out of the way, so that his hands can reach the typewriter unencumbered, he can write darned good stories.

One of them, "Or All the Seas with Oysters," won for him the Hugo at the 16th Convention (Los Angeles, 1958) at which point, I have been told (I wasn't there in person) his Beard turned momentarily red with joy.

5

OR ALL THE SEAS WITH OYSTERS

When the man came in to the F & O Bike Shop, Oscar greeted him with a hearty "Hi, there!" Then, as he looked closer at the middle-aged visitor with the eyeglasses and business suit, his forehead creased and he began to snap his thick fingers.

"Oh, say, I know you," he muttered. "Mr. — um — name's on the tip of my tongue, doggone it . . ." Oscar was a barrel-chested fellow. He had orange hair.

"Why, sure you do," the man said. There was a Lion's emblem in his lapel. "Remember, you sold me a girl's bicycle with gears, for my daughter? We got to talking about that red French racing bike your partner was working on—"

Oscar slapped his big hand down on the cash register. He raised his head and rolled his eyes up. "Mr. Whatney!" Mr. Whatney beamed. "Oh, *sure.* Gee, how could I forget? And we went across the street afterward and had a couple a beers. Well, how you *been,* Mr. Whatney? I guess the bike—it was an English model, wasn't it? Yeah. It must of given satisfaction or you would of been back, huh?"

Mr. Whatney said the bicycle was fine, just fine. Then he said, "I understand there's been a change, though. You're all by yourself now. Your partner . . ."

Oscar looked down, pushed his lower lip out, nodded. "You heard, huh? Ee-up. I'm all by myself now. Over three months now."

The partnership had come to an end three months ago, but it had been faltering long before then. Ferd liked books, long-playing records and high-level conversation. Oscar liked beer, bowling and women. Any women. Any time.

The shop was located near the park; it did a big trade in renting bicycles to picnickers. If a woman was barely old enough to be *called* a woman, and not quite old enough to be called an *old* woman, or if she was anywhere in between, and if she was alone, Oscar would ask, "How does that machine feel to you? All right?"

"Why . . . I guess so."

Taking another bicycle, Oscar would say, "Well, I'll just ride along a little bit with you, to make sure. Be right back, Ferd." Ferd always nodded gloomily. He knew that Oscar would not be right back. Later, Oscar would say, "Hope you made out in the shop as good as I did in the park."

"Leaving me all alone here all that time," Ferd grumbled.

And Oscar usually flared up. "Okay, then, next time *you* go and leave *me* stay here. See if I begrudge you a little fun." But he knew, of course, that Ferd—tall, thin, pop-eyed Ferd—would never go. "Do you good," Oscar said, slapping his sternum. "Put hair on your chest."

Ferd muttered that he had all the hair on his chest that he needed. He would glance down covertly at his lower arms; they were thick with long black hair, though his upper arms were slick and white. It was already like that when he was in high school, and some of the others would laugh at him—call him "Ferdie the Birdie." They knew it bothered him, but they did it anyway. How was it possible—he wondered then; he still did now—for people deliberately to hurt someone else who hadn't hurt them? How was it possible?

He worried over other things. All the time.

"The Communists—" He shook his head over the newspaper. Oscar offered an advice about the Communists in two short words. Or it might be capital punishment. "Oh, what a terrible thing if an innocent man was to be executed," Ferd moaned. Oscar said that was the guy's tough luck.

"Hand me that tire-iron," Oscar said.

And Ferd worried even about other people's minor concerns. Like the time the couple came in with the tandem and the baby-basket on it. Free air was all they took; then the woman decided to change the diaper and one of the safety pins broke.

"Why are there never any safety pins?" the woman fretted, rummaging here and rummaging there. "There are *never* any safety pins."

Ferd made sympathetic noises, went to see if he had any; but, though he was sure there'd been some in the office, he couldn't find them. So they drove off with one side of the diaper tied in a clumsy knot.

At lunch, Ferd said it was too bad about the safety pins. Oscar dug his teeth into a sandwich, tugged, tore, chewed, swallowed. Ferd liked to experiment with sandwich spreads—the one he liked most was cream-cheese, olives, anchovy and avocado, mashed up with a little mayonnaise—but Oscar always had the same pink luncheon-meat.

"It must be difficult with a baby." Ferd nibbled. "Not just traveling, but raising it."

Oscar said, "Jeez, there's drugstores in every block, and if you can't read, you can at least reckernize them."

"Drugstores? Oh, to buy safety pins, you mean."

"Yeah. Safety pins."

"But . . . you know . . . it's true . . . there's never any safety pins when you look."

Oscar uncapped his beer, rinsed the first mouthful around. "Aha! Always plenny of clothes hangers, though. Throw 'em out every month, next month same closet's full of 'm again. Now whatcha wanna do in your spare time, you invent a device which it'll make safety pins outa clothes hangers."

Ferd nodded abstractedly. "But in my spare time I'm working on the French racer . . ." It was a beautiful machine, light, low-slung, swift, red and shining. You felt like a bird when you rode it. But, good as it was, Ferd knew he could make it better. He showed it to everybody who came in the place until his interest slackened.

Nature was his latest hobby, or, rather, reading about Nature. Some kids had wandered by from the park one day with tin cans in which they had put salamanders and toads, and they proudly showed them to Ferd. After that, the work on the red racer slowed down and he spent his spare time on natural history books.

"Mimicry!" he cried to Oscar. "A wonderful thing!"

Oscar looked up interestedly from the bowling scores in the paper. "I seen Edie Adams on TV the other night, doing her imitation of Marilyn Monroe. Boy, oh, boy."

Ferd was irritated, shook his head. "Not that kind of mimicry. I mean how insects and arachnids will mimic the shapes of leaves and twigs and so on, to escape being eaten by birds or other insects and arachnids."

A scowl of disbelief passed over Oscar's heavy face. "You mean they change their *shapes?* What you giving me?"

"Oh, it's true. Sometimes the mimicry is for aggressive purposes, though—like a South African turtle that looks like a rock and so the fish swim up to it and then it catches them. Or that spider in Sumatra. When it lies on its back, it looks like a bird dropping. Catches butterflies that way."

Oscar laughed, a disgusted and incredulous noise. It died away as he turned back to the bowling scores. One hand groped at his pocket, came away, scratched absently at the orange thicket under the shirt, then went patting his hip pocket.

"Where's that pencil?" he muttered, got up, stomped into the office, pulled open drawers. His loud cry of "Hey!" brought Ferd into the tiny room.

"What's the matter?" Ferd asked.

Oscar pointed to a drawer. "Remember that time you claimed there were no safety pins here? Look—whole gahdamn drawer is full of 'em."

Ferd stared, scratched his head, said feebly that he was certain he'd looked there before . . .

A contralto voice from outside asked, "Anybody here?"

Oscar at once forgot the desk and its contents, called, "Be right with you," and was gone. Ferd followed him slowly.

There was a young woman in the shop, a rather massively built young woman, with muscular calves and a deep chest. She was pointing out the seat of her bicycle to Oscar, who was saying "Uh-huh" and looking more at her than at anything else. "It's just a little too far forward ("Uh-huh"), as you can see. A wrench is all I need ("Uh-huh"). It was silly of me to forget my tools."

Oscar repeated, "Uh-huh" automatically, then snapped to. "Fix it in a jiffy," he said, and—despite her insistence that she could do it herself—he did fix it. Though not quite in a jiffy. He refused money. He prolonged the conversation as long as he could.

"Well, thank *you*," the young woman said. "And now I've got to go."

"That machine feel all right to you now?"

"Perfectly. Thanks—"

"Tell you what, I'll just ride along with you a little bit, just—"

Pear-shaped notes of laughter lifted the young woman's bosom. "Oh, you couldn't keep up with me! My machine is a *racer!*"

The moment he saw Oscar's eye flit to the corner, Ferd knew what he had in mind. He stepped forward. His cry of "No" was drowned out by his partner's loud, "Well, I guess this racer here can keep up with yours!"

The young woman giggled richly, said, well, they would see about that, and was off. Oscar, ignoring Ferd's outstretched hand, jumped on the French bike and was gone. Ferd stood in the doorway, watching the two figures, hunched over their handlebars, vanish down the road into the park. He went slowly back inside.

It was almost evening before Oscar returned, sweaty but smiling. Smiling broadly. "Hey, what a babe!" he cried. He wagged his head, he whistled, he made gestures, noises like escaping steam. "Boy, oh, boy, what an afternoon!"

"Give me the bike," Ferd demanded.

Oscar said, yeah, sure; turned it over to him and went to wash. Ferd looked at the machine. The red enamel was covered with dust; there was mud spattered and dirt and bits of dried grass. It seemed soiled—degraded. He had felt like a swift bird when he rode it . . .

Oscar came out wet and beaming. He gave a cry of dismay, ran over.

"Stand away," said Ferd, gesturing with the knife. He slashed the tires, the seat and seat cover, again and again.

"You crazy?" Oscar yelled. "You outa your mind? Ferd, no, don't, Ferd—"

Ferd cut the spokes, bent them, twisted them. He took the heaviest hammer and pounded the frame into shapelessness, and then he kept on pounding till his breath was gasping.

G

"You're not only crazy," Oscar said bitterly, "you're rotten jealous. You can go to hell." He stomped away.

Ferd, feeling sick and stiff, locked up, went slowly home. He had no taste for reading, turned out the light and fell into bed, where he lay awake for hours, listening to the rustling noises of the night and thinking hot, twisted thoughts.

They didn't speak to each other for days after that, except for the necessities of the work. The wreckage of the French racer lay behind the shop. For about two weeks, neither wanted to go out back where he'd have to see it.

One morning Ferd arrived to be greeted by his partner, who began to shake his head in astonishment even before he started speaking. "How did you *do* it, how did you *do* it, Ferd? Jeez, what a beautiful job—I gotta hand it to you—no more hard feelings, huh, Ferd?"

Ferd took his hand. "Sure, sure. But what are you talking about?"

Oscar led him out back. There was the red racer, all in one piece, not a mark or scratch on it, its enamel bright as ever. Ferd gaped. He squatted down and examined it. It *was* his machine. Every change, every improvement he had made, was there.

He straightened up slowly. "Regeneration . . ."

"Huh? What say?" Oscar asked. Then, "Hey, kiddo, you're all white. Whad you do, stay up all night and didn't get no sleep? Come on in and siddown. But I still don't see how you done it."

Inside, Ferd sat down. He wet his lips. He said, "Oscar—listen—"

"Yeah?"

"Oscar. You know what regeneration is? No? Listen. Some kinds of lizards, you grab them by the tail, the tail breaks off and they grow a new one. If a lobster loses a claw, it regenerates another one. Some kinds of worms—and hydras and starfish—you cut them into pieces, each piece will grow back the missing parts. Salamanders can regenerate lost hands, and frogs can grow legs back."

"No kidding, Ferd. But, uh, I mean: Nature. Very interesting. But to get back to the bike now—how'd you manage to fix it so good?"

"I never touched it. It regenerated. Like a newt. Or a lobster."

Oscar considered this. He lowered his head, looked up at Ferd from under his eyebrows. "Well, now, Ferd . . . Look . . . How come all broke bikes don't do that?"

"This isn't an ordinary bike. I mean it isn't a real bike." Catching Oscar's look, he shouted, "Well, it's *true!*"

The shout changed Oscar's attitude from bafflement to incredulity. He got up. "So for the sake of argument, let's say all that stuff about the bugs and the eels or whatever the hell you were talking about is true. But they're alive. A bike ain't." He looked down triumphantly.

Ferd shook his leg from side to side, looked at it. "A crystal isn't, either, but a broken crystal can regenerate itself if the conditions are right. Oscar, go see if the safety pins are still in the desk. Please, Oscar?"

He listened as Oscar, muttering, pulled the desk drawers out, rummaged in them, slammed them shut, tramped back.

"Naa," he said. "All gone. Like that lady said that time, and you said, there never are any safety pins when you want 'em. They disap—Ferd? What're—"

Ferd jerked open the closet door, jumped back as a shoal of clothes hangers clattered out.

"And like *you* say," Ferd said with a twist of his mouth, "on the other hand, there are always plenty of clothes hangers. There weren't any here before."

Oscar shrugged. "I don't see what you're getting at. But anybody could of got in here and took the pins and left the hangers. *I* could of—but I didn't. Or *you* could of. Maybe—" He narrowed his eyes. "Maybe you walked in your sleep and done it. You better see a doctor. Jeez, you look rotten."

Ferd went back and sat down, put his head in his hands. "I *feel* rotten. I'm scared, Oscar. Scared of what?" He breathed noisily. "I'll tell you. Like I explained before, about how things that live in the wild places, they mimic other things there. Twigs, leaves . . . toads that look like rocks. Well, suppose there are . . . things . . . that live in people places. Cities. Houses. These things could imitate—well, other kinds of things you find in people places—"

"*People* places, for crise sake!"

"Maybe they're a different kind of life-form. Maybe they get their nourishment out of the elements in the air. You know what safety pins *are*—these other kinds of them? Oscar, the safety pins are the pupa-forms and then they, like, *hatch*. Into the larval-forms. Which look just like coat hangers. They feel like them, even, but they're not. Oscar, they're not, not really, not really, not . . ."

He began to cry into his hands. Oscar looked at him. He shook his head.

After a minute, Ferd controlled himself somewhat. He snuffled. "All these bicycles the cops find, and they hold them waiting for owners to show up, and then we buy them at the sale because no owners show up because there aren't any, and the same with the ones the kids are always trying to sell us, and they say they just found them, and they really did because they were never made in a factory. They grew. They grow. You smash them and throw them away, they regenerate."

Oscar turned to someone who wasn't there and waggled his head. "Hoo, boy," he said. Then, to Ferd: "You mean one day there's a safety pin and the next day instead there s a coat hanger?"

Ferd said, "One day there's a cocoon; the next day there's a moth. One day there's an egg; the next day there's a chicken. But with . . . these it doesn't happen in the open daytime where you can see it. But at night, Oscar—at night you can *hear* it happening. All the little noises in the nighttime, Oscar—"

Oscar said, "Then how come we ain't up to our belly-button in bikes? If I had a bike for every coat hanger—"

But Ferd had considered that, too. If every codfish egg, he explained, or every oyster spawn grew to maturity, a man could walk across the ocean on the backs of all the codfish or oysters there'd be. So many died, so many were eaten by predatory creatures, that Nature had to produce a maximum in order to allow a minimum to arrive at maturity. And Oscar's question was: then who, uh, eats the, uh, coat hangers?

Ferd's eyes focused through wall, buildings, park, more buildings, to the horizon. "You got to get the picture. I'm not talking about real pins or hangers. I got a name for the others—'false friends,' I call them. In high school French, we had to watch out for French words that looked like English words, but really were different. '*Faux amis,*' they call them. False friends. Pseudo-pins. Pseudo-hangers . . . Who eats them? I don't know for sure. Pseudo-vacuum cleaners, maybe?"

His partner, with a loud groan, slapped his hands against his thighs. He said, "Ferd, Ferd, for crise sake. You know what's the trouble with you? You talk about oysters, but you forgot what they're good for. You forgot there's two kinds of people in the world. Close up them books, them bug books and French books. Get out, mingle, meet people. Soak up some brew. You know what? The next time Norma—that's this broad's name with the racing bike—the next time she comes here, *you* take the red racer and *you* go out in the woods with her. I won't mind. And I don't think she will, either. Not *too* much."

But Ferd said no. "I never want to touch the red racer again. I'm afraid of it."

At this, Oscar pulled him to his feet, dragged him protestingly out to the back and forced him to get on the French machine. "Only way to conquer your fear of it!"

Ferd started off, white-faced, wobbling. And in a moment was on the ground, rolling and thrashing, screaming.

Oscar pulled him away from the machine.

"It threw me!" Ferd yelled. "It tried to kill me! Look—blood!"

His partner said it was a bump that threw him—it was his own fear. The blood? A broken spoke. Grazed his cheek. And he insisted Ferd get on the bicycle again, to conquer his fear.

But Ferd had grown hysterical. He shouted that no man was safe—that mankind had to be warned. It took Oscar a long time to pacify him and to get him to go home and into bed.

He didn't tell all this to Mr. Whatney, of course. He merely said that his partner had gotten fed up with the bicycle business.

"It don't pay to worry and try to change the world," he pointed out. "I always say take things the way they are. If you can't lick 'em, join 'em."

Mr. Whatney said that was his philosophy, exactly. He asked how things were, since.

"Well . . . not *too* bad. I'm engaged, you know Name's Norma. Crazy about bicycles. Everything considered, things aren't bad at all. More work, yes, but I can do things all my own way, so . . ."

Mr. Whatney nodded. He glanced around the shop. "I see they're still making drop-frame bikes," he said, "though, with so many women wearing slacks, I wonder they bother."

Oscar said, "Well, I dunno. I kinda like it that way. Ever stop to think that bicycles are like people? I mean, of all the machines in the world, only bikes come male and female."

Mr. Whatney gave a little giggle, said that was *right*, he had never thought of it like that before. Then Oscar asked if Mr. Whatney had anything in particular in mind—not that he wasn't always welcome.

"Well, I wanted to look over what you've got. My boy's birthday is coming up—"

Oscar nodded sagely. "Now here's a job," he said, "which you can't get it in any other place but here. Specialty of the house. Combines the best features of the French racer and the American standard, but it's made right here, and it comes in three models —Junior, Intermediate and Regular. Beautiful, ain't it?"

Mr. Whatney observed that, say, that might be just the ticket. "By the way," he asked, "what's become of the French racer, the red one, used to be here?"

Oscar's face twitched. Then it grew bland and innocent and he leaned over and nudged his customer. "Oh, *that* one. Old Frenchy? Why, I put *him* out to stud!"

And they laughed and they laughed, and after they told a few more stories they concluded the sale, and they had a few beers and they laughed some more. And then they said what a shame it was about poor Ferd, poor old Ferd, who had been found in his own closet with an unraveled coat hanger coiled tightly around his neck.

1959
17th Convention
Detroit

Clifford D. Simak

Clifford D. Simak is one of the oldest and most nearly invisible of my friends. It came to pass after this fashion.

In 1938, before I had published any stories of my own, I, like all science fiction fans, considered myself a redoubtable critic of the medium, and I never hesitated to write letters to the editor denouncing those stories I disliked, and doing so, moreover, in the most uncompromising tones imaginable. I did so in connection with a story entitled "Rule 18" by Clifford D. Simak.

Cliff promptly wrote me a letter asking me for more details of what he had done wrong so that he could improve himself. (No, he was not being sarcastic; he really meant it. That's the kind of guy he is.) This forced me to reread the story and to realize that what really bothered me was Cliff's habit of jumping suddenly from one scene to the next, changing time, place and personnel in complete abandon.

At first reading, this was unsettling, but the second time round, I saw the point. It introduced a sense of swift action and, properly handled, it lent a mood of heightened drama. I wrote a letter of apology and, without even a twinge of conscience, adopted the device myself in the stories I was then trying to write.

Our friendship was established and we corresponded thereafter for over twenty years without once meeting each other. As the fates would have it, those conventions I attended, he could not, and those which he attended, I could not. Even at the 17th Convention (Detroit, 1959) when I handed out the Hugo awarded his story "The Big Front Yard," it was accepted by proxy.

And then, finally, on October 20, 1961, we both found ourselves in New York simultaneously. I had forgiven him, by then, his lack of consideration in winning a Hugo, and we had lunch together. After 23 years, I met Cliff in the flesh.

Now I know very well what the proper denouement should be: Old time pen-pals meet after many years and long-held illusions are shattered.

Sorry. Truth is duller than fiction. It was as though we had always known each other in person. We had a delightful lunch together; a pair of old friends communicating for once in a slightly modified fashion, by sound-waves rather than through marks on paper.

And we still correspond.

6

THE BIG FRONT YARD

Hiram Taine came awake and sat up in his bed.

Towser was barking and scratching at the floor.

"Shut up," Taine told the dog.

Towser cocked quizzical ears at him and then resumed the barking and scratching at the floor.

Taine rubbed his eyes. He ran a hand through his rat's-nest head of hair. He considered lying down again and pulling up the covers.

But not with Towser barking.

"What's the matter with you, anyhow?" he asked Towser, with not a little wrath.

"*Whuff*," said Towser, industriously proceeding with his scratching at the floor.

"If you want out," said Taine, "all you got to do is open the screen door. You know how it is done. You do it all the time."

Towser quit his barking and sat down heavily, watching his master getting out of bed.

Taine put on his shirt and pulled on his trousers, but didn't bother with his shoes.

Towser ambled over to a corner, put his nose down to the baseboard and snuffled moistly.

"You got a mouse?" asked Taine.

"*Whuff*," said Towser, most emphatically.

"I can't ever remember you making such a row about a mouse," Taine said, slightly puzzled. "You must be off your rocker."

It was a beautiful summer morning. Sunlight was pouring through the open window.

Good day for fishing, Taine told himself, then remembered that there'd be no fishing, for he had to go out and look up that old four-poster maple bed that he had heard about up Woodman way. More than likely, he thought, they'd want twice as much as it was worth. It was getting so, he told himself, that a man couldn't make an honest dollar. Everyone was getting smart about antiques.

He got up off the bed and headed for the living room.

"Come on," he said to Towser.

Towser came along, pausing now and then to snuffle into corners and to whuffle at the floor.

"You got it bad," said Taine.

Maybe it's a rat, he thought. The house was getting old.

He opened the screen door and Towser went outside.

"Leave that woodchuck be today," Taine advised him. "It's a losing battle. You'll never dig him out."

Towser went around the corner of the house.

Taine noticed that something had happened to the sign that hung on the post beside the driveway. One of the chains had become unhooked and the sign was dangling.

He padded out across the driveway slab and the grass, still wet with dew, to fix the sign. There was nothing wrong with it—just the unhooked chain. Might have been the wind, he thought, or some passing urchin. Although probably not an urchin. He got along with kids. They never bothered him, like they did some others in the village. Banker Stevens, for example. They were always pestering Stevens.

He stood back a way to be sure the sign was straight.

It read, in big letters:

HANDY MAN

And under that, in smaller lettering:

I fix anything

And under that:

ANTIQUES FOR SALE

What have you got to trade?

Maybe, he told himself, he'd ought to have two signs, one for his fix-it shop and one for antiques and trading. Some day, when he had the time, he thought, he'd paint a couple of new ones. One for each side of the driveway. It would look neat that way.

He turned around and looked across the road at Turner's Woods. It was a pretty sight, he thought. A sizable piece of woods like that right at the edge of town. It was a place for birds and rabbits and woodchucks and squirrels and it was full of forts built through generations by the boys of Willow Bend.

Some day, of course, some smart operator would buy it up and start a housing development or something equally objectionable and when that happened a big slice of his own boyhood would be cut out of his life.

Towser came around the corner of the house. He was sidling along, sniffing at the lowest row of siding and his ears were cocked with interest.

"That dog is nuts," said Taine and went inside.

He went into the kitchen, his bare feet slapping on the floor. He filled the teakettle, set it on the stove and turned the burner on underneath the kettle.

He turned on the radio, forgetting that it was out of kilter.

When it didn't make a sound, he remembered and, disgusted, snapped it off. That was the way it went, he thought. He fixed other people's stuff, but never got around to fixing any of his own.

He went into the bedroom and put on his shoes. He threw the bed together.

Back in the kitchen the stove had failed to work again. The burner beneath the kettle still was cold.

Taine hauled off and kicked the stove. He lifted the kettle and held his palm above the burner. In a few seconds he could detect some heat.

"Worked again," he told himself.

Some day, he knew, kicking the stove would fail to work. When that happened, he'd have to get to work on it. Probably wasn't more than a loose connection.

He put the kettle back onto the stove.

There was a clatter out in front and Taine went out to see what was going on.

Beasly, the Horton's yardboy-chauffeur-gardener-et cetera was backing a rickety old truck up the driveway. Beside him sat Abbie Horton, the wife of H. Henry Horton, the village's most important citizen. In the back of the truck, lashed on with ropes and half-protected by a garish red and purple quilt, stood a mammoth television set. Taine recognized it from of old. It was a good ten years out of date and still, by any standard, it was the most expensive set ever to grace any home in Willow Bend.

Abbie hopped out of the truck. She was an energetic, bustling, bossy woman.

"Good morning, Hiram," she said. "Can you fix this set again?"

"Never saw anything that I couldn't fix," said Taine, but nevertheless he eyed the set with something like dismay. It was not the first time he had tangled with it and he knew what was ahead.

"It might cost you more than it's worth," he warned her. "What you really need is a new one. This set is getting old and—"

"That's just what Henry said," Abbie told him, tartly. "Henry wants to get one of the color sets. But I won't part with this one. It's not just TV, you know. It's a combination with radio and a record player and the wood and style are just right for the other furniture, and besides—"

"Yes, I know," said Taine, who'd heard it all before.

Poor old Henry, he thought. What a life the man must lead. Up at that computer plant all day long, shooting off his face and bossing everyone, then coming home to a life of petty tyranny.

"Beasly," said Abbie, in her best drill-sergeant voice, "you get right up there and get that thing untied."

"Yes'm," Beasly said. He was a gangling, loose-jointed man who didn't look too bright.

"And see you be careful with it. I don't want it all scratched up."

"Yes'm," said Beasly.

"I'll help," Taine offered.

The two climbed into the truck and began unlashing the old monstrosity.

"It's heavy," Abbie warned. "You two be careful of it."

"Yes'm," said Beasly.

It was heavy and it was an awkward thing to boot, but Beasly and Taine horsed it around to the back of the house and up the stoop and through the back door and down the basement stairs, with Abbie following eagle-eyed behind them, alert to the slightest scratch.

The basement was Taine's combination workshop and display room for antiques. One end of it was filled with benches and with tools and machinery and boxes full of odds and ends and piles of just plain junk were scattered everywhere. The other end housed a collection of rickety chairs, sagging bedposts, ancient highboys, equally ancient lowboys, old coal scuttles painted gold, heavy iron fireplace screens and a lot of other stuff that he had collected from far and wide for as little as he could possibly pay for it.

He and Beasly set the TV down carefully on the floor. Abbie watched them narrowly from the stairs.

"Why, Hiram," she said, excited, "you put a ceiling in the basement. It looks a whole lot better."

"Huh?" asked Taine.

"The ceiling. I said you put in a ceiling."

Taine jerked his head up and what she said was true. There was a ceiling there, but he'd never put it in.

He gulped a little and lowered his head, then jerked it quickly up and had another look. The ceiling was still there.

"It's not that block stuff," said Abbie with open admiration. "You can't see any joints at all. How did you manage it?"

Taine gulped again and got back his voice. "Something I thought up," he told her weakly.

"You'll have to come over and do it to our basement. Our basement is a sight. Beasly put the ceiling in the amusement room, but Beasly is all thumbs."

"Yes'm," Beasly said contritely.

"When I get the time," Taine promised, ready to promise anything to get them out of there.

"You'd have a lot more time," Abbie told him acidly, "if you weren't gadding around all over the country buying up that broken-down old furniture that you call antiques. Maybe you can fool the city folks when they come driving out here, but you can't fool me."

"I make a lot of money out of some of it," Taine told her calmly.

"And lose your shirt on the rest of it," she said.

"I got some old china that is just the kind of stuff you are looking for," said Taine. "Picked it up just a day or two ago. Made a good buy on it. I can let you have it cheap."

"I'm not interested," she said and clamped her mouth tight shut.

She turned around and went back up the stairs.

"She's on the prod today," Beasly said to Taine. "It will be a bad day. It always is when she starts early in the morning."

"Don't pay attention to her," Taine advised.

"I try not to, but it ain't possible. You sure you don't need a man? I'd work for you cheap."

"Sorry, Beasly. Tell you what—come over some night soon and we'll play some checkers."

"I'll do that, Hiram. You're the only one who ever asks me over. All the others ever do is laugh at me or shout."

Abbie's voice came bellowing down the stairs. "Beasly, are you coming? Don't go standing there all day. I have rugs to beat."

"Yes'm," said Beasly, starting up the stairs.

At the truck, Abbie turned on Taine with determination: "You'll get that set fixed right away? I'm lost without it."

"Immediately," said Taine.

He stood and watched them off, then looked around for Towser, but the dog had disappeared. More than likely he was at the woodchuck hole again, in the woods across the road. Gone off, thought Taine, without his breakfast, too.

The teakettle was boiling furiously when Taine got back to the kitchen. He put coffee in the maker and poured in the water. Then he went downstairs.

The ceiling was still there.

He turned on all the lights and walked around the basement, staring up at it.

It was a dazzling white material and it appeared to be translucent—up to a point, that is. One could see into it, but he could not see through it. And there were no signs of seams. It was fitted neatly and tightly around the water pipes and the ceiling lights.

Taine stood on a chair and rapped his knuckles against it sharply. It gave out a bell-like sound, almost exactly as if he'd rapped a fingernail against a thinly-blown goblet.

He got down off the chair and stood there, shaking his head. The whole thing was beyond him. He had spent part of the evening repairing Banker Stevens' lawn mower and there'd been no ceiling then.

He rummaged in a box and found a drill. He dug out one of the smaller bits and fitted it in the drill. He plugged in the cord and climbed on the chair again and tried the bit against the ceiling. The whirling steel slid wildly back and forth. It didn't make a scratch. He switched off the drill and looked closely at the ceiling. There was not a mark upon it. He tried again, pressing against the drill with all his strength. The bit went *ping* and the broken end flew across the basement and hit the wall.

Taine stepped down off the chair. He found another bit and fitted it in the drill and went slowly up the stairs, trying to think. But he was too confused to think. That ceiling should not be up there, but there it was. And unless he went stark, staring crazy and forgetful as well, he had not put it there.

In the living room, he folded back one corner of the worn and faded carpeting and plugged in the drill. He knelt and started drilling in the floor. The bit went smoothly through the old oak flooring, then stopped. He put on more pressure and the drill spun without getting any bite.

And there wasn't supposed to be anything underneath that wood! Nothing to stop a drill. Once through the flooring, it should have dropped into the space between the joists.

Taine disengaged the drill and laid it to one side.

He went into the kitchen and the coffee now was ready. But before he poured it, he pawed through a cabinet drawer and found a pencil flashlight. Back in the living room he shone the light into the hole that the drill had made.

There was something shiny at the bottom of the hole.

He went back to the kitchen and found some day-old doughnuts and poured a cup of coffee. He sat at the kitchen table, eating doughnuts and wondering what to do.

There didn't appear, for the moment at least, much that he

could do. He could putter around all day trying to figure out what
had happened to his basement and probably not be any wiser
than he was right now.

His money-making Yankee soul rebelled against such a horrid
waste of time.

There was, he told himself, that maple four-poster that he
should be getting to before some unprincipled city antique dealer
should run afoul of it. A piece like that, he figured, if a man had
any luck at all, should sell at a right good price. He might turn a
handsome profit on it if he only worked it right.

Maybe, he thought, he could turn a trade on it. There was the
table model TV set that he had traded a pair of ice skates for last
winter. Those folks out Woodman way might conceivably be
happy to trade the bed for a reconditioned TV set, almost like
brand new. After all, they probably weren't using the bed and,
he hoped fervently, had no idea of the value of it.

He ate the doughnuts hurriedly and gulped down an extra cup
of coffee. He fixed a plate of scraps for Towser and set it outside
the door. Then he went down into the basement and got the
table TV set and put it in the pickup truck. As an afterthought,
he added a reconditioned shotgun which would be perfectly all
right if a man were careful not to use these far-reaching, powerful shells, and a few other odds and ends that might come in
handy on a trade.

He got back late, for it had been a busy and quite satisfactory
day. Not only did he have the four-poster loaded on the truck,
but he had as well a rocking chair, a fire screen, a bundle of
ancient magazines, an old-fashioned barrel churn, a walnut high-
boy and a Governor Winthrop on which some half-baked, slap-
happy decorator had applied a coat of apple-green paint. The
television set, the shotgun and five dollars had gone into the
trade. And what was better yet, he'd managed it so well that the
Woodman family probably was dying of laughter at this very
moment about how they'd taken him.

He felt a little ashamed of it—they'd been such friendly people.
They had treated him so kindly and had him stay for dinner and
had sat and talked with him and shown him about the farm and
even asked him to stop by if he went through that way again.

He's wasted the entire day, he thought, and he rather hated that, but maybe it had been worth it to build up his reputation out that way as the sort of character who had softening of the head and didn't know the value of a dollar. That way, maybe some other day, he could do some more business in the neighborhood.

He heard the television set as he opened the back door, sounding loud and clear, and he went clattering down the basement stairs in something close to a panic. For now that he'd traded off the table model, Abbie's set was the only one downstairs and Abbie's set was broken.

It was Abbie's set, all right. It stood just where he and Beasly had put it down that morning and there was nothing wrong with it—nothing wrong at all. It was even televising color.

Televising color!

He stopped at the bottom of the stairs and leaned against the railing for support.

The set kept right on televising color.

Taine stalked the set and walked around behind it.

The back of the cabinet was off, leaning against a bench that stood behind the set, and he could see the innards of it glowing cheerily.

He squatted on the basement floor and squinted at the lighted innards and they seemed a good deal different from the way that they should be. He'd repaired the set many times before and he thought he had a good idea of what the working parts would look like. And now they all seemed different, although just how he couldn't tell.

A heavy step sounded on the stairs and a hearty voice came booming down to him.

"Well, Hiram, I see you got it fixed."

Taine jackknifed upright and stood there slightly frozen and completely speechless.

Henry Horton stood foursquarely and happily on the stairs, looking very pleased.

"I told Abbie that you wouldn't have it done, but she said for me to come over anyway— Hey, Hiram, it's in color! How did you do it, man?"

Taine grinned sickly. "I just got fiddling around," he said.

Henry came down the rest of the stairs with a stately step and stood before the set, with his hands behind his back, staring at it fixedly in his best executive manner.

He slowly shook his head. "I never would have thought," he said, "that it was possible."

"Abbie mentioned that you wanted color."

"Well, sure. Of course I did. But not on this old set. I never would have expected to get color on this set. How did you do it, Hiram?"

Taine told the solemn truth. "I can't rightly say," he said.

Henry found a nail keg standing in front of one of the benches and rolled it out in front of the old-fashioned set. He sat down warily and relaxed into solid comfort.

"That's the way it goes," he said. "There are men like you, but not very many of them. Just Yankee tinkerers. You keep messing around with things, trying one thing here and another there and before you know it you come up with something."

He sat on the nail keg, staring at the set.

"It's sure a pretty thing," he said. "It's better than the color they have in Minneapolis. I dropped in at a couple of the places the last time I was there and looked at the color sets. And I tell you honest, Hiram, there wasn't one of them that was as good as this."

Taine wiped his brow with his shirt sleeve. Somehow or other, the basement seemed to be getting warm. He was fine sweat all over.

Henry found a big cigar in one of his pockets and held it out to Taine.

"No, thanks. I never smoke."

"Perhaps you're wise," said Henry. "It's a nasty habit."

He stuck the cigar into his mouth and rolled it east to west.

"Each man to his own," he proclaimed expansively. "When it comes to a thing like this, you're the man to do it. You seem to think in mechanical contraptions and electronic circuits. Me, I don't know a thing about it. Even in the computer game, I still don't know a thing about it; I hire men who do. I can't even saw a board or drive a nail. But I can organize. You remember, Hiram, how everybody snickered when I started up the plant?"

"Well, I guess some of them did, at that."

"You're darn tooting they did. They went around for weeks with their hands up to their faces to hide smart-aleck grins. They said, what does Henry think he's doing, starting up a computer factory out here in the sticks; he doesn't think he can compete with those big companies in the east, does he? And they didn't stop their grinning until I sold a couple of dozen units and had orders for a year or two ahead."

He fished a lighter from his pocket and lit the cigar carefully, never taking his eyes off the television set.

"You got something there," he said, judiciously, "that may be worth a mint of money. Some simple adaptation that will fit on any set. If you can get color on this old wreck, you can get color on any set that's made."

He chuckled moistly around the mouthful of cigar. "If RCA knew what was happening here this minute, they'd go out and cut their throats."

"But I don't know what I did," protested Taine.

"Well, that's all right," said Henry, happily. "I'll take this set up to the plant tomorrow and turn loose some of the boys on it. They'll find out what you have here before they're through with it."

He took the cigar out of his mouth and studied it intently, then popped it back in again.

"As I was saying, Hiram, that's the difference in us. You can do the stuff, but you miss the possibilities. I can't do a thing, but I can organize it once the thing is done. Before we get through with this, you'll be wading in twenty dollar bills clear up to your knees."

"But I don't have—"

"Don't worry. Just leave it all to me. I've got the plant and whatever money we may need. We'll figure out a split."

"That's fine of you," said Taine mechanically.

"Not at all," Henry insisted, grandly. "It's just my aggressive, grasping sense of profit. I should be ashamed of myself, cutting in on this."

He sat on the keg, smoking and watching the TV perform in exquisite color.

"You know, Hiram," he said, "I've often thought of this, but never got around to doing anything about it. I've got an old computer up at the plant that we will have to junk because it's taking up room that we really need. It's one of our early models, a sort of experimental job that went completely sour. It sure is a screwy thing. No one's ever been able to make much out of it. We tried some approaches that probably were wrong—or maybe they were right, but we didn't know enough to make them quite come off. It's been standing in a corner all these years and I should have junked it long ago. But I sort of hate to do it. I wonder if you might not like it—just to tinker with."

"Well, I don't know," said Taine.

Henry assumed an expansive air. "No obligation, mind you. You may not be able to do a thing with it—I'd frankly be surprised if you could, but there's no harm in trying. Maybe you'll decide to tear it down for the salvage you can get. There are several thousand dollars worth of equipment in it. Probably you could use most of it one way or another."

"It might be interesting," conceded Taine, but not too enthusiastically.

"Good," said Henry, with an enthusiasm that made up for Taine's lack of it. "I'll have the boys cart it over tomorrow. It's a heavy thing. I'll send along plenty of help to get it unloaded and down into the basement and set up."

Henry stood up carefully and brushed cigar ashes off his lap.

"I'll have the boys pick up the TV set at the same time," he said. "I'll have to tell Abbie you haven't got it fixed yet. If I ever let it get into the house, the way it's working now, she'd hold onto it."

Henry climbed the stairs heavily and Taine saw him out the door into the summer night.

Taine stood in the shadow, watching Henry's shadowed figure go across the Widow Taylor's yard to the next street behind his house. He took a deep breath of the fresh night air and shook his head to try to clear his buzzing brain, but the buzzing went right on.

Too much had happened, he told himself. Too much for any single day—first the ceiling and now the TV set. Once he had a good night's sleep he might be in some sort of shape to try to wrestle with it.

Towser came around the corner of the house and limped slowly up the steps to stand beside his master. He was mud up to his ears.

"You had a day of it, I see," said Taine. "And, just like I told you, you didn't get the woodchuck."

"*Woof*," said Towser, sadly.

"You're just like a lot of the rest of us," Taine told him, severely. "Like me and Henry Horton and all the rest of us. You're chasing something and you think you know what you're chasing, but you really don't. And what's even worse, you have no faint idea of why you're chasing it."

Towser thumped a tired tail upon the stoop.

Taine opened the door and stood to one side to let Towser in, then went in himself.

He went through the refrigerator and found part of a roast, a slice or two of luncheon meat, a dried-out slab of cheese and half a bowl of cooked spaghetti. He made a pot of coffee and shared the food with Towser.

Then Taine went back downstairs and shut off the television set. He found a trouble lamp and plugged it in and poked the light into the innards of the set.

He squatted on the floor, holding the lamp, trying to puzzle out what had been done to the set. It was different, of course, but it was a little hard to figure out in just what ways it was different. Someone had tinkered with the tubes and had them twisted out of shape and there were little white cubes of metal tucked here and there in what seemed to be an entirely haphazard and illogical manner—although, Taine admitted to himself, there probably was no haphazardness. And the circuit, he saw, had been rewired and a good deal of wiring had been added.

But the most puzzling thing about it was that the whole thing seemed to be just jury-rigged—as if someone had done no more than a hurried, patch-up job to get the set back in working order on an emergency and temporary basis.

Someone, he thought!

And who had that someone been?

He hunched around and peered into the dark corners of the basement and he felt innumerable and many-legged imaginary insects running on his body.

Someone had taken the back off the cabinet and leaned it against the bench and had left the screws which held the back laid neatly in a row upon the floor. Then they had jury-rigged the set and jury-rigged it far better than it had ever been before.

If this was a jury-job, he wondered, just what kind of job would it have been if they had had the time to do it up in style?

They hadn't had the time, of course. Maybe they had been scared off when he had come home—scared off even before they could get the back on the set again.

He stood up and moved stiffly away.

First the ceiling in the morning—and now, in the evening, Abbie's television set.

And the ceiling, come to think of it, was not a ceiling only. Another liner, if that was the proper term for it, of the same material as the ceiling, had been laid beneath the floor, forming a sort of boxed-in area between the joists. He had struck that liner when he had tried to drill into the floor.

And what, he asked himself, if all the house were like that, too?

There was just one answer to it all: *There was something in the house with him!*

Towser had heard that *something* or smelled it or in some other manner sensed it and had dug frantically at the floor in an attempt to dig it out, as if it were a woodchuck.

Except that this, whatever it might be, certainly was no woodchuck.

He put away the trouble light and went upstairs.

Towser was curled up on a rug in the living room beside the easy chair and beat his tail in polite decorum in greeting to his master.

Taine stood and stared down at the dog. Towser looked back at him with satisfied and sleepy eyes, then heaved a doggish sigh and settled down to sleep.

Whatever Towser might have heard or smelled or sensed this morning, it was quite evident that as of this moment he was aware of it no longer.

Then Taine remembered something else.

He had filled the kettle to make water for the coffee and had set it on the stove. He had turned on the burner and it had worked the first time.

He hadn't had to kick the stove to get the burner going.

He woke in the morning and someone was holding down his feet and he sat up quickly to see what was going on.

But there was nothing to be alarmed about; it was only Towser who had crawled into bed with him and now lay sprawled across his feet.

Towser whined softly and his back legs twitched as he chased dream rabbits.

Taine eased his feet from beneath the dog and sat up, reaching for his clothes. It was early, but he remembered suddenly that he had left all of the furniture he had picked up the day before out there in the truck and should be getting downstairs where he could start reconditioning it.

Towser went on sleeping.

Taine stumbled to the kitchen and looked out of the window and there, squatted on the back stoop, was Beasly, the Horton man-of-all-work.

Taine went to the back door to see what was going on.

"I quit them, Hiram," Beasly told him. "She kept on pecking at me every minute of the day and I couldn't do a thing to please her, so I up and quit."

"Well, come on in," said Taine. "I suppose you'd like a bite to eat and a cup of coffee."

"I was kind of wondering if I could stay here, Hiram. Just for my keep until I can find something else."

"Let's have breakfast first," said Taine, "then we can talk about it."

He didn't like it, he told himself. He didn't like it at all. In another hour or so Abbie would show up and start stirring up a ruckus about how he'd lured Beasly off. Because, no matter how dumb Beasly might be, he did a lot of work and took a lot of nagging and there wasn't anyone else in town who would work for Abbie Horton.

"Your ma used to give me cookies all the time," said Beasly. "Your ma was a real good woman, Hiram."

"Yes, she was," said Taine.

"My ma used to say that you folks were quality, not like the rest in town, no matter what kind of airs they were always putting on. She said your family was among the first settlers. Is that really true, Hiram?"

"Well, not exactly first settlers, I guess, but this house has stood here for almost a hundred years. My father used to say there never was a night during all those years that there wasn't at least one Taine beneath its roof. Things like that, it seems, meant a lot to father."

"It must be nice," said Beasly, wistfully, "to have a feeling like that. You must be proud of this house, Hiram."

"Not really proud; more like belonging. I can't imagine living in any other house."

Taine turned on the burner and filled the kettle. Carrying the kettle back, he kicked the stove. But there wasn't any need to kick it; the burner was already beginning to take on a rosy glow.

Twice in a row, Taine thought. This thing is getting better!

"Gee, Hiram," said Beasly, "this is a dandy radio."

"It's no good," said Taine. "It's broke. Haven't had the time to fix it."

"I don't think so, Hiram. I just turned it on. It's beginning to warm up."

"It's beginning to— Hey, let me see!" yelled Taine.

Beasly told the truth. A faint hum was coming from the tubes. A voice came in, gaining in volume as the set warmed up. It was speaking gibberish.

"What kind of talk is that?" asked Beasly.

"I don't know," said Taine, close to panic now.

First the television set, then the stove and now the radio!

He spun the tuning knob and the pointer crawled slowly across the dial face instead of spinning across as he remembered it, and station after station sputtered and went past.

He tuned in the next station that came up and it was strange lingo, too—and he knew by then exactly what he had.

Instead of a $39.50 job, he had here on the kitchen table an all-band receiver like they advertised in the fancy magazines.

He straightened up and said to Beasly: "See if you can get someone speaking English. I'll get on with the eggs."

He turned on the second burner and got out the frying pan. He put it on the stove and found eggs and bacon in the refrigerator.

Beasly got a station that had band music playing.

"How's that?" he asked.

"That's fine," said Taine.

Towser came out from the bedroom, stretching and yawning. He went to the door and showed he wanted out.

Taine let him out.

"If I were you," he told the dog, "I'd lay off that woodchuck. You'll have all the woods dug up."

"He ain't digging after any woodchuck, Hiram."

"Well, a rabbit, then."

"Not a rabbit, either. I snuck off yesterday when I was supposed to be beating rugs. That's what Abbie got so sore about."

Taine grunted, breaking eggs into the skillet.

"I snuck away and went over to where Towser was. I talked with him and he told me it wasn't a woodchuck or a rabbit. He said it was something else. I pitched in and helped him dig. Looks to me like he found an old tank of some sort buried out there in the woods."

"Towser wouldn't dig up any tank," protested Taine. "He wouldn't care about anything except a rabbit or a woodchuck."

"He was working hard," insisted Beasly. "He seemed to be excited."

"Maybe the woodchuck just dug his hole under this old tank or whatever it might be."

"Maybe so," Beasly agreed. He fiddled with the radio some more. He got a disk jockey who was pretty terrible.

Taine shoveled eggs and bacon onto plates and brought them to the table. He poured big cups of coffee and began buttering the toast.

"Dive in," he said to Beasly.

"This is good of you, Hiram, to take me in like this. I won't stay no longer than it takes to find a job."

"Well, I didn't exactly say—"

"There are times," said Beasly, "when I get to thinking I haven't got a friend and then I remember your ma, how nice she was to me and all—"

"Oh, all right," said Taine.

He knew when he was licked.

He brought the toast and a jar of jam to the table and sat down, beginning to eat.

"Maybe you got something I could help you with," suggested Beasly, using the back of his hand to wipe egg off his chin.

"I have a load of furniture out in the driveway. I could use a man to help me get it down into the basement."

"I'll be glad to do that," said Beasly. "I am good and strong. I don't mind work at all. I just don't like people jawing at me."

They finished breakfast and then carried the furniture down into the basement. They had some trouble with the Governor Winthrop, for it was an unwieldy thing to handle.

When they finally horsed it down, Taine stood off and looked at it. The man, he told himself, who slapped paint onto that beautiful cherrywood had a lot to answer for.

He said to Beasly: "We have to get the paint off that thing there. And we must do it carefully. Use paint remover and a rag wrapped around a spatula and just sort of roll it off. Would you like to try it?"

"Sure, I would. Say, Hiram, what will we have for lunch?"

"I don't know," said Taine. "We'll throw something together. Don't tell me you're hungry."

"Well, it was sort of hard work, getting all that stuff down here."

"There are cookies in the jar on the kitchen shelf," said Taine. "Go and help yourself."

When Beasly went upstairs, Taine walked slowly around the basement. The ceiling, he saw, was still intact. Nothing else seemed to be disturbed.

Maybe that television set and the stove and radio, he thought, was just their way of paying rent to me. And if that were the case, he told himself, whoever they might be, he'd be more than willing to let them stay right on.

He looked around some more and could find nothing wrong.

He went upstairs and called to Beasly in the kitchen.

"Come on out to the garage, where I keep the paint. We'll hunt up some remover and show you how to use it."

Beasly, a supply of cookies clutched in his hand, trotted willingly behind him.

As they rounded the corner of the house they could hear Towser's muffled barking. Listening to him, it seemed to Taine that he was getting hoarse.

Three days, he thought—or was it four?

"If we don't do something about it," he said, "that fool dog is going to get himself wore out."

He went into the garage and came back with two shovels and a pick.

"Come on," he said to Beasly. "We have to put a stop to this before we have any peace."

Towser had done himself a noble job of excavation. He was almost completely out of sight. Only the end of his considerably bedraggled tail showed out of the hole he had clawed in the forest floor.

Beasly had been right about the tanklike thing. One edge of it showed out of one side of the hole.

Towser backed out of the hole and sat down heavily, his whiskers dripping clay, his tongue hanging out of the side of his mouth.

"He says that it's about time that we showed up," said Beasly.

Taine walked around the hole and knelt down. He reached down a hand to brush the dirt off the projecting edge of Beasly's tank. The clay was stubborn and hard to wipe away, but from the feel of it the tank was heavy metal.

Taine picked up a shovel and rapped it against the tank. The tank gave out a clang.

They got to work, shoveling away a foot or so of topsoil that lay above the object. It was hard work and the thing was bigger than they had thought and it took some time to get it uncovered, even roughly.

"I'm hungry," Beasly complained.

Taine glanced at his watch. It was almost one o'clock.

"Run on back to the house," he said to Beasly. "You'll find something in the refrigerator and there's milk to drink."

"How about you, Hiram? Ain't you ever hungry?"

"You could bring me back a sandwich and see if you can find a trowel."

"What you want a trowel for?"

"I want to scrape the dirt off this thing and see what it is."

He squatted down beside the thing they had unearthed and watched Beasly disappear into the woods.

"Towser," he said, "this is the strangest animal you ever put to ground."

A man, he told himself, might better joke about it—if to do no more than keep his fear away.

Beasly wasn't scared, of course. Beasly didn't have the sense to be scared of a thing like this.

Twelve feet wide by twenty long and oval shaped. About the size, he thought, of a good-size living room. And there never had been a tank of that shape or size in all of Willow Bend.

He fished his jackknife out of his pocket and started to scratch away the dirt at one point on the surface of the thing. He got a square inch of free dirt and it was no metal such as he had ever seen. It looked for all the world like glass.

He kept on scraping at the dirt until he had a clean place as big as an outstretched hand.

It wasn't any metal. He'd almost swear to that. It looked like cloudy glass—like the milk-glass goblets and bowls he was always on the lookout for. There were a lot of people who were plain nuts about it and they'd pay fancy prices for it.

He closed the knife and put it back into his pocket and squatted, looking at the oval shape that Towser had discovered.

And the conviction grew: Whatever it was that had come to live with him undoubtedly had arrived in this same contraption. From space or time, he thought, and was astonished that he thought it, for he'd never thought such a thing before.

He picked up his shovel and began to dig again, digging down this time, following the curving side of this alien thing that lay within the earth.

And as he dug, he wondered. What should he say about this—or should he say anything? Maybe the smartest course would be to cover it again and never breathe a word about it to a living soul.

Beasly would talk about it, naturally. But no one in the village would pay attention to anything that Beasly said. Everyone in Willow Bend knew Beasly was cracked.

Beasly finally came back. He carried three inexpertly-made sandwiches wrapped in an old newspaper and a quart bottle almost full of milk.

"You certainly took your time," said Taine, slightly irritated.

"I got interested," Beasly explained.

"Interested in what?"

"Well, there were three big trucks and they were lugging a lot of heavy stuff down into the basement. Two or three big cabinets and a lot of other junk. And you know Abbie's television set? Well, they took the set away. I told them that they shouldn't, but they took it anyway."

"I forgot," said Taine. "Henry said he'd send the computer over and I plumb forgot."

Taine ate the sandwiches, sharing them with Towser, who was very grateful in a muddy way.

Finished, Taine rose and picked up his shovel.

"Let's get to work," he said.

"But you got all that stuff down in the basement."

"That can wait," said Taine. "This job we have to finish."

It was getting dusk by the time they finished.

Taine leaned wearily on his shovel.

Twelve feet by twenty across the top and ten feet deep—and all of it, every bit of it, made of the milk-glass stuff that sounded like a bell when you whacked it with a shovel.

They'd have to be small, he thought, if there were many of them, to live in a space that size, especially if they had to stay there very long. And that fitted in, of course, for if they weren't small they couldn't now be living in the space between the basement joists.

If they were really living there, thought Taine. If it wasn't all just a lot of supposition.

Maybe, he thought, even if they had been living in the house, they might be there no longer—for Towser had smelled or heard or somehow sensed them in the morning, but by that very night he'd paid them no attention.

Taine slung his shovel across his shoulder and hoisted the pick.

"Come on," he said, "let's go. We've put in a long, hard day."

They tramped out through the brush and reached the road. Fireflies were flickering off and on in the woody darkness and the street lamps were swaying in the summer breeze. The stars were hard and bright.

Maybe they still were in the house, thought Taine. Maybe when they found out that Towser had objected to them, they had fixed it so he'd be aware of them no longer.

They probably were highly adaptive. It stood to good reason they would have to be. It hadn't taken them too long, he told himself grimly, to adapt to a human house.

He and Beasly went up the gravel driveway in the dark to put the tools away in the garage and there was something funny going on, for there was no garage.

There was no garage and there was no front on the house and the driveway was cut off abruptly and there was nothing but the curving wall of what apparently had been the end of the garage.

They came up to the curving wall and stopped, squinting unbelieving in the summer dark.

There was no garage, no porch, no front of the house at all. It was as if someone had taken the opposite corners of the front of the house and bent them together until they touched, folding the entire front of the building inside the curvature of the bent-together corners.

Taine now had a curved-front house. Although it was, actually, not as simple as all that, for the curvature was not in proportion to what actually would have happened in case of such a feat. The curve was long and graceful and somehow not quite apparent. It was as if the front of the house had been eliminated and an illusion of the rest of the house had been summoned to mask the disappearance.

Taine dropped the shovel and the pick and they clattered on the driveway gravel. He put his hand up to his face and wiped it across his eyes, as if to clear his eyes of something that could not possibly be there.

And when he took the hand away it had not changed a bit.

There was no front to the house.

Then he was running around the house, hardly knowing he was running, and there was a fear inside of him at what had happened to the house.

But the back of the house was all right. It was exactly as it had always been.

He clattered up the stoop with Beasly and Towser running close behind him. He pushed open the door and burst into the entry and scrambled up the stairs into the kitchen and went across the kitchen in three strides to see what had happened to the front of the house.

At the door between the kitchen and the living room he stopped and his hands went out to grasp the door jamb as he stared in disbelief at the windows of the living room.

It was night outside. There could be no doubt of that. He had seen the fireflies flickering in the brush and weeds and the street lamps had been lit and the stars were out.

But a flood of sunlight was pouring through the windows of the living room and out beyond the windows lay a land that was not Willow Bend.

"Beasly," he gasped, "look out there in front!"

Beasly looked.

"What place is that?" he asked.

"That's what I'd like to know."

Towser had found his dish and was pushing it around the kitchen floor with his nose, by way of telling Taine that it was time to eat.

Taine went across the living room and opened the front door. The garage, he saw, was there. The pickup stood with its nose against the open garage door and the car was safe inside.

There was nothing wrong with the front of the house at all.

But if the front of the house was all right, that was all that was.

For the driveway was chopped off just a few feet beyond the tail end of the pickup and there was no yard or woods or road. There was just a desert—a flat, far-reaching desert, level as a floor, with occasional boulder piles and haphazard clumps of vegetation and all of the ground covered with sand and pebbles. A big blinding sun hung just above a horizon that seemed much too far away and a funny thing about it was that the sun was in the north, where no proper sun should be. It had a peculiar whiteness, too.

Beasly stepped out on the porch and Taine saw that he was shivering like a frightened dog.

"Maybe," Taine told him, kindly, "you'd better go back in and start making us some supper."

"But, Hiram—"

"It's all right," said Taine. "It's bound to be all right."

"If you say so, Hiram."

He went in and the screen door banged behind him and in a minute Taine heard him in the kitchen.

He didn't blame Beasly for shivering, he admitted to himself. It was a sort of shock to step out of your front door into an

H

unknown land. A man might eventually get used to it, of course, but it would take some doing.

He stepped down off the porch and walked around the truck and around the garage corner and when he rounded the corner he was half prepared to walk back into familiar Willow Bend—for when he had gone in the back door the village had been there.

There was no Willow Bend. There was more of the desert, a great deal more of it.

He walked around the house and there was no back to the house. The back of the house now was just the same as the front had been before—the same smooth curve pulling the sides of the house together.

He walked on around the house to the front again and there was desert all the way. And the front was still all right. It hadn't changed at all. The truck was there on the chopped-off driveway and the garage was open and the car inside.

Taine walked out a way into the desert and hunkered down and scooped up a handful of the pebbles and the pebbles were just pebbles.

He squatted there and let the pebbles trickle through his fingers.

In Willow Bend there was a back door and there wasn't any front. Here, wherever here might be, there was a front door, but there wasn't any back.

He stood up and tossed the rest of the pebbles away and wiped his dusty hands upon his breeches.

Out of the corner of his eye he caught a sense of movement on the porch and there they were.

A line of tiny animals, if animals they were, came marching down the steps, one behind another. They were four inches high or so and they went on all four feet, although it was plain to see that their front feet were really hands, not feet. They had ratlike faces that were vaguely human, with noses long and pointed. They looked as if they might have scales instead of hide, for their bodies glistened with a rippling motion as they walked. And all of them had tails that looked very much like the coiled-wire tails one finds on certain toys and the tails stuck straight up above them, quivering as they walked.

They came down the steps in single file, in perfect military order, with half a foot or so of spacing between each one of them.

They came down the steps and walked out into the desert in a straight, undeviating line as if they knew exactly where they might be bound. There was something deadly purposeful about them and yet they didn't hurry.

Taine counted sixteen of them and he watched them go out into the desert until they were almost lost to sight.

There go the ones, he thought, who came to live with me. They are the ones who fixed up the ceiling and who repaired Abbie's television set and jiggered up the stove and radio. And more than likely, too, they were the ones who had come to Earth in the strange milk-glass contraption out there in the woods.

And if they had come to Earth in that deal out in the woods, then what sort of place was this?

He climbed the porch and opened the screen door and saw the neat, six-inch circle his departing guests had achieved in the screen to get out of the house. He made a mental note that some day, when he had the time, he would have to fix it.

He went in and slammed the door behind him.

"Beasly," he shouted.

There was no answer.

Towser crawled from beneath the love seat and apologized.

"It's all right, pal," said Taine. "That outfit scared me, too."

He went into the kitchen. The dim ceiling light shone on the overturned coffee pot, the broken cup in the center of the floor, the upset bowl of eggs. One broken egg was a white and yellow gob on the linoleum.

He stepped down on the landing and saw that the screen door in the back was wrecked beyond repair. Its rusty mesh was broken—exploded might have been a better word—and a part of the frame was smashed.

Taine looked at it in wondering admiration.

"The poor fool," he said. "He went straight through it without opening it at all."

He snapped on the light and went down the basement stairs. Halfway down he stopped in utter wonderment.

To his left was a wall—a wall of the same sort of material as had been used to put in the ceiling.

He stooped and saw that the wall ran clear across the basement, floor to ceiling, shutting off the workshop area.

And inside the workshop, what?

For one thing, he remembered, the computer that Henry had sent over just this morning. Three trucks, Beasly had said—three truckloads of equipment delivered straight into their paws!

Taine sat down weakly on the steps.

They must have thought, he told himself, that he was co-operating! Maybe they had figured that he knew what they were about and so went along with them. Or perhaps they thought he was paying them for fixing up the TV set and the stove and radio.

But to tackle first things first, why had they repaired the TV set and the stove and radio? As a sort of rental payment? As a friendly gesture? Or as a sort of practice run to find out what they could about this world's technology? To find, perhaps, how their technology could be adapted to the materials and conditions on this planet they had found?

Taine raised a hand and rapped with his knuckles on the wall beside the stairs and the smooth white surface gave out a pinging sound.

He laid his ear against the wall and listened closely and it seemed to him he could hear a low-key humming, but if so it was so faint he could not be absolutely sure.

Banker Stevens' lawn mower was in there, behind the wall, and a lot of other stuff waiting for repair. They'd take the hide right off him, he thought, especially Banker Stevens. Stevens was a tight man.

Beasly must have been half-crazed with fear, he thought. When he had seen those things coming up out of the basement, he'd gone clean off his rocker. He'd gone straight through the door without even bothering to try to open it and now he was down in the village yapping to anyone who'd stop to listen to him.

No one ordinarily would pay Beasly much attention, but if he yapped long enough and wild enough, they'd probably do some checking. They'd come storming up here and they'd give the place a going over and they'd stand goggle-eyed at what they found in front and pretty soon some of them would have worked their way around to sort of running things.

And it was none of their business, Taine stubbornly told himself, his ever-present business sense rising to the fore. There was a lot of real estate lying around out there in his front yard and the only way anyone could get to it was by going through the house. That being the case, it stood to reason that all that land out there was his. Maybe it wasn't any good at all. There might be nothing there. But before he had other people overrunning it, he'd better check and see.

He went up the stairs and out into the garage.

The sun was still just above the northern horizon and there was nothing moving.

He found a hammer and some nails and a few short lengths of plank in the garage and took them in the house.

Towser, he saw, had taken advantage of the situation and was sleeping in the gold-upholstered chair. Taine didn't bother him.

Taine locked the back door and nailed some planks across it. He locked the kitchen and the bedroom windows and nailed planks across them, too.

That would hold the villagers for a while, he told himself, when they came tearing up here to see what was going on.

He got his deer rifle, a box of cartridges, a pair of binoculars and an old canteen out of a closet. He filled the canteen at the kitchen tap and stuffed a sack with food for him and Towser to eat along the way, for there was no time to wait and eat.

Then he went into the living room and dumped Towser out of the gold-upholstered chair.

"Come on, Tows," he said. "We'll go and look things over."

He checked the gasoline in the pickup and the tank was almost full.

He and the dog got in and he put the rifle within easy reach. Then he backed the truck and swung it around and headed out, north, across the desert.

It was easy traveling. The desert was as level as a floor. At times it got a little rough, but no worse than a lot of the back roads he traveled hunting down antiques.

The scenery didn't change. Here and there were low hills, but the desert itself kept on mostly level, unraveling itself into that far-off horizon. Taine kept on driving north, straight into the sun.

He hit some sandy stretches, but the sand was firm and hard and he had no trouble.

Half an hour out he caught up with the band of things—all sixteen of them—that had left the house. They were still traveling in line at their steady pace.

Slowing down the truck, Taine traveled parallel with them for a time, but there was no profit in it; they kept on traveling their course, looking neither right or left.

Speeding up, Taine left them behind.

The sun stayed in the north, unmoving, and that certainly was queer. Perhaps, Taine told himself, this world spun on its axis far more slowly than the Earth and the day was longer. From the way the sun appeared to be standing still, perhaps a good deal longer.

Hunched above the wheel, staring out into the endless stretch of desert, the strangeness of it struck him for the first time with its full impact.

This was another world—there could be no doubt of that—another planet circling another star, and where it was in actual space no one on Earth could have the least idea. And yet, through some machination of those sixteen things walking straight in line, it also was lying just outside the front door of his house.

Ahead of him a somewhat larger hill loomed out of the flatness of the desert. As he drew nearer to it, he made out a row of shining objects lined upon its crest. After a time he stopped the truck and got out with the binoculars.

Through the glasses, he saw that the shining things were the same sort of milk-glass contraptions as had been in the woods. He counted eight of them, shining in the sun, perched upon some sort of rock-gray cradles. And there were other cradles empty.

He took the binoculars from his eyes and stood there for a moment, considering the advisibility of climbing the hill and investigating closely. But he shook his head. There'd be time for that later on. He'd better keep on moving. This was not a real exploring foray, but a quick reconnaissance.

He climbed into the truck and drove on, keeping watch upon the gas gauge. When it came close to half full he'd have to turn around and go back home again.

Ahead of him he saw a faint whiteness above the dim horizon

line and he watched it narrowly. At times it faded away and then came in again, but whatever it might be was so far off he could make nothing of it.

He glanced down at the gas gauge and it was close to the half-way mark. He stopped the pickup and got out with the binoculars.

As he moved around to the front of the machine he was puzzled at how slow and tired his legs were and then remembered—he should have been in bed many hours ago. He looked at his watch and it was two o'clock and that meant, back on Earth, two o'clock in the morning. He had been awake for more than twenty hours and much of that time he had been engaged in the back-breaking work of digging out the strange thing in the woods.

He put up the binoculars and the elusive white line that he had been seeing turned out to be a range of mountains. The great, blue, craggy mass towered up above the desert with the gleam of snow on its peaks and ridges. They were a long way off, for even the powerful glasses brought them in as little more than a misty blueness.

He swept the glasses slowly back and forth and the mountains extended for a long distance above the horizon line.

He brought the glasses down off the mountains and examined the desert that stretched ahead of him. There was more of the same that he had been seeing—the same floorlike levelness, the same occasional mounds, the self-same scraggy vegetation.

And a house!

His hands trembled and he lowered the glasses, then put them up to his face again and had another look. It was a house, all right. A funny-looking house standing at the foot of one of the hillocks, still shadowed by the hillock so that one could not pick it out with the naked eye.

It seemed to be a small house. Its roof was like a blunted cone and it lay tight against the ground, as if it hugged or crouched against the ground. There was an oval opening that probably was a door, but there was no sign of windows.

He took the binoculars down again and stared at the hillock. Four or five miles away, he thought. The gas would stretch that far and even if it didn't he could walk the last few miles into Willow Bend.

It was queer, he thought, that a house should be all alone out
here. In all the miles he'd traveled in the desert he'd seen no
sign of life beyond the sixteen little ratlike things that marched
in single file, no sign of artificial structure other than the eight
milk-glass contraptions resting in their cradles.

He climbed into the pickup and put it into gear. Ten minutes
later he drew up in front of the house, which still lay within the
shadow of the hillock.

He got out of the pickup and hauled his rifle after him. Towser
leaped to the ground and stood with his hackles up, a deep growl
in his throat.

"What's the matter, boy?" asked Taine.

Towser growled again.

The house stood silent. It seemed to be deserted.

The walls were built, Taine saw, of rude, rough masonry
crudely set together, with a crumbling, mudlike substance used
in lieu of mortar. The roof originally had been of sod and that
was queer, indeed, for there was nothing that came close to sod
upon this expanse of desert. But now, although one could see
the lines where the sod strips had been fitted together, it was
nothing more than earth baked hard by the desert sun.

The house itself was featureless, entirely devoid of any orna-
ment, with no attempt at all to soften the harsh utility of it as a
simple shelter. It was the sort of thing that a shepherd people
might have put together. It had the look of age about it; the stone
had flaked and crumbled in the weather.

Rifle slung beneath his arm, Taine paced toward it. He reached
the door and glanced inside and there was darkness and no movement.

He glanced back for Towser and saw that the dog had crawled
beneath the truck and was peering out and growling.

"You stick around," said Taine. "Don't go running off."

With the rifle thrust before him, Taine stepped through the
door into the darkness. He stood for a long moment to allow his
eyes to become accustomed to the gloom.

Finally he could make out the room in which he stood. It was
plain and rough, with a rude stone bench along one wall and
queer unfunctional niches hollowed in another. One rickety piece

of wooden furniture stood in a corner, but Taine could not make out what its use might be.

An old and deserted place, he thought, abandoned long ago. Perhaps a shepherd people might have lived here in some long-gone age, when the desert had been a rich and grassy plain.

There was a door into another room and as he stepped through it he heard the faint, far-off booming sound and something else as well—the sound of pouring rain! From the open door that led out through the back he caught a whiff of salty breeze and he stood there frozen in the center of that second room.

Another one!

Another house that led to another world!

He walked slowly forward, drawn toward the outer door, and he stepped out into a cloudy, darkling day with the rain streaming down from wildly racing clouds. Half a mile away, across a field of jumbled broken, iron-gray boulders, lay a pounding sea that raged upon the coast, throwing great spumes of angry spray high into the air.

He walked out from the door and looked up at the sky, and the rain drops pounded at his face with a stinging fury. There was a chill and a dampness in the air and the place was eldritch —a world jerked straight from some ancient Gothic tale of goblin and of sprite.

He glanced around and there was nothing he could see, for the rain blotted out the world beyond this stretch of coast, but behind the rain he could sense or seemed to sense a presence that sent shivers down his spine. Gulping in fright, Taine turned around and stumbled back again through the door into the house.

One world away, he thought, was far enough; two worlds away was more than one could take. He trembled at the sense of utter loneliness that tumbled in his skull and suddenly this long-forsaken house became unbearable and he dashed out of it.

Outside the sun was bright and there was welcome warmth. His clothes were damp from rain and little beads of moisture lay on the rifle barrel.

He looked around for Towser and there was no sign of the dog. He was not underneath the pickup; he was nowhere in sight.

Taine called and there was no answer. His voice sounded lone and hollow in the emptiness and silence.

He walked around the house, looking for the dog, and there was no back door to the house. The rough rock walls of the sides of the house pulled in with that funny curvature and there was no back to the house at all.

But Taine was not interested; he had known how it would be. Right now he was looking for his dog and he felt the panic rising in him. Somehow it felt a long way from home.

He spent three hours at it. He went back into the house and Towser was not there. He went into the other world again and searched among the tumbled rocks and Towser was not there. He went back to the desert and walked around the hillock and then he climbed to the crest of it and used the binoculars and saw nothing but the lifeless desert, stretching far in all directions.

Dead-beat with weariness, stumbling, half asleep even as he walked, he went back to the pickup.

He leaned against it and tried to pull his wits together.

Continuing as he was would be a useless effort. He had to get some sleep. He had to go back to Willow Bend and fill the tank and get some extra gasoline so that he could range farther afield in his search for Towser.

He couldn't leave the dog out here—that was unthinkable. But he had to plan, he had to act intelligently. He would be doing Towser no good by stumbling around in his present shape.

He pulled himself into the truck and headed back for Willow Bend, following the occasional faint impressions that his tires had made in the sandy places, fighting a half-dead drowsiness that tried to seal his eyes shut.

Passing the higher hill on which the milk-glass things had stood, he stopped to walk around a bit so he wouldn't fall asleep behind the wheel. And now, he saw, there were only seven of the things resting in their cradles.

But that meant nothing to him now. All that meant anything was to hold off the fatigue that was closing down upon him, to cling to the wheel and wear off the miles, to get back to Willow Bend and get some sleep and then come back again to look for Towser.

Slightly more than halfway home he saw the other car and watched it in numb befuddlement, for this truck that he was

driving and the car at home in his garage were the only two
vehicles this side of his house.

He pulled the pickup to a halt and tumbled out of it.

The car drew up and Henry Horton and Beasly and a man
who wore a star leaped quickly out of it.

"Thank God we found you, man!" cried Henry, striding over
to him.

"I wasn't lost," protested Taine. "I was coming back."

"He's all beat out," said the man who wore the star.

"This is Sheriff Hanson," Henry said. "We were following your
tracks."

"I lost Towser," Taine mumbled. "I had to go and leave him.
Just leave me be and go and hunt for Towser. I can make it
home."

He reached out and grabbed the edge of the pickup's door to
hold himself erect.

"You broke down the door," he said to Henry. "You broke into
my house and you took my car—"

"We had to do it, Hiram. We were afraid that something might
have happened to you. The way that Beasly told it, it stood your
hair on end."

"You better get him in the car," the sheriff said. "I'll drive the
pickup back."

"But I have to hunt for Towser!"

"You can't do anything until you've had some rest."

Henry grabbed him by the arm and led him to the car and
Beasly held the rear door open.

"You got any idea what this place is?" Henry whispered con-
spiratorially.

"I don't positively know," Taine mumbled. "Might be some
other—"

Henry chuckled. "Well, I guess it doesn't really matter. Whatever it may be, it's put us on the map. We're in all the news-
casts and the papers are plastering us in headlines and the town
is swarming with reporters and cameramen and there are big
officials coming. Yes, sir, I tell you, Hiram, this will be the making
of us—"

Taine heard no more. He was fast asleep before he hit the seat.

He came awake and lay quietly in the bed and he saw the shades were drawn and the room was cool and peaceful.

It was good, he thought, to wake in a room you knew—in a room that one had known for his entire life, in a house that had been the Taine house for almost a hundred years.

Then memory clouted him and he sat bolt upright.

And now he heard it—the insistent murmur from outside the window.

He vaulted from the bed and pulled one shade aside. Peering out, he saw the cordon of troops that held back the crowd that overflowed his back yard and the back yards back of that.

He let the shade drop back and started hunting for his shoes, for he was fully dressed. Probably Henry and Beasly, he told himself, had dumped him into bed and pulled off his shoes and let it go at that. But he couldn't remember a single thing of it. He must have gone dead to the world the minute Henry had bundled him into the back seat of the car.

He found the shoes on the floor at the end of the bed and sat down upon the bed to pull them on.

And his mind was racing on what he had to do.

He'd have to get some gasoline somehow and fill up the truck and stash an extra can or two into the back and he'd have to take some food and water and perhaps his sleeping bag. For he wasn't coming back until he found his dog.

He got on his shoes and tied them, then went out into the living room. There was no one there, but there were voices in the kitchen.

He looked out the window and the desert lay outside, unchanged. The sun, he noticed, had climbed higher in the sky, but out in his front yard it was still forenoon.

He looked at his watch and it was six o'clock and from the way the shadows had been falling when he'd peered out of the bedroom window, he knew that it was 6:00 P.M. He realized with a guilty start that he must have slept almost around the clock. He had not meant to sleep that long. He hadn't meant to leave Towser out there that long.

He headed for the kitchen and there were three persons there— Abbie and Henry Horton and a man in military garb.

"There you are," cried Abbie merrily. "We were wondering when you would wake up."

"You have some coffee cooking, Abbie?"

"Yes, a whole pot full of it. And I'll cook up something else for you."

"Just some toast," said Taine. "I haven't got much time. I have to hunt for Towser."

"Hiram," said Henry, "this is Colonel Ryan, National Guard. He has his boys outside."

"Yes, I saw them through the window."

"Necessary," said Henry. "Absolutely necessary. The sheriff couldn't handle it. The people came rushing in and they'd have torn the place apart. So I called the governor."

"Taine," the colonel said, "sit down. I want to talk with you."

"Certainly," said Taine, taking a chair. "Sorry to be in such a rush, but I lost my dog out there."

"This business," said the colonel, smugly, "is vastly more important than any dog could be."

"Well, colonel, that just goes to show that you don't know Towser. He's the best dog I ever had and I've had a lot of them. Raised him from a pup and he's been a good friend all these years—"

"All right," the colonel said, "so he is a friend. But still I have to talk with you."

"You just sit and talk," Abbie said to Taine. "I'll fix up some cakes and Henry brought over some of that sausage that we get out on the farm."

The back door opened and Beasly staggered in to the accompaniment of a terrific metallic banging. He was carrying three empty five-gallon gas cans in one hand and two in the other hand and they were bumping and banging together as he moved.

"Say," yelled Taine, "what's going on here?"

"Now, just take it easy," Henry said. "You have no idea the problems that we have. We wanted to get a big gas tank moved through here, but we couldn't do it. We tried to rip out the back of the kitchen to get it through, but we couldn't—"

"You did what!"

"We tried to rip out the back of the kitchen," Henry told him calmly. "You can't get one of those big storage tanks through an

ordinary door. But when we tried, we found that the entire
house is boarded up inside with the same kind of material that
you used down in the basement. You hit it with an axe and it
blunts the steel—"

"But, Henry, this is my house and there isn't anyone who has
the right to start tearing it apart."

"Fat chance," the colonel said. "What I would like to know,
Taine, what is that stuff that we couldn't break through?"

"Now you take it easy, Hiram," cautioned Henry. "We have a
big new world waiting for us out there—"

"It isn't waiting for you or anyone," yelled Taine.

"And we have to explore it and to explore it we need a stock-
pile of gasoline. So since we can't have a storage tank, we're getting together as many gas cans as possible and then we'll run a
hose through here—"

"But, Henry—"

"I wish," said Henry sternly, "that you'd quit interrupting me
and let me have my say. You can't even imagine the logistics that
we face. We're bottlenecked by the size of a regulation door. We
have to get supplies out there and we have to get transport. Cars
and trucks won't be so bad. We can disassemble them and lug
them through piecemeal, but a plane will be a problem."

"You listen to me, Henry. There isn't anyone going to haul a
plane through here. This house has been in my family for almost
a hundred years and I own it and I have a right to it and you
can't come in high-handed and start hauling stuff through it."

"But," said Henry plaintively, "we need a plane real bad. You
can cover so much more ground when you have a plane."

Beasly went banging through the kitchen with his cans and out
into the living room.

The colonel sighed. "I had hoped, Mr. Taine, that you would
understand how the matter stood. To me it seems very plain that
it's your patriotic duty to co-operate with us in this. The government, of course, could exercise the right of eminent domain and
start condemnation action, but it would rather not do that. I'm
speaking unofficially, of course, but I think it's safe to say the
government would much prefer to arrive at an amicable agreement."

"I doubt," Taine said, bluffing, not knowing anything about it, "that the right to eminent domain would be applicable. As I understand it, it applies to buildings and to roads—"

"This is a road," the colonel told him flatly. "A road right through your house to another world."

"First," Taine declared, "the government would have to show it was in the public interest and that refusal of the owner to relinquish title amounted to an interference in government procedure and—"

"I think," the colonel said, "that the government can prove it is in the public interest."

"I think," Taine said angrily, "I better get a lawyer."

"If you really mean that," Henry offered, ever helpful, "and you want to get a good one—and I presume you do—I would be pleased to recommend a firm that I am sure would represent your interests most ably and be, at the same time, fairly reasonable in cost."

The colonel stood up, seething. "You'll have a lot to answer, Taine. There'll be a lot of things the government will want to know. First of all, they'll want to know just how you engineered this. Are you ready to tell that?"

"No," said Taine, "I don't believe I am."

And he thought with some alarm: They think that I'm the one who did it and they'll be down on me like a pack of wolves to find out just how I did it. He had visions of the FBI and the state department and the Pentagon and, even sitting down, he felt shaky in the knees.

The colonel turned around and marched stiffly from the kitchen. He went out the back and slammed the door behind him.

Henry looked at Taine speculatively.

"Do you really mean it?" he demanded. "Do you intend to stand up to them?"

"I'm getting sore," said Taine. "They can't come in here and take over without even asking me. I don't care what anyone may think, this is my house. I was born here and I've lived here all my life and I like the place and—"

"Sure," said Henry. "I know just how you feel."

"I suppose it's childish of me, but I wouldn't mind so much if they showed a willingness to sit down and talk about what they meant to do once they'd taken over. But there seems no disposition to even ask me what I think about it. And I tell you, Henry, this is different than it seems. This isn't a place where we can walk in and take over, no matter what Washington may think. There's something out there and we better watch our step—"

"I was thinking," Henry interrupted, "as I was sitting here, that your attitude is most commendable and deserving of support. It has occurred to me that it would be most unneighborly of me to go on sitting here and leave you in the fight alone. We could hire ourselves a fine array of legal talent and we could fight the case and in the meantime we could form a land and development company and that way we could make sure that this new world of yours is used the way it should be used.

"It stands to reason, Hiram, that I am the one to stand beside you, shoulder to shoulder, in this business since we're already partners in this TV deal."

"What's this about TV?" shrilled Abbie, slapping a plate of cakes down in front of Taine.

"Now, Abbie," Henry said patiently, "I have explained to you already that your TV set is back of that partition down in the basement and there isn't any telling when we can get it out."

"Yes, I know," said Abbie, bringing a platter of sausages and pouring a cup of coffee.

Beasly came in from the living room and went bumbling out the back.

"After all," said Henry, pressing his advantage, "I would suppose I had some hand in it. I doubt you could have done much without the computer I sent over."

And there it was again, thought Taine. Even Henry thought he'd been the one who did it.

"But didn't Beasly tell you?"

"Beasly said a lot, but you know how Beasly is."

And that was it, of course. To the villagers it would be no more than another Beasly story—another whopper that Beasly had dreamed up. There was no one who believed a word that Beasly said.

Taine picked up the cup and drank his coffee, gaining time to shape an answer and there wasn't any answer. If he told the truth, it would sound far less believable than any lie he'd tell.

"You can tell me, Hiram. After all, we're partners."

He's playing me for a fool, thought Taine. Henry thinks he can play anyone he wants for a fool and sucker.

"You wouldn't believe me if I told you, Henry."

"Well," Henry said, resignedly, getting to his feet, "I guess that part of it can wait."

Beasly came tramping and banging through the kitchen with another load of cans.

"I'll have to have some gasoline," said Taine, "if I'm going out for Towser."

"I'll take care of that right away," Henry promised smoothly. "I'll send Ernie over with his tank wagon and we can run a hose through here and fill up those cans. And I'll see if I can find someone who'll go along with you."

"That's not necessary. I can go alone."

"If we had a radio transmitter. Then you could keep in touch."

"But we haven't any. And, Henry, I can't wait. Towser's out there somewhere—"

"Sure, I know how much you thought of him. You go out and look for him if you think you have to and I'll get started on this other business. I'll get some lawyers lined up and we'll draw up some sort of corporate papers for our land development—"

"And, Hiram," Abbie said, "will you do something for me, please?"

"Why, certainly," said Taine.

"Would you speak to Beasly. It's senseless the way he's acting. There wasn't any call for him to up and leave us. I might have been a little sharp with him, but he's so simple-minded he's infuriating. He ran off and spent half a day helping Towser at digging out that woodchuck and—"

"I'll speak to him," said Taine.

"Thanks, Hiram. He'll listen to you. You're the only one he'll listen to. And I wish you could have fixed my TV set before all this came about. I'm just lost without it. It leaves a hole in the living room. It matched my other furniture, you know."

"Yes I know," said Taine.

"Coming, Abbie?" Henry asked, standing at the door.

He lifted a hand in a confidential farewell to Taine. "I'll see you later, Hiram. I'll get it all fixed up."

I just bet you will, thought Taine.

He went back to the table, after they were gone, and sat down heavily in a chair.

The front door slammed and Beasly came panting in, excited.

"Towser's back!" he yelled. "He's coming back and he's driving in the biggest woodchuck you ever clapped your eyes on."

Taine leaped to his feet.

"Woodchuck! That's an alien planet. It hasn't any woodchucks."

"You come and see," yelled Beasly.

He turned and raced back out again, with Taine following close behind.

It certainly looked considerably like a woodchuck—a sort of man-size woodchuck. More like a woodchuck out of a children's book, perhaps, for it was walking on its hind legs and trying to look dignified even while it kept a weather eye on Towser.

Towser was back a hundred feet or so, keeping a wary distance from the massive chuck. He had the pose of a good sheep-herding dog, walking in a crouch, alert to head off any break that the chuck might make.

The chuck came up close to the house and stopped. Then it did an about-face so that it looked back across the desert and it hunkered down.

It swung its massive head to gaze at Beasly and Taine and in the limpid brown eyes Taine saw more than the eyes of an animal.

Taine walked swiftly out and picked up the dog in his arms and hugged him tight against him. Towser twisted his head around and slapped a sloppy tongue across his master's face.

Taine stood with the dog in his arms and looked at the man-size chuck and felt a great relief and an utter thankfulness.

Everything was all right now, he thought. Towser had come back.

He headed for the house and out into the kitchen.

He put Towser down and got a dish and filled it at the tap. He placed it on the floor and Towser lapped at it thirstily, slopping water all over the linoleum.

"Take it easy, there," warned Taine. "You don't want to overdo it."

He hunted in the refrigerator and found some scraps and put them in Towser's dish.

Towser wagged his tail with doggish happiness.

"By rights," said Taine, "I ought to take a rope to you, running off like that."

Beasly came ambling in.

"That chuck is a friendly cuss," he announced. "He's waiting for someone."

"That's nice," said Taine, paying no attention.

He glanced at the clock.

"It's seven-thirty," he said. "We can catch the news. You want to get it Beasly?"

"Sure. I know right where to get it. That fellow from New York."

"That's the one," said Taine.

He walked into the living room and looked out the window. The man-size chuck had not moved. He was sitting with his back to the house, looking back the way he'd come.

Waiting for someone, Beasly had said, and it looked as if he might be, but probably it was all just in Beasly's head.

And if he were waiting for someone, Taine wondered, who might that someone be? *What* might that someone be? Certainly by now the word had spread out that there was a door into another world. And how many doors, he wondered, had been opened through the ages?

Henry had said that there was a big new world out there waiting for Earthmen to move in. And that wasn't it at all. It was the other way around.

The voice of the news commentator came blasting from the radio in the middle of a sentence:

". . . finally got into the act. Radio Moscow said this evening that the Soviet delegate will make representations in the U.N. tomorrow for the internationalization of this other world and the gateway to it.

"From that gateway itself, the home of a man named Hiram Taine, there is no news. Complete security had been clamped down and a cordon of troops form a solid wall around the house, holding back the crowds. Attempts to telephone the residence are blocked by a curt voice which says that no calls are being accepted for that number. And Taine himself has not stepped from the house."

Taine walked back into the kitchen and sat down.

"He's talking about you," Beasly said importantly.

"Rumor circulated this morning that Taine, a quiet village repair man and dealer in antiques, and until yesterday a relative unknown, had finally returned from a trip which he made out into this new and unknown land. But what he found, if anything, no one yet can say. Nor is there any further information about this other place beyond the fact that it is a desert and, to the moment, lifeless.

"A small flurry of excitement was occasioned late yesterday by the finding of some strange object in the woods across the road from the residence, but this area likewise was swiftly cordoned off and to the moment Colonel Ryan, who commands the troops, will say nothing of what actually was found.

"Mystery man of the entire situation is one Henry Horton, who seems to be the only unofficial person to have entry to the Taine house. Horton, questioned earlier today, had little to say, but managed to suggest an air of great conspiracy. He hinted he and Taine were partners in some mysterious venture and left hanging in midair the half impression that he and Taine had collaborated in opening the new world.

"Horton, it is interesting to note, operates a small computer plant and it is understood on good authority that only recently he delivered a computer to Taine, or at least some sort of machine to which considerable mystery is attached. One story is that this particular machine had been in the process of development for six or seven years.

"Some of the answers to the matter of how all this did happen and what actually did happen must wait upon the findings of a team of scientists who left Washington this evening after an all-day conference at the White House, which was attended by representatives from the military, the state department, the security division and the special weapons section.

"Throughout the world the impact of what happened yesterday at Willow Bend can only be compared to the sensation of the news, almost twenty years ago, of the dropping of the first atomic bomb. There is some tendency among many observers to believe that the implications of Willow Bend, in fact, may be even more earth-shaking than were those at Hiroshima.

"Washington insists, as is only natural, that this matter is of internal concern only and that it intends to handle the situation as it best affects the national welfare.

"But abroad there is a rising storm of insistence that this is not a matter of national policy concerning one nation, but that it necessarily must be a matter of worldwide concern.

"There is an unconfirmed report that a U.N. observer will arrive in Willow Bend almost momentarily. France, Britain, Bolivia, Mexico and India have already requested permission of Washington to send observers to the scene and other nations undoubtedly plan to file similar requests.

"The world sits on edge tonight, waiting for the word from Willow Bend and—"

Taine reached out and clicked the radio to silence.

"From the sound of it," said Beasly, "we're going to be overrun by a batch of foreigners."

Yes, thought Taine, there might be a batch of foreigners, but not exactly in the sense that Beasly meant. The use of the word, he told himself, so far as any human was concerned, must be outdated now. No man of Earth ever again could be called a foreigner with alien life next door—literally next door. What were the people of the stone house?

And perhaps not the alien life of one planet only, but the alien life of many. For he himself had found another door into yet another planet and there might be many more such doors and what would these other worlds be like, and what was the purpose of the doors?

Someone, *something*, had found a way of going to another planet short of spanning light-years of lonely space—a simpler and a shorter way than flying through the gulfs of space. And once the way was open, then the way stayed open and it was as easy as walking from one room to another.

But one thing—one ridiculous thing—kept puzzling him and that was the spinning and the movement of the connected planets, of all the planets that must be linked together. You could not, he argued, establish solid, factual links between two objects that move independently of one another.

And yet, a couple of days ago, he would have contended just as stolidly that the whole idea on the face of it was fantastic and impossible. Still it had been done. And once one impossibility was accomplished, what logical man could say with sincerity that the second could not be?

The doorbell rang and he got up to answer it.

It was Ernie, the oil man.

"Henry said you wanted some gas and I came to tell you I can't get it until morning."

"That's all right," said Taine. "I don't need it now."

And swiftly slammed the door.

He leaned against it, thinking: I'll have to face them sometime. I can't keep the door locked against the world. Sometime, soon or late, the Earth and I will have to have this out.

And it was foolish, he thought, for him to think like this, but that was the way it was.

He had something here that the Earth demanded; something that Earth wanted or thought it wanted. And yet, in the last analysis, it was his responsibility. It had happened on his land, it had happened in his house; unwittingly, perhaps, he'd even aided and abetted it.

And the land and house are mine, he fiercely told himself, and that world out there was an extension of his yard. No matter how far or where it went, an extension of his yard.

Beasly had left the kitchen and Taine walked into the living room. Towser was curled up and snoring gently in the gold-upholstered chair.

Taine decided he would let him stay there. After all, he thought, Towser had won the right to sleep anywhere he wished.

He walked past the chair to the window and the desert stretched to its far horizon and there before the window sat the man-size woodchuck and Beasly side by side, with their backs turned to the window and staring out across the desert.

Somehow it seemed natural that the chuck and Beasly should be sitting there together—the two of them, it appeared to Taine, might have a lot in common.

And it was a good beginning—that a man and an alien creature from this other world should sit down companionably together.

He tried to envision the setup of these linked worlds, of which Earth was now a part, and the possibilities that lay inherent in the fact of linkage rolled thunder through his brain.

There would be contact between the Earth and these other worlds and what would come of it?

And come to think of it, the contact had been made already, but so naturally, so undramatically, that it failed to register as a great, important meeting. For Beasly and the chuck out there were contact and if it all should go like that, there was absolutely nothing for one to worry over.

This was no haphazard business, he reminded himself. It had been planned and executed with the smoothness of long practice. This was not the first world to be opened and it would not be the last.

The little ratlike things had spanned space—how many light-years of space one could not even guess—in the vehicle which he had unearthed out in the woods. They then had buried it, perhaps as a child might hide a dish by shoving it into a pile of sand. Then they had come to this very house and had set up the apparatus that had made this house a tunnel between one world and another. And once that had been done, the need of crossing space had been canceled out forever. There need be but one crossing and that one crossing would serve to link the planets.

And once the job was done the little ratlike things had left, but not before they had made certain that this gateway to their planet would stand against no matter what assault. They had sheathed the house inside the studdings with a wonder-material that would resist an ax and that, undoubtedly, would resist much more than a simple ax.

And they had marched in drill-order single file out to the hill where eight more of the space machines had rested in their cradles. And now there were only seven there, in their cradles on the hill, and the ratlike things were gone and, perhaps, in time to come, they'd land on another planet and another doorway would be opened, a link to yet another world.

But more, Taine thought, than the linking of mere worlds. It would be, as well, the linking of the peoples of those worlds.

The little ratlike creatures were the explorers and the pioneers who sought out other Earthlike planets and the creature waiting with Beasly just outside the window must also serve its purpose and perhaps in time to come there would be a purpose which man would also serve.

He turned away from the window and looked around the room and the room was exactly as it had been ever since he could remember it. With all the change outside, with all that was happening outside, the room remained unchanged.

This is the reality, thought Taine, this is all the reality there is. Whatever else may happen, this is where I stand—this room with its fireplace blackened by many winter fires, the bookshelves with the old thumbed volumes, the easy-chair, the ancient worn carpet —worn by beloved and unforgotten feet through the many years.

And this also, he knew, was the lull before the storm.

In just a little while the brass would start arriving—the team of scientists, the governmental functionaries, the military, the observers from the other countries, the officials from the U.N.

And against all these, he realized, he stood weaponless and shorn of his strength. No matter what a man might say or think, he could not stand off the world.

This was the last day that this would be the Taine house. After almost a hundred years, it would have another destiny.

And for the first time in all those years there'd be no Taine asleep beneath its roof.

He stood looking at the fireplace and the shelves of books and he sensed the old, pale ghosts walking in the room and he lifted a hesitant hand as if to wave farewell, not only to the ghosts but to the room as well. But before he got it up, he dropped it to his side.

What was the use, he thought.

He went out to the porch and sat down on the steps.

Beasly heard him and turned around.

"He's nice," he said to Taine, patting the chuck upon the back. "He's exactly like a great big teddy bear."

"Yes, I see," said Taine.

"And best of all, I can talk with him."

"Yes, I know," said Taine, remembering that Beasly could talk with Towser, too.

He wondered what it would be like to live in the simple world of Beasly. At times, he decided, it would be comfortable.

The ratlike things had come in the spaceship, but why had they come to Willow Bend, why had they picked this house, the only house in all the village where they would have found the equipment that they needed to build their apparatus so easily and so quickly? For there was no doubt that they had cannibalized the computer to get the equipment they needed. In that, at least, Henry had been right. Thinking back on it, Henry, after all, had played quite a part in it.

Could they have foreseen that on this particular week in this particular house the probability of quickly and easily doing what they had come to do had stood very high?

Did they, with all their other talents and technology, have clairvoyance as well?

"There's someone coming," Beasly said.

"I don't see a thing."

"Neither do I," said Beasly, "but Chuck told me that he saw them."

"Told you!"

"I told you we been talking. There, I can see them too."

They were far off, but they were coming fast—three dots rode rapidly out of the desert.

He sat and watched them come and he thought of going in to get the rifle, but he didn't stir from his seat upon the steps. The rifle would do no good, he told himself. It would be a senseless thing to get it; more than that, a senseless attitude. The least that man could do, he thought, was to meet these creatures of another world with clean and empty hands.

They were closer now and it seemed to him that they were sitting in invisible chairs that traveled very fast.

He saw that they were humanoid, to a degree at least, and there were only three of them.

They came in with a rush and stopped very suddenly a hundred feet or so from where he sat upon the steps.

He didn't move or say a word—there was nothing he could say. It was too ridiculous.

They were, perhaps, a little smaller than himself, and black as the ace of spades, and they wore skin tight shorts and vests that were somewhat oversize and both the shorts and vests were the blue of April skies.

But that was not the worst of it.

They sat on saddles, with horns in front and stirrups and a sort of bedroll tied on the back, but they had no horses.

The saddles floated in the air, with the stirrups about three feet above the ground and the aliens sat easily in the saddles and stared at him and he stared back at them.

Finally he got up and moved forward a step or two and when he did that the three swung from the saddles and moved forward, too, while the saddles hung there in the air, exactly as they'd left them.

Taine walked forward and the three walked forward until they were no more than six feet apart.

"They say hello to you," said Beasly. "They say welcome to you."

"Well, all right, then, tell them— Say, how do you know all this!"

"Chuck tells me what they say and I tell you. You tell me and I tell him and he tells them. That's the way it works. That is what he's here for."

"Well, I'll be—," said Taine. "So you can really talk to him."

"I told you that I could," stormed Beasly. "I told you that I could talk to Towser, too, but you thought that I was crazy."

"Telepathy!" said Taine. And it was worse than ever now. Not only had the ratlike things known all the rest of it, but they'd known of Beasly, too.

"What was that you said, Hiram?"

"Never mind," said Taine. "Tell that friend of yours to tell them I'm glad to meet them and what can I do for them?"

He stood uncomfortably and stared at the three and he saw that their vests had many pockets and that the pockets were crammed, probably with their equivalent of tobacco and handkerchiefs and pocket knives and such.

"They say," said Beasly, "that they want to dicker."

"Dicker?"

"Sure, Hiram. You know, trade."

Beasly chuckled thinly. "Imagine them laying themselves open to a Yankee trader. That's what Henry says you are. He says you can skin a man on the slickest—"

"Leave Henry out of this," snapped Taine. "Let's leave Henry out of something."

He sat down on the ground and the three sat down to face him.

"Ask them what they have in mind to trade."

"Ideas," Beasly said.

"Ideas! That's a crazy thing—"

And then he saw it wasn't.

Of all the commodities that might be exchanged by an alien people, ideas would be the most valuable and the easiest to handle. They'd take no cargo room and they'd upset no economies —not immediately, that is—and they'd make a bigger contribution to the welfare of the cultures than trade in actual goods.

"Ask them," said Taine, "what they'll take for the idea back of those saddles they are riding."

"They say, what have you to offer?"

And that was the stumper. That was the one that would be hard to answer.

Automobiles and trucks, the internal gas engine—well, probably not. Because they already had the saddles. Earth was out of date in transportation from the viewpoint of these people.

Housing architecture—no, that was hardly an idea and, anyhow, there was that other house, so they knew of houses.

Cloth? No, they had cloth.

Paint, he thought. Maybe paint was it.

"See if they are interested in paint," Taine told Beasly.

"They say, what is it? Please explain yourself."

"O.K., then. Let's see. It's a protective device to be spread over almost any surface. Easily packaged and easily applied. Protects against weather and corrosion. It's decorative, too. Comes in all sorts of colors. And it's cheap to make."

"They shrug in their mind," said Beasly. "They're just slightly interested. But they'll listen more. Go ahead and tell them."

And that was more like it, thought Taine.

That was the kind of language that he could understand.

He settled himself more firmly on the ground and bent forward slightly, flicking his eyes across the three deadpan, ebony faces, trying to make out what they might be thinking.

There was no making out. Those were three of the deadest pans he had ever seen.

It was all familiar. It made him feel at home. He was in his element.

And in the three across from him, he felt somehow subconsciously, he had the best dickering opposition he had ever met. And that made him feel good too.

"Tell them," he said, "that I'm not quite sure. I may have spoken up too hastily. Paint, after all, is a mighty valuable idea."

"They say, just as a favor to them, not that they're really interested, would you tell them a little more."

Got them hooked, Taine told himself. If he could only play it right—

He settled down to dickering in earnest.

Hours later Henry Horton showed up. He was accompanied by a very urbane gentleman, who was faultlessly turned out and who carried beneath his arm an impressive attaché case.

Henry and the man stopped on the steps in sheer astonishment.

Taine was squatted on the ground with a length of board and he was daubing paint on it while the aliens watched. From the daubs here and there upon their anatomies, it was plain to see the aliens had been doing some daubing of their own. Spread all over the ground were other lengths of half-painted boards and a couple of dozen old cans of paint.

Taine looked up and saw Henry and the man.

"I was hoping," he said, "that someone would show up."

"Hiram," said Henry, with more importance than usual, "may I present Mr. Lancaster. He is a special representative of the United Nations."

"I'm glad to meet you, sir," said Taine. "I wonder if you would—"

"Mr. Lancaster," Henry explained grandly, "was having some slight difficulty getting through the lines outside, so I volunteered my services. I've already explained to him our joint interest in this matter."

"It was very kind of Mr. Horton," Lancaster said. "There was this stupid sergeant—"

"It's all in knowing," Henry said, "how to handle people."

The remark, Taine noticed, was not appreciated by the man from the U.N.

"May I inquire, Mr. Taine," asked Lancaster, "exactly what you're doing?"

"I'm dickering," said Taine.

"Dickering. What a quaint way of expressing—"

"An old Yankee word," said Henry quickly, "with certain connotations of its own. When you trade with someone you are exchanging goods, but if you're dickering with him you're out to get his hide."

"Interesting," said Lancaster. "And I suppose you're out to skin these gentlemen in the sky-blue vests—"

"Hiram," said Henry, proudly, "is the sharpest dickerer in these parts. He runs an antique business and he has to dicker hard—"

"And may I ask," said Lancaster, ignoring Henry finally, "what you might be doing with these cans of paint? Are these gentlemen potential customers for paint or—"

Taine threw down the board and rose angrily to his feet.

"If you'd both shut up!" he shouted. "I've been trying to say something ever since you got here and I can't get in a word. And I tell you, it's important—"

"Hiram!" Henry exclaimed in horror.

"It's quite all right," said the U.N. man. "We *have* been jabbering. And now, Mr. Taine?"

"I'm backed into a corner," Taine told him, "and I need some help. I've sold these fellows on the idea of paint, but I don't know a thing about it—the principle back of it or how it's made or what goes into it or—"

"But, Mr. Taine, if you're selling them the paint, what difference does it make—"

"I'm not selling them the paint," yelled Taine. "Can't you understand that? They don't want the paint. They want the *idea* of paint, the principle of paint. It's something that they never thought of and they're interested. I offered them the paint idea for the idea of their saddles and I've almost got it—"

"Saddles? You mean those things over there, hanging in the air?"

"That is right. Beasly, would you ask one of our friends to demonstrate a saddle?"

"You bet I will," said Beasly.

"What," demanded Henry, "has Beasly got to do with this?"

"Beasly in an interpreter. I guess you'd call him a telepath. You remember how he always claimed he could talk with Towser?"

"Beasly was always claiming things."

"But this time he was right. He tells Chuck, that funny-looking monster, what I want to say and Chuck tells these aliens. And these aliens tell Chuck and Chuck tells Beasly and Beasly tells me."

"Ridiculous!" snorted Henry. "Beasly hasn't got the sense to be . . . what did you say he was?"

"A telepath," said Taine.

One of the aliens had gotten up and climbed into a saddle. He rode it forth and back. Then he swung out of it and sat down again.

"Remarkable," said the U.N. man. "Some sort of antigravity unit, with complete control. We could make use of that, indeed."

He scraped his hand across his chin.

"And you're going to exchange the idea of paint for the idea of that saddle?"

"That's exactly it," said Taine, "but I need some help. I need a chemist or a paint manufacturer or someone to explain how paint is made. And I need some professor or other who'll understand what they're talking about when they tell me the idea of the saddle."

"I see," said Lancaster. "Yes, indeed, you have a problem. Mr. Taine, you seem to me a man of some discernment—"

"Oh, he's all of that," interrupted Henry. "Hiram's quite astute."

"So I suppose you'll understand," said the U.N. man, "that this whole procedure is quite irregular—"

"But it's not," exploded Taine. "That's the way they operate. They open up a planet and then they exchange ideas. They've been doing that with other planets for a long, long, time. And ideas are all they want, just the new ideas, because that is the way to keep on building a technology and culture. And they have a lot of ideas, sir, that the human race can use."

"That is just the point," said Lancaster. "This is perhaps the most important thing that has ever happened to us humans. In just a short year's time we can obtain data and ideas that will put us ahead—theoretically, at least—by a thousand years. And in a thing that is so important, we should have experts on the job—"

"But," protested Henry, "you can't find a man who'll do a better dickering job than Hiram. When you dicker with him your back teeth aren't safe. Why don't you leave him be? He'll do a job for you. You can get your experts and your planning groups together and let Hiram front for you. These folks have accepted him and have proved they'll do business with him and what more do you want? All he needs is a little help."

Beasly came over and faced the U.N. man.

"I won't work with no one else," he said. "If you kick Hiram out of here, then I go with him. Hiram's the only person who ever treated me like a human—"

"There, you see!" Henry said, triumphantly.

"Now, wait a second, Beasly," said the U.N. man. "We could make it worth your while. I should imagine that an interpreter in a situation such as this could command a handsome salary."

"Money don't mean a thing to me," said Beasly. "It won't buy me friends. People still will laugh at me."

"He means it, mister," Henry warned. "There isn't anyone who can be as stubborn as Beasly. I know; he used to work for us."

The U.N. man looked flabbergasted and not a little desperate.

"It will take you quite some time," Henry pointed out, "to find another telepath—leastwise one who can talk to these people here."

The U.N. man looked as if he were strangling. "I doubt," he said, "there's another one on Earth."

"Well, all right," said Beasly, brutally, "let's make up our minds. I ain't standing here all day."

"All right," cried the U.N. man. "You two go ahead. Please, will you go ahead? This is a chance we can't let slip through our fingers. Is there anything you want? Anything I can do for you?"

"Yes, there is," said Taine. "There'll be the boys from Washington and bigwigs from other countries. Just keep them off my back."

"I'll explain most carefully to everyone. There'll be no interference."

"And I need that chemist and someone who'll know about the saddles. And I need them quick. I can stall these boys a little longer, but not for too much longer."

"Anyone you need," said the U.N. man. "Anyone at all. I'll have them here in hours. And in a day or two there'll be a pool of experts waiting for whenever you may need them—on a moment's notice."

"Sir," said Henry, unctuously, "that's most co-operative. Both Hiram and I appreciate it greatly. And now, since this is settled, I understand that there are reporters waiting. They'll be interested in your statement."

The U.N. man, it seemed, didn't have it in him to protest. He and Henry went tramping up the stairs.

Taine turned around and looked out across the desert.

"It's a big front yard," he said.

Robert Bloch

Robert Bloch likes to say that he has the heart of a little boy—pickled in alcohol on his desk.

And I think he has, for this mild, gentle soul, who gazes benignly at the world from his lanky, sharp-featured height, writes the most grisly tales imaginable. Notably, he wrote the story entitled "Alfred Hitchcock's Psycho" which, when it was first written, was known simply as *Psycho*.

I met Bob rather slightly at the 11th Convention (Philadelphia, 1953) but our real friendship dates from the 13th Convention (Cleveland, 1955). Thereafter we carried on a correspondence that saw weekly letters exchanged for four years—until Bob was carried by the tidal wave of "Alfred Hitchcock's Psycho" into the engulfing arms of Hollywood where he disappeared (I hope, not forever) from the ken of mortal man.

Bob is one of the three science fiction personalities who, for his wit, humor, presence of mind and general amiability, serves as perennial toastmaster at the conventions. (Anthony Boucher, mystery reviewer for the New York *Times*, and beloved one-time editor of *The Magazine of Fantasy and Science Fiction* is the second.)

On the occasion of the 17th Convention (Detroit, 1959), Bob and I shared the role of toastmaster. Influenced by the usual course of events at the Academy Award dinner in Hollywood we got up after the banquet in our glisten and glitter and announced the Hugo winners in alternation.

It was Bob's turn when we came to the short-story award and he opened the envelope and remained standing and staring, his eyes slightly protruding and his Adam's apple bobbing slowly up and down. I looked over his shoulder and the card he held announced his own story, "The Hell-Bound Train" to be the winner.

I

With a gay laugh, I plucked the card from his nerveless fingers, and announced the result. I placed the Hugo in his trembling hands and guided him to a seat where he might for just a moment be alone with his glory.

7

THE HELL-BOUND TRAIN

When Martin was a little boy, his Daddy was a Railroad Man. Daddy never rode the high iron, but he walked the tracks for the *CB&Q*, and he was proud of his job. And every night when he got drunk, he sang this old song about *That Hell-Bound Train*.

Martin didn't quite remember any of the words, but he couldn't forget the way his Daddy sang them out. And when Daddy made the mistake of getting drunk in the afternoon and got squeezed between a Pennsy tank-car and an *AT&SF* gondola, Martin sort of wondered why the Brotherhood didn't sing the song at his funeral.

After that, things didn't go so good for Martin, but somehow he always recalled Daddy's song. When Mom up and ran off with a traveling salesman from Keokuk (Daddy must have turned over in his grave, knowing she'd done such a thing, and with a *passenger*, too!) Martin hummed the tune to himself every night in the Orphan Home. And after Martin himself ran away, he used to whistle the song softly at night in the jungles, after the other bindlestiffs were asleep.

Martin was on the road for four-five years before he realized he wasn't getting anyplace. Of course he'd tried his hand at a lot of things—picking fruit in Oregon, washing dishes in a Montana hash-house, stealing hub-caps in Denver and tires in Oklahoma City—but by the time he'd put in six months on the chain-gang down in Alabama he knew he had no future drifting around this way on his own.

So he tried to get on the railroad like his Daddy had and they told him that times were bad.

But Martin couldn't keep away from the railroads. Wherever he traveled, he rode the rods; he'd rather hop a freight heading north in sub-zero weather than lift his thumb to hitch a ride with a Cadillac headed for Florida. Whenever he managed to get hold of a can of Sterno, he'd sit there under a nice warm culvert, think about the old days, and often as not he'd hum the song about *That Hell-Bound Train.* That was the train the drunks and the sinners rode—the gambling men and the grifters, the big-time spenders, the skirt-chasers, and all the jolly crew. It would be really fine to take a trip in such good company, but Martin didn't like to think of what happened when that train finally pulled into the Depot Way Down Yonder. He didn't figure on spending eternity stoking boilers in Hell, without even a Company Union to protect him. Still, it would be a lovely ride. If there was *such* a thing as a Hell-Bound Train. Which, of course, there wasn't.

At least Martin didn't *think* there was, until that evening when he found himself walking the tracks heading south, just outside of Appleton Junction. The night was cold and dark, the way November nights are in the Fox River Valley, and he knew he'd have to work his way down to New Orleans for the winter, or maybe even Texas. Somehow he didn't much feel like going, even though he'd heard tell that a lot of those Texas automobiles had solid gold hub-caps.

No sir, he just wasn't cut out for petty larceny. It was worse than a sin—it was unprofitable, too. Bad enough to do the Devil's work, but then to get such miserable pay on top of it! Maybe he'd better let the Salvation Army convert him.

Martin trudged along humming Daddy's song, waiting for a rattler to pull out of the Junction behind him. He'd have to catch it—there was nothing else for him to do.

But the first train to come along came from the other direction, roaring towards him along the track from the south.

Martin peered ahead, but his eyes couldn't match his ears, and so far all he could recognize was the sound. It *was* a train, though; he felt the steel shudder and sing beneath his feet.

And yet, how could it be? The next station south was Neenah-Menasha, and there was nothing due out of there for hours.

The clouds were thick overhead, and the field-mists rolled like a cold fog in a November midnight. Even so, Martin should have been able to see the headlight as the train rushed on. But there was only the whistle, screaming out of the black throat of the night. Martin could recognize the equipment of just about any locomotive ever built, but he'd never heard a whistle that sounded like this one. It wasn't signalling; it was screaming like a lost soul.

He stepped to one side, for the train was almost on top of him now. And suddenly there it was, looming along the tracks and grinding to a stop in less time than he'd believed possible. The wheels hadn't been oiled, because they screamed too, screamed like the damned. But the train slid to a halt and the screams died away into a series of low, groaning sounds, and Martin looked up and saw that this was a passenger train. It was big and black, without a single light shining in the engine cab or any of the long string of cars; Martin couldn't read any lettering on the sides, but he was pretty sure this train didn't belong on the Northwestern Road.

He was even more sure when he saw the man clamber down out of the forward car. There was something wrong about the way he walked, as though one of his feet dragged, and about the lantern he carried. The lantern was dark, and the man held it up to his mouth and blew, and instantly it glowed redly. You don't have to be a member of the Railway Brotherhood to know that this is a mighty peculiar way of lighting a lantern.

As the figure approached, Martin recognized the conductor's cap perched on his head, and this made him feel a little better for a moment—until he noticed that it was worn a bit too high, as though there might be something sticking up on the forehead underneath it.

Still, Martin knew his manners, and when the man smiled at him, he said, "Good evening, Mr. Conductor."

"Good evening, Martin."

"How did you know my name?"

The man shrugged. "How did you know I was the Conductor?"

"You *are*, aren't you?"

"To you, yes. Although other people, in other walks of life, may recognize me in different roles. For instance, you ought to see

what I look like to the folks out in Hollywood." The man grinned.
"I travel a great deal," he explained.

"What brings you here?" Martin asked.

"Why, you ought to know the answer to that, Martin. I came
because you needed me. Tonight, I suddenly realized you were
backsliding. Thinking of joining the Salvation Army, weren't
you?"

"Well—" Martin hesitated.

"Don't be ashamed. To err is human, as somebody-or-other
once said. *Reader's Digest*, wasn't it? Never mind. The point is,
I felt you needed me. So I switched over and came your way."

"What for?"

"Why, to offer you a ride, of course. Isn't it better to travel
comfortably by train than to march along the cold streets behind
a Salvation Army band? Hard on the feet, they tell me, and even
harder on the eardrums."

"I'm not sure I'd care to ride your train, sir," Martin said. "Considering where I'm likely to end up."

"Ah, yes. The old argument." The Conductor sighed. "I suppose
you'd prefer some sort of bargain, is that it?"

"Exactly," Martin answered.

"Well, I'm afraid I'm all through with that sort of thing. There's
no shortage of prospective passengers any more. Why should I
offer you any special inducements?"

"You must want me, or else you wouldn't have bothered to go
out of your way to find me."

The Conductor sighed again. "There you have a point. Pride
was always my besetting weakness, I admit. And somehow I'd
hate to lose you to the competition, after thinking of you as my
own all these years." He hesitated. "Yes, I'm prepared to deal
with you on your own terms, if you insist."

"The terms?" Martin asked.

"Standard proposition. Anything you want."

"Ah," said Martin.

"But I warn you in advance, there'll be no tricks. I'll grant you
any wish you can name—but in return, you must promise to ride
the train when the time comes."

"Suppose it never comes?"

"It will."

"Suppose I've got the kind of a wish that will keep me off forever?"

"There is no such wish."

"Don't be too sure."

"Let me worry about that," the Conductor told him. "No matter what you have in mind, I warn you that I'll collect in the end. And there'll be none of this last-minute hocus-pocus, either. No last-hour repentances, no blonde *frauleins* or fancy lawyers showing up to get you off. I offer a clean deal. That is to say, you'll get what you want, and I'll get what I want."

"I've heard you trick people. They say you're worse than a used-car salesman."

"Now, wait a minute—"

"I apologize," Martin said, hastily. "But it *is* supposed to be a fact that you can't be trusted."

"I admit it. On the other hand, you seem to think you have found a way out."

"A sure-fire proposition."

"Sure-fire? Very funny!" The man began to chuckle, then halted. "But we waste valuable time, Martin. Let's get down to cases. What do you want from me?"

Martin took a deep breath. "I want to be able to stop Time."

"Right now?"

"No. Not yet. And not for everybody. I realize that would be impossible, of course. But I want to be able to stop Time for myself. Just once, in the future. Whenever I get to a point where I know I'm happy and contented, that's where I'd like to stop. So I can just keep on being happy forever."

"That's quite a proposition," the Conductor mused. "I've got to admit I've never heard anything just like it before—and believe me, I've listened to some lulus in my day." He grinned at Martin. "You've really been thinking about this, haven't you?"

"For years," Martin admitted. Then he coughed. "Well, what do you say?"

"It's not impossible, in terms of your own *subjective* time-sense," the Conductor murmured. "Yes, I think it could be arranged."

"But I mean *really* to stop. Not for me just to *imagine* it."

"I understand. And it can be done."

"Then you'll agree?"

"Why not? I promised you, didn't I? Give me your hand."

Martin hesitated. "Will it hurt very much? I mean, I don't like the sight of blood, and—"

"Nonsense! You've been listening to a lot of poppycock. We already have made our bargain, my boy. I merely intend to put something into your hand. The ways and means of fulfilling your wish. After all, there's no telling at just what moment you may decide to exercise the agreement, and I can't drop everything and come running. So it's better if you can regulate matters for yourself."

"You're going to give me a Time-stopper?"

"That's the general idea. As soon as I can decide what would be practical." The Conductor hesitated. "Ah, the very thing! Here, take my watch."

He pulled it out of his vest-pocket; a railroad watch in a silver case. He opened the back and made a delicate adjustment; Martin tried to see just exactly what he was doing, but the fingers moved in a blinding blur.

"There we are," the Conductor smiled. "It's all set, now. When you finally decide where you'd like to call a halt, merely turn the stem in reverse and unwind the watch until it stops. When it stops, Time stops, for you. Simple enough?" And the Conductor dropped the watch into Martin's hand.

The young man closed his fingers tightly around the case. "That's all there is to it, eh?"

"Absolutely. But remember—you can stop the watch only once. So you'd better make sure that you're satisfied with the moment you choose to prolong. I caution you in all fairness; make very certain of your choice."

"I will." Martin grinned. "And since you've been so fair about it, I'll be fair, too. There's one thing you seem to have forgotten. It doesn't really matter *what* moment I choose. Because once I stop Time for myself, that means I stay where I am forever. I'll never have to get any older. And if I don't get any older, I'll never die. And if I never die, then I'll never have to take a ride on your train."

The Conductor turned away. His shoulders shook convulsively, and he may have been crying. "And you said *I* was worse than a used-car salesman," he gasped, in a strangled voice.

Then he wandered off into the fog, and the train-whistle gave an impatient shriek, and all at once it was moving swiftly down the track, rumbling out of sight in the darkness.

Martin stood there, blinking down at the silver watch in his hand. If it wasn't that he could actually see it and feel it there, and if he couldn't smell that peculiar odor, he might have thought he'd imagined the whole thing from start to finish—train, Conductor, bargain, and all.

But he had the watch, and he could recognize the scent left by the train as it departed, even though there aren't many locomotives around that use sulphur and brimstone as fuel.

And he had no doubts about his bargain. That's what came of thinking things through to a logical conclusion. Some fools would have settled for wealth, or power, or Kim Novak. Daddy might have sold out for a fifth of whiskey.

Martin knew that he'd made a better deal. Better? It was foolproof. All he needed to do now was choose his moment.

He put the watch in his pocket and started back down the railroad track. He hadn't really had a destination in mind before, but he did now. He was going to find a moment of happiness. . . .

Now young Martin wasn't altogether a ninny. He realized perfectly well that happiness is a relative thing; there are conditions and degrees of contentment, and they vary with one's lot in life. As a hobo, he was often satisfied with a warm handout, a double-length bench in the park, or a can of Sterno made in 1957 (a vintage year). Many a time he had reached a state of momentary bliss through such simple agencies, but he was aware that there were better things. Martin determined to seek them out.

Within two days he was in the great city of Chicago. Quite naturally, he drifted over to West Madison Street, and there he took steps to elevate his role in life. He became a city bum, a panhandler, a moocher. Within a week he had risen to the point where happiness was a meal in a regular one-arm luncheon joint, a two-bit flop on a real army cot in a real flophouse, and a full fifth of muscatel.

There was a night, after enjoying all three of these luxuries to the full, when Martin thought of unwinding his watch at the pinnacle of intoxication. But he also thought of the faces of the honest johns he'd braced for a handout today. Sure, they were squares, but they were prosperous. They wore good clothes, held good jobs, drove nice cars. And for them, happiness was even more ecstatic—they ate dinner in fine hotels, they slept on inner-spring mattresses, they drank blended whiskey.

Squares or no, they had something there. Martin fingered his watch, put aside the temptation to hock it for another bottle of muscatel, and went to sleep determined to get himself a job and improve his happiness-quotient.

When he awoke he had a hangover, but the determination was still with him. Before the month was out Martin was working for a general contractor over on the South Side, at one of the big rehabilitation projects. He hated the grind, but the pay was good, and pretty soon he got himself a one-room apartment out on Blue Island Avenue. He was accustomed to eating in decent restaurants now, and he bought himself a comfortable bed, and every Saturday night he went down to the corner tavern. It was all very pleasant, but—

The foreman liked his work and promised him a raise in a month. If he waited around, the raise would mean that he could afford a second-hand car. With a car, he could even start picking up a girl for a date now and then. Other fellows on the job did, and they seemed pretty happy.

So Martin kept on working, and the raise came through and the car came through and pretty soon a couple of girls came through.

The first time it happened, he wanted to unwind his watch immediately. Until he got to thinking about what some of the older men always said. There was a guy named Charlie, for example, who worked alongside him on the hoist. "When you're young and don't know the score, maybe you get a kick out of running around with those pigs. But after a while, you want something better. A nice girl of your own. That's the ticket."

Martin felt he owed it to himself to find out. If he didn't like it better, he could always go back to what he had.

Almost six months went by before Martin met Lillian Gillis.

By that time he'd had another promotion and was working inside, in the office. They made him go to night school to learn how to do simple book-keeping, but it meant another fifteen bucks extra a week, and it was nicer working indoors.

And Lillian *was* a lot of fun. When she told him she'd marry him, Martin was almost sure that the time was now. Except that she was sort of—well, she was a *nice* girl, and she said they'd have to wait until they were married. Of course, Martin couldn't expect to marry her until he had a little more money saved up, and another raise would help, too.

That took a year. Martin was patient, because he knew it was going to be worth it. Every time he had any doubts, he took out his watch and looked at it. But he never showed it to Lillian, or anybody else. Most of the other men wore expensive wristwatches and the old silver railroad watch looked just a little cheap.

Martin smiled as he gazed at the stem. Just a few twists and he'd have something none of these other poor working slobs would ever have. Permanent satisfaction, with his blushing bride—

Only getting married turned out to be just the beginning. Sure, it was wonderful, but Lillian told him how much better things would be if they could move into a new place and fix it up. Martin wanted decent furniture, a TV set, a nice car.

So he started taking night courses and got a promotion to the front office. With the baby coming, he wanted to stick around and see his son arrive. And when it came, he realized he'd have to wait until it got a little older, started to walk and talk and develop a personality of its own.

About this time the company sent him out on the road as a trouble-shooter on some of those other jobs, and now he *was* eating at those good hotels, living high on the hog and the expense-account. More than once he was tempted to unwind his watch. This was the good life. . . . Of course, it would be even better if he just didn't have to *work*. Sooner or later, if he could cut in on one of the company deals, he could make a pile and retire. Then everything would be ideal.

It happened, but it took time. Martin's son was going to high school before he really got up there into the chips. Martin got a

strong hunch that it was now or never, because he wasn't exactly
a kid any more.

But right about then he met Sherry Westcott, and she didn't
seem to think he was middle-aged at all, in spite of the way he
was losing hair and adding stomach. She taught him that a *toupee*
could cover the bald spot and a cummerbund could cover the
potgut. In fact, she taught him quite a lot and he so enjoyed
learning that he actually took out his watch and prepared to unwind it.

Unfortunately, he chose the very moment that the private de-
tectives broke down the door of the hotel room, and then there
was a long stretch of time when Martin was so busy fighting the
divorce action that he couldn't honestly say he was enjoying any
given moment.

When he made the final settlement with Lil he was broke
again, and Sherry didn't seem to think he was so young, after all.
So he squared his shoulders and went back to work.

He made his pile, eventually, but it took longer this time, and
there wasn't much chance to have fun along the way. The fancy
dames in the fancy cocktail lounges didn't seem to interest him
any more, and neither did the liquor. Besides, the Doc had
warned him off that.

But there were other pleasures for a rich man to investigate.
Travel, for instance—and not riding the rods from one hick burg
to another, either. Martin went around the world by plane and
luxury liner. For a while it seemed as though he would find his
moment after all, visiting the Taj Mahal by moonlight. Martin
pulled out the battered old watchcase, and got ready to unwind
it. Nobody else was there to watch him—

And that's why he hesitated. Sure, this was an enjoyable moment, but he was alone. Lil and the kid were gone, Sherry was
gone, and somehow he'd never had time to make any friends.
Maybe if he found new congenial people, he'd have the ultimate
happiness. That must be the answer—it wasn't just money or
power or sex or seeing beautiful things. The real satisfaction lay
in friendship.

So on the boat trip home, Martin tried to strike up a few ac-
quaintances at the ship's bar. But all these people were much
younger, and Martin had nothing in common with them. Also

they wanted to dance and drink, and Martin wasn't in condition to appreciate such pastimes. Nevertheless, he tried.

Perhaps that's why he had the little accident the day before they docked in San Francisco. "Little accident" was the ship's doctor's way of describing it, but Martin noticed he looked very grave when he told him to stay in bed, and he'd called an ambulance to meet the liner at the dock and take the patient right to the hospital.

At the hospital, all the expensive treatment and the expensive smiles and the expensive words didn't fool Martin any. He was an old man with a bad heart, and they thought he was going to die.

But he could fool them. He still had the watch. He found it in his coat when he put on his clothes and sneaked out of the hospital.

He didn't have to die. He could cheat death with a single gesture—and he intended to do it as a free man, out there under a free sky.

That was the real secret of happiness. He understood it now. Not even friendship meant as much as freedom. This was the best thing of all—to be free of friends or family or the furies of the flesh.

Martin walked slowly beside the embankment under the night sky. Come to think of it, he was just about back where he'd started, so many years ago. But the moment was good, good enough to prolong forever. Once a bum, always a bum.

He smiled as he thought about it, and then the smile twisted sharply and suddenly, like the pain twisting sharply and suddenly in his chest. The world began to spin and he fell down on the side of the embankment.

He couldn't see very well, but he was still conscious, and he knew what had happened. Another stroke, and a bad one. Maybe this was it. Except that he wouldn't be a fool any longer. He wouldn't wait to see what was still around the corner.

Right now was his chance to use his power and save his life. And he was going to do it. He could still move, nothing could stop him.

He groped in his pocket and pulled out the old silver watch, fumbling with the stem. A few twists and he'd cheat death, he'd

never have to ride that Hell-Bound Train. He could go on forever.

Forever.

Martin had never really considered the word before. To go on
forever—but *how?* Did he *want* to go on forever, like this; a sick
old man, lying helplessly here in the grass?

No. He couldn't do it. He wouldn't do it. And suddenly he
wanted very much to cry, because he knew that somewhere along
the line he'd outsmarted himself. And now it was too late. His
eyes dimmed, there was a roaring in his ears . . .

He recognized the roaring, of course, and he wasn't at all surprised to see the train come rushing out of the fog up there on
the embankment. He wasn't surprised when it stopped, either, or
when the Conductor climbed off and walked slowly towards
him.

The Conductor hadn't changed a bit. Even his grin was still
the same.

"Hello, Martin," he said. "All aboard."

"I know," Martin whispered. "But you'll have to carry me. I
can't walk. I'm not even really talking any more, am I?"

"Yes you are," the Conductor said. "I can hear you fine. And
you can walk, too." He leaned down and placed his hand on
Martin's chest. There was a moment of icy numbness, and then,
sure enough, Martin could walk after all.

He got up and followed the Conductor along the slope, moving to the side of the train.

"In here?" he asked.

"No, the next car," the Conductor murmured. "I guess you're
entitled to ride Pullman. After all, you're quite a successful man.
You've tasted the joys of wealth and position and prestige. You've
known the pleasures of marriage and fatherhood. You've sampled
the delights of dining and drinking and debauchery, too, and
you traveled high, wide and handsome. So let's not have any
last-minute recriminations."

"All right," Martin sighed. "I can't blame you for my mistakes.
On the other hand, you can't take credit for what happened,
either. I worked for everything I got. I did it all on my own. I
didn't even need your watch."

"So you didn't," the Conductor said, smiling. "But would you mind giving it back to me now?"

"Need it for the next sucker, eh?" Martin muttered.

"Perhaps."

Something about the way he said it made Martin look up. He tried to see the Conductor's eyes, but the brim of his cap cast a shadow. So Martin looked down at the watch instead.

"Tell me something," he said, softly. "If I give you the watch, what will you do with it?"

"Why, throw it into the ditch," the Conductor told him. "That's all I'll do with it." And he held out his hand.

"What if somebody comes along and finds it? And twists the stem backwards, and stops Time?"

"Nobody would do that," the Conductor murmured. "Even if they knew."

"You mean, it was all a trick? This is only an ordinary, cheap watch?"

"I didn't say that," whispered the Conductor. "I only said that no one has ever twisted the stem backwards. They've all been like you, Martin—looking ahead to find that perfect happiness. Waiting for the moment that never comes."

The Conductor held out his hand again.

Martin sighed and shook his head. "You cheated me after all."

"You cheated yourself, Martin. And now you're going to ride that Hell-Bound Train."

He pushed Martin up the steps and into the car ahead. As he entered, the train began to move and the whistle screamed. And Martin stood there in the swaying Pullman, gazing down the aisle at the other passengers. He could see them sitting there, and somehow it didn't seem strange at all.

Here they were; the drunks and the sinners, the gambling men and the grifters, the big-time spenders, the skirt-chasers, and all the jolly crew. They knew where they were going, of course, but they didn't seem to give a damn. The blinds were drawn on the windows, yet it was light inside, and they were all living it up—singing and passing the bottle and roaring with laughter, throwing the dice and telling their jokes and bragging their big brags, just the way Daddy used to sing about them in the old song.

"**Mighty** nice traveling companions," Martin said. "Why, I've never seen such a pleasant bunch of people. I mean, they seem to be really enjoying themselves!"

The Conductor shrugged. "I'm afraid things won't be quite so jazzy when we pull into that Depot Way Down Yonder."

For the third time, he held out his hand. "Now, before you sit down, if you'll just give me that watch. A bargain's a bargain—"

Martin smiled. "A bargain's a bargain," he echoed. "I agreed to ride your train if I could stop Time when I found the right moment of happiness. And I think I'm about as happy right here as I've ever been."

Very slowly, Martin took hold of the silver watch-stem.

"No!" gasped the Conductor. "No!"

But the watch-stem turned.

"Do you realize what you've done?" the Conductor yelled. "Now we'll never reach the Depot! We'll just go on riding, all of us—forever!"

Martin grinned. "I know," he said. "But the fun is in the trip, not the destination. You taught me that. And I'm looking forward to a wonderful trip. Look, maybe I can even help. If you were to find me another one of those caps, now, and let me keep this watch—"

And that's the way it finally worked out. Wearing his cap and carrying his battered old silver watch, there's no happier person in or out of this world—now and forever—than Martin. Martin, the new Brakeman on That Hell-Bound Train.

1960
18th Convention
Pittsburgh

Daniel Keyes

It is difficult, as you all by now realize, for me to hand out Hugos, convinced as I am that in any one year, any of half a dozen stories of my own, rightly deserved the victory. Naturally, I mask this feeling with consummate skill and I believe I gave myself away only once.

That was at the 18th Convention (Pittsburgh, 1960)—a convention which, I might say as a purely personal opinion, was the best and most wonderful convention of all—when I found myself handing out the Hugo to Daniel Keyes for the story "Flowers for Algernon."

Now here was a story which struck me so forcefully that I was actually lost in admiration as I read it. So lost in admiration was I for the delicacy of his feeling, for the sure way in which he plucked at my heartstrings, for the skill with which he handled the remarkable *tour de force* involved in his method of telling the story, that I completely forgot to hate him.

When I announced the Hugo for that story in Pittsburgh, therefore, a sudden access of warmth entered my tones which must have shown, by comparison, that the cheer with which I handed out the other Hugos was synthetic.

My winged words cleft the air impassionedly as I delivered an impromptu encomium on the manifold excellences of Daniel Keyes. "How did he do it?" I demanded of the Muses. "How did he do it?"

I then looked up at a level about nine or ten feet from the floor in order to encounter the face of this giant whom I had never, until that moment, met.

A hand plucked at my elbow and I brought my eyes down to ordinary man-height. And, from the round and gentle face of Daniel Keyes, issued the immortal words: "Listen, when you find out how I did it, let me know, will you? I want to do it again."

8

FLOWERS FOR ALGERNON

progris riport 1—martch 5, 1965

Dr. Strauss says I shud rite down what I think and evrey thing that happins to me from now on. I dont know why but he says its importint so they will see if they will use me. I hope they use me. Miss Kinnian says maybe they can make me smart. I want to be smart. My name is Charlie Gordon. I am 37 years old. I have nuthing more to rite now so I will close for today.

progris riport 2--martch 6

I had a test today. I think I faled it. And I think maybe now they wont use me. What happind is a nice young man was in the room and he had some white cards and ink spilled all over them. He sed Charlie what do yo see on this card. I was very skared even tho I had my rabits foot in my pockit because when I was a kid I always faled tests in school and I spillled ink to.

I told him I saw a inkblot. He said yes and it made me feel good. I thot that was all but when I got up to go he said Charlie we are not thru yet. Then I dont remember so good but he wantid me to say what was in the ink. I dint see nuthing in the ink but he said there was picturs there other pepul saw some picturs. I couldnt see any picturs. I reely tryed. I held the card close up and then far away. Then I said if I had my glases I coud

see better I usally only ware my glases in the movies or TV but
I said they are in the closit in the hall. I got them. Then I said
let me see that card agen I bet Ill find it now.

I tryed hard but I only saw the ink. I told him maybe I need
new glases. He rote something down on a paper and I got skared
of faling the test. I told him it was a very nice inkblot with littel
points all around the edges. He looked very sad so that wasnt it.
I said please let me try agen. Ill get it in a few minits becaus
Im not so fast somtimes. Im a slow reeder too in Miss Kinnians
class for slow adults but I'm trying very hard.

He gave me a chance with another card that had 2 kinds of
ink spilled on it red and blue.

He was very nice and talked slow like Miss Kinnian does and
he explaned it to me that it was a *raw shok*. He said pepul see
things in the ink. I said show me where. He said think. I told him
I think a inkblot but that wasn't rite eather. He said what does
it remind you—pretend something. I closed my eyes for a long
time to pretend. I told him I pretend a fowntan pen with ink
leeking all over a table cloth.

I dont think I passed the *raw shok* test

progris riport 3—martch 7

Dr Strauss and Dr Nemur say it dont matter about the inkblots.
They said that maybe they will still use me. I said Miss Kinnian
never gave me tests like that one only spelling and reading. They
said Miss Kinnian told that I was her bestist pupil in the adult
nite school becaus I tryed the hardist and I reely wantid to lern.
They said how come you went to the adult nite scool all by yourself Charlie. How did you find it. I said I asked pepul and
sumbody told me where I shud go to lern to read and spell good.
They said why did you want to. I told them becaus all my life I
wantid to be smart and not dumb. But its very hard to be smart.
They said you know it will probly be tempirery. I said yes. Miss
Kinnian told me. I dont care if it herts.

Later I had more crazy tests today. The nice lady who gave it
to me told me the name and I asked her how do you spellit so I
can rite it my progris riport. THEMATIC APPERCEPTION
TEST. I dont know the frist 2 words but I know what *test* means.

You got to pass it or you get bad marks. This test lookd easy becaus I coud see the picturs. Only this time she dint want me to tell her the picturs. That mixd me up. She said make up storys about the pepul in the picturs.

I told her how can you tell storys about pepul you never met. I said why shud I make up lies. I never tell lies any more becaus I always get caut.

She told me this test and the other one the raw-shok was for getting personality. I laffed so hard. I said how can you get that thing from inkblots and fotos. She got sore and put her picturs away. I don't care. It was sily. I gess I faled that test too.

Later some men in white coats took me to a difernt part of the hospitil and gave me a game to play. It was like a race with a white mouse. They called the mouse Algernon. Algernon was in a box with a lot of twists and turns like all kinds of walls and they gave me a pencil and a paper with lines and lots of boxes. On one side it said START and on the other end it said FINISH. They said it was *amazed* and that Algernon and me had the same *amazed* to do. I dint see how we could have the same *amazed* if Algernon had a box and I had a paper but I dint say nothing. Anyway there wasnt time because the race started.

One of the men had a watch he was trying to hide so I wouldnt see it so I tryed not to look and that made me nervus.

Anyway that test made me feel worser than all the others because they did it over 10 times with different *amazeds* and Algernon won every time. I dint know that mice were so smart. Maybe thats because Algernon is a white mouse. Maybe white mice are smarter than other mice.

progris riport 4—Mar 8

Their going to use me! Im so excited I can hardly write. Dr Nemur and Dr Strauss had a argament about it first. Dr Nemur was in the office when Dr Strauss brot me in. Dr Nemur was worryed about using me but Dr Strauss told him Miss Kinnian rekemmended me the best from all the people who she was teaching. I like Miss Kinnian becaus shes a very smart teacher. And she said Charlie your going to have a second chance. If you volenteer for this experament you mite get smart. They dont know if it will be perminint but theirs a chance. Thats why I said ok even when I was scared because she said it was an oper- ashun. She said dont be scared Charlie you done so much with so little I think you deserv it most of all.

So I got scaird when Dr. Nemur and Dr. Strauss argud about it. Dr. Strauss said I had something that was very good. He said I had a good *motorvation*. I never even knew I had that. I felt proud when he said that not every body with an eye-q of 68 had that thing. I dant know what it is or where I got it but he said Algernon had it too. Algernons *motor-vation* is the cheese they put in his box. But it cant be that because I didn't eat any cheese this week.

Then he told Dr Nemur something I dint understand so while they were talking I wrote down some of the words.

He said Dr. Nemur I know Charlie is not what you had in mind as the first of your new brede of intelek** (coudnt get the word) superman. But most people of his low ment** are host** and uncoop** they are usually dull apath** and hard to reach. He has a good natcher hes intristed and eager to please.

Dr Nemur said remember he will be the first human beeng ever to have his intelijence tripled by surgicle meens.

Dr. Strauss said exakly. Look at how well hes lerned to read and write for his low mentel age its as grate an acheve** as you and I lerning einstines therey of **vity without help. That shows the inteness motor-vation. Its comparat** a tremen** achev** I say we use Charlie.

I dint get all the words but it sounded like Dr Strauss was on my side and like the other one wasnt.

Then Dr Nemur nodded he said all right maybe your right. We will use Charlie. When he said that I got so exited I jumped up and shook his hand for being so good to me. I told him thank you doc you wont be sorry for giving me a second chance. And I mean it like I told him. After the operashun Im gonna try to be smart. Im gonna try awful hard.

progris riport 5—Mar 10

Im skared. Lots of the nurses and the people who gave me the tests came to bring me candy and wish me luck. I hope I have luck. I got my rabits foot and my lucky penny. Only a black cat crossed me when I was comming to the hospitil. Dr Strauss says dont be supersitis Charlie this is science. Anyway Im keeping my rabits foot with me.

I asked Dr Strauss if Ill beat Algernon in the race after the operashun and he said maybe. If the operashun works Ill show that mouse I can be as smart as he is. Maybe smarter. Then Ill be abel to read better and spell the words good and know lots of things and be like other people. I want to be smart like other people. If it works perminint they will make everybody smart all over the wurld.

They dint give me anything to eat this morning. I dont know what that eating has to do with getting smart. Im very hungry and Dr. Nemur took away my box of candy. That Dr Nemur is a grouch. Dr Strauss says I can have it back after the operashun. You cant eat befor a operashun . . .

progress report 6—Mar 15

The operashun dint hurt. He did it while I was sleeping. They took off the bandijis from my head today so I can make a PROGRESS REPORT. Dr. Nemur who looked at some of my other ones says I spell PROGRESS wrong and told me how to spell it and REPORT too. I got to try and remember that.

I have a very bad memary for spelling. Dr Strauss says its ok to tell about all the things that happin to me but he says I should tell more about what I feel and what I think. When I told him I dont know how to think he said try. All the time when the bandijis were on my eyes I tryed to think. Nothing happened. I dont know what to think about. Maybe if I ask him he will tell me how I can think now that Im suppose to get smart. What do smart people think about. Fancy things I suppose. I wish I knew some fancy things alredy.

progress report 7—mar 19

Nothing is happining. I had lots of tests and different kinds of races with Algernon. I hate that mouse. He always beats me. Dr. Strauss said I got to play those games. And he said some time I got to take those tests over again. Those inkblots are stupid. And those pictures are stupid too. I like to draw a picture of a man and a woman but I wont make up lies about people.

I got a headache from trying to think so much. I thot Dr Strauss was my frend but he dont help me. He dont tell me what to think or when Ill get smart. Miss Kinnian dint come to see me. I think writing these progress reports are stupid too.

progress report 8—Mar 23

Im going back to work at the factory. They said it was better I shud go back to work but I cant tell anyone what the operashun was for and I have to come to the hospitil for an hour evry night after work. They are gonna pay me mony every month for learning to be smart.

Im glad Im going back to work because I miss my job and all my frends and all the fun we have there.

Dr Strauss says I shud keep writing things down but I dont have to do it every day just when I think of something or something speshul happins. He says dont get discoridged because it takes time and it happins slow. He says it took a long time with Algernon before he got 3 times smarter than he was before. Thats why Algernon beats me all the time because he had that operashun too. That makes me feel better. I coud probly do that *amazed* faster than a reglar mouse. Maybe some day Ill beat him. That would be something. So far Algernon looks smart perminent.

Mar 25 (I dont have to write PROGRESS REPORT on top any more just when I hand it in once a week for Dr Nemur. I just have to put the date on. That saves time)

We had a lot of fun at the factery today. Joe Carp said hey look where Charlie had his operashun what did they do Charlie put some brains in. I was going to tell him but I remembered Dr Strauss said no. Then Frank Reilly said what did you do Charlie forget your key and open your door the hard way. That made me laff. Their really my friends and they like me.

Sometimes somebody will say hey look at Joe or Frank or George he really pulled a Charlie Gordon. I dont know why they say that but they always laff. This morning Amos Borg who is the

4 man at Donnegans used my name when he shouted at Ernie the office boy. Ernie lost a packige. He said Ernie for godsake what are you trying to be a Charlie Gordon. I dont understand why he said that.

Mar 28 Dr Strauss came to my room tonight to see why I dint come in like I was suppose to. I told him I dont like to race with Algernon any more. He said I dont have to for a while but I shud come in. He had a present for me. I thot it was a little television but it wasnt. He said I got to turn it on when I go to sleep. I said your kidding why shud I turn it on when Im going to sleep. Who ever herd of a thing like that. But he said if I want to get smart I got to do what he says. I told him I dint think I was going to get smart and he puts his hand on my sholder and said Charlie you dont know it yet but your getting smarter all the time. You wont notice for a while. I think he was just being nice to make me feel good because I dont look any smarter.

Oh yes I almost forgot. I asked him when I can go back to the class at Miss Kinnians school. He said I wont go their. He said that soon Miss Kinnian will come to the hospitil to start and teach me speshul.

Mar 29 That crazy TV kept up all night. How can I sleep with something yelling crazy things all night in my ears. And the nutty pictures. Wow. I don't know what it says when Im up so how am I going to know when Im sleeping.

Dr Strauss says its ok. He says my brains are lerning when I sleep and that will help me when Miss Kinnian starts my lessons in the hospitl (only I found out it isn't a hospitil its a labatory.) I think its all crazy. If you can get smart when your sleeping why do people go to school. That thing I don't think will work. I use to watch the late show and the late late show on TV all the time and it never made me smart. Maybe you have to sleep while you watch it.

progress report 9—April 3

Dr Strauss showed me how to keep the TV turned low so now I can sleep. I don't hear a thing. And I still dont understand what it says. A few times I play it over in the morning to find out what

I lerned when I was sleeping and I don't think so. Miss Kinnian says Maybe its another langwidge. But most times it sounds american. It talks faster then even Miss Gold who was my teacher in 6 grade.

I told Dr. Strauss what good is it to get smart in my sleep. I want to be smart when Im awake. He says its the same thing and I have two minds. Theres the *subconscious* and the *conscious* (thats how you spell it). And one dont tell the other one what its doing. They dont even talk to each other. Thats why I dream. And boy have I been having crazy dreams. Wow. Ever since that night TV. The late late late show.

I forgot to ask him if it was only me or if everybody had those two minds.

(I just looked up the word in the dictionary Dr Strauss gave me. The word is *subconscious. adj. Of the nature of mental operations yet not present in consciousness; as, subconscious conflict of desires.*) There's more but I still dont know what it means. This isnt a very good dictionary for dumb people like me.

Anyway the headache is from the party. My friends from the factery Joe Carp and Frank Reilly invited me to go to Muggsys Saloon for some drinks. I don't like to drink but they said we will have lots of fun. I had a good time.

Joe Carp said I shoud show the girls how I mop out the toilet in the factory and he got me a mop. I showed them and everyone laffed when I told that Mr. Donnegan said I was the best janiter he ever had because I like my job and do it good and never miss a day except for my operashun.

I said Miss Kinnian always said Charlie be proud of your job because you do it good.

Everybody laffed and we had a good time and they gave me lots of drinks and Joe said Charlie is a card when hes potted. I dont know what that means but everybody likes me and we have fun. I cant wait to be smart like my best friends Joe Carp and Frank Reilly.

I dont remember how the party was over but I think I went out to buy a newspaper and coffe for Joe and Frank and when I came back there was no one their. I looked for them all over till late. Then I dont remember so good but I think I got sleepy or sick. A nice cop brot me back home Thats what my landlady Mrs Flynn says.

But I got a headache and a big lump on my head. I think maybe I fell but Joe Carp says it was the cop they beat up drunks some times. I don't think so. Miss Kinnian says cops are to help people. Anyway I got a bad headache and Im sick and hurt all over. I dont think Ill drink anymore.

April 6 I beat Algernon! I dint even know I beat him until Burt the tester told me. Then the second time I lost because I got so exited I fell off the chair before I finished. But after that I beat him 8 more times. I must be getting smart to beat a smart mouse like Algernon. But I dont *feel* smarter.

I wanted to race Algernon some more but Burt said thats enough for one day. They let me hold him for a minit. Hes not so bad. Hes soft like a ball of cotton. He blinks and when he opens his eyes their black and pink on the eges.

I said can I feed him because I felt bad to beat him and I wanted to be nice and make friends. Burt said no Algernon is a very specshul mouse with an operashun like mine, and he was the first of all the animals to stay smart so long. He told me Algernon is so smart that every day he has to solve a test to get his food. Its a thing like a lock on a door that changes every time Algernon goes in to eat so he has to lern something new to get his food. That made me sad because if he coudnt lern he woud be hungry.

I don't think its right to make you pass a test to eat. How woud Dr Nemur like it to have to pass a test every time he wants to eat. I think Ill be friends with Algernon.

April 9 Tonight after work Miss Kinnian was at the laboratory. She looked like she was glad to see me but scared. I told her dont worry Miss Kinnian Im not smart yet and she laffed. She said I have confidence in you Charlie the way you struggled so hard to read and right better than all the others. At werst you will have it for a littel wile and your doing somthing for science.

We are reading a very hard book. Its called *Robinson Crusoe* about a man who gets merooned on a dessert Iland. Hes smart and figers out all kinds of things so he can have a house and food and hes a good swimmer. Only I feel sorry because hes all alone and has no frends. But I think their must be somebody else on the iland because theres a picture with his funny umbrella looking at footprints. I hope he gets a frend and not be lonly.

April 10 Miss Kinnian teaches me to spell better. She says look at a word and close your eyes and say it over and over until you remember. I have lots of truble with *through* that you say *threw* and *enough* and *tough* that you dont say *enew and tew.* You got to say *enuff* and *tuff.* Thats how I use to write it before I started to get smart. Im confused but Miss Kinnian says theres no reason in spelling.

Apr 14 Finished *Robinson Crusoe.* I want to find out more about what happens to him but Miss Kinnian says thats all there is. *Why.*

Apr 15 Miss Kinnian says Im lerning fast. She read some of the Progress Reports and she looked at me kind of funny. She says Im a fine person and Ill show them all. I asked her why. She said never mind but I shouldnt feel bad if I find out everybody isnt nice like I think. She said for a person who god gave so little to you done more then a lot of people with brains they never even used. I said all my friends are smart people but there good. They like me and they never did anything that wasnt nice. Then she got something in her eye and she had to run out to the ladys room.

Apr 16 Today, I lerned, the *comma,* this is a comma (,) a period, with a tail, Miss Kinnian, says its importent, because, it makes writing, better, she said, somebody, coud lose, a lot of money, if a comma, isnt, in the, right place, I dont have, any money, and I dont see, how a comma, keeps you, from losing it,

Apr 17 I used the comma wrong. Its punctuation. Miss Kinnian told me to look up long words in the dictionary to lern to spell them. I said whats the difference if you can read it anyway. She said its part of your education so now on Ill look up all the words

Im not sure how to spell. It takes a long time to write that way but I only have to look up once and after that I get it right.

You got to mix them up, she showed? me" how. to mix! them (and now; I can! mix up all kinds" of punctuation, in! my writing? There, are lots! of rules? to lern; but Im gettin'g them in my head.

One thing I like about, Dear Miss Kinnian: (thats the way it goes in a business letter if I ever go into business) is she, always gives me' a reason" when—I ask. She's a gen'ius! I wish I cou'd be smart" like, her;

(Puncuation, is; fun!)

April 18 What a dope I am! I didn't even understand what she was talking about. I read the grammar book last night and it explanes the whole thing. Then I saw it was the same way as Miss Kinnian was trying to tell me, but I didn't get it.

Miss Kinnian said that the TV working in my sleep helped out. She and I reached a plateau. Thats a flat hill.

After I figured out how puncuation worked, I read over all my old Progress Reports from the beginning. Boy, did I have crazy spelling and punctuation! I told Miss Kinnian I ought to go over the pages and fix all the mistakes but she said, "No, Charlie, Dr. Nemur wants them just as they are. That's why he let you keep them after they were photostated, to see your own progress. You're coming along fast, Charlie."

That made me feel good. After the lesson I went down and played with Algernon. We don't race any more.

April 20 I feel sick inside. Not sick like for a doctor, but inside my chest it feels empty like getting punched and a heartburn at the same time. I wasn't going to write about it, but I guess I got to, because its important. Today was the first time I ever stayed home from work.

Last night Joe Carp and Frank Reilly invited me to a party. There were lots of girls and some men from the factory. I remembered how sick I got last time I drank too much, so I told Joe I didn't want anything to drink. He gave me a plain coke instead.

We had a lot of fun for a while. Joe said I should dance with Ellen and she would teach me the steps. I fell a few times and I

couldn't understand why because no one else was dancing besides Ellen and me. And all the time I was tripping because
somebody's foot was always sticking out.

Then when I got up I saw the look on Joe's face and it gave me
a funny feeling in my stomack. "He's a scream," one of the girls
said. Everybody was laughing.

"Look at him. He's blushing. Charlie is blushing."

"Hey, Ellen, what'd you do to Charlie? I never saw him act
like that before."

I didn't know what to do or where to turn. Everyone was looking at me and laughing and I felt naked. I wanted to hide. I ran
outside and I threw up. Then I walked home. It's a funny thing
I never knew that Joe and Frank and the others liked to have
me around all the time to make fun of me.

Now I know what it means when they say "to pull a Charlie
Gordon."

I'm ashamed.

progress report 11

April 21 Still didn't go into the factory. I told Mrs. Flynn my
landlady to call and tell Mr. Donnegan I was sick. Mrs. Flynn
looks at me very funny lately like she's scared.

I think it's a good thing about finding out how everybody
laughs at me. I thought about it a lot. It's because I'm so dumb
and I don't even know when I'm doing something dumb. People
think it's funny when a dumb person can't do things the same
way they can.

Anyway, now I know I'm getting smarter every day. I know
punctuation and I can spell good. I like to look up all the hard
words in the dictionary and I remember them. I'm reading a lot
now, and Miss Kinnian says I read very fast. Sometimes I even
understand what I'm reading about, and it stays in my mind.
There are times when I can close my eyes and think of a page
and it all comes back like a picture.

Besides history, geography and arithmetic, Miss Kinnian said
I should start to learn foreign languages. Dr. Strauss gave me
some more tapes to play while I sleep. I still don't understand
how that conscious and unconscious mind works, but Dr. Strauss

says not to worry yet. He asked me to promise that when I start learning college subjects next week I wouldn't read any books on psychology—that is, until he gives me permission.

I feel a lot better today, but I guess I'm still a little angry that all the time people were laughing and making fun of me because I wasn't so smart. When I become intelligent like Dr. Strauss says, with three times my I.Q. of 68, then maybe I'll be like everyone else and people will like me.

I'm not sure what an I.Q. is. Dr. Nemur said it was something that measured how intelligent you were—like a scale in the drugstore weighs pounds. But Dr. Strauss had a big argument with him and said an I.Q. didn't weigh intelligence at all. He said an I.Q. showed how much intelligence you could get, like the numbers on the outside of a measuring cup. You still had to fill the cup up with stuff.

Then when I asked Burt, who gives me my intelligence tests and works with Algernon, he said that both of them were wrong (only I had to promise not to tell them he said so). Burt says that the I.Q. measures a lot of different things including some of the things you learned already, and it really isn't any good at all.

So I still don't know what I.Q. is except that mine is going to be over 200 soon. I didn't want to say anything, but I don't see how if they don't know *what* it is, or *where* it is—I don't see how they know *how much* of it you've got.

Dr. Nemur says I have to take a *Rorshach Test* tomorrow. I wonder what *that* is.

April 22 I found out what a Rorshach is. It's the test I took before the operation—the one with the inkblots on the pieces of cardboard.

I was scared to death of those inkblots. I knew the man was going to ask me to find the pictures and I knew I couldn't. I was thinking to myself, if only there was some way of knowing what kind of pictures were hidden there. Maybe there weren't any pictures at all. Maybe it was just a trick to see if I was dumb enough to look for something that wasn't there. Just thinking about that made me sore at him.

"All right, Charlie," he said, "you've seen these cards before, remember?"

J

"Of course I remember."

The way I said it, he knew I was angry, and he looked surprised. "Yes, of course. Now I want you to look at this. What might this be? What do you see on this card? People see all sorts of things in these inkblots. Tell me what it might be for you—what it makes you think of."

I was shocked. That wasn't what I had expected him to say. "You mean there are no pictures hidden in those inkblots?"

He frowned and took off his glasses. "What?"

"Pictures. Hidden in the inkblots. Last time you told me everyone could see them and you wanted me to find them too."

He explained to me that the last time he had used almost the exact same words he was using now. I didn't believe it, and I still have the suspicion that he misled me at the time just for the fun of it. Unless—I don't know any more—could I have been *that* feeble-minded?

We went through the cards slowly. One looked like a pair of bats tugging at something. Another one looked like two men fencing with swords. I imagined all sorts of things. I guess I got carried away. But I didn't trust him any more, and I kept turning them around, even looking on the back to see if there was anything there I was supposed to catch. While he was making his notes, I peeked out of the corner of my eye to read it. But it was all in code that looked like this:

$$WF + A \qquad DdF - Ad \; orig. \qquad WF - A$$
$$SF + obj$$

The test still doesn't make sense to me. It seems to me that anyone could make up lies about things that they didn't really imagine? Maybe I'll understand it when Dr. Strauss lets me read up on psychology.

April 25 I figured out a new way to line up the machines in the factory, and Mr. Donnegan says it will save him ten thousand dollars a year in labor and increased production. He gave me a $25 bonus.

I wanted to take Joe Carp and Frank Reilly out to lunch to celebrate, but Joe said he had to buy some things for his wife, and Frank said he was meeting his cousin for lunch. I guess it'll take a little time for them to get used to the changes in me. Everybody seems to be frightened of me. When I went over to Amos Borg and tapped him, he jumped up in the air.

People don't talk to me much any more or kid around the way they used to. It makes the job kind of lonely.

April 27 I got up the nerve today to ask Miss Kinnian to have dinner with me tomorrow night to celebrate my bonus.

At first she wasn't sure it was right, but I asked Dr. Strauss and he said it was okay. Dr. Strauss and Dr. Nemur don't seem to be getting along so well. They're arguing all the time. This evening I heard them shouting. Dr. Nemur was saying that it was *his* experiment and *his* research, and Dr. Strauss shouted back that he contributed just as much, because he found me through Miss Kinnian and he performed the operation. Dr. Strauss said that someday thousands of neuro-surgeons might be using his technique all over the world.

Dr. Nemur wanted to publish the results of the experiment at the end of this month. Dr. Strauss wanted to wait a while to be sure. Dr. Strauss said Dr. Nemur was more interested in the Chair of Psychology at Princeton than he was in the experiment. Dr. Nemur said Dr. Strauss was nothing but an opportunist trying to ride to glory on *his* coattails.

When I left afterwards, I found myself trembling. I don't know why for sure, but it was as if I'd seen both men clearly for the first time. I remember hearing Burt say Dr. Nemur had a shrew of a wife who was pushing him all the time to get things published so he could become famous. Burt said that the dream of her life was to have a big shot husband.

April 28 I don't understand why I never noticed how beautiful Miss Kinnian really is. She has brown eyes and feathery brown hair that comes to the top of her neck. She's only thirty-four! I think from the beginning I had the feeling that she was an unreachable genius—and very, very old. Now, every time I see her she grows younger and more lovely.

We had dinner and a long talk. When she said I was coming along so fast I'd be leaving her behind, I laughed.

"It's true, Charlie. You're already a better reader than I am. You can read a whole page at a glance while I can take in only a few lines at a time. And you remember every single thing you read. I'm lucky if I can recall the main thoughts and the general meaning."

"I don't feel intelligent. There are so many things I don't understand."

She took out a cigarette and I lit it for her. "You've got to be a *little* patient. You're accomplishing in days and weeks what it takes normal people to do in a lifetime. That's what makes it so amazing. You're like a giant sponge now, soaking things in. Facts, figures, general knowledge. And soon you'll begin to connect them, too. You'll see how different branches of learning are related. There are many levels, Charlie, like steps on a giant ladder that take you up higher and higher to see more and more of the world around you.

"I can see only a little bit of that, Charlie, and I won't go much higher than I am now, but you'll keep climbing up and up, and see more and more, and each step will open new worlds that you never even knew existed." She frowned. "I hope . . . I just hope to God—"

"What?"

"Never mind, Charles. I just hope I wasn't wrong to advise you to go into this in the first place."

I laughed. "How could that be? It worked, didn't it? Even Algernon is still smart."

We sat there silently for a while and I knew what she was thinking about as she watched me toying with the chain of my rabbit's foot and my keys. I didn't want to think of that possibility any more than elderly people want to think of death. I *knew* that this was only the beginning. I knew what she meant about levels because I'd seen some of them already. The thought of leaving her behind made me sad.

I'm in love with Miss Kinnian.

progress report 12

April 30 I've quit my job with Donnegan's Plastic Box Company. Mr. Donnegan insisted it would be better for all concerned if I left. What did I do to make them hate me so?

The first I knew of it was when Mr. Donnegan showed me the

petition. Eight hundred names, everyone in the factory, except Fanny Girden. Scanning the list quickly, I saw at once that hers was the only missing name. All the rest demanded that I be fired.

Joe Carp and Frank Reilly wouldn't talk to me about it. No one else would either, except Fanny. She was one of the few people I'd known who set her mind to something and believed it no matter what the rest of the world proved, said or did—and Fanny did not believe that I should have been fired. She had been against the petition on principle and despite the pressure and threats she'd held out.

"Which don't mean to say," she remarked, "that I don't think there's something mighty strange about you, Charlie. Them changes. I don't know. You used to be a good, dependable, ordinary man—not too bright maybe, but honest. Who knows what you done to yourself to get so smart all of a sudden. Like everybody around here's been saying, Charlie, it's not right."

"But how can you say that, Fanny? What's wrong with a man becoming intelligent and wanting to acquire knowledge and understanding of the world around him?"

She stared down at her work and I turned to leave. Without looking at me, she said: "It was evil when Eve listened to the snake and ate from the tree of knowledge. It was evil when she saw that she was naked. If not for that none of us would ever have to grow old and sick, and die."

Once again, now, I have the feeling of shame burning inside me. This intelligence has driven a wedge between me and all the people I once knew and loved. Before, they laughed at me and despised me for my ignorance and dullness; now, they hate me for my knowledge and understanding. What in God's name do they want of me?

They've driven me out of the factory. Now I'm more alone than ever before. . . .

May 15 Dr. Strauss is very angry at me for not having written any progress reports in two weeks. He's justified because the lab is now paying me a regular salary. I told him I was too busy thinking and reading. When I pointed out that writing was such a slow process that it made me impatient with my poor handwriting, he suggested I learn to type. It's much easier to write now because I can type seventy-five words a minute. Dr. Strauss continually reminds me of the need to speak and write simply so people will be able to understand me.

I'll try to review all the things that happened to me during the last two weeks. Algernon and I were presented to the *American Psychological Association* sitting in convention with the *World Psychological Association*. We created quite a sensation. Dr. Nemur and Dr. Strauss were proud of us.

I suspect that Dr. Nemur, who is sixty—ten years older than Dr. Strauss—finds it necessary to see tangible results of his work. Undoubtedly the result of pressure by Mrs. Nemur.

Contrary to my earlier impressions of him, I realize that Dr. Nemur is not at all a genius. He has a very good mind, but it struggles under the spectre of self-doubt. He wants people to take him for a genius. Therefore it is important for him to feel that his work is accepted by the world. I believe that Dr. Nemur was afraid of further delay because he worried that someone else might make a discovery along these lines and take the credit from him.

Dr. Strauss on the other hand might be called a genius, although I feel his areas of knowledge are too limited. He was educated in the tradition of narrow specialization; the broader aspects of background were neglected far more than necessary —even for a neuro-surgeon.

I was shocked to learn the only ancient languages he could read were Latin, Greek and Hebrew, and that he knows almost nothing of mathematics beyond the elementary levels of the calculus of variations. When he admitted this to me, I found myself almost annoyed. It was as if he'd hidden this part of himself in order to deceive me, pretending—as do many people I've discovered—to be what he is not. No one I've ever known is what he appears to be on the surface.

Dr. Nemur appears to be uncomfortable around me. Sometimes when I try to talk to him, he just looks at me strangely and turns away. I was angry at first when Dr. Strauss told me I was giving Dr. Nemur an inferiority complex. I thought he was mocking me and I'm oversensitive at being made fun of.

How was I to know that a highly respected psycho-experimentalist like Nemur was unacquainted with Hindustani and Chinese? It's absurd when you consider the work that is being done in India and China today in the very field of his study.

I asked Dr. Strauss how Nemur could refute Rahajamati's attack on his method if Nemur couldn't even read them in the first place. That strange look on Strauss' face can mean only one of two things. Either he doesn't want to tell Nemur what they're saying in India, or else—and this worries me—Dr. Strauss doesn't know either. I must be careful to speak and write clearly and simply so people won't laugh.

May 18 I am very disturbed. I saw Miss Kinnian last night for the first time in over a week. I tried to avoid all discussions of intellectual concepts and to keep the conversation on a simple, everyday level, but she just stared at me blankly and asked me what I meant about the mathematical variance equivalent in Dorbermann's *Fifth Concerto.*

When I tried to explain she stopped me and laughed. I guess I got angry, but I suspect I'm approaching her on the wrong level. No matter what I try to discuss with her, I am unable to communicate. I must review Vrostadt's equations on *Levels of Semantic Progression.* I find I don't communicate with people much any more. Thank God for books and music and things I can think about. I am alone at Mrs. Flynn's boarding house most of the time and seldom speak to anyone.

May 20 I would not have noticed the new dishwasher, a boy of about sixteen, at the corner diner where I take my evening meals if not for the incident of the broken dishes.

They crashed to the floor, sending bits of white china under the tables. The boy stood there, dazed and frightened, holding the empty tray in his hand. The catcalls from the customers (the cries of "hey, there go the profits!" . . . *"Mazeltov!"* . . . and "well, *he* didn't work here very long . . ." which invariably seems to follow the breaking of glass or dishware in a public restaurant) all seemed to confuse him.

When the owner came to see what the excitement was about, the boy cowered as if he expected to be struck. "All right! All right, you dope," shouted the owner, "don't just stand there! Get the broom and sweep that mess up. A broom . . . a broom, you idiot! It's in the kitchen!"

The boy saw he was not going to be punished. His frightened expression disappeared and he smiled as he came back with the broom to sweep the floor. A few of the rowdier customers kept up the remarks, amusing themselves at his expense.

"Here, sonny, over here there's a nice piece behind you . . ."

"He's not so dumb. It's easier to break 'em than wash 'em!"

As his vacant eyes moved across the crowd of onlookers, he slowly mirrored their smiles and finally broke into an uncertain grin at the joke he obviously did not understand.

I felt sick inside as I looked at his dull, vacuous smile, the wide, bright eyes of a child, uncertain but eager to please. They were laughing at him because he was mentally retarded.

And I had been laughing at him too.

Suddenly I was furious at myself and all those who were smirking at him. I jumped up and shouted, "Shut up! Leave him alone! It's not his fault he can't understand! He can't help what he is! But he's still a human being!"

The room grew silent. I cursed myself for losing control. I tried not to look at the boy as I walked out without touching my food. I felt ashamed for both of us.

How strange that people of honest feelings and sensibility, who would not take advantage of a man born without arms or eyes —how such people think nothing of abusing a man born with low intelligence. It infuriated me to think that not too long ago I had foolishly played the clown.

And I had almost forgotten.

I'd hidden the picture of the old Charlie Gordon from myself because now that I was intelligent it was something that had to be pushed out of my mind. But today in looking at that boy, for the first time I saw what I had been. *I was just like him!*

Only a short time ago, I learned that people laughed at me. Now I can see that unknowingly I joined with them in laughing at myself. That hurts most of all.

I have often reread my progress reports and seen the illiteracy, the childish naïveté, the mind of low intelligence peering from a dark room, through the keyhole at the dazzling light outside. I see that even in my dullness I knew I was inferior, and that other people had something I lacked—something denied me. In my mental blindness, I thought it was somehow connected with the ability to read and write, and I was sure that if I could get those skills I would automatically have intelligence too.

Even a feeble-minded man wants to be like other men.

A child may not know how to feed itself, or what to eat, yet it knows of hunger.

This then is what I was like. I never knew. Even with my gift of intellectual awareness, I never really knew.

This day was good for me. Seeing the past more clearly, I've decided to use my knowledge and skills to work in the field of increasing human intelligence levels. Who is better equipped for this work? Who else has lived in both worlds? These are my people. Let me use my gift to do something for them.

Tomorrow, I will discuss with Dr. Strauss how I can work in this area. I may be able to help him work out the problems of widespread use of the technique which was used on me. I have several good ideas of my own.

There is so much that might be done with this technique. If I could be made into a genius, what about thousands of others like myself? What fantastic levels might be achieved by using this technique on normal people? On *geniuses?*

There are so many doors to open. I am impatient to begin.

progress report 13

May 23 It happened today. Algernon bit me. I visited the lab to see him as I do occasionally, and when I took him out of his cage, he snapped at my hand. I put him back and watched him for a while. He was unusually disturbed and vicious.

May 24 Burt, who is in charge of the experimental animals, tells me that Algernon is changing. He is less co-operative; he refuses to run the maze any more; general motivation has decreased. And he hasn't been eating. Everyone is upset about what this may mean.

May 25 They've been feeding Algernon, who now refuses to work the shifting-lock problem. Everyone identifies me with

Algernon. In a way we're both the first of our kind. They're all pretending that Algernon's behavior is not necessarily significant for me. But it's hard to hide the fact that some of the other animals who were used in this experiment are showing strange behavior.

Dr. Strauss and Dr. Nemur have asked me not to come to the lab any more. I know what they're thinking but I can't accept it. I am going ahead with my plans to carry their research forward. With all due respect to both these fine scientists, I am well aware of their limitations. If there is an answer, I'll have to find it out for myself. Suddenly, time has become very important to me.

May 29 I have been given a lab of my own and permission to go ahead with the research. I'm onto something. Working day and night. I've had a cot moved into the lab. Most of my writing time is spent on the notes which I keep in a separate folder, but from time to time I feel it necessary to put down my moods and thoughts from sheer habit.

I find the *calculus of intelligence* to be a fascinating study. Here is the place for the application of all the knowledge I have acquired.

May 31 Dr. Strauss thinks I'm working too hard. Dr. Nemur says I'm trying to cram a lifetime of research and thought into a few weeks. I know I should rest, but I'm driven on by something inside that won't let me stop. I've got to find the reason for the sharp regression in Algernon. I've got to know *if* and *when* it will happen to me.

June 4

LETTER TO DR. STRAUSS (*copy*)

Dear Dr. Strauss:

Under separate cover I am sending you a copy of my report entitled, "The Algernon-Gordon Effect: A Study of Structure and Function of Increased Intelligence," which I would like to have published.

As you see, my experiments are completed. I have included in my report all of my formulae, as well as mathematical analysis in the appendix. Of course, these should be verified.

Because of its importance to both you and Dr. Nemur (and need I say to myself, too?) I have checked and rechecked my results a dozen times in the hope of finding an error. I am sorry to say the results must stand. Yet for the sake of science, I am grateful for the little bit that I here add to the knowledge of the function of the human mind and of the laws governing the artificial increase of human intelligence.

I recall your once saying to me that an experimental *failure* or the *disproving* of a theory was as important to the advancement of learning as a success would be. I know now that this is true. I am sorry, however, that my own contribution to the field must rest upon the ashes of the work of two men I regard so highly.

Yours truly,
Charles Gordon

June 5 I must not become emotional. The facts and the results of my experiments are clear, and the more sensational aspects of my own rapid climb cannot obscure the fact that the tripling of intelligence by the surgical technique developed by Drs. Strauss and Nemur must be viewed as having little or no practical applicability (at the present time) to be the increase of human intelligence.

As I review the records and data on Algernon, I see that although he is still in his physical infancy, he has regressed mentally. Motor activity is impaired; there is a general reduction of glandular activity; there is an accelerated loss of coordination.

There are also strong indications of progressive amnesia.

As will be seen by my report, these and other physical and mental deterioration syndromes can be predicted with significant results by the application of my formula.

The surgical stimulus to which we were both subjected has resulted in an intensification and acceleration of all mental processes. The unforeseen development, which I have taken the liberty of calling the *Algernon-Gordon Effect*, is the logical extension of the entire intelligence speed-up. The hypothesis here proven may be described simply in the following terms: Artificially increased intelligence deteriorates at a rate of time directly proportional to the quantity of the increase.

I feel that this, in itself, is an important discovery.

As long as I am able to write, I will continue to record my thoughts in these progress reports. It is one of my few pleasures. However, by all indications, my own mental deterioration will be very rapid.

I have already begun to notice signs of emotional instability and forgetfulness, the first symptoms of the burnout.

June 10 Deterioration progressing. I have become absent-minded. Algernon died two days ago. Dissection shows my predictions were right. His brain had decreased in weight and there was a general smoothing out of cerebral convolutions, as well as a deepening and broadening of brain fissures.

I guess the same thing is or will soon be happening to me. Now that it's definite, I don't want it to happen.

I put Algernon's body in a cheese box and buried him in the back yard. I cried.

June 15 Dr. Strauss came to see me again. I wouldn't open the door and I told him to go away. I want to be left to myself. I am touchy and irritable. I feel the darkness closing in. It's hard to throw off thoughts of suicide. I keep telling myself how important this journal will be.

It's a strange sensation to pick up a book you enjoyed just a few months ago and discover you don't remember it. I remembered how great I thought John Milton was, but when I picked up *Paradise Lost* I couldn't understand it at all. I got so angry I threw the book across the room.

I've got to try to hold on to some of it. Some of the things I've learned. Oh, God, please don't take it all away.

June 19 Sometimes, at night, I go out for a walk. Last night, I couldn't remember where I lived. A policeman took me home. I have the strange feeling that this has all happened to me before—a long time ago. I keep telling myself I'm the only person in the world who can describe what's happening to me.

June 21 Why can't I remember? I've got to fight. I lie in bed for days and I don't know who or where I am. Then it all comes back to me in a flash. Fugues of amnesia. Symptoms of senility— second childhood. I can watch them coming on. It's so cruelly logical. I learned so much and so fast. Now my mind is deteriorating rapidly. I won't let it happen. I'll fight it. I can't help thinking of the boy in the restaurant, the blank expression, the silly smile, the people laughing at him. No—please—not that again. . . .

June 22 I'm forgetting things that I learned recently. It seems to be following the classic pattern—the last things learned are the first things forgotten. Or is that the pattern? I'd better look it up again. . . .

I re-read my paper on the *Algernon-Gordon Effect* and I get the strange feeling that it was written by someone else. There are parts I don't even understand.

Motor activity impaired. I keep tripping over things, and it becomes increasingly difficult to type.

June 23 I've given up using the typewriter. My coordination is bad. I feel I'm moving slower and slower. Had a terrible shock today. I picked up a copy of an article I used in my research, Krueger's *Uber psychische Ganzheit,* to see if it would help me understand what I had done. First I thought there was something wrong with my eyes. Then I realized I could no longer read German. I tested myself in other languages. All gone.

June 30 A week since I dared to write again. It's slipping away like sand through my fingers. Most of the books I have are too hard for me now. I get angry with them because I know that I read and understood them just a few weeks ago.

I keep telling myself I must keep writing these reports so that somebody will know what is happening to me. But it gets harder to form the words and remember spellings. I have to look up even simple words in the dictionary now and it makes me impatient with myself.

Dr. Strauss comes around almost every day, but I told him I wouldn't see or speak to anybody. He feels guilty. They all do. But I don't blame anyone. I knew what might happen. But how it hurts.

July 7 I don't know where the week went. Todays Sunday I know because I can see through my window people going to church. I think I stayed in bed all week but I remember Mrs. Flynn bringing food to me a few times. I keep saying over and over I've got to do something but then I forget or maybe its just easier not to do what I say I'm going to do.

I think of my mother and father a lot these days. I found a picture of them with me taken at a beach. My father has a big ball under his arm and my mother is holding me by the hand. I dont remember them the way they are in the picture. All I remember is my father drunk most of the time and arguing with mom about money.

He never shaved much and he used to scratch my face when he hugged me. My Mother said he died but Cousin Miltie said he heard his dad say that my father ran away with another woman. When I asked my mother she slapped me and said my father was dead. I dont think I ever found out the truth but I dont care much. (He said he was going to take me to see cows on a farm once but he never did. He never kept his promises. . . .)

July 10 My landlady Mrs. Flynn is very worried about me. She says the way I lay around all day and dont do anything I remind her of her son before she threw him out of the house. She said she doesn't like loafers. If Im sick its one thing, but if Im a loafer thats another thing and she won't have it. I told her I think Im sick.

I try to read a little bit every day, mostly stories, but sometimes I have to read the same thing over and over again because I don't know what it means. And its hard to write. I know I should look up all the words in the dictionary but its so hard and Im so tired all the time.

Then I got the idea that I would only use the easy words instead of the long hard ones. That saves time. I put flowers on Algernons grave about once a week. Mrs Flynn thinks Im crazy to put flowers on a mouses grave but I told her that Algernon was special.

July 14 Its sunday again. I dont have anything to do to keep me busy now because my television set is broke and I dont have any money to get it fixed. (I think I lost this months check from the lab. I dont remember)

I get awful headaches and asperin doesnt help me much. Mrs. Flynn knows Im really sick and she feels very sorry for me. Shes a wonderful woman whenever someone is sick.

July 22 Mrs. Flynn called a strange doctor to see me. She was afraid I was going to die. I told the doctor I wasnt too sick and I only forget sometimes. He asked me did I have any friends or relatives and I said no I dont have any. I told him I had a friend called Algernon once but he was a mouse and we used to run races together. He looked at me kind of funny like he thought I was crazy. He smiled when I told him I used to be a genius. He talked to me like I was a baby and he winked at Mrs. Flynn. I got mad and chased him out because he was making fun of me the way they all used to.

July 24 I have no more money and Mrs Flynn says I got to go to work somewhere and pay the rent because I havent paid for two months. I dont know any work but the job I used to have at Donnegans Box Company. I dont want to go back because they all knew me when I was smart and maybe they'll laugh at me. But I dont know what else to do to get money.

July 25 I was looking at some of my old progress reports and its very funny but I cant read what I wrote. I can make out some of the words but they dont make sense.

Miss Kinnian came to the door but I said go away I dont want to see you. She cried and I cried too but I wouldnt let her in because I didn't want her to laugh at me. I told her I didnt like her any more. I told her I didnt want to be smart any more. Thats not true. I still love her and I still want to be smart but I had to say that so shed go away. She gave Mrs. Flynn money to pay the rent. I dont want that. I got to get a job.

Please . . . please let me not forget how to read and write. . . .

July 27 Mr. Donnegan was very nice when I came back and asked him for my old job of janitor. First he was very suspicious but I told him what happened to me then he looked very sad and put his hand on my shoulder and said Charlie Gordon you got guts.

Everybody looked at me when I came downstairs and started working in the toilet sweeping it out like I used to. I told myself Charlie if they make fun of you dont get sore because you remember their not so smart as you once thot they were. And besides they were once your friends and if they laughted at you that doesnt mean anything because they liked you too.

One of the new men who came to work there after I went away made a nasty crack he said hey Charlie I hear your a very smart fella a real quiz kid. Say something intelligent. I felt bad but Joe Carp came over and grabbed him by the shirt and said leave him alone you lousy cracker or I'll break your neck. I didnt expect Joe to take my part so I guess hes really my friend.

Later Frank Reilly came over and said Charlie if anybody bothers you or trys to take advantage you call me or Joe and we will set em straight. I said thanks Frank and I got choked up so I had to turn around and go into the supply room so he wouldnt see me cry. Its good to have friends.

July 28 I did a dumb thing today I forgot I wasnt in Miss Kinnians class at the adult center any more like I use to be. I went in and sat down in my old seat in the back of the room and she looked at me funny and she said Charles. I dint remember she ever called me that before only Charlie so I said hello Miss Kinnian Im redy for my lesin today only I lost my reader that we was using. She startid to cry and run out of the room and everybody looked at me and I saw they wasnt the same pepul who use to be in my class.

Then all of a suddin I remembered some things about the operashun and me getting smart and I said holy smoke I reely pulled a Charlie Gordon that time. I went away before she come back to the room.

Thats why Im going away from New York for good. I dont want to do nothing like that agen. I dont want Miss Kinnian to feel sorry for me. Evry body feels sorry at the factery and I dont want that eather so Im going someplace where nobody knows that Charlie Gordon was once a genus and now he cant even reed a book or rite good.

Im taking a cuple of books along and even if I cant reed them Ill practise hard and maybe I wont forget every thing I lerned. If I try reel hard maybe Ill be a littel bit smarter than I was before the operashun. I got my rabits foot and my luky penny and maybe they will help me.

If you ever reed this Miss Kinnian dont be sorry for me Im glad I got a second chanse to be smart becaus I lerned a lot of things that I never even new were in this world and Im grateful that I saw it all for a littel bit. I dont know why Im dumb agen or what I did wrong maybe its because I dint try hard enuff. But if I try and practis very hard maybe Ill get a littl smarter and know what all the words are. I remember a littel bit how nice I had a feeling with the blue book that has the torn cover when I red it. Thats why Im gonna keep trying to get smart so I can have that feeling agen. Its a good feeling to know things and be smart. I wish I had it rite now if I did I would sit down and reed all the time. Anyway I bet Im the first dumb person in the world who ever found out somthing importent for science. I remember I did somthing but I dont remember what. So I gess its like I did it for all the dumb pepul like me.

Goodbye Miss Kinnian and Dr. Strauss and evreybody. And P.S. please tell Dr Nemur not to be such a grouch when pepul laff at him and he would have more frends. Its easy to make frends if you let pepul laff at you. Im going to have lots of frends where I go.

P.P.S. Please if you get a chanse put some flowrs on Algernons grave in the bak yard. . . .

1961
19th Convention
Seattle

Poul Anderson

There is a secret to the pronunciation of Poul Anderson's first name that only Scandinavians know.

In the summer of 1959, Poul Anderson and his wife were crossing the country by car and decided to stop off for a visit at the Asimovs. (It was either that or run into the Atlantic Ocean.)

This gave me a chance to see him; a chance that doesn't happen often, for he lives on "the Coast," while I live in a Boston suburb.

In any case, we had a pleasant time of it and a sizable portion of the evening was spent in alternately reciting his first name. First he would say it, then I would say it, then he would say it, then I would say it, and so on. I distinctly heard the pronunciation *he* gave it (a delicate perversion of the vowel which must be heard to be believed) but all I could come up with was "Pole."

Poor Poul gave up at last with a smile of forbearance on his face and admitted that everyone said "Pole."

It was about this time that I was coming to admire all things Scandinavian with great intensity (you ought to hear me tell of my experiences at a smorgasbord-type restaurant at which I committed such heroic carnage that there were moments afterward when it seemed that an operation would be necessary) and Poul may have had much to do with it. He is tall, has blond wavy hair and an incredibly youthful appearance. There is much of the Viking in him and it breathes through all his stories. Yet he is, withal, a gentle soul whose conversation is a particular delight for he is equally at home in the sciences and in the humanities.

That fall we met again at the 17th Convention (Detroit, 1959) and, as Toastmaster, it was my delight and pleasure to introduce Poul as Guest of Honor.

His great moment, however, came at the 19th Convention

(Seattle, 1961) when his novelette, "The Longest Voyage," won the Hugo. I could not attend that convention, so I did not witness the award, and my love and affection for Poul has therefore remained without alloy.

9

THE LONGEST VOYAGE

When first we heard of the Sky Ship, we were on an island whose name, as nearly as Montalirian tongues can wrap themselves about so barbarous a noise, was Yarzik. That was almost a year after the *Golden Leaper* sailed from Lavre Town, and we judged we had come halfway round the world. So befouled was our poor caravel with weeds and shells that all sail could scarce drag her across the sea. What drinking water remained in the butts was turned green and evil, the biscuit was full of worms, and the first signs of scurvy had appeared on certain crewmen.

"Hazard or no," decreed Captain Rovic, "we must land somewhere." A gleam I remembered appeared in his eyes. He stroked his red beard and murmured, "Besides, it's long since we asked for the Aureate Cities. Perhaps this time they'll have intelligence of such a place."

Steering by that ogre planet which climbed daily higher as we bore westward, we crossed such an emptiness that mutinous talk broke out afresh. In my heart I could not blame the crew. Imagine, my lords. Day upon day upon day where we saw naught but blue waters, white foam, high clouds in a tropic sky; heard only the wind, *whoosh* of waves, creak of timbers, sometimes at night the huge sucking and rushing as a sea monster breached. These were terrible enough to common sailors, unlettered men who still thought the world must be flat. But then to have Tambur hang forever above the bowsprit, and climb, so that all could see we must eventually pass directly beneath that brooding thing . . . and what upbore it? the crew mumbled in the forecastle. Would an angered God not let fall down on us?

So a deputation waited on Captain Rovic. Very timid and respectful they were, those rough burly men, as they asked him to turn about. But their comrades massed below, muscled sun-blackened bodies taut in the ragged kilts, with daggers and belaying pins ready to hand. We officers on the quarterdeck had swords and pistols, true. But we numbered a mere six, including that frightened boy who was myself, and aged Froad the astrologue, whose robe and white beard were reverend to see but of small use in a fight.

Rovic stood mute for a long while after the spokesman had voiced this demand. The stillness grew, until the empty shriek of wind in our shrouds, the empty glitter of ocean out to the world's rim, became all there was. Most splendid our master looked, for he had donned scarlet hose and bell-tipped shoon when he knew the deputation was coming: as well as helmet and corselet polished to mirror brightness. The plumes blew around that blinding steel head and the diamonds on his fingers flashed against the rubies in his sword hilt. Yet when at last he spoke, it was not as a knight of the Queen's court, but in the broad Anday of his fisher boyhood.

"So 'tis back ye'd wend, lads? Wi' a fair wind an' a warm sun, liefer ye'd come about an' beat half round the globe? How ye're changed from yere fathers! Ken ye nay the legend, that once all things did as man commanded, an' 'twas an Andayman's lazy fault that now men must work? For see ye, 'twas nay too much that he told his ax to cut down a tree for him, an' told the faggots to walk home, but when he told 'em to carry him, then God was wroth an' took the power away. Though to be sure, as recompense God gave all Andaymen sea-luck, dice-luck, an' love-luck. What more d'ye ask for, lads?"

Bewildered at this response, the spokesman wrung his hands, flushed, looked at the deck, and stammered that we'd all perish miserably . . . starve, or thirst, or drown, or be crushed under that horrible moon, or sail off the world's edge . . . the *Golden Leaper* had come farther than ship had sailed since the Fall of Man, and if we returned at once, our fame would live forever—

"But can ye eat fame, Etien?" asked Rovic, still mild and smiling. "We've had fights an' storms, aye, an' merry carouses too; but devil an Aureate City we've seen, though well ye ken they lie out here someplace, stuffed wi' treasure for the first bold man who'll come plunder 'em. What ails yere gutworks, lad? Is't nay an easy cruise? What would the foreigners say? How will yon arrogant cavaliers o' Sathayn, yon grubby chapmen o' Woodland, laugh—nay alone at us, but at all Montalir—did we turn back!"

Thus he jollied them. Only once did he touch his sword, half drawing it, as if absent-mindedly, when he recalled how we had weathered the hurricane off Xingu. But they remembered the mutiny that followed then, and how that same sword had pierced three armed sailors who attacked him together. His dialect told them he would let bygones lie forgotten: if they would. His bawdy promises of sport among lascivious heathen tribes yet to be discovered, his recital of treasure legends, his appeal to their pride as seamen and Montalirians, soothed fear. And then in the end, when he saw them malleable, he dropped the provincial speech. He stood forth on the quarterdeck with burning casque and tossing plumes, and the flag of Montalir blew its sea-faded colors above him, and he said as the knights of the Queen say:

"Now you know I do not propose to turn back until the great globe has been rounded and we bring to Her Majesty that gift which is most peculiarly ours to give. The which is not gold or slaves, nor even that lore of far places that she and her most excellent Company of Merchant Adventurers desire. No, what we shall lift in our hands to give her, on that day when again we lie by the long docks of Lavre, shall be our achievement: that we did this thing which no men have dared in all the world erenow, and did it to her glory."

A while longer he stood, through a silence full of the sea's noise. Then he said quietly, "Dismissed," turned on his heel and went back into his cabin.

So we continued for some days more, the men subdued but not uncheerful, the officers taking care to hide their doubts. I found myself busied, not so much with the clerical duties for which I was paid or the study of captaincy for which I was apprenticed —both these amounting to little by now—as with assisting Froad the astrologue. In these balmy airs he could carry on his work even on shipboard. To him it scarce mattered whether we sank or swam; he had lived more than a common span of years already. But the knowledge of the heavens to be gained here, that was something else. At night, standing on the foredeck with quadrant, astrolabe, and telescope, drenched in the radiance from above, he resembled some frosty-bearded saint in the windows of Provien Minster.

"See there, Zhean." His thin hand pointed above seas that glowed and rippled with light, past the purple sky and the few stars still daring to show themselves, toward Tambur. Huge it was in full phase at midnight, sprawling over seven degrees of sky, a shield or barry of soft vert and azure, splotched with angry sable that could be seen to move across its face. The firefly moon we had named Siett twinkled near the hazy edge of the giant. Balant, espied rarely and low on the horizon in our part of the world, here stood high: a crescent, but with the dark part of the disk tinged by luminous Tambur.

"Observe," declared Froad, "there's no doubt left, one can *see* how it rotates on an axis, and how storms boil up in its air. Tambur is no longer the dimmest of frightened legends, nor a dreadful apparition seen to rise as we entered unknown waters; Tambur is real. A world like our own. Immensely bigger, certes, but still a spheroid in space: around which our own world moves, always turning the same hemisphere to her monarch. The conjectures of the ancients are triumphantly confirmed. Not merely that our world is round, *pouf*, that's obvious to anyone . . . but that we move about a greater center, which in turn has an annual path about the sun. But, then, how big is the sun?"

"Siett and Balant are inner satellites of Tambur," I rehearsed, struggling for comprehension. "Vieng, Darou, and the other moons commonly seen at home, have paths outside our own world's. Aye. But what holds it all up?"

"That I don't know. Mayhap the crystal sphere containing the stars exerts an inward pressure. The same pressure, maybe, that hurled mankind down onto the earth, at the time of the Fall From Heaven."

That night was warm, but I shivered, as if those had been winter stars. "Then," I breathed, "there may also be men on . . . Siett, Balant, Vieng . . . even on Tambur?"

"Who knows? We'll need many lifetimes to find out. And what

lifetimes they'll be! Thank the good God, Zhean, that you were born in this dawn of the coming age."

Froad returned to making measurements. A dull business, the other officers thought; but by now I had learned enough of the mathematic arts to understand that from these endless tabulations might come the true size of the earth, of Tambur, sun and moons and stars, the path they took through space and the direction of Paradise. So the common sailors, who muttered and made signs against evil as they passed our instruments, were closer to fact than Rovic's gentlemen: for indeed Froad practiced a most potent gramarye.

At length we saw weeds floating on the sea, birds, towering cloud masses, all the signs of land. Three days later we raised an island. It was an intense green under those calm skies. Surf, still more violent than in our hemisphere, flung against high cliffs, burst in a smother of foam and roared back down again. We coasted carefully, the palomers aloft to seek an approach, the gunners standing by our cannon with lighted matches. For not only were there unknown currents and shoals—familiar hazards— but we had had brushes with canoe-sailing cannibals in the past. Especially did we fear the eclipses. My lords can visualize how in that hemisphere the sun each day must go behind Tambur. In that longitude the occurrence was about midafternoon and lasted nearly ten minutes. An awesome sight: the primary planet —for so Froad now called it, a planet akin to Diell or Coint, with our own world humbled to a mere satellite thereof!—become a black disk encircled with red, up in a sky suddenly full of stars. A cold wind blew across the sea, and even the breakers seemed hushed. Yet so impudent is the soul of man that we continued about our duties, stopping only for the briefest prayer as the sun disappeared, thinking more about the chance of shipwreck in the gloom than of God's Majesty.

So bright is Tambur that we continued to work our way around the island at night. From sunup to sunup, twelve mortal hours, we kept the *Golden Leaper* slowly moving. Toward the second noon, Captain Rovic's persistence was rewarded. An opening in the cliffs revealed a long fjord. Swampy shores overgrown with saltwater trees told us that while the tides rose high in that bay, it was not one of those roosts so dreaded by mariners. The wind being against us, we furled sail and lowered the boats, towing in our caravel by the power of oars. This was a vulnerable moment, especially since we had perceived a village within the fjord. "Should we not stand out, master, and let them come first to us?" I ventured.

Rovic spat over the rail. "I've found it best never to show doubt," said he. "If a canoe fleet should assail us, we'll give 'em a whiff of grapeshot and trust to break their nerve. But I think, thus showing ourselves fearless of them from the very first, we're less likely to meet treacherous ambuscade later."

He proved right.

In the course of time, we learned we had come upon the eastern end of a large archipelago. The inhabitants were mighty seafarers, considering that they had only outrigger dugouts to travel in. These, however, were often a hundred feet long. With forty paddles, or with three bast-sailed masts, such a vessel could almost match our best speed, and was more maneuverable. However, the small cargo space limited their range of travel.

Though they lived in houses of wood and thatch, possessing only stone tools, the natives were cultivated folk. They farmed as well as fished; their priests had an alphabet. Tall and vigorous, somewhat darker and less hairy than we, they were impressive to behold: whether nude as was common, or in full panoply of cloth and feathers and shell ornaments. They had formed a loose empire throughout the archipelago, raided islands lying farther north and carried on a brisk trade within their own borders. Their whole nation they called the Hisagazi, and the island on which we had chanced was Yarzik.

This we learned slowly, as we mastered somewhat their tongue. For we were several weeks at that town. The duke of the island, Guzan, made us welcome, supplying us with food, shelter, and helpers as we required. For our part, we pleased them with glassware, bolts of Wondish cloth, and suchlike trade goods. Nonetheless we encountered many difficulties. The shore above high-water mark being too swampy for beaching a vessel as heavy as ours, we must build a drydock before we could careen. Numerous of us took a flux from some disease, though all recovered in time, and this slowed us further.

"Yet I think our troubles will prove a blessing," Rovic told me one night. As had become his habit, once he learned I was a discreet amanuensis, he confided certain thoughts in me. The captain is ever a lonely man; and Rovic, fisher lad, freebooter, self-taught navigator, victor over the Grand Fleet of Sathayn and ennobled by the Queen herself, must have found the keeping of that necessary aloofness harder than would a gentleman born.

I waited silent, there in the grass hut they had given him. A soapstone lamp threw wavering light and enormous shadows over us; something rustled the thatch. Outside, the damp ground sloped past houses on stilts and murmurous fronded trees, to the fjord where it shimmered under Tambur. Faintly I heard drums throb, a chant and stamping of feet around some sacrificial fire. Indeed the cool hills of Montalir seemed far.

Rovic leaned back his muscular form, y-clad a mere seaman's kilt in this heat. He had had them fetch him a civilized chair from the ship. "For see you, young fellow," he continued, "at other times we'd have established just enough communication to ask about gold. Well, we might also try to get a few sailing directions. But all in all, we'd hear little except the old story—'aye, foreign lord, indeed there's a kingdom where the very streets are paved with gold . . . a hundred miles west'—anything to get rid of us, eh? But in this prolonged stay, I've asked out the duke and the idolater priests more subtly. I've been so coy about whence we came and what we already know, that they've let slip a gobbet of knowledge they'd not otherwise have disgorged on the rack itself."

"The Aureate Cities?" I cried.

"Hush! I'd not have the crew get excited and out of hand. Not yet."

His leathery, hooknosed face turned strange with thought. "I've always believed those cities an old wives' tale," he said. My shock must have been mirrored to his gaze, for he grinned and went on, "A useful one. Like a lodestone on a stick, it's dragging us around the world." His mirth faded. Again he got that look, which was not unlike the look of Froad considering the heavens. "Aye, of course I want gold, too. But if we find none on this voyage, I'll not care. I'll just capture a few ships of Eralia or Sathayn when we're back in home waters, and pay for the voyage thus. I spoke

God's truth that day on the quarterdeck, Zhean, that this journey was its own goal; until I can give it to Queen Odela, who once gave me the kiss of ennoblement."

He shook himself out of his reverie and said in a brisk tone: "Having led him to believe I already knew the most of it, I teased from Duke Guzan the admission that on the main island of this Hisagazi empire is something I scarce dare think about. A ship of the gods, he says, and an actual live god who came from the stars therein. Any of the natives will tell you this much. The secret reserved to the noble folk is that this is no legend or mummery, but sober fact. Or so Guzan claims. I know not what to think. But . . . he took me to a holy cave and showed me an object from that ship. It was some kind of clockwork mechanism, I believe. What, I know not. But of a shining silvery metal such as I've never seen before. The priest challenged me to break it. The metal was not heavy; must have been thin. But it blunted my sword, splintered a rock I pounded with, and my diamond ring would not scratch it."

I made signs against evil. A chill went along me, spine and skin and scalp, until I prickled all over. For the drums were muttering in a jungle dark, and the waters lay like quicksilver beneath gibbous Tambur, and each afternoon that planet ate the sun. Oh, for the bells of Provien, across windswept Anday downs!

When the *Golden Leaper* was seaworthy again, Rovic had no trouble gaining permission to visit the Hisagazian emperor on the main island. He would, indeed, have found difficulty in not doing so. By now the canoes had borne word of us from one end of the realm to another, and the great lords were all agog to see these blue-eyed strangers. Sleek and content once more, we disentangled ourselves from the arms of tawny wenches and embarked. Up anchor, up sail, with chanties whose echoes sent sea birds whirling above the steeps, and we stood out to sea. This time we were escorted. Guzan himself was our pilot, a big middle-aged man whose handsomeness was not much injured by the livid green tattoos his folk affected on face and body. Several of his sons spread their pallets on our decks, while a swarm of warriors paddled alongside.

Rovic summoned Etien the boatswain to him in his cabin.

"You're a man of some wit," he said. "I give you charge of keeping our crew alert, weapons ready, however peaceful this may look."

"Why, master!" The scarred brown face sagged with near dismay. "Think you the natives plot a treachery?"

"Who can tell?" said Rovic. "Now, say naught to the crew. They've no skill in dissembling. Did greed or fear rise among 'em, the natives would sense as much, and grow uneasy—which would worsen the attitude of our own men, until none but God's Daughter could tell what'd happen. Only see to it, as casually as you're able, that our arms are ever close by and that our folk stay together."

Etien collected himself, bowed, and left the cabin. I made bold to ask what Rovic had in mind.

"Nothing, yet," said he. "However, I did hold in these fists a piece of clockwork such as the Grand Ban of Giair never imagined; and yarns were spun me of a Ship which flew down from heaven, bearing a god or a prophet. Guzan thinks I know more than I do, and hopes we'll be a new, disturbing element in the balance of things, by which he may further his own ambitions. He did not take all those fighting men along by accident. As for me . . . I intend to learn more about this."

He sat a while at his table, staring at a sunbeam which sickled up and down the wainscot as the ship rocked. Finally: "Scripture tells us man dwelt beyond the stars before the Fall. The astrologues of the past generation or two have told us the planets are corporeal bodies like this earth. A traveler from Paradise—"

I left with my head in a roar.

We made an easy passage among scores of islands. After several days we raised the main one, Ulas-Erkila. It is about a hundred miles long, forty miles across at the widest, rising steep and green toward central mountains dominated by a volcanic cone. The Hisagazi worship two sorts of gods, watery and fiery, and believe this Mount Ulas houses the latter. When I saw that snowpeak afloat in the sky above emerald ridges, staining the blue with smoke, I could feel what the pagans did. The holiest act a man can perform among them is to cast himself into the burning crater of Ulas, and many an aged warrior is carried up the mountain that he may do so. Women are not allowed on the slopes.

Nikum, the royal seat, is situated at the head of a fjord like
the village where we had been staying. But Nikum is rich and
extensive, being about the size of Roann. Many houses are made
from timber rather than thatch; there is also a massive basalt
temple atop a cliff, overlooking the city, with orchards, jungle,
and mountains at its back. So great are the tree trunks available
to them for pilings, the Hisagazi have built here a regular set of
docks like those at Lavre—instead of moorings and floats that can
rise or fall with the tides, such as most harbors throughout the
world are content with. We were offered a berth of honor at the
central wharf, but Rovic made the excuse that our ship was awkward to handle and got us tied at the far end.

"In the middle, we'd have the watchtower straight above us,"
he muttered to me. "And they may not have discovered the bow
here, but their javelin throwers are good. Also, we'd have an
easy approach to our ship, plus a clutter of moored canoes between us and the bay mouth. Here, though, a few of us could
hold the pier whilst the others ready for quick departure."

"But have we anything to fear, master?" I asked.

He gnawed his mustache. "I know not. Much depends on what
they really believe about this god-ship of theirs . . . as well as
what the truth is. But come all death and hell against us, we'll
not return without that truth for Queen Odela."

Drums rolled and feathered spearmen leaped as our officers
disembarked. A royal catwalk had been erected above high-
water level. (Common townsfolk in this realm swim from house
to house when the tide laps their thresholds, or take a coracle if
they have burdens to carry.) Across the graceful span of vines
and canes lay the palace, which was a long building made from
logs, the roof pillars carved into fantastic god-shapes.

Iskilip, Priest-Emperor of the Hisagazi, was an old and corpu-
lent man. A soaring headdress of plumes, a feather robe, a
wooden scepter topped with a human skull, his own facial tattoos, his motionlessness, all made him seem unhuman. He sat on a
dais, under sweet-smelling torches. His sons sat crosslegged at
his feet, his courtiers on either side. Down the long walls were
ranged his guardsmen. They had not our custom of standing to
attention; but they were big supple young men, with shields and

corselets of scaly seamonster leather, with flint axes and obsidian spears that could kill as easily as iron. Their heads were shaven, which made them look the fiercer.

Iskilip greeted us well, called for refreshment, bade us be seated on a bench not much lower than his dais. He asked many perceptive questions. Wide-ranging, the Hisagazi knew of islands far beyond their own chain. They could even point the direction and tell us roughly the distance of a many-castled country they named Yurakadak, though one of them had traveled that far himself. Judging by their third-hand description, what could this be but Giair, which the Wondish adventurer Hanas Tolasson had reached overland? It blazed in me that we were indeed rounding the world. Only after that glory had faded a little did I again heed the talk.

"As I told Guzan," Rovic was saying, "another thing which drew us hither was the tale that you were blessed with a Ship from heaven. And he showed me this was true."

A hissing went down the hall. The princes grew stiff, the courtiers blanked their countenances, even the guardsmen stirred and muttered. Remotely through the walls I heard the rumbling, nearing tide. When Iskilip spoke, through the mask of himself, his voice had gone whetted: "Have you forgotten that these things are not for the uninitiate to see, Guzan?"

"No, Holy One," said the duke. Sweat sprang forth among the devils on his face, but it was not the sweat of fear. "However, this captain knew. His people also . . . as nearly as I could learn . . . he still has trouble speaking so I can understand . . . his people are initiate too. The claim seems reasonable, Holy One. Look at the marvels they brought. The hard, shining stone-which-is-not-stone, as in this long knife I was given, is that not like the stuff of which the Ship is built? The tubes which make distant things look close at hand, such as he has given you, Holy One, is this not akin to the far-seer the Messenger possesses?"

Iskilip leaned forward, toward Rovic. His scepter hand trembled so much that the pegged jaws of the skull clattered together. "Did the Star People themselves teach you to make all this?" he cried. "I never imagined . . . The Messenger never spoke of any others—"

Rovic held up both palms. "Not so fast, Holy One, I pray you,"

K

said he. "We are poorly versed in your tongue. I couldn't recognize a word just now."

This was his deceit. All his officers had been ordered to feign a knowledge of Hisagazi less than they really possessed. (We had improved our command of it by secret practicing with each other.) Thus he had an unimpeachable device for equivocation.

"Best we talk of this in private, Holy One," suggested Guzan, with a glance at the courtiers. They returned him a jealous glare.

Iskilip slouched in his gorgeous regalia. His words fell blunt enough, but in the weak tone of an old, uncertain man. "I know not. If these strangers are already initiate, certes we can show them what we have. But otherwise—if profane ears heard the Messenger's own tale—"

Guzan raised a dominator's hand. Bold and ambitious, long thwarted in his petty province, he had taken fire this day. "Holy One," he said, "why has the full story been withheld all these years? In part to keep the commoners obedient, aye. But also, did you and your councillors not fear that all the world might swarm hither, greedy for knowledge, if it knew, and we should then be overwhelmed? Well, if we let the blue-eyed men go home with curiosity unsatisfied, I think they are sure to return in strength. So we have naught to lose by revealing the truth to them. If they have never had a Messenger of their own, if they can be of no real use to us, time enough to kill them. But if they have indeed been visited like us, what might we and they not do together!"

This was spoken fast and softly, so that we Montalirians should not understand. And indeed our gentlemen failed to do so. I, having young ears, got the gist; and Rovic preserved such a fatuous smile of incomprehension that I knew he was seizing every word.

So in the end they decided to take our leader—and my insignificant self, for no Hisagazian magnate goes anywhere quite unattended—up to the temple. Iskilip led the way in person, with Guzan and two brawny princes behind. A dozen spearmen brought up the rear. I thought Rovic's blade would be scant use if trouble came, but set my lips firmly together and made myself walk behind him. He looked as eager as a child on Thanksday

Morning, teeth agleam in the pointed beard, a plumed bonnet slanted rakish over his brow. None would have thought him aware of any peril.

We left about sundown; in Tambur's hemisphere, folk make less distinction between day and night than our people must. Having observed Siett and Balant in high tide position, I was not surprised that Nikum lay nearly drowned. And yet, as we wound up the cliff trail toward the temple, methought I had never seen a view more alien.

Below us lay a sheet of water, on which the long grass roofs of the city appeared to float; the crowded docks, where our own ship's masts and spars raked above heathen figureheads; the fjord, winding between precipices toward its mouth, where the surf broke white and terrible on the skerries. The heights above us seemed altogether black, against a fire-colored sunset that filled nigh half the sky and bloodied the waters. Wan through those clouds I glimpsed the thick crescent of Tambur, banded in a heraldry no man could read. A basalt column chipped into the shape of a head loomed in outline athwart the planet. Right and left of the path grew sawtoothed grasses, summer-dry. The sky was pale at the zenith, dark purple in the east, where the first few stars had appeared. Tonight I found no comfort in the stars. We all walked silent. The bare native feet made no noise. My own shoes went *pad-pad* and the bells on Rovic's toes raised a tiny jingle.

The temple was a bold piece of work. Within a quadrangle of basalt walls guarded by tall stone heads lay several buildings of the same material. Only the fresh-cut fronds that roofed them were alive. With Iskilip to lead us, we brushed past acolytes and priests to a wooden cabin behind the sanctum. Two guardsmen stood watch at its door, but they knelt for Iskilip. The emperor rapped with his curious scepter.

My mouth was dry and my heart thunderous. I expected almost any being hideous or radiant to stand in the doorway as it was opened. Astonishing, then, to see just a man, and of no great stature. By lamplight within I discerned his room, clean, austere, but not uncomfortable; this could have been any Hisagazian dwelling. He himself wore a simple bast skirt. The legs beneath were bent and thin, old man's shanks. His body was also thin, but still erect, the white head proudly carried. In complexion he was darker than a Montalirian, lighter than a Hisagazian, with brown eyes and thin beard. His visage differed subtly, in nose and lips and slope of jaw, from any other race I had ever encountered. But he was human.

Naught else.

We entered the cabin, shutting out the spearmen. Iskilip doddered through a half-religious ceremony of introduction. I saw Guzan and the princes shift their stance, restless and unawed. Their class had long been party to this. Rovic's face was unreadable. He bowed with full courtliness to Val Nira, Messenger of Heaven, and explained our presence in a few words. But as he spoke, their eyes met and I saw him take the star man's measure.

"Aye, this in my home," said Val Nira. Habit spoke for him; he had given this account to so many young nobles that the edges were worn off it. As yet he had not observed our metallic instruments, or else had not grasped their significance to him. "For . . . forty-three years, is that right, Iskilip? I have been treated as well as might be. If at times I was near screaming from loneliness, that is what an oracle must expect."

The emperor stirred, uneasy in his robe. "His demon left him," he explained. "Now he is simple human flesh. That's the real secret we keep. It was not ever thus. I remember when he first came. He prophesied immense things, and all the people wailed and went on their faces. But sithence his demon has gone back to the stars, and the once potent weapon he bore has equally been emptied of its force. The people would not believe this, however, so we still pretend otherwise, or there would be unrest among them."

"Affecting your own privileges," said Val Nira. His tone was tired and sardonic. "Iskilip was young then," he added to Rovic, "and the imperial succession was in doubt. I gave him my influence. He promised in return to do certain things for me."

"I tried, Messenger," said the monarch. "Ask all the sunken canoes and drowned men if I did not try. But the will of the gods was otherwise."

"Evidently." Val Nira shrugged. "These islands have few ores, Captain Rovic, and no person capable of recognizing those I required. It's too far to the mainland for Hisagazian canoes. But I don't deny you tried, Iskilip . . . then." He cocked an eyebrow back at us. "This is the first time foreigners have been taken so deeply into the imperial confidence, my friends. Are you certain you can get back out again, alive?"

"Why, why, why, they're our guests!" blustered Iskilip and Guzan, almost in each other's mouths.

"Besides," smiled Rovic, "I had most of the secret already. My own country has secrets of its own, to set against this. Yes, I think we might well do business, Holy One."

The emperor trembled. His voice cracked across. "Have you indeed a Messenger too?"

"*What?*" For a numbed moment Val Nira stared at us. Red and white pursued each other across his countenance. Then he sat down on the bench and began to weep.

"Well, not precisely." Rovic laid a hand on the shaking shoulder, "I confess no heavenly vessel had docked at Montalir. But we've certain other secrets, belike equally valuable." Only I, who knew his moods somewhat, could sense the tautness in him. He locked eyes with Guzan and stared the duke down as a wild animal tamer does. And all the while, motherly gentle, he spoke with Val Nira. "I take it, friend, your Ship was wrecked on these shores, but could be repaired if you had certain materials?"

"Yes . . . yes . . . listen—" Stammering and gulping at the thought he might see his home again ere he died, Val Nira tried to explain.

The doctrinal implications of what he said are so astounding, even dangerous, that I feel sure my lords would not wish me to repeat much. However, I do not believe they are false. If the stars are indeed suns like our own, each attended by planets like our own, this demolishes the crystal-sphere theory. But Froad, when he was told later, did not think that mattered to the true religion. Scripture has never said in so many words that Paradise lies directly above the birthplace of God's Daughter; this was merely assumed, during those centuries when the earth was believed to be flat. Why should Paradise not be those planets of other suns, where men dwell in magnificence, men who possess all the ancient arts and flit from star to star as casually as we might go from Lavre to West Alayn?

Val Nira believed our ancestors had been cast away on this world, several thousand years ago. They must have been fleeing the consequences of some crime or heresy, to come so far from any human domain. Somehow their ship was wrecked, the survivors went back to savagery, only by degrees have their descendants regained a little knowledge. I cannot see where this explanation contradicts the dogma of the Fall. Rather, it amplifies it. The Fall was not the portion of all mankind, but only of a few—our own tainted blood—while the others continued to dwell prosperous and content in the heavens.

Even today, our world lies far off the trade lanes of the Paradise folk. Very few of them nowadays have any interest in seeking new worlds. Val Nira, though, was such a one. He traveled at hazard for months until he chanced upon our earth. Then the curse seized him, too. Something went wrong. He descended upon Ulas-Erkila, and the Ship would fly no more.

"I know what the damage is," he said ardently. "I've not forgotten. How could I? No day has passed in all these years that I didn't recite to myself what must be done. A certain subtle engine in the Ship requires quicksilver." (He and Rovic must spend some time talking ere they deduced this must be what he meant by the word he used.) "When the engine failed, I landed so hard that its tanks burst. All the quicksilver, what I had in reserve as well as what I was employing, poured forth. So much, in that hot enclosed space, would have poisoned me. I fled outside, forgetting to close the doorway. The deck being canted, the quicksilver ran after me. By the time I had recovered from blind panic, a tropical rainstorm had carried off all the fluid metal. A series of unlikely accidents, yes, that's what's condemned me to a life's exile. It really would have made more sense to perish outright!"

He clutched Rovic's hand, staring up from his seat at the captain who stood over him. "Can you actually get quicksilver?" he begged. "I need no more than the volume of a man's head. Only that, and a few repairs easily made with tools in the Ship. When this cult grew up around me, I must needs release certain things I possessed, that each provincial temple might have a relic. But

I took care never to give away anything important. Whatever I need is all there. A gallon of quicksilver, and— Oh, God, my wife may even be alive, on Terra!"

Guzan, at least, had begun to understand the situation. He gestured to the princes, who hefted their axes and stepped a little closer. The door was shut on the guard escort, but a shout would bring their spears into this cabin. Rovic looked from Val Nira to Guzan, whose face was grown ugly with tension. My captain laid hand on hilt. In no other way did he seem to feel any nearness of trouble.

"I take it, milord," he said lightly, "you're willing that the Heaven Ship be made to fly again."

Guzan was jarred. He had never expected this. "Why, of course," he exclaimed. "Why not?"

"Your tame god would depart you. What then becomes of your power in Hisagazia?"

"I . . . I'd not thought of that," Iskilip stuttered.

Val Nira's eyes shuttled among us, as if watching a game of paddleball. His thin body shook. "No," he whimpered. "You can't. You can't keep me!"

Guzan nodded. "In a few more years," he said, not unkindly, "you would depart in death's canoe anyhow. If meanwhile we held you against your will, you might not speak the right oracles for us. Nay, be at ease; we'll get your flowing stone." With a slitted glance at Rovic: "Who shall fetch it?"

"My own folk," said the knight. "Our ship can readily reach Giair, where there are civilized nations who surely have the quicksilver. We could return within a year, I think."

"Accompanied by a fleet of adventurers, to help you seize the sacred vessel?" asked Guzan bluntly. "Or . . . once out of our islands . . . you might not proceed to Yurakadak at all. You might continue the whole way home, and tell your Queen, and return with all the power she commands."

Rovic lounged against a roof post, like a big pouncecat at its ease in ruffles and hose and scarlet cape. His right hand continued to rest on his sword pommel. "Only Val Nira could make that Ship go, I suppose," he drawled. "Does it matter who aids him in making repairs? Surely you don't think either of our nations could conquer Paradise!"

"The Ship is very easy to operate," chattered Val Nira. "Anyone can fly it in air. I showed many nobles what levers to use. It's navigating among the stars which is more difficult. No nation on this world could even reach my people unaided—let alone fight them—but why should you think of fighting? I've told you a thousand times, Iskilip, the dwellers in the Milky Way are dangerous to none, helpful to all. They have so much wealth they're hard put to find a use for most of it. Gladly would they spend large amounts to help all the peoples on this world become civilized again." With an anxious, half hysterical look at Rovic: "Fully civilized, I mean. We'll teach you our arts. We'll give you engines, automata, homunculi, that do all the toilsome work; and boats that fly through the air; and regular passenger service on those ships that ply between the stars—"

"These things you have promised for forty years," said Iskilip. "We've only your word."

"And, finally, a chance to confirm his word," I blurted.

Guzan said with calculated grimness: "Matters are not that simple, Holy One. I've watched these men from across the ocean for weeks, while they lived on Yarzik. Even on their best behavior, they're a fierce and greedy lot. I trust them no further than my eyes reach. This very night I see how they've befooled us. They know our language better than they ever admitted. And they misled us to believe they might have some inkling of a Messenger. If the Ship were indeed made to fly again, with them in possession, who knows what they might choose to do?"

Rovic's tone softened still further, "What do you propose, Guzan?"

"We can discuss that another time."

I saw knuckles tighten around stone axes. For a moment, only Val Nira's unsteady breathing was heard. Guzan stood heavy in the lamplight, rubbing his chin, the small black eyes turned downward in thoughtfulness. At last he shook himself. "Perhaps," he said crisply, "a crew mainly Hisagazian could sail your ship, Rovic, and fetch the flowing stone. A few of your men could go along to instruct ours. The rest could remain here as hostages."

My captain made no reply. Val Nira groaned, "You don't understand! You're squabbling over nothing! Wnen my people come here, there'll be no more war, no more oppression, they'll cure you of all such diseases. They'll show friendship to all and favor to none. I beg you—"

"Enough," said Iskilip. His own words fell ragged. "We shall sleep on all this. If anyone can sleep after so much strangeness."

Rovic looked past the emperor's plumes, into the face of Guzan. "Before we decide anything—" His fingers tightened on the sword hilt till the nails turned white. Some thought had sprung up within him. But he kept his tone even. "First I want to see that Ship. Can we go there tomorrow?"

Iskilip was the Holy One, but he stood huddled in his feather robe. Guzan nodded agreement.

We bade our goodnights and went forth under Tambur. The planet was waxing toward full, flooding the courtyard with cold luminance, but the hut was shadowed by the temple. It remained a black outline, with a narrow lamplight rectangle of doorway in the middle. There was etched the frail body of Val Nira, who had come from the stars. He watched us till we had gone out of sight.

On the way down the path, Guzan and Rovic bargained in curt words. The Ship lay two days' march inland, on the slopes of Mount Ulas. We would go in a joint party to inspect it, but a mere dozen Montalirians were to be allowed. Afterward we would debate our course of action.

Lanthorns glowed yellow at our caravel's poop. Refusing Iskilip's hospitality, Rovic and I returned thither for the night. A pikeman on guard at the gangway inquired what I had learned. "Ask me tomorrow," I said feebly. "My head's in too much of a whirl."

"Come into my cabin, lad, for a stoup ere we retire," the captain invited me.

God knows I needed wine. We entered the low little room, crowded with nautical instruments, with books, and with printed charts that looked quaint to me now I had seen a little of those spaces where the cartographer drew mermaids and windsprites. Rovic sat down behind his table, gestured me to a chair opposite, and poured from a carafe into two goblets of Quaynish crystal.

Then I knew he had momentous thoughts in his head—far more than the problem of saving our lives.

We sipped a while, unspeaking. I heard the *lap-lap* of wavelets on our hull, the tramp of men on watch, the rustle of distant surf: otherwise nothing. At last Rovic leaned back, staring at the ruby wine on the table. I could not read his expression.

"Well, lad," said he, "what do you think?"

"I know not what to think, master."

"You and Froad are a little prepared for this idea that the stars are other suns. You're educated. As for me, I've seen so much eldritch in my day that this seems quite believable. The rest of our people, though—"

"An irony that barbarians like Guzan should long have been familiar with the concept—having had the old man from the sky to preach it privily to their class for more than forty years— Is he indeed a prophet, master?"

"He denies it. He plays prophet because he must, but it's evident all the dukes and earls of this realm know it's a trick. Iskilip is senile, more than half converted to his own artificial creed. He was mumbling about prophecies Val Nira made long ago, true prophecies. Bah! Tricks of memory and wishfulness. Val Nira is as human and fallible as I am. We Montalirians are the same flesh as these Hisagazi, even if we have learned the use of metal before they did. Val Nira's people know more in turn than us; but they're still mortals, by Heaven. I *must* remember that they are."

"Guzan remembers."

"Bravo, lad!" Rovic's mouth bent upward, one-sidedly. "He's a clever one, and bold. When he came, he saw his chance to stop stagnating as the petty lord of an outlying island. He'll not let that chance slip without a fight. Like many a double-dealer before him, he accuses us of plotting the very things he hopes to do."

"But what does he hope for?"

"My guess would be, he wants the Ship for himself. Val Nira said it was easy to fly. Navigation between the stars would be too difficult for anyone save him; nor could any man in his right mind hope to play pirate along the Milky Way. However . . . if the Ship stayed right here, on this earth, rising no higher than a mile above ground . . . the warlord who used it might conquer more widely than Lame Darveth himself."

I was aghast. "Do you mean Guzan would not even try to seek out Paradise?"

Rovic scowled so blackly at his wine that I saw he wanted aloneness. I stole off to my bunk in the poop.

The captain was up before dawn, readying our folk. Plainly he had reached some decision, and it was not pleasant. But once he set a course, he seldom left it. He was long in conference with Etien, who came out of the cabin looking frightened. As if to reassure himself, the boatswain ordered the men about all the more harshly.

Our allowed dozen were to be Rovic, Froad, myself, Etien, and eight crewmen. All were supplied with helmets and corselets, muskets and edged weapons. Since Guzan had told us there was a beaten path to the Ship, we assembled a supply cart on the dock. Etien supervised its lading. I was astonished to see that nearly all it carried, till the axles groaned, was barrels of gunpowder. "But we're not taking cannon!" I protested.

"Skipper's orders," rapped Etien. He turned his back on me. After a glance at Rovic's face, no one ventured to ask him the reason. I remembered we would be going up a mountainside. A wagonful of powder, with lit fuse, set rolling down toward a hostile army, might win a battle. But did Rovic anticipate open conflict so soon?

Certes his orders to the men and officers remaining behind suggested as much. They were to stay aboard the *Golden Leaper*, holding her ready for instant fight or flight.

As the sun rose, we said our morning prayers to God's Daughter and marched down the docks. The wood banged hollow under our boots. A few thin mists drifted on the bay; Tambur's crescent hung wan above. Nikum Town was hushed as we passed through.

Guzan met us at the temple. A son of Iskilip was supposedly in charge, but the duke ignored that youth as much as we did. They had a hundred guardsmen with them, scaly-coated, shavenheaded, tattooed with storms and dragons. The early sunlight gleamed off obsidian spearheads. Our approach was watched in silence. But when we drew up before those disorderly ranks, Guzan trod forth. He was also y-clad in leather, and carried the sword Rovic had given him on Yarzik. The dew shimmered on his feather cloak. "What have you in that wagon?" he demanded.

"Supplies," Rovic answered.

"For four days?"

"Send home all but ten of your men," said Rovic coolly, "and I'll send back this cart."

Their eyes clashed, until Guzan turned and gave his orders. We started off, a few Montalirians surrounded by pagan warriors. The jungle lay ahead of us, a deep and burning green, rising halfway up the slope of Ulas. Then the mountain became naked black, up to the snow that edged its smoking crater.

Val Nira walked between Rovic and Guzan. Strange, I thought, that the instrument of God's will for us was so shriveled. He ought to have walked tall and haughty, with a star on his brow.

During the day, at night when we made camp, and again the next day, Rovic and Froad questioned him eagerly about his home. Of course, all their talk was in fragments. Nor did I hear everything, since I must take my turn at pulling our wagon along that narrow, upward, damnable trail. The Hisagazi have no draft animals, therefore they make very little use of the wheel and have no proper roads. But what I did hear kept me long awake.

Ah, greater marvels than the poets have imagined for Elf Land! Entire cities built in a single tower half a mile high. The sky made to glow so that there is no true darkness after sunset. Food not grown in the earth, but manufactured in alchemical elaboratories. The lowest peasant owning a score of machines which serve him more subtly and humbly than might a thousand slaves —owning an aerial carriage which can fly him around his world in less than a day—owning a crystal window on which theatrical images appear, to beguile his abundant leisure. Argosies between suns, stuffed with the wealth of a thousand planets; yet every ship unarmed and unescorted, for there are no pirates and this realm has long ago come to such good terms with the other starfaring nations that war has also ceased. (These other countries, it seems, are more akin to the supernatural than Val Nira's, in that the races composing them are not human, though able to speak and reason.) In this happy land there is little crime. When it does occur, the criminal is soon captured by the arts of the provost corps; yet he is not hanged, nor even transported overseas. Instead, his mind is cured of the wish to violate any law. He returns home to live as an especially honored citizen, since all know he is now completely trustworthy. As for the government —but here I lost the thread of discourse. I believe it is in form a republic, but in practice a devoted fellowship of men, chosen by examination, who see to the welfare of everyone else.

Surely, I thought, this was Paradise!

Our sailors listened with mouths agape. Rovic's mien was reserved, but he gnawed his mustaches incessantly. Guzan, to whom this was an old tale, grew rough of manner. Plain to see, he disliked our intimacy with Val Nira, and the ease wherewith we grasped ideas that were spoken.

But then, we came of a nation which has long encouraged natural philosophy and improvement of all mechanic arts. I myself, in my short lifetime, had witnessed the replacement of the waterwheel in regions where there are few streams, by the modern form of windmill. The pendulum clock was invented the year before I was born. I had read many romances about the flying machines which no few men have tried to devise. Living at such a dizzy pace of progress, we Montalirians were well prepared to entertain still vaster concepts.

At night, sitting up with Froad and Etien around a campfire, I spoke somewhat of this to the savant. "Ah," he crooned, "today Truth stood unveiled before me. Did you hear what the starman said? The three laws of planetary motion about a sun, and the one great law of attraction which explains them? Dear saints, that law can be put in a single short sentence, and yet the development will keep mathematicians busy for three hundred years!"

He stared past the flames, and the other fires around which the heathen men slept, and the jungle gloom, and the angry volcanic glow in heaven. I started to query him. "Leave be, lad," grunted Etien. "Can ye nay tell when a man's in love?"

I shifted my position, a little closer to the boatswain's stolid, comforting bulk. "What do you think of all this?" I asked, softly, for the jungle whispered and croaked on every side.

"Me, I stopped thinking a while back," he said. "After yon day on the quarterdeck, when the skipper jested us into sailing wi'

him though we went off the world's edge an' tumbled down in
foam amongst the nether stars . . . well, I'm but a poor sailor
man, an' my one chance o' regaining home is to follow the
skipper."

"Even beyond the sky?"

"Less hazard to that, maybe, than sailing on around the world.
The little man swore his vessel was safe, an' that there're no
storms between the suns."

"Can you trust his word?"

"Oh, aye. Even a knocked-about old palomer like me has seen
enough o' men to ken when a one's too timid an' eagersome to
stand by a lie. I fear not the folk in Paradise, nor does the skipper. Except in some way—" Etien rubbed his bearded jaw, scowling. "In some way I can nay wholly grasp, they affright Rovic. He
fears nay they'll come hither wi' torch an' sword; but there's somewhat else about 'em that frets him."

I felt the ground shudder, ever so faintly. Ulas had cleared
his throat. "It does seem we'd be daring God's anger—"

"That's nay what gnaws on the skipper's mind. He was never
an over-pious man." Etien scratched himself, yawned, and
climbed to his feet. "Glad I am to be nay the skipper. Let him
think over what's best to do. Time ye an' me was asleep."

But I slept little that night.

Rovic, I think, rested well. Yet as the next day wore on, I could
see haggardness on him. I wondered why. Did he think the
Hisagazi would turn on us? If so, why had he come at all? As
the slope steepened, the wagon grew so toilsome to push and
drag that my fears died for lack of breath.

Yet when we came upon the Ship, toward evening, I forgot my
weariness. And after one amazed volley of oaths, our mariners
rested silent on their pikes. The Hisagazi, never talkative,
crouched low in token of awe. Only Guzan remained erect among
them. I glimpsed his expression as he stared at the marvel. It
was a look of lust.

Wild was that place. We had gone above timberline, so the
land was a green sea below us, edged with silvery ocean. Here
we stood among tumbled black boulders, with cinders and spongy
tufa underfoot. The mountain rose in steeps and scarps and ra-

vines, up to the snows and the smoke, which rose another mile into a pale chilly sky. And here stood the Ship.

And the Ship was beauty.

I remember. In length—height, rather, since it stood on its tail—it was about equal to our own caravel, in form not unlike a lance head, in color a shining white untarnished after forty years. That was all. But words are paltry, my lord. What can they show of clean soaring curves, of iridescence on burnished metal, of a thing which was proud and lovely and in its very shape aquiver to be off? How can I conjure back the glamor which hazed that Ship whose keel had cloven starlight?

We stood there a long time. My vision blurred. I wiped my eyes, angry to be seen so affected, until I noticed one tear glisten in Rovic's red beard. But the captain's visage was quite blank. When he spoke, he said merely, in a flat voice, "Come, let's make camp."

The Hisagazian guardsmen dared approach no closer than these several hundred yards, to so potent an idol as the Ship had become. Our own mariners were glad enough to maintain the same distance. But after dark, when all else was in order, Val Nira led Rovic, Froad, Guzan, and myself to the vessel.

As we approached, a double door in the side swung noiselessly open and a metal gangplank descended therefrom. Glowing in Tambur's light, and in the dull clotted red reflected off the smoke clouds, the Ship was already as strange as I could endure. When it thus opened itself to me, as if a ghost stood guard, I whimpered and fled. The cinders crunched beneath my boots; I caught a whiff of sulfurous air.

But at the edge of camp I rallied myself enough to look again. The dark ground blotted all light, so that the Ship appeared alone with its grandeur. Presently I went back.

The interior was lit by luminous panels, cool to the touch. Val Nira explained that the great engine which drove it—as if the troll of folklore were put on a treadmill—was intact, and would furnish power at the flick of a lever. As nearly as I could understand what he said, this was done by changing the metallic part of ordinary salt into light . . . so I do not understand after all. The quicksilver was required for a part of the controls, which channeled power from the engine into another mechanism that hurtled the Ship skyward. We inspected the broken container. Enormous indeed had been the impact of landing, to twist and bend that thick alloy so. And yet Val Nira had been shielded by invisible forces, and the rest of the Ship had not suffered important damage. He fetched some tools, which flamed and hummed and whirled, and demonstrated a few repair operations on the broken part. Obviously he would have no trouble completing the work—and then he need only pour in a gallon of quicksilver, to bring his vessel alive again.

Much else did he show us that night. I shall say naught of this, for I cannot even remember such strangeness very clearly, let alone find words. Suffice it that Rovic, Froad, and Zhean spent a few hours in Elf Hill.

So, too, did Guzan. Though he had been taken here once before, as part of his initiation, he had never been shown this much erenow. Watching him, however, I saw less marveling in him than greed.

No doubt Rovic observed the same. There was little which Rovic did not observe. When we departed the Ship, his silence was not stunned like Froad's or my own. At the time, I thought in a vague fashion that he fretted over the trouble Guzan was certain to make. Now, looking back, I believe his mood was sadness.

Sure it is that long after we others were in our bedrolls, he stood alone, looking at the planetlit Ship.

Early in a cold dawn, Etien shook me awake. "Up, lad, we've work to do. Load yere pistols an' belt on yere dirk."

"What? What's to happen?" I fumbled with a hoarfrosted blanket. Last night seemed a dream.

"The skipper's nay said, but plainly he awaits a fight. Report to the wagon an' help us move into yon flying tower." Etien's thick form heelsquatted a moment longer beside me. Then, slowly: "Methinks Guzan has some idea o' murdering us all, here on the mountain. One officer an' a few crewmen can be made to sail the *Golden Leaper* for him, to Giair an' back. The rest o' us would be less trouble to him wi' our weasands slit."

I crawled forth, teeth clattering in my head. After arming myself, I snatched some food from the common store. The Hisagazi on the march carry dried fish and a sort of bread made from a powdered weed. Only the saints knew when I'd next get a chance to eat. I was the last to join Rovic at the cart. The natives were drifting sullenly toward us, unsure what we intended.

"Let's go, lads," said Rovic. He gave his orders. Four men started manhandling the wagon across the rocky trail toward the Ship, where this gleamed among mists. We others stood by, weapons ready. Almost at once Guzan hastened toward us, with Val Nira toiling in his wake.

Anger darkened his countenance. "What are you doing?" he barked.

Rovic gave him a calm stare. "Why, milord, as we may be here for some time, inspecting the wonders aboard the Ship—"

"What?" interrupted Guzan. "What do you mean? Have you not seen enough for one visit? We must get home again, and prepare to sail after the flowing stone."

"Go if you wish," said Rovic. "I choose to linger. And since you don't trust me, I reciprocate the feeling. My folk will stay in the Ship, which can be defended if necessary."

Guzan stormed and raged, but Rovic ignored him. Our men continued hauling the cart over the uneven ground. Guzan signaled his spearmen, who approached in a disordered but alert mass. Etien spoke a command. We fell into line. Pikes slanted forward, muskets took aim.

Guzan stepped back. We had demonstrated firearms for him at his own home island. Doubtless he could overwhelm us with sheer numbers, were he determined enough, but the cost would be heavy. "No reason to fight, is there?" purred Rovic. "I am only taking a sensible precaution. The Ship is a most valuable prize. It could bring Paradise for all . . . or dominion over this earth for one. There are those who'd prefer the latter. I've not accused you of being among them. However, in prudence I'd liefer keep the Ship for my hostage and my fortress, as long as it pleases me to remain here."

I think then I was convinced of Guzan's real intentions, not as a surmise of ours but as plain fact. Had he truly wished to attain the stars, his one concern would have been to keep the Ship safe. He would not have reached out, snatched little Val Nira in his powerful hands, and dragged the starman backward like a shield against our fire. Not that his intent matters, save to my own conscience. Wrath distorted his patterned visage. He screamed at us, "Then I'll keep a hostage too! And much good may your shelter do you!"

The Hisagazi milled about, muttering, hefting their spears and axes, but not prepared to follow us. We grunted our way across the black mountainside. The sun strengthened. Froad twisted his beard. "Dear me, master captain," he said, "think you they'll lay siege to us?"

"I'd not advise anyone to venture forth alone," said Rovic dryly.

"But without Val Nira to explain things, what use for us to stay at the Ship? Best we go back. I've mathematic texts to consult —my head's aspin with the law that binds the turning planets— I must ask the man from Paradise what he knows of—"

Rovic interrupted with a gruff order to three men, that they help lift a wheel wedged between two stones. He was in a savage temper. I confess his action seemed mad to me. If Guzan intended treachery, we had gained little by immobilizing ourselves in the Ship, where he could starve us. Better to let him attack in the open, where we would have a chance of fighting our way through. On the other hand, if Guzan did not plan to fall on us in the jungle—or any other time—then this was senseless provocation on our part. But I dared not question.

When we had brought our wagon up to the Ship, its gangplank again descended for us. The sailors started and cursed. Rovic forced himself out of his own bitterness, to speak soothing words. "Easy, lads. I've been aboard already, ye ken. Naught harmful within. Now we must tote our powder thither, an' stow it as I've planned."

Being slight of frame, I was not set to carrying the heavy casks, but put at the foot of the gangplank to watch the Hisagazi. We were too far away to distinguish words, but I saw how Guzan stood up on a boulder and harangued them. They shook their weapons at us and whooped. But they did not venture to attack. I wondered wretchedly what this was all about. If Rovic had foreseen us besieged, that would explain why he brought so much powder along . . . no, it would not, for there was more than a dozen men could shoot off in weeks of musketry, even had we had enough lead along . . . and we had almost no food! I looked past the poisonous volcano clouds, to Tambur where storms raged that could engulf all our earth, and wondered what demons lurked here to possess men.

I sprang to alertness at an indignant shout from within. Froad! Almost, I ran up the gangway, then remembered my duty. I heard Rovic roar him down and order the crewfolk to carry on. Froad and Rovic must have gone alone into the pilot's compartment and talked for an hour or more. When the old man emerged, he protested no longer. But as he walked down the gangway, he wept.

Rovic followed, grimmer of countenance than I had ever seen a man erenow. The sailors filed after, some looking appalled, some relieved, but chiefly watching the Hisagazian camp. They were simple mariners; the Ship was little to them save an alien and disquieting thing. Last came Etien, walking backward down the metal plank as he uncoiled a long string.

"Form square!" barked Rovic. The men snapped into position. "Best get within, Zhean and Froad," said the captain. "You can better carry extra ammunition than fight." He placed himself in the van.

I tugged Froad's sleeve. "Please, I beg you, master, what's happening?" But he sobbed too much to answer.

Etien crouched with flint and steel in his hands. He heard me —for otherwise we were all deathly silent—and said in a hard voice: "We placed casks o' powder throughout this hull, lad, wi' powder trains to join 'em. Here's the fuse to the whole."

I could not speak, could not even think, so monstrous was this. As if from immensely far away, I heard the click of stone on steel in Etien's fingers, heard him blow on the spark and add: "A good idea, methinks. I said t'other eventide, I'd follow the skipper wi'out fear o' God's curse—but better 'tis not to tempt Him overmuch."

"Forward march!" Rovic's sword blazed clear of the scabbard. Our feet scrunched loud and horrible on the mountain as we quick-stepped away. I did not look back. I could not. I was still fumbling in a nightmare. Since Guzan would have moved to intercept us anyhow, we proceeded straight toward his band. He stepped forward as we halted at the camp's edge. Val Nira slunk shivering after him. I heard the words dimly:

"Well, Rovic, what now? Are you ready to go home?"

"Yes," said the captain. His voice was dull. "All the way home."

Guzan squinted in rising suspiciousness. "Why did you abandon your wagon? What did you leave behind?"

"Supplies. Come, let's march."

Val Nira stared at the cruel shapes of our pikes. He must wet his lips a few times ere he could quaver, "What are you talking about? There's no reason to leave food there. It would spoil in all the time until . . . until—" He faltered as he looked into Rovic's eyes. The blood drained from him.

"What have you done?" he whispered.

Suddenly Rovic's free hand went up, to cover his face. "What I must," he said thickly. "Daughter of God, forgive me."

The starman regarded us an instant more. Then he turned and ran. Past the astonished warriors he burst, out onto the cindery slope, toward his Ship.

"Come back!" bellowed Rovic. "You fool you'll never—"

He swallowed hard. As he looked after that small, stumbling, lonely shape, hurrying across a fire mountain toward the Beautiful One, the sword sank in his grasp. "Perhaps it's best," he said, like a benediction.

Guzan raised his own sword. In scaly coat and blowing feathers, he was a figure as impressive as steel-clad Rovic. "Tell me what you've done," he snarled, "or I'll kill you this moment!"

He paid our muskets no heed. He, too, had had dreams.

He, too, saw them end, when the Ship exploded.

Even that adamantine hull could not withstand a wagonload of carefully placed gunpowder, set off at one time. There came a crash that knocked me to my knees, and the hull cracked open. White-hot chunks of metal screamed across the slopes. I saw one of them strike a boulder and split it in twain. Val Nira vanished, destroyed too quickly to have seen what happened; so in the ultimate, God was merciful to him. Through the flames and smokes and the doomsday noise which followed, I saw the Ship fall. It rolled down the slope, strewing its own mangled guts behind. Then the mountainside grumbled and slid in pursuit, and buried it, and dust hid the sky.

More than this, I have no heart to remember.

The Hisagazi shrieked and fled. They must have thought all hell come to earth. Guzan stood his ground. As the dust enveloped us, hiding the grave of the Ship and the white volcano crater, turning the sun red, he sprang at Rovic. A musketeer raised his weapon. Etien slapped it down. We stood and watched those two men fight, up and over the shaken cinder land, and knew in our private darkness that this was their right. Sparks flew where the blades clamored together. At last Rovic's skill prevailed. He took Guzan in the throat.

We gave Guzan decent burial and went down through the jungle.

That night the guardsmen rallied their courage enough to attack us. We were aided by our muskets, but must chiefly use sword and pike. We hewed our way through them because we had no other place to go than the sea.

They gave up, but carried word ahead of us. When we reached Nikum, all the forces Iskilip could raise were besieging the *Golden Leaper* and waiting to oppose Rovic's entry. We formed a square again, and no matter how many thousands they had, only a score or so could reach us at any time. Nonetheless, we left six good men in the crimsoned mud of those streets. When our people on the caravel realized Rovic was coming back, they bombarded the town. This ignited the thatch roofs and distracted the enemy enough that a sortie from the ship was able to effect a juncture with us. We chopped our way to the pier, got aboard, and manned the capstan.

Outraged and very brave, the Hisagazi paddled their canoes up to our hull, where our cannon could not be brought to bear. They stood on each other's shoulders to reach our rail. One band forced itself aboard, and the fight was fierce which cleared them from the decks. That was when I got the shattered collarbone which plagues me to this day.

But in the end, we came out of the fjord. A fresh east wind was blowing. With all sail aloft, we outran the foe. We counted our dead, bound our wounds, and slept.

Next dawning, awakened by the pain of my shoulder and the

worse pain within, I mounted the quarterdeck. The sky was overcast. The wind had stiffened; the sea ran cold and green, whitecaps out to a cloud-gray horizon. Timbers groaned and rigging skirled. I stood an hour facing aft, into the chill wind that numbs pain.

When I heard boots behind me, I did not turn around. I knew they were Rovic's. He stood beside me a long while, bareheaded. I noticed that he was starting to turn gray.

Finally, not yet regarding me, still squinting into the air that lashed tears from our eyes, he said: "I had a chance to talk Froad over, that day. He was grieved, but owned I was right. Has he spoken to you about it?"

"No," I said.

"None of us are ever likely to speak of it much," said Rovic.

After another time: "I was not afraid Guzan or anyone else would seize the Ship and try to turn conqueror. We men of Montalir should well be able to deal with any such rogues. Nor was I afraid of the Paradise dwellers. That poor little man could only have been telling truth. They would never have harmed us . . . willingly. They would have brought precious gifts, and taught us their own esoteric arts, and let us visit all their stars."

"Then why?" I got out.

"Someday Froad's successors will solve the riddles of the universe," he said. "Someday our descendants will build their own Ship, and go forth to whatever destiny they wish."

Spume blew up and around us, until our hair was wet. I tasted the salt on my lips.

"Meanwhile," said Rovic, "we'll sail the seas of this earth, and walk its mountains, and chart and subdue and come to understand it. Do you see, Zhean? That is what the Ship would have taken from us."

Then I was also made able to weep. He laid his hand on my uninjured shoulder and stood with me while the *Golden Leaper*, all sail set, proceeded westward.

I can't resist having the final word . . .

Every good story reflects credit upon its author and all the authors I know, without exception, cheerfully accept such credit, and do not willingly allow any of it to escape.

In particular, any suggestion that the editor of a magazine deserves any specific credit for the good writing of the stories appearing in it, is met with unfavorable reactions ranging from gently derisive to violently negative.

However, I will let you into a professional secret if you will promise not to reveal the source of your information. An editor, whether he wants to or not, places his mark upon the magazine and every story in it. He selects the stories that are to appear and thus sets the tone for the magazine. He talks endlessly to authors who come to visit him and writes letters to those who do not. He encourages, inspires, offers suggestions, donates ideas. He asks for revision and points out room for improvement even at the cost of securing for himself a vaster and more articulate unpopularity than human flesh and blood ought to be required to endure.

Let me list, then, the editors responsible for seeing the Hugo winners in print, before they became Hugo winners.

For "The Darfsteller," "Allamagoosa," "Exploration Team," "The Big Front Yard," and "The Longest Voyage," we have John

W. Campbell, Jr., to thank. John is large, indecently intelligent, fearfully articulate and dreadfully opinionated on every conceivable subject. He is a dangerous man to argue with for he will convince you that white is plaid and when you are ready to die for your new belief, will turn about and as painstakingly convince you that plaid is black. No one has so influenced the field as has he.

The editorial responsibility for "The Star" belongs to Larry T. Shaw. Larry is short and very soft-spoken, so that it is necessary to lean your ear against his mouth to realize that he has lost his temper and is shouting. He wears glasses thicker than he is and smokes a pipe somewhat longer than he is; and on a very small budget ran a darned good magazine for as long as money held out at all.

"Or All the Seas with Oysters" appeared in Horace L. Gold's magazine. Horace's personality, quite different from that of John Campbell, is nevertheless just as overpowering. His tongue-lashings of authors who have failed to live up to their own standards are notorious but when the author, smarting and bleeding, condescended to patch his story as suggested, he was generally rewarded with the knowledge that somehow his story had been greatly improved. (I can testify to this of personal knowledge for no author smarts as sharply or bleeds as copiously under such conditions as do I—or finds his stories as drastically changed for the better.)

For "The Hell-Bound Train," we have Anthony Boucher; witty, genial, understanding, and the composer of the gentlest and most soothing letters of rejection that can possibly exist. He, more than anyone else, learned how to give science fiction the delicate aura of literature. Tony earned love under the most unfavorable possible conditions for he was loved even by the authors whose stories he rejected.

Finally, Robert P. Mills can move up as the editor responsible for "Flowers for Algernon." He stepped into Anthony Boucher's shoes when Tony retired as editor. They weren't easy shoes to wear properly but Bob managed to do it well. Tall and gangling, a keeper of his temper under the most trying of circumstances, Bob doesn't really look the part of science fiction editor. He is widely felt to be "too normal" for this role, and that gives rise to a sense of uneasiness among science fiction authors who have never in their lives suffered from being "too normal." But the uneasiness is unjustified. Under that normal and good-looking exterior, there beats a warm and screwball heart.

I know all these gentlemen personally. They have all, on one occasion or another, told me what a lousy writer I was; and I invariably answered by telling them what lousy editors they were (prudently waiting till they were out of earshot, of course). But every one of them (plus some others who are not represented in this anthology) helped me often and, I am sure, helped every author they could reach.

This help should be acknowledged far more often and far more publicly than it is, and I am glad to have an opportunity here to strike a blow for justice and right-thinking.

Isaac Asimov

THE HUGO

The notion of a science fiction award arose in early 1953 in Philadelphia. A gentleman by the name of Hal Lynch, having watched the Academy Awards on television, was struck by the idea, which he passed on at once to those fans who were organizing the 11th Convention (Philadelphia, 1953).

After numerous misadventures, the awards were designed and handmachined by Jack McKnight of Lansdale, Pennsylvania. He produced them deftly, racing against time, in a remarkable demonstration of skillful labor-of-love. The awards were small stainless-steel rocketships, finned at base and center and set on a cylindrical wooden base on which an appropriately inscribed plaque was set.

There was no feeling at the time that such an award ought to be repeated and, in fact, at the 12th Convention (San Francisco, 1954) there were no awards. The 13th Convention (Cleveland, 1955), however, decided to present what was officially termed "The Second Annual Science Fiction Achievement Award," and that was the true beginning of the Hugo as an annual feature.

The manufacture of the Hugos for the 13th Convention was once again an Odyssey of complication and near-despair, for the Conventions are one and all conducted by impecunious fans who must raise money by squeezing blood out of turnips. And while money won't buy happiness, lack of money won't buy Hugos.

A new Hugo was designed by Ben Jason of Cleveland. It differed from the McKnight version in appearance chiefly in that it was larger, lacked the central fins and was set on a cubical base. The crucial difference, however, was that the Jason design could be mass-produced, while the McKnight design could not be.

The annual production of standardized Hugos was now possible. Ben Jason plugged hard for this and, in the main, won his point. Most Conventions since 1955 have used his design, which is now considered standard. Mr. Jason possesses the original mold and has personally supervised the construction for a number of the post-Cleveland Conventions. He has been commissioned to do the work for the 20th Convention (Chicago, 1962) and the 21st Convention (Washington, 1963).

The Jason-designed Hugo is that which decorates the cover-jacket of this book.

A full list of the Hugo winners through 1962 has been prepared by Ed Wood, of Idaho Falls, Idaho, a prominent science fiction fan with an encyclopedic knowledge of the field.

Here is the list:

11TH CONVENTION—PHILADELPHIA, 1953

#1 FAN PERSONALITY—Forrest J. Ackerman
INTERIOR ILLUSTRATOR—Virgil Finlay
COVER ARTIST—Ed Emshwiller; Hannes Bok (tie)
EXCELLENCE IN FACT ARTICLES—Willy Ley
NEW SCIENCE FICTION AUTHOR OR ARTIST—Philip José Farmer
PROFESSIONAL MAGAZINE—*Galaxy* and *Astounding Science Fiction* (tie)
NOVEL—*The Demolished Man* by Alfred Bester

13TH CONVENTION—CLEVELAND, 1955

NOVEL—*They'd Rather Be Right* by Mark Clifton and Frank Riley
*NOVELETTE—"The Darfsteller" by Walter M. Miller, Jr.
*SHORT STORY—"Allamagoosa" by Eric Frank Russell
PROFESSIONAL MAGAZINE—*Astounding Science Fiction*
ILLUSTRATOR—Frank Kelly Freas
AMATEUR PUBLICATION—*Fantasy Times*

14TH CONVENTION—NEW YORK, 1956

NOVEL—*Double Star* by Robert A. Heinlein
*NOVELETTE—"Exploration Team" by Murray Leinster
*SHORT STORY—"The Star" by Arthur C. Clarke
FEATURE WRITER—Willy Ley
PROFESSIONAL MAGAZINE—*Astounding Science Fiction*
ILLUSTRATOR—Frank Kelly Freas
MOST PROMISING NEW AUTHOR—Robert Silverberg
AMATEUR PUBLICATION—*Inside & Science Fiction Advertiser*
CRITIC—Damon Knight

15TH CONVENTION—LONDON, 1957

PROFESSIONAL MAGAZINE, AMERICAN—*Astounding Science Fiction*
PROFESSIONAL MAGAZINE, BRITISH—*New Worlds Science Fiction*
AMATEUR PUBLICATION—*Science Fiction Times*

16TH CONVENTION—LOS ANGELES, 1958

NOVEL—*The Big Time* by Fritz Leiber
*SHORT STORY—"Or All the Seas with Oysters," by Avram Davidson
PROFESSIONAL MAGAZINE—*Magazine of Fantasy and Science Fiction*
ILLUSTRATOR—Frank Kelly Freas
MOTION PICTURE—*The Incredible Shrinking Man* by Richard Matheson
MOST OUTSTANDING ACTIFAN—Walter A. Willis

17TH CONVENTION—DETROIT, 1959

NOVEL—*A Case of Conscience* by James Blish
*NOVELETTE—"The Big Front Yard" by Clifford D. Simak
*SHORT STORY—"The Hell-Bound Train" by Robert Bloch
ILLUSTRATOR—Frank Kelly Freas
PROFESSIONAL MAGAZINE—*Magazine of Fantasy and Science Fiction*
AMATEUR PUBLICATION—*FANAC*
MOST PROMISING NEW AUTHOR—Brian W. Aldiss

18TH CONVENTION—PITTSBURGH, 1960

NOVEL—*Starship Trooper,* by Robert A. Heinlein
*SHORT FICTION—"Flowers for Algernon," by Daniel Keyes
PROFESSIONAL MAGAZINE—*Magazine of Fantasy and Science Fiction*
AMATEUR PUBLICATION—*Cry of the Nameless*
ILLUSTRATOR—Ed Emshwiller
DRAMATIC PRESENTATION—*The Twilight Zone,* by Rod Serling
SPECIAL AWARD—Hugo Gernsback as "The Father of Magazine Science Fiction"

19TH CONVENTION—SEATTLE, 1961

NOVEL—*A Canticle for Leibowitz* by Walter M. Miller, Jr.
*SHORT STORY—"The Longest Voyage," by Poul Anderson
PROFESSIONAL MAGAZINE—*Analog Science Fact and Fiction*
AMATEUR PUBLICATION—*Who Killed Science Fiction?* by Earl
  Kemp
ILLUSTRATOR—Ed Emshwiller
DRAMATIC PRESENTATION—*The Twilight Zone* by Rod Serling

20TH CONVENTION—CHICAGO, 1962

NOVEL—*Stranger in a Strange Land* by Robert Heinlein
SHORT FICTION—'*Hothouse*' Stories by Brian Aldiss *in The Magazine
  of Fantasy & Science Fiction*
DRAMATIC PRESENTATION—*The Twilight Zone* by Rod Serling
PROFESSIONAL ARTIST—Ed Emshwiller
PROFESSIONAL MAGAZINE—*Analog*
AMATEUR MAGAZINE—Richard Bergeron's *Warhoon*

*Winners presented in this anthology